MYTHOLOGIA

FIRST OMNIBUS EDITION

ADAM ALEXANDER HAVIARAS

Sign-up for the Eagles and Dragons Publishing Newsletter and get a FREE BOOK today.

Subscribers get first access to new releases, special offers, and much more.

Visit:
www.eaglesanddragonspublishing.com

CHARIOT OF THE SON

THE STORY OF PHAETHON

And Theia was subject in love to Hyperion and bare great Helios and clear Selene and Eos who shine upon all that are on earth and upon the deathless Gods who live in the wide heaven.

— HESIOD, *THEOGONY*

HYMN I

OUTCASTS

1

THE RISING SUN

On a high rock overlooking the grassy plain of Ethiopia, a young man waited.

Everyday since he was old enough to do so, Phaethon left the safety of the palace of King Merops while darkness still blanketed the world and some light yet lingered in the constellations.

With spear and bow in hand, he crossed the open spaces of the grassland, and forded the broad rivers, risking lion and crocodile to reach the edge of the forest where the land rose and rocks from the last great making of the world thrust upward to the sky.

The climb to his chosen eyrie was not an easy one, but he had strength in his limbs and a will to reach the top.

Phaethon, golden-skinned and auburn-haired, waited not for beasts to hunt, nor enemies to waylay, nor the young women carrying water upon their heads that he might abuse them.

He waited for the sun.

· · ·

THE WHOLE of Phaethon's existence revolved around that first, soul-warming glimpse of golden light to pour out of the East every day with divine constancy. Never wavering in his devotion, he watched it, his hands gripping the edge of the rock above the deadly precipice, anticipating that first brilliant crack at the far edge of the world.

It was with a longing, and a lingering sadness, that Phaethon watched the light of the world turn all to colour - the emerald of the plains, the silver of the rivers, the blue of the lakes, and the browns and yellows of earth and mountain. He needed to feel that light as his body needed air to breathe or water to drink. The light was sustenance for his very spirit, and when it rushed upon Phaethon, he felt it rejuvenate him, fill him with power, and pride, and other inexplicable emotions. All about him life exploded, and he revelled in it.

Flowers blossomed, flights of birds shot into the skies, and beasts crawled from their dens to welcome each new day. The rising sun drove them all, created anew with each rosy dawn.

Phaethon stood, his tunic thrown down, his arms outspread to the world until, having reached its zenith, he could feel the sun moving on. The young man breathed slowly in and out, images of rushing rivers and snow-capped mountains flashing suddenly behind his closed lids - wheels turning, as of fire and streaks across a singed sky.

Then, blinding light.

When he awoke, he was on his perch near to the edge.

He sighed and gathered his belongings - his tunic, bow, and the spear around which a serpent had wrapped itself. Gently, Phaethon slid it off and the serpent lay there in the last light of the sun.

·   ·   ·

ON THE PLAIN where the antelope leapt, and wild horses cropped at the tall grasses, a rider in a plumed head-dress came toward him. Phaethon recognized his eldest brother Niobis' haughty manner.

As Merops' heir, Niobis treated all his brothers and sisters as subjects, but none more so than Phaethon.

"Phaethon!" he called out.

"Yes, brother," Phaethon answered, stopping and leaning casually upon his spear.

"You've been gone most of the day. Mother is worried."

"She knows where I go. Why worry?"

"Father sent me to collect you. Come now."

"As you can see, I am already coming."

"You're always so impudent!"

"And you're as puffed up as a peacock, Niobis. Get yourself back! I come when the sun sets."

Without warning, Niobis kicked his dark stallion hard at Phaethon, his spear out for attack.

Phaethon dropped his things and grabbed hold of the oncoming spear shaft just in time, throwing Niobis into the mud.

"Curse you!" Niobis sputtered full of rage.

Phaethon held the spear toward his brother and then with three long strides sent the shaft into the brown water of the river where it stuck in the mud and then toppled over beneath the surface.

He picked up his things, turned his back on his brother, and walked away in the direction of the palace.

.   .   .

THE PALACE CAME into view a short while later, its gilded peaks and walls of red and yellow stone appearing as deep shades of earth in the angling light.

Phaethon nodded to the guards as he passed and saw them tense at his approach.

In the inner courtyard stood all of his brothers and sisters in a circle. Their voices were like a muttering of seals on a too-little beach. All tall, and slim, and dark, Phaethon never felt at one with them. He was pale, and thickly muscled, his brown-red hair always having been a source of amusement.

At his approach, the circle broke to reveal Niobis sitting in the centre. His other brothers stood about him, fists clenched, their royal robes angry and wrinkled from bending over the eldest.

"Phaethon!" cried Teros, a younger of the boys. "Why did you try to kill Niobis?"

"Me?" Phaethon returned. "He charged me from horse-back with his spear!"

"You lie!" Niobis rose and came forward, brushing off the hands of his concerned sisters. "You tried to kill me."

"Careful, little king. Else you may eat more mud."

"You're a bastard!" The words exploded full force from Niobis' mouth to echo throughout the palace.

Phaethon held back, his fists wanting to swing up, but he controlled them. Instead, he looked upon his brothers and sisters, all beautiful, all smooth as ebony, with gold about their arms, necks, and ankles. Their eyes were wide with wonder, and he knew they believed it too, that he was not one of them. He never would be.

Niobis smiled broadly, sensing that his shot had hit home. "You know it's true. You're a bastard. You...don't...belong... here."

"What's the meaning of this?"

The voice of King Merops crashed down on them, and all the children cowered before their father. All except Phaethon.

Merops' tall form swept in among them, a full head taller than Niobis. His yellow and purple robes rustling as he swished a horse-hair flail at a few stray flies. He came between Niobis and Phaethon.

"I asked you both a question. What is the meaning of this?"

Phaethon looked up into the king's big white eyes, held his gaze, but said nothing.

"Niobis?" the king asked. "Why are you covered in mud? It is unseemly for a prince."

"I fell from my horse."

"How?"

"I..." Niobis looked at Phaethon, his eyes narrowing. "I went to fetch Phaethon as you asked, but when I approached him he unhorsed me and threw me into the mud."

"Father," Phaethon spoke up. "I merely grabbed the spear that he had levelled at me."

"But Father-"

"Silence!" Merops' thick hand fastened on Niobis' shoulder, silencing him.

"Father," Teros stepped up. "Niobis called Phaethon bastard before all here."

Merops looked down on the little boy, his countenance grave. He was silent a moment, breathing deeply.

"Phaethon," the king began. "It is time for you to go to your mother. She would have words with you, and she has been worried."

"Yes, father." Phaethon looked at one of the upper

windows of Queen Clymene's apartments. He could see her blond head framed within, her stormy blue eyes taking in the scene below.

Merops looked up at the window, nodded, and spoke loud enough for her to hear him. "It is time she told you what you need to know."

With that, King Merops swept from the courtyard with Niobis and the rest following.

Phaethon stood alone looking up at his mother.

2

SECRETS REVEALED

"Mother?" Phaethon's voice was soft in the upper corridor of the palace. Red walls led to a blue door at the end. "Mother, may I enter?"

The door swung open and a young girl, one of his mother's handmaidens, bowed to him.

"Leave us, Anthi," the queen's voice commanded, and the girl went out, closing the door behind her as Phaethon watched.

He stood still, taking in the rooms, a place he loved second only to his eyrie on the other side of the plain.

Queen Clymene's royal rooms were nothing like the earthly elsewheres of Merops' palace. There were no browns or greys or blacks. Rather, Clymene's world was one of blues and brilliant greens, pink, white, and the light of the sun. The walls were painted in shades of turquoise with depictions of dolphins and sea horses, and glimpses of Poseidon's world. Temples wavered in the wine-dark realm, and oceanids roamed freely, including one that looked very much like Clymene.

Above it all, rising over the sea and the earth, shone the sun, brilliant and blinding. The likeness was as though captured sunlight had been embedded in the wall of the queen's apartments.

Clymene sat on a couch of pure white marble, draped with sea-blue cushions that matched her robes. The blond waves of her hair fell about her shoulders to frame the pink seashell that hung about her neck. She stroked the latter with a finger, and her eyes met her son's.

"I was worried for you this morning."

"I'm well," Phaethon answered. "I wanted to linger in the sun longer today. That's all."

"Yes," she replied, her eyes closing then opening. He thought that she would say more, but she only beckoned for him to sit next to her.

Clymene took her son's hand in both of hers and bent her forehead to touch it. Phaethon felt cool tears run onto his hand, and sensed an odour of sea spray in the air, though he knew little of the sea, never having experienced that particular joy.

"What's wrong, Mother?" he asked, letting her weep without making any motion to comfort her.

Clymene regained her composure and sat straight, the salt tears soaking back into her skin like water upon a soft, sandy beach. In truth, something in her majestic eyes now worried Phaethon, and he pulled his hand away.

"I heard all that transpired in the courtyard, my son," she finally said.

Phaethon jumped up, his anger back as he stared at the sun upon the wall.

"Niobis called me a bastard in front of my brothers and sisters, even in front of the servants! Father said nothing...did nothing!" Phaethon's arms and shoulders flexed, his jaw tensed.

When did my beautiful boy become a man? Clymene thought as she looked upon him. *How the tides do flow without notice... It is time.*

"They are not your brothers and sisters," Clymene said. "And Merops is...not your father." *It is done...*

Phaethon whirled around as though he had been struck, and for a moment he was confused as to whether his anger stemmed from the words his mother had spoken, or because he realized Niobis had spoken true.

"And you?" Fear and sadness welled inside of Phaethon's golden eyes, their brilliance momentarily dim and dark. "Are you not my mother?"

"I *am* your mother," Clymene answered without hesitation, her voice strong like a crashing wave. "And I am proud of that fact. I am your mother, Phaethon. It was I who gave birth to you, who brought you to the light."

The young man was relieved, but the great question hung like a double-headed axe between them.

"Then...who *is* my father?"

Clymene rose from her couch and walked to the fresco of the sun on her wall. Phaethon noticed that her lips moved, but she uttered no words.

"Mother, please. I must know."

"Your father," she began, "is the Shining One. He who lights the world." She turned to face her son. "You, my lovely Phaethon, are the son of Helios."

Phaethon stepped back until he felt the couch, then sat. He saw his mother standing before him, the image of the sun illuminating the space behind her.

"Helios? The Great Charioteer is my father?"

Clymene nodded, sad, wistful, and longing. He would have questions, she knew. First, she moved to a box of carved olive wood which rested upon a table. She opened it and removed a gold medallion with an image of the sun upon it. She handed it to her son, dangling it by the braided leather rope.

"This is yours now," she said.

Phaethon took it in his hands and looked at the image of the charioteer on the back, then at the face on the obverse. A handsome, golden visage stared back at him, hair long and wild as sunlight, smiling.

"My father..."

"Yes, he is."

"But why...I don't understand. Why are we here in this land with Merops? Why are we not with my father? Do you not love him?"

His mother's face told him the truth immediately. There was a great sadness, untold pain at the remark, a wound that had not healed.

"He is my truest love, incomparable to Iapetus, or Merops."

"Then why are you not with him?"

"Zeus forbade it."

The mention of the king of the Olympians silenced Phaethon. Now he waited, listened.

"From the realm of my own father, Oceanus, I used to watch Helios drive his team across the sky. I would sing to him from the deep, and from the shore. I would call to him. One day, he stopped and we, for but a few minutes, stared at each other. We knew we loved one another, and every day after that I sang and he stopped, always for an instant. Then, one night while your aunt Selene lashed her blacks across the world, your father came to my shore in a gilded boat. He was dressed all in white." She smiled. "Even by night he was brilliant and beautiful."

Clymene roamed about the large room in remembrance, her hand straying to objects now and then as if to ground herself back in reality.

"Beneath the constellations we lay together, and I begot you."

"What of your then husband?" Phaethon had known that much of the time before Merops, that his mother had been wed to another.

"Iapetus was a Titan, and had other interests than a mere oceanid such as me. I had not seen him for an age, and our sons, your brothers, were all grown."

"I have brothers?"

"Atlas, Menoetius, Prometheus, and Epimetheus are your half-brothers, yes."

Phaethon knew their names. "You never told me?"

"Again, Zeus forbade it, and all are bound to obey or bear his wrath." Clymene touched the fire of a lamp that burned nearby when she said it, remembering her beloved Prometheus. "When you were born, Zeus commanded your father to stay away from us. He knew, by the word of Aphrodite, that your father loved us more than anything, and so he feared for the timely rising and setting of the sun. I was commanded to marry Merops, and banished to this dry place of earth and heat so far from the life-giving sea."

Phaethon went to his mother's side at the west-facing window where they both watched the last rays of sun bleed over the edge of the world.

"That's why I long for the sun, why I'm so different here," Phaethon said in a low voice.

"Yes. In your heart, you have always known the light, and been drawn to your father's strength." She placed her hands on Phaethon's shoulders. "One thing you can be sure of is that you were never without him in the light of day, for he sees all from his heights, and was surely watching you as he passed."

"Am I the only child you had by him?"

Clymene hesitated, then turned to the window again.

"No. Your father and I, we disobeyed Zeus and met again. I had to see him. I had to show you to him." She looked her son in his brilliant, confused eyes. "You have three sisters, Phaethon. They are the Heliades: Phoebe, Merope, and Aetheria. Long have they waited to meet you."

"Where are they?" Phaethon's emotions welled fiercely inside. He had felt alone for so long, ignorant of all.

"They linger by the seas, and are charged with the return of your father's gilded boat when he is not in need of it."

"They see him?"

"Rarely. They have their purpose as decreed."

"And I have no purpose!" Phaethon pushed away from her and went to another window where he looked down into the courtyard and saw Niobis and the other boys practicing with sword and spear in the torchlight. "I'll kill them for their insults," he muttered.

"No! You shall not. You are no murderer, and Merops has been good to us."

"A good jailer!"

"No. A good friend and kindly husband. He protected us when no other would have received us beneath their roof for fear of angering Zeus."

Phaethon turned back to the window, quiet and angry, his mind whirling like the starlit heavens.

Darkness hung heavier on the world that night, it seemed. The stars burned fiercely. The son of Helios suddenly hated the world in which he found himself, in which his mother was imprisoned. The sounds of his step-brothers and sisters out the window annoyed him like the braying of hyenas on the plain. The lake waters beyond the palace smelled stale, and the plains that had once appeared to him green and fresh were now dank, and dark, and soiled.

"Why would Zeus do this to us...to me? He doesn't even know me."

Clymene reached out a lithe but shaking hand to her son's shoulder. He did not pull away this time.

"Zeus rules all the world, and must think of the whole - gods, men, beasts, and those in between. It does not seem fair or just, that is true. Many a night did I cry myself to a sleep with nightmares and loneliness. But...each morning, with the rising of the sun, I would pick you up from your crib, hold you to my breast, and feel the true well of love that existed. You are what has kept me close to my true love. You are a product of that love."

Phaethon heard the warm words pouring from his mother's heart, and a measure of guilt crept in upon him. He had not fully listened to her meaning. There was one thought which he then clung to, and would not release.

"I want to go to my father."

Clymene had been waiting for it, had known he would wish it. She sat down, nodding her head absently. This was the moment she had dreaded in her heart. The time had come to bid her son farewell.

"I cannot stop you. You are a man now, and able to roam this earth as you will."

"Come with me." A small remnant of the naive boy asked. "Be with Father." He said it as if it was a simple matter.

"If I were to go, I would be defying Zeus who forbade me to ever see your father again. Were I caught, and I would be, I would be chained in the darkest depths of Tartarus, never to see you or feel you father's light upon my face again."

"And I?"

"There were no such laws placed upon you. All that was commanded was that you would be reared here, away from your father. And now you are a man, and free to go."

Sad rivulets ran from Clymene's eyes. Oceanids had ever been full of emotion, storm-tossed.

Phaethon could see her struggling to right herself and he held both her hands in his.

"I would go, Mother, though it crushes me to leave you in this place."

Silence hung between them for several heartbeats.

"How do I get there? I mean...where will I find him?"

"Your father dwells in the Palace of the Sun, far, far to the East, beyond the world's edge. Few venture there or find it."

"Then how will I?"

Clymene's eyes strayed to the medallion about his neck.

"That is your key, your guide. Your sisters will take you to the other side of the world in the gilded boat, and with the medallion of the sun, his palace shall appear to you."

"Appear? Is it a magical place?"

"It is god-made, the home of the Sun."

"And my sisters? Where do I find them?"

"You will need to travel to the sea east of here. Wait upon the shore while holding the medallion and they will come to you."

Phaethon stood up and paced excitedly, scarcely able to

contain the new-found life and hope that burned within his veins.

"There is one thing you must do for me, Phaethon, before you go to your father." She stood now, determined, emboldened by his own fervour.

"Yes?"

"I wish for you to go to your half-brother, Prometheus, high in the Caucasus."

"What shall I say to him?"

"After yourself, he is one of my most beloved." Clymene stared into dark memories then, to a time when Zeus had meted out punishment to her sons by Iapetus - Atlas holding up the heavens, and Prometheus chained at the top of the world while the others went down into darkness. "Tell him I love him, and forever shall. That I am proud of him for what he did to champion men. Tell him that I think of him every day, and hope that my prayers somewhat ease his suffering."

"But how do I get to the top of the world? Where is the Caucasus?"

She had forgotten that Phaethon's only world had ever been the one of Merops' palace, and the plain beyond. To be released from imprisonment would be daunting in itself, a terrifying event.

"You must go north before you seek your father's palace. Your sisters know the way." Clymene went to a carved cupboard and removed another box decorated with a relief of Olympus. "Give this to Prometheus for me."

"What's in it?" Phaethon opened the lid to see two gold, covered bowls, and a small phial. "It smells wonderful, sweet."

"The bowls contain ambrosia and nectar. They will give him strength for a long time."

"And the phial?"

"An alternative to his imprisonment." Clymene looked down and then directly at Phaethon. "You must not touch the phial, for any reason."

He looked at it and closed the lid, wary. "Very well."

There was little else to say. How does one express a whole sea of emotion in a few days, hours, or even minutes. Clymene threw her arms about him, tried to breathe him in, remember how it felt to hold her dearest son.

"I'm afraid," she whispered.

"I must see him, meet him. If I do not, I shall never rest or be able to gaze upon the sun again for fear of the pain in my heart. I'll never fit in here, Mother."

She stood back and looked upon him. He was a man, handsome, strong, a descendant of gods. Such were not meant to be chained.

"You are right. You must go if your heart tells you. Remember, the world is not always kind, even to gods. Listen to your sisters and they will take you where you need to go. When you travel with them, time speeds itself, and so you will be able to cover great distances. Take all that you need from the palace stores - food, weapons. I will speak with Merops."

"I love you, Mother. I will come to you before I leave tomorrow."

"Tomorrow?" she began to protest, but stopped herself. "Yes. Tomorrow. Please do come to see me."

Phaethon hugged her again, kissed her hand, and left her rooms with the carved box beneath his arm.

When he was gone, Clymene lay down upon her bed and cried herself to sleep as she had not done for an age.

· · ·

"Will you miss me?" the girl, Anthi, asked as she and Phaethon lay naked together in his room.

"Of course I will," he answered, his fingers tracing the swell of her breasts, and the curve of her hips. "I shall think on you always." It sounded hollow to him and her resigned sigh confirmed it. However, she was the only girl he had ever known. She possessed a small part of him, but he found it difficult to imagine missing the girl whom he had first kissed and made love to. All he could think of, as he gazed from her naked body to the collection of his things in the corner of the room, was his long journey on the morrow to the top of the world and beyond, to the Palace of the Sun where he would finally meet his father.

"I love you, Phaethon," Anthi whispered, her tears falling on his chest.

He held her tight, silent in the dying lamplight.

When next Anthi awoke, Phaethon was gone.

As the sun rose the next morning, Phaethon was already making his way across the plain toward the sea. He walked quickly, eager to meet his sisters, eager to get away from Merops' palace.

He had seen King Merops that morning, and the truth was that the king had been kindly toward him. He always had been. When Phaethon told him he was leaving, Merops placed a thick hand upon his shoulder.

"I wish you well on your journey to see your father, Phaethon. Though you are not my own, it has been a pleasure seeing you grow into a man. Take whatever you need from the palace for your journey, and if your path ever leads you back this way, your mother and I shall bless the day."

"Thank you, sire. Please...take care of my mother for me."

"Never fear, Phaethon. For she is dear to me, though I know her heart has never been mine."

The king looked sad then. He turned, beckoning all his own children. They followed without another word. Only Teros lingered a moment, his glassy eyes taking one last look at Phaethon.

When he was alone with Clymene, Phaethon embraced her and hoisted his satchel and spears.

"You have the medallion and box?" she asked.

"Yes."

"Go then, with my love, my son. The sun is rising, and you must rush to meet it."

And that had been it. Phaethon had gathered his things and left by the large wooden gates of the palace. He glanced back only once to see Clymene's dark outline upon the parapet of the palace gatehouse.

Ahead, the dirt road was flanked by the green grass of the plain, and as the sun rose higher and higher, antelope, buffalo, zebras, and other beasts ranged all about him.

HYMN II

CHILDREN OF THE SUN

3

THE HELIADES

It took Phaethon three days to reach the sea, and the anticipation of seeing it deepened with each step.

His mother's true home... He could smell it, and hear it more and more until the crash of waves matched the beating of his own heart.

All the world seemed fresh to Phaethon, each new experience empowering. At night, he slept beneath the stars, sword close in case of lions, but none came. He dreamed of meeting his father, and woke to his light in the dawn sky.

On the day when he finally reached the seashore, a place of soft golden sand, he waded into the foam and breathed deeply of the salt air that reminded him of his mother's tears. He tasted it and marvelled at the feeling of comfort it gave him.

After exploring the shore and washing himself in the sea's embrace, Phaethon lit a fire and lay back against a sand dune to wait as darkness fell. His sisters had not come.

. . .

LULLED BY THE SEA, as if its music were a long-forgotten lullaby, Phaethon drifted away on a tide of dreams, not of the deep, or of Merops' palace, nor even of his mother.

He dreamed of light, so intense, so powerful, that fear shook his sleeping form. The light grew bigger and hotter, even louder in his ears. Behind it all, a crash of waves, a neighing of horses, and weeping. When the white light slammed into him, he awoke with a cry, his eyes wider than a frightened child's.

"Be at peace, Brother." The voice was soft as a trickling spring, or shower of misty rain. "You are safe."

When the fear and confusion bled away from his eyes, Phaethon took in the scene around him. He was no longer on the beach. It was a ship of polished wood and hammered gold, and it cut swiftly through the water, though there was no one at the helm.

The young man's eyes fell on three girls, and he knew them at once.

"Sisters?"

They smiled and nodded, each beautiful and bright, one with hair of gold, one of black, and one of auburn, each with eyes to match.

"I am Phoebe," said the first, who had spoken already.

"I am Merope," added the second.

"And I am Aetheria," said the last.

"We are the Heliades," Phoebe said. "Our mother told us to come and get you."

"How?" Phaethon sat up. "You speak with her?"

"Of course," Merope handed him a cup of fresh water. "We hear her prayers, and she ours, when we are at sea."

"And our father?" Phaethon asked, hopeful. "Do you see and speak with him?"

All three girls hung their heads, and Aetheria answered.

"Rarely. Zeus decreed that we should bring the golden boat to where father needs it, but we do not see him take it. We are always made to sleep, and when we awake, the boat is returned, and he is gone."

"Will you take me to him? Please, sisters!"

The girls looked at each other, and then at once each pulled a golden medallion from her silken robes.

"Yes," Phoebe answered. "We will journey together to the Palace of the Sun, and there you will meet our father."

Their voices were as a welcome home, a farewell to solitude. Phaethon looked at the sisters he had never known, and try as he might, he could not stay the tears that had, for so long, been dammed up behind the walls of his soul.

He turned his face away from them, his eyes on the glittering sea. He spied the world below clearly, a world of sea nymphs and oceanids, of coral palaces and temples, and chariots drawn by teams of hippocampi.

I have missed so much.

"Do not weep, Brother." Phoebe sat beside him and she cradled his head on her shoulder, her tenderness lightening his heart. "Long have we wanted to see you, our only brother. We are your sisters, and now that we are together -"

"Nothing shall separate us," continued Merope.

"Ever," added Aetheria.

Brother and sisters sat then, close in the middle of the sacred boat, and looked in wonder to the sun crossing the heavens above them.

PHAETHON SLEPT AGAIN, and when he awoke, it was dusk. He was on the shore of a long-flowing river among reeds and tall grass. For a moment he panicked, wishing it had not all been a dream.

When his sisters' laughter splashed into his hearing, relief washed over him. All of their things had been laid out on the beach, and a pavilion of white and blue with golden suns had been erected. In the distance, north, loomed a mass of jagged mountains that seemed to pierce the very clouds and sky.

Phaethon stood up, the sound of insects ringing all about him. The air smelled of fresh water and clean mud as he went down the path through the grasses to the water.

The boat was gone, and the Heliades splashed naked in the shallows.

Phaethon noticed how the angling orange light covered their bodies and turned away.

"Come, Brother!" Aetheria called, laughing. "The river water is so different!"

His sisters were beautiful, but he still did not move. Never did he see his step-sisters in Merops' palace in their full nakedness.

"We must not embarrass Phaethon, sisters," Phoebe said as she came out of the water and donned her robe. "Come. We will go to the pavilion while he bathes."

When all three were gone, Phaethon undressed and plunged into the river. It was fresher than the lake before Merops' palace, and tasted sweet. He dove, and surfaced, and dove again, washing the dust off and reviving himself. He floated on his back for a time, his hand on a nearby rock, and stared at the sky.

Phaethon wondered where his father was, what it must be like to drive the Chariot of the Sun across the heavens.

As the sun descended and the stars lifted their veils, a sadness came over him. It always did.

He remembered his mother speaking of all the nights she had cried herself to sleep.

In darkness, I feel the same, he realized.

When he reached the pavilion, his sisters were seated about a table with a carved relief of the sun in the middle. It was set with bowls of fruit and nuts, and boards of cheese and bread. Into four cups, Merope had poured crimson wine.

Phaethon sat upon a cushion and accepted a plate and cup. "What are we doing here?" he asked.

"Waiting," Phoebe answered.

"For what?"

"For the boat to return. When father needs it, it is there for him. Then it is returned to us."

"But he could be anywhere!"

"It is no matter. It always returns to us."

"But how?"

The Heliades were silent. Then Merope spoke.

"We forget, brother, that you have been raised in a mortal world among Merops' children."

"It is easier if you trust in the boat to return," Phoebe continued. "It is part of the natural order of things."

Phaethon sipped his wine, his brow creased.

Phoebe smiled. "We are also to remain here until you complete your task."

"I am to see our half-brother, Prometheus, in the Caucasus. But we have only travelled a day! How am I to reach the top of the world?"

"Again," said Aetheria, "You must trust in this. Believe, Phaethon."

"Look outside," Merope said.

They all looked out the entrance of the pavilion where the folds were pulled aside.

There, visible from where they sat, all four siblings gazed upon the tallest peak to the North where it shot upward out of a grassy world to touch the heavens.

"The snow-covered peak," Phoebe whispered. "That is where you will find him."

Phaethon felt a chill run through his body.

"It's so high... So far..."

"Yes," Merope said. "Prometheus is up there, and that is where you must go."

"Mother should never have asked this of you!" Aetheria said, struggling to control her fear.

"But she did," Phaethon said. "And I must do as I promised."

They ate in silence after that. The mountain seemed to have cast a pall over their reunion, and so all each of them wished for was to fall into sleep's embrace.

Only Phaethon found it difficult to sleep. To him, it seemed, there was an echo of constant, pained moaning on the wind in the world outside.

4

THE CHAINED TITAN

Sunlight filtered through the fabric of the pavilion, soft and diffused.

Phaethon awoke to see Merope and Aetheria sleeping still, the rise and fall of their breaths soothing and melodic.

He rose, strapped on his sandals and cloak, and went outside. There he found Phoebe facing the rising sun, a silhouette of white and gold. He approached quietly from behind.

"Good morning, Phaethon."

"Sister."

"Did you sleep?" she continued to stare east.

"Not really. Well...a little. I don't sleep very well."

Phoebe turned to him.

"Could you hear him? Up there?" Her eyes went to the snow-capped peak in the sky.

"Yes. I could hear him."

"I always hear him." Phoebe's eyes were pained then,

small wisps of golden hair falling about her face, loose in the morning breeze.

"You weep?"

She looked back at him, surprised. "Of course. He is our brother, our mother's son." She walked a few paces as if toward the mountain. "For seeking to help mortals and wanting them to be better than themselves, Zeus punished Prometheus with eternal torment and pain. The eagle devours our brother's liver daily, only for it to grow back and have the torture repeated the next day."

Phaethon came up beside her, the echo of the previous night's pained anthem in his mind.

"He suffers for us all," she said.

"Mother gave me things for him."

"I know." Phoebe faced him. "Are you prepared to make this journey?"

Phaethon looked up again. "Yes. But how do I find my way? I could get lost."

"You will know the way."

"What about all of you? There may be bandits in these parts."

"Worry not, Brother," came Aetheria's voice, followed by Merope's.

"The Heliades are needed and respected by all. The sun is our emblem, and our shield. None harm us, for all rely upon us."

"What of me?" he asked.

"You must take your weapons with you," Phoebe said.

A SHORT TIME LATER, Phaethon was walking north along the river, with his sisters watching his back from the pavilion.

He was wrapped in his cloak, the box from his mother strapped to his back. With his sword, shield, and spears, he was well-armed. Defending himself was not his biggest worry. Getting lost was.

However, his feet felt light as he went. The mountains approached him at an alarming rate until he found himself in the foothills. The wind became stronger, colder. In fact the wind blew so much louder than on the plain that it seemed to Phaethon it was masking something.

The path became steeper, rockier, with tufts of purple, blue, and yellow wildflowers cropping up. A mountain stream trickled down beside his chosen path as Phaethon went up and up, first among beech and oak, and then among tall wavering pines that seemed to whisper as he passed.

The sun was angling west soon, and Phaethon realized that he would need to find shelter for the night. When Selene came into the sky with the darkness, Phaethon was perched beneath a rocky outcrop, his shield before him, his spear in his hand.

Moonlight painted the forest slopes with silver, and soon a howling of wolves could be heard all over the mountainside.

THE NIGHT WAS one of terror.

Apart from the incessant wind and howling of wolves, his brother's moans haunted the slopes of that high place.

Phaethon wondered if Prometheus was not exaggerating his condition, being cowardly.

He soon realized the cruelty of that thought, wondered if the wolves were also feasting on his brother in the dark.

With his shield before him, spear levelled, he went out

into the moonlight to look up the path. The stream trickled like a black line through the snow-frosted ground, and the path disappeared into the steeper reaches.

A deep resonant growling came up behind Phaethon.

The darkness seemed to deepen as he turned to see three wolves spreading out around him. Their teeth gleamed like polished bronze as they bared them.

Phaethon crouched.

He had hunted lions in Ethiopia, but always one at a time, and always with Merops' sons.

Now he was alone in the dark.

Phaethon backed up the path, trying to keep the wolves in front of him. It seemed to him that the forest floor rumbled with their threats.

The wolf on the right stepped into the small stream and yanked its paw out quickly.

As Phaethon watched, the wolf on the left lunged, its teeth grating on the large round shield that he held before him. He drove his spear down on top of the wolf's neck and felt the bone snap. When the other by the stream came, Phaethon swung the spear that way to slash across its chest.

The beast roared in pain and clamped its jaws on the spear shaft, wrenching it from Phaethon's grip. When it lunged again, Phaethon's sword slid free and drove into the opened chest wound. They both tumbled into the stream.

Phaethon turned quickly, the last wolf almost upon him, its jaws gaping for the kill.

It was a sound to chill the soul that stopped the beast and sent it back into the darkness. A cry so full of terror, pain, and lamenting that Phaethon too cowered, covered his ears, and scrambled out of the stream.

He retrieved his shield and sword and made for the rocks

where he had been taking shelter. The wind battered down the howling of wolves and the cries of all other beasts until, clutching his shield and medallion about his neck, Phaethon lost consciousness there, in the dark upon the mountain.

It was a bird that woke him, and pecked at the rim of his shield while he slept beneath it.

Phaethon shivered as he awoke, stiff and confused. The wind had died. He stood and looked down the mountain between the trees to the green plains beyond, the rivers running south like molten silver.

Did I come all that way in one day?

The thought unnerved and encouraged him at once. Even without the boat or his sisters, he had moved through the world unlike any mortal.

I am the son of Helios, he told himself and hoisted his belongings.

He paused when his eyes fell on his blood-stained hands and forearms, the legs of his breeches. The two wolf bodies on the ground nearby were frozen, as if sleeping.

Phaethon stepped around the bodies, and went to kneel beside the stream to drink.

Just as he put his lips to his cupped hands, he was spitting the blood from his mouth. He fell back from the stream, crabbing backwards from the red current.

Phaethon looked at his hands and legs and remembered falling into the stream.

It can't be...

He looked up the mountain. Phoebe's lonely figure the previous morning came to his mind then. *He suffers for us all,* she had said.

Phaethon picked up his shield and spear, and with what strength he had, he pressed on up the path.

THE LIGHT WAS full upon the mountain as he broke from the tree line onto the rocky, snow-capped heights. As he did so, thunder crashed in the distance, though the sky was purest blue but for the sun.

Phaethon stood still.

All sound had gone out of the world - the wind, the birds, the tumble of frozen rock. All was utterly still. Even his own breath was silent, though he was certain he breathed.

Walk on... came a hushed voice at the back of his consciousness. *Keep moving, Phaethon...*

"Mother? Phoebe?"

He could not figure out who had spoken, but whomever it was had given him courage so that he was able to climb one step at a time along that silent, crimson stream that steamed in the cold mountain air like fire.

Higher and higher Phaethon went. At one point, he spotted a giant bird circling the highest peak and then land.

"The eagle..." he muttered to himself, his words swallowed by the air. "I promised her..." he reminded himself as he went faster, despite the crushing feeling hammering in his young lungs.

The bloody stream ran faster now, as Phaethon came to the bottom of the last peak. He struggled to keep his footing on the snow, and shielded his eyes against the white glare.

He came to a cliff face near twice his height, next to which a rich red spray fluted into the air to join the stream below. With no other way up, Phaethon lunged for the ledge above him, and with frozen hands, grasped the jagged rocks.

His eyrie in Ethiopia had been a more difficult jump to master, but here it seemed all of his strength was being sapped. He strained, and pulled, and with one leg thrown up and over, attained the top.

Phaethon stood, dizzy from the effort. The air smelled of blood and fire at once, and he fought back the urge to vomit.

A path slick with blood wound away from him, around a corner. He followed it and turned the corner, his hand upon the rock face.

PHAETHON WANTED to weep at the sight that met him, and his hand went to his mouth to stifle a cry.

Sound had returned, though he wished it had not. For all he could hear was the sound of tearing flesh, a muffled squelching, and the occasional flutter of great feathers that blew slaughter-scented wind in his face.

Phaethon looked upon the massive rock face where his brother, the Titan Prometheus, hung in chains of adamant. Blood ran in a river from the tear in his body where Zeus' eagle devoured his liver, slowly, endlessly.

He stepped up to where Prometheus was chained, his muscular body hanging limp and uncovered.

Prometheus was perfect, strong and young, despite being ages old. His handsome face, framed by long auburn hair, was frozen in an agonized sleep.

Just when Phaethon began to wonder if he was indeed dead, Prometheus let out a groan which shook that peak at the top of the world.

"Brother?" Phaethon spoke to the tortured Titan.

The muscles of that massive form strained momentarily.

Prometheus' head raised, an ear cocked, and then he opened his tired eyes.

"Phaethon?"

"Yes. It's me."

To Phaethon's surprise, Prometheus closed his eyes again and wept softly.

The eagle continued about its business, plunging its beak into his side, and ripping out tiny bits of flesh.

Phaethon drew his sword and moved to kill the animal.

"NO!" Prometheus' eyes shot open, and he shook his head urgently. "You mustn't!"

"But why?" Phaethon asked, tears burning his own eyes. "I can't just let it do that to you."

Prometheus smiled. "Dear, brother. It's not for you to end my punishment, but for Zeus alone."

"I don't understand." Phaethon collapsed upon a rock, utterly spent from his trek. He looked up at the clouds in the sky, cold and grisly now that he was here among the dark rock and despair that was his brother's everyday. The snows ran away from that spot, through the trees to the rivers far below. And Prometheus' blood mingled with it all, leaching from the heavens.

Prometheus sensed Phaethon's tired bewilderment.

"When I gave man the secret of fire, I knew I was defying Zeus. And I knew there would be consequences. But in so doing, I have given man hope, a better future."

"While you stay up here, chained and tortured for all time?"

Prometheus' golden eyes met Phaethon's, and it seemed to the latter then that fear and sorrow dwelt alongside determination and courage beyond measure.

"It is my fate, Brother."

The eagle then stopped its savage feast to look from the one to the other. Its beautiful all-knowing, all-seeing eyes were in distinct contrast to its gore-besmirched head and talons.

"I'm glad to see you, Phaethon," Prometheus finally said. "I had begun to wonder if ever I would."

"I would have come sooner, but-"

"No. Now was the time."

Phaethon nodded and looked away as steaming blood poured away again from his brother's side.

"Phoebe, Merope, and Aetheria send you their love, especially Phoebe."

"Yes," the Titan smiled. "We talk sometimes when the world permits. She in her dreams, and I when the pain is at its least."

"Mother wanted me to bring this to you." Phaethon unhitched the wooden box from his back, unwrapped and opened it.

Prometheus' eyes gazed into it with curiosity, and he smiled.

"Even now she wishes to feed me. Please, Phaethon. Can you raise the ambrosia to my lips first?"

Phaethon glanced at the eagle a moment where it watched him intently. A distant rumble of thunder peeled across the valleys, but the bird allowed Phaethon to approach. He climbed up the rock, holding the slack of one chain, and held out the fire-coloured ambrosia.

Prometheus ate, and ate, until the bowl was empty, and Phaethon could feel a greater intensity of heat radiating from his brother's body. The Titan motioned to the other bowl.

"The nectar, please."

Phaethon did the same with the nectar, feeding it to his brother carefully so as not to loose a single drop.

Prometheus sighed and breathed deeply so that his chest and ribs heaved. He strained his arms and legs against the chains, testing their strength. His muscles doubled in size, and for a moment Phaethon thought he would break his god-made bonds.

But it was not meant to be.

"What is that small phial within the box?" Prometheus asked.

"Mother told me not to touch it, but that it was an alternative to imprisonment."

"Hydra's blood." Sadness crept across Prometheus' features. "I wish she had not tempted me so."

"Will it kill you?"

"Yes. And you or anyone else who touches it. You must close the box and cast it down the mountainside when you leave."

"You don't want to...you don't want to be free of this?" Phaethon looked at the eagle, the chains, that desolate place at the top of the world.

"Brother, the very actions that put me here are what made me free. If I escape these chains, I will not be free. As I said, it is my destiny to be here."

Phaethon was quiet, and watched as the sun tipped westward to the edge of the world. "What of my destiny? I've been living in ignorance, never knowing who I was, by the order of Zeus."

"Our mother kept you safe, in accordance with her own destiny."

"But what am I to do with my life now?" Phaethon's voice was pleading, but Prometheus shook his head.

"I cannot tell you that, for in so doing, you would not be free." Prometheus strained at his chains, ignoring the feasting eagle to lean closer to Phaethon. "Listen to me. You must decide what to do, Brother. We *are* our choices, both gods and men." He looked at the sun then, arcing across the sky. "Just remember that we are all held to account for our choices, for all time." He rattled the heavy adamant links that had imprisoned him. "Think on what you want, what you feel you *must* do, and then do that."

Phaethon's eyes strayed again to the setting sun.

Dread entered Prometheus' heart, but he remained silent.

"You must go now. Night approaches and you should not remain here with me too long. Zeus knows all, and sees all."

Just then the eagle pulled back from Prometheus' body, flapped its great wings, and soared into the western sky.

"Go now," the Titan urged. "I have enjoyed meeting you. You have given me strength, Phaethon. In my heart. But I must rest for the morrow."

Phaethon nodded. "Will I ever see you again?"

Prometheus merely shook his head. "Go now, and tell our sisters I love and cherish them."

"I will." Phaethon took up the box, and made his way down the path, pausing at the turn for one last glimpse, a wave. He could not see the tears in the Titan's eyes then, nor hear the prayers Prometheus muttered to the sky in his favour.

When Phaethon retrieved his sword, spear, and shield, and once more made his way onto the snows before the tree line, he crept toward a cliff overlooking a canyon of crags far below, and cast the wooden box over the precipice as his brother had requested.

He then followed the bloody stream down the mountain, through the snow and trees. He pressed on through the night, wanting only to get as far as he could from the Caucasus. The pain he felt in his throat, his heart, was too much to bear.

Sound returned, and he could hear the nocturne of the wood as he went, including the wolves. He was grateful that they stayed away from him. He had come far to see Prometheus.

And yet only to leave him there.

The thoughts pressed upon him as his footsteps came onto the soft grasses of the foothills. He could hear singing in his mind, and stopped to look about. It was beautiful, sad.

The red stream had bled into the earth some way back, and now Phaethon could see the smooth line of the river pouring south.

He listened again to the song as the sun broke over the horizon in myriad shades of yellow, pink, and fire, its rays covering the sky in magnificent strokes.

The voices intensified in their sonorous rhythm and beauty, and Phaethon knew it was his sisters, the Heliades, singing to their father as he raced across the world.

Phaethon closed his eyes and let the blessed light wash over his weary body. He dropped his shield and spear and held his arms wide as he looked over the broad green plains laced with fresh rivers as far as the eye could see, flowing to the deserts of the South.

The light gave him strength as the nectar and ambrosia had done for Prometheus. With a great bound from the boulder upon which he stood, Phaethon leapt down the path and ran the rest of the way back to his sisters and the camp.

I'm coming, Father! I am coming...

AETHERIA AND MEROPE each ran to him as he appeared on the path flanked by tall grasses. The light and warmth of the river valley set all about them in gold, and in the angling light, birds, butterflies, and other insects flit about them.

Aetheria launched herself at Phaethon, divine laughter bursting forth.

Merope's dark hair fell over his shoulder as she held him, tight and intense. "We were worried," she said in his ear.

"Where is Phoebe?"

"She has seen the boat off again," Aetheria answered, her smile lightening Phaethon's heart.

The two girls led him back to the pavilion where Phoebe was just setting out food and wine.

Without a word, Phaethon let fall his belongings and rushed to her.

Her golden eyes swelled with relief, and she held him to her, tears falling gently onto his neck. "I'm glad you are safe."

"I have much to tell you," he answered, happy beyond measure to be back among them.

As they ate, Phaethon recounted the journey, and it was no small shock to him that he had been gone for seven days.

"But I was only gone for two nights!"

"Time moves differently upon the Caucasus, brother," Merope said, sipping her wine from a golden cup.

Phaethon grew quiet and stared out the tent flaps into the night.

"What is it?" Phoebe asked.

"The box that mother sent with me contained ambrosia and nectar."

"Oh, that must have helped poor Prometheus," Aetheria put in.

"It also contained a phial of hydra's blood."

Each of the girls' hands went to their mouths in horror.

"I didn't know what it was."

"Phaethon," Phoebe was kneeling before him now, her eyes intense. "Did you give Prometheus the phial?"

"No."

She slumped down.

"He told me he could not take it, would not, because he would not be free if he did. That only Zeus could free him."

"What did you do with it?" Aetheria asked.

"I threw it over the cliff as he asked me to." Phaethon stood and moved to the tent flaps to feel the cool breeze. "Even as the eagle tore at his flesh, Prometheus told me that it was his destiny to be there, and that I needed to find what I want to do if I want to achieve my own destiny."

The Heliades were silent as they looked at their brother, framed by the darkness of the night. Beyond him, their aunt Selene cast her silver glow upon the land.

None of them spoke again that night. On learning of what had gone before them, of what Prometheus had done, suffered, and believed, each of them now questioned the very purpose of their existence.

When they each lay down upon their pallets, the sound of Prometheus' sighs trickled down the mountain to blend with the earth, the water, the trees, and the air. It was everywhere, and the sound of his suffering would echo in their hearts for all time.

.   .   .

At dawn, the golden boat was waiting for them in the river near their camp. It shone in the early morning light beside the shore where water snakes glided and dragon flies hovered among the rushes.

When the boat was loaded, Phaethon helped each of his sisters on board. Standing in the water and holding the prow with one hand, he gazed into the sky toward that peak at the top of the world. He imagined Prometheus there on that cold, soundless precipice, and did not want to leave.

Phoebe came to the prow and placed her hand on his.

"We must go now. It's time."

"I don't know if I can. He's all alone up there. Forever."

"Zeus may yet relent," she hoped.

You must both go...

Phaethon looked quickly to his sister who nodded as her eyes went to the mountain.

Then Phaethon climbed into the boat, and as soon as they were all seated, it moved into the river's current of its own accord, south, toward the great river Ocean, their mother's realm. From thence, they would be taken to the far edge of the world to the Palace of the Sun.

HYMN III

THE SHINING FATHER

5

THE PALACE OF THE SUN

The journey was as a dream for the four siblings, even for the Heliades whose lives revolved about the comings and goings of that golden barge.

Few beings, god or man, ever journeyed to the Palace of the Sun.

The Heliades knew not what they needed to do, for they had never set foot in their father's home. The golden boat drifted over the great distance with unimaginable ease, casting its passengers into a deep slumber after a short time.

As the boat passed, nymphs, oceanids, and nereids ensured its safety, singing to the children of their one-time mistress and the God of Light.

Before he lay himself down in the hull, Phaethon remembered seeing herds of centaurs rushing to the river's edge, and waving as they passed. Flights of eagles cast shadows upon water and land, and pink river dolphins surfaced beside the boat, their laughter seeing them into the great blue of the writhing River Ocean.

Then all was sleep, deep and peaceful.

. . .

PHAETHON, Phoebe, Merope, and Aetheria knew not how long they had travelled, nor what remote shores of the world they had skirted in the sun's barge.

When they awoke, the boat bobbed gently on the swells like a child upon its slumbering mother's breast.

There was no land in sight.

"What's this?" Merope said, rubbing her eyes. "Where are we? Phoebe, Aetheria, Phaethon, wake up!"

The siblings pulled themselves from out of their dreams. Slowly, they all knelt, looking about at the blue expanse.

Panic began to set in.

"Perhaps the boat took us to the wrong place?" Phaethon wondered.

"It's not possible." Aetheria shook her head.

"The boat does not misguide itself," Merope assured them. "Phoebe?" Merope looked to the prow where Phoebe stood staring silently at the sea as a soft wind blew her golden hair around her face.

"I dreamed..." Phoebe said.

"Of what?" her sisters asked.

Phaethon remained silent.

"I dreamed a song." She turned to look at them. Their eyes were wide. "A song to calm the raging seas, to give life..."

"Me too," Aetheria whispered.

"And I." Merope stood and moved toward Phoebe. "Come, Aetheria."

Phaethon helped them to the prow and sat back as the Heliades clasped hands.

As the boat bobbed gently, the three sisters closed their eyes. At once, sweet notes from heaven filled the air.

The melody of their voices rose, soft and bright as the sun itself, and Phaethon felt his heart swell with emotions for which he had no name. The beauty of their paean was something he could not have conceived of in any realm of men or gods.

In the near distance, the River Ocean began to bubble, more and more, until Phaethon feared a great beast or tidal wave was upon them. Perhaps Poseidon himself had come to punish them for their daring?

But the Heliades sang on calmly, and no destruction came. Instead, from the writhing mass of sea-foam, five great golden spires came out of the depths to reveal the image of their father, Helios, and his chariot team. It rose higher and higher to reveal the palace for which it served as a crown.

To the right of it rose an image of a woman and a team of horses, not of gold, but of purest black, rising into the sky and crowning a twin palace.

Now the Heliades struggled to hold their tune, overcome as they were by the sight before them.

Two titanic mounds of rock rose out of the foaming water, each covered in palaces of pure marble, set and splashed with gold, the one white, and the other black.

The Palaces of the Sun and Moon.

Phaethon stared in disbelief. Had he come so far?

His eyes rested on his father's palace, gleaming columns holding up porticos and towers that flanked a great hall. Upon each tower was set a golden sun, and a massive door gaped beneath the colossal golden chariot at the zenith.

The ocean calmed and the Heliades stopped their song, tears streaming from their eyes.

"They're beautiful," Aetheria said.

The palaces had risen to their full height, and glinted in

the last light of day. Great waterfalls poured off of them, and brilliant suns and moons glinted where they were set into the very rock.

"Something's happening," Phaethon said, parting his tunic at the top to reveal the medallion of the sun about his neck. "It's glowing!"

Phaethon's sisters pulled out their own medallions and found the same.

"Look!" Phoebe pointed to the base of the palace rock and there, in the shape of a rayed sun, was an entrance.

The boat began to move directly toward it, and as they approached, the gateway glowed the same as their medallions, pulling them in.

"I never imagined anything so big," Phaethon's voice was hoarse.

"Or beautiful," Phoebe added.

They all looked up as the boat approached, their eyes taking in the ancient pocked rock, and then straying up along mighty columns to windows, and towers, and balconies bearing polished sun discs.

They were not afraid, for they were in the home of their father, the Charioteer of the Sun.

Phoebe took Phaethon's hand, and he helped her and the others to disembark at a mooring where polished bronze horses flanked a marble landing platform.

Torches were alight everywhere within the cavern and up a long corridor which they followed.

The ceiling of that long, winding corridor was higher than a temple and adorned with paintings of godly skill, depictions of the sun and moon, rising and setting, of the wars between the Gods and the Titans.

When they reached the end of the corridor, they entered

a long room with a colonnade that looked west over the River Ocean.

"He's not here?" Phaethon asked.

"The sun is still up," Merope said.

"Helios will return soon."

All four of them turned quickly from the wide, light-giving window to see a tall, powerful, and lithe woman dressed all in black.

Her bare arms and face were of purest white, and her eyes were a deep, brilliant blue.

They all froze, but then she smiled and came toward them, her long black hair streaming in her wake.

"Thea Selene," Merope said, and all four of them bowed to their father's sister, the Goddess of the Moon.

"Heliades?" She moved to each of them and bent to caress their cheeks and kiss their foreheads. "I've been watching you for so long, girls. And you, Phaethon..." Selene held him at arm's length. "I never thought to see my nephew so near."

Selene stepped back, her eyes full of love and care for her brother's children.

"Does my father know we are coming, Thea?"

Selene smiled at Phaethon. "Your father knows and sees all, Nephew. And he will be back soon." Selene looked out to the West where the sun dipped over the edge of the world.

Then, an enormous conch horn shook the palace rock, and Selene's eyes darted.

"I must go now, children. My team awaits me. There is wine and food in the next room." She smiled one last time. "The Palaces of the Sun and Moon want for nothing. Especially now."

With that, she was gone, like a shadow when the final lights are extinguished.

In the world outside, they heard the sound of a soft horn, and the crack of a whip as Selene drove her team from her palace into the night sky. They rushed to the window and watched as heaven's canopy of stars burst into brilliance in the wake of her black chariot.

PHAETHON and his sisters sat upon couches, eating and drinking, but sparingly. The Heliades had rarely met their father, though they served him faithfully. Helios, to them, was more a longing, a hope in the daytime sky. They each sought his approval from a forced distance.

For Phaethon, the moment he had been dreaming of since leaving Ethiopia was upon him. For all his pacing and gazing outside, for all his eagerness to meet his true father, he felt his own shortcomings more acutely than ever.

"What if father doesn't like me?" Phaethon burst out.

His sisters stopped eating and looked up. Phoebe spoke.

"How could he not but love you? Our mother is his greatest love, and you are the son he has never met."

Phaethon sat down and accepted a cup of wine from Aetheria.

"Isn't it odd that the sea about the palace is ever calm?" Merope said.

"Yes." Phoebe went to the window to look out. The ocean was a glossy black expanse of reflected star and moon light, a wondrous sight. She had wanted to speak more with Selene, but she knew the burden of being one of the charioteers of sun and moon. All depended on their timing, the accurate and consistent cycle of their teams across the sky.

A great rushing of air collided with the palace then, and

Aetheria and Merope jumped to their feet to stand beside Phoebe and Phaethon.

The four of them, for a moment, believed the palace would plunge back into the midnight depths of Ocean, but then they heard the trample of hooves above them, the rock of wheels coming to a sudden halt.

A loud neighing of horses caused Phaethon to cover his ears.

The Heliades smiled, and Aetheria spoke.

"He is here!"

6

WITH THE SUNSET

The sound of titanic, hurried footsteps rang within the palace walls until a doorway at the back of the room glowed orange and yellow all about its edges. When the door burst open, a great wave of light crashed forth like a blast of lightning. After a few moments, the glare receded to reveal Helios himself standing before them.

Phoebe, Aetheria, Merope, and Phaethon unshielded their eyes to see their father standing there smiling.

To Phaethon, Helios was a Titan greater than all. Taller than any man, perfectly proportioned, and of a might only to be imagined. His muscles thrived beneath his sun-dark skin, full of strength, action, and vitality. His long auburn hair framed his godly face, alive with light and flame. It seemed to shift with his very mood.

But, for all this, it was the eyes of the father, alighted upon his children, that Phaethon took to heart. Such a look of warmth, love, and pride shone forth from Helios' golden gaze that for the first time in his life, Phaethon did not feel sadness lurking beneath the surface of his being.

"Heliades!" Helios rushed to his daughters, calling them each by name, kissing their foreheads gently, and holding them all for a measure of time long-needed by each.

Phaethon watched, awed and afraid by the tightness wringing his chest. What had he done to deserve a glorious father? What deeds could he boast of?

Then his father's eyes fell upon him, and the sun rose brighter than it ever had for Phaethon. Without a word, Helios approached the son he had never met, silent, his smile less, but still warm.

He took Phaethon by the shoulders and looked him over.

"Phaethon," Helios whispered as he pulled the young man close and held him tightly.

All Phaethon felt was love. That is all. Pure and all-accepting.

All those years of unguided loneliness in Ethiopia vanished then, and all that was left was a boy holding on with all his might to his true father.

For several moments they stayed like that with the Heliades encircling them.

In her dream that night, far away, Clymene wept for joy that her son had finally met her love, and for sadness that she could never be there with them.

"All these years that I have been watching you, my son. And now, you've come." Helios clapped his massive hands. "Let us sit, and talk, and let me hear of your journey to the Palace of the Sun!" He laughed and they followed him to sit together.

They sat as a family that night, eating, drinking, and laughing. Helios listened with joy to the sparkling voices of his daughters as they spoke of their days, and of discovering they had a brother.

Phaethon spoke of the sad years in Ethiopia, and Helios knew he was partly to blame for it, for not appealing to Zeus more forcefully. But when Phaethon spoke of his visit to Prometheus, he was reminded of Zeus' wroth which may well have been turned on Clymene or their children.

How could I even tempt such a thing? Helios thought as he looked upon them all sitting with him.

"You are all here now, my children. And that has filled me with unimaginable joy."

ONE BY ONE, Aetheria, Merope, Phoebe, and Phaethon all drifted into contented slumber about their father who sat watching the rise and fall of their breathing.

When they slept deeply, Helios moved to the pillared balcony overlooking the River Ocean.

Despite the joy he now felt, a sharp spearpoint of dread pricked at the back of his immortal thoughts, and thunder rumbled in the night.

Let them stay awhile... Not long. The Sun will not fail... I promise.

He spent the entire night gazing upon his sleeping children. He had seen many wonders of the world, and yet it amazed him that those four youths upon the couches before him awed him more than anything else.

For so long Helios had put them out of his mind as soon as the hurt would set in. Those who thought that gods were immune to sadness and pain were going through time with their eyes shut tight.

He knew that now. He hoped that time would be allowed to them.

· · ·

WHEN THE GREAT conch sounded and Selene's team came home to the Palace of the Moon, Helios left his children sleeping.

He raced up to his four horses and the golden chariot, hopped into the cab, and sped out to give the world as bright a sunrise as ever it bore witness to.

Phaethon awoke with the sun on his face and rushed to the open windows looking west. The light sparkled so intensely on the ocean that he had to shield his sleepy eyes.

"You're awake," said Selene, coming into the room. "I thought you might be." She paused and looked out like a captain at sea, searching the horizon. "The night has ever been mine, and I do so love it. But the day is beauty beyond imagining."

Phaethon was silent beside his aunt. She was tall, and dark, and her beauty was overwhelming up close. She smiled and took his hand.

"Come. Let me introduce you to my team."

Selene led Phaethon to the side of the palace where a door opened onto a bridge of hewn stone that arced over the cliffs and the sea to join to the Palace of the Moon.

The height was dizzying, but Phaethon felt safe with Selene. Her calm confidence lent him courage.

He followed her through corridors of black marble veined with crimson, and then up a staircase to a large door decorated with a golden moon.

Phaethon expected a strong smell of stable as Selene opened the door, but the odour that did meet him was one of jasmine and dew, scents of the night.

Four large paddocks held four magnificent steeds who stood several hands taller than Selene and Phaethon. The horses' bodies were smooth and black as night, and they each looked up when their mistress approached with her soothing voice. She stopped at the fourth.

"This is Xanthus. He is the team leader, the heart of them all. He helps me to keep them all reigned in so that we do not pass over the world too quickly. Selene stroked the stallion's soft muzzle, her cheek upon his.

Phaethon reached out and the stallion lifted its head.

"Shh. Shh," Selene soothed. "He's our friend. It's all right."

The stallion leaned down to allow Phaethon to greet him.

"He's cold?"

"Yes. The night is cold and dark, and so are they." Selene smiled. "But they are quick as shadows."

"Are they immortal?" Phaethon asked.

"Yes. As are you father's. They were given to us by Zeus himself so that we might keep order in the world, that day and night might never fade or fail in the passing of time."

"I would love to ride them," Phaethon mused.

Selene's face grew serious.

"They listen only to me, as I am the only one bound to them."

"I see. I have ridden for much of my life though. I'm quite skilled."

Selene laughed at his sudden excitement. "I'm sure you are. But immortal horses possess a power beyond that of worldly ones." She closed the door to Xanthus' paddock. "Come, let us wake your sisters and have food together." Selene led Phaethon out of the torchlit stables and back to the Palace of the Sun. As they walked, she observed the great strength in his limbs, but she knew he would never be able to handle her team, or his father's.

·   ·   ·

FOR THE WHOLE of that day, Phaethon wandered the corridors of his father's palace while Phoebe sang to the sea. She loved to do that, and he loved to listen. Her voice calmed him as it calmed the unfathomable depths that stretched as far as the eye could see.

"Where are Aetheria and Merope?" he asked as he came up beside her.

"With Selene, at the Palace of the Moon."

"You didn't want to go?"

"I would rather watch the day here with you. In father's palace, it truly feels like home."

Phaethon's thoughts went immediately to Prometheus who was having his liver torn out even as he and Phoebe stood comfortably in the Palace of the Sun.

"Do not dwell on him, Phaethon," she said, his thoughts as clear to her as a cup of spring water. "It will bring you nothing but grief, and he would not want that."

"How can he be so selfless?" *How can I even approach his greatness?* he thought.

"There are few like our brother." Phoebe began her song again and it seemed that all the world slowed only to listen to her.

7

A BURNING PURPOSE

Days and weeks passed upon the earth with Phaethon and the Heliades sitting with their father during the night, and with Selene in the empty Palace of the Sun during the day.

During that time, a yearning began in Phaethon's heart. It took root, and grew in strength.

He wanted to know why his father had not contacted him before, how and when he spoke with Clymene. He wanted to know what it was like, exactly, to drive the Chariot of the Sun.

Phaethon had been too timid at first to approach his father on these things, but now, after many long talks into the night, in which Helios had asked him all about his own life, he found the courage to ask.

The five of them were sitting on couches, drinking wine and eating food from the cornucopia in their midst.

"Father?" Phaethon began.

"Yes, my son?" Helios' gaze turned on him, bright, and clear, and happy as a spring dawn.

"Why did you never contact me? Every morning since I

was old enough to go alone, I was sitting on that rock above the plains of Ethiopia, waiting. I was watching for something I was unaware of, and yet you knew. You see all and you never once stopped for me. Why?"

Though he did not realize it, Phaethon was standing, his fists clenched, tears streaming down his face. He had missed years of family warmth, and now he felt the loss of time acutely.

Helios set down his golden cup and stood. He walked to the balustrade and looked out into the night.

They do not understand the loneliness of my existence... Then he turned to speak.

"I wanted to. Truly, Phaethon. I could see you there every day of your life, and I tried to give you all the greatest of days. But I could not, can never, stop for any reason. The constancy of my chariot across the daytime sky is written in the laws of this world. All depend upon the light for food, for health - humans, animals, plants... Life itself holds me to account. If I blunder, the consequences could be disastrous for gods and men." Helios' smile was gone, replaced by a dread look. "That is why I never stopped."

Phaethon hung his head.

"But I was always watching you, all of you." He smiled again, at his daughters, and back at Phaethon. "Come. There is...something I would show you."

Helios went with Phoebe beside him, Merope, Aetheria, and Phaethon following. He led them up a winding staircase that led to one of the sun-capped towers flanking the Stables of the Sun.

They came to a circular room that was empty save for a pedestal in the middle. Upon this was a wide, shallow bowl of silver. The water in the bowl was absolutely still, like oil by the light of the torch.

Helios looked at it a moment, and then dipped his finger in.

Before their eyes, the water began to glow and shimmer. A veil lifted and Clymene appeared before them, sleeping but restless, tears running sideways from her eyes as she slept.

"Mother?" Aetheria gasped.

"Yes," Helios said, his hair shading his eyes as he looked down. "You asked how I could see you. This is how. I have watched you all in the long lonely nights of my life. I speak to your mother as she sleeps, and I tell her how I love her."

"Oh, Mother," Merope suddenly said, approaching the bowl. "Is it really her?"

"Yes. She is sleeping now. If you speak, she will hear." Helios reached out and touched Clymene's cheek as it was in the water, and spoke. "My love? It is me. Our children are here."

Helios, my love? Clymene whispered as she slept.

"Yes."

"Mother?"

Merope? My darling. Is that you?

"Yes, Mother. I love you."

I love you... Clymene answered, smiling now.

"And I, Mother. I am here too," Aetheria said. "I miss you so."

Aetheria? I miss you too. And Phoebe? Where is she?

"I am here. We are all well. I love you."

And I love you, Phoebe. Sweet girl.

"Mother?" Phaethon stepped up.

Phaethon? Clymene's voice was suddenly strained. *Please don't do it, my son. Do not.*

"Do what?"

I had a dream, of fire and sadness.

"Prometheus is brave, Mother. He says he loves you, and that he is fulfilling his destiny."

Clymene shook her head violently as she slept.

No! I had a dream. Fire!

"Please, Mother. All is well," Phaethon pleaded. "Do not worry. I miss you and love you."

Then Helios stepped up to the bowl and touched Clymene's brow.

"Sleep, my life. Sleep. Soon the sun's light shall kiss you."

Clymene fell back into peaceful slumber then, and Phaethon and his sisters gazed in amazement at the bowl.

"That is how I have watched you when I am here, my children. I have whispered to you in your dreams. There is only one other such vessel in the world, and that rests with Zeus on the heights of Olympus."

"Can you speak to mother again?" Merope asked.

"Not tonight. Too much and she could go mad." Helios looked out the window. "Come. The night is nearly at an end."

"I would help you harness your team, Father." Phaethon had not yet been invited to see the horses of the sun. The had all been so busy talking into the nights.

"Yes," Helios answered. "I have waited because my horses are much more wild than your aunt's, but now is the time. Follow me, all of you."

Phaethon had come to accept all of the wonders he had seen since leaving Ethiopia without question. Indeed, much of it had felt normal to his very soul. But when the great gilded doors of the stables swung open, it was as though he had settled on Olympus itself.

The stables were bright and decorated with golden suns and columns holding up a roof painted like the sky. Beneath that sky, four massive paddocks held Helios' team of whites, two on either side of a wide path that led out into the sky from the very top of the palace.

Sitting in the middle of the path was Helios' titanic chariot, glinting brighter than any star in the heavens. It leaned forward from its two massive wheels as if ready to speed away of its own accord. On its surface, reliefs of the battles of the Gods and Titans moved and blazed, and Phaethon thought he could hear the crack of thunder, the clang of god-made weapons, and the crash of waves on rock. Phaethon's eyes looked over every inch of the chariot with longing and wonder.

Helios whistled and all four horses turned to him. They were tall, larger than Selene's, leaving no doubt of their divinity. Their manes shone like sunlight upon water, and their eyes blazed with life.

Phaethon and the Heliades stood gaping from the doorway.

"Come in," Helios told them. "Come and meet them." He went to the first. "This is... Eous. She loves to run and play." He smiled. "This second is Aethon. She is the determined one. Pyrois here is the brightest in the sky." Helios smiled at the awed look upon his children's faces as he moved to the last paddock near the mouth of the stables. "And this, this is Plegon, my strength. He is the power that binds them all and drives us across the heavens."

"Can I get closer?"

"Yes, my son. I've dreamed of the day you might meet

them. They are my constant companions." Helios opened the paddock so that Phaethon could approach the stallion.

The young man reached up, above his head, to stroke the stallion's smooth white jaw. The horse nudged him, stamped his massive hoof, and leaned in closer to Phaethon.

Helios smiled. "He likes you." The father stood proud, arms crossed as he watched his children with the members of his team. They were all his family, and if he could die, he could have done it then for all the joy he felt.

In the world outside, the stars began to fade, and Helios set about his business.

"Dawn approaches. Merope, Aetheria, Phoebe, and Phaethon, please open the paddocks. They will know what to do."

Helios' children did as their father bid and instantly the three mares and the stallion thundered out of their stalls to line up before the Chariot of the Sun.

With a speed that came of ages of repetition, Helios harnessed his team and they stomped and whinnied with excitement. The floor beneath their hooves shook as though the palace would crumble into the sea, but it did not. A harness of golden adamant was hung on each horse, and Helios inspected each carefully.

While his father checked the team, Phaethon climbed into the chariot's cab.

He felt the power flowing through his arms and legs as he stood in the Chariot of the Sun. The reins felt good in his hands, like he had come to the place where he belonged.

"Come down, Phaethon." Helios' voice was stern. He stood below Phaethon, his tunic thrown aside and his torso bared for his ride.

"Let me come with you."

"There is room for only one. Come."

The great horn sounded within and without the palace then, and Helios leapt into the chariot as Phaethon came down.

"Cover your eyes!" Helios warned as he took the reins.

A great rush of fire filled the stables then, and just before he closed his eyes, Phaethon saw his father's entire body alight from within. Helios' muscles expanded and writhed with unheard of strength, and in a flash of heat and light the Chariot of the Sun burst forth from the palace to herald a new day.

WHEN PHAETHON and his sisters opened their eyes, all was still, and clean, and white in the stables.

"I never thought to witness it," Phoebe said to the others.

They were all silent as they made their way back down to the palace rooms.

How can one describe the first glimpse of sunlight, its birth? It was then that the Heliades realized their importance, the support they gave to Helios as his offspring, his representatives in the world of men. All respected them and kept an awed distance, and as such, remembered and honoured their father. Their songs were of the sun and filled the world with a joy that was a part of life's flow. As they sailed in the sun's boat, they spread that joy through time. The golden boat was not their father's. It was theirs. Helios did not need it. They did.

Phoebe, Aetheria, and Merope went down to eat and watch with new wonder as their father raced across the sky.

For Phaethon, there was no such affirmation or sense of

fulfillment. Having stood in the Chariot of the Sun, he knew what he wanted more than anything.

Phaethon wanted to be his father's son, to show the world a day that it would never forget, a day that it would remember always as the most beautiful day that had ever dawned.

He wanted to be the one to drive his father's chariot across the sky and make Helios, Zeus, and all the others see that he was worthy of his parentage. He wanted the Gods to sit up and take notice from those lofty olympian heights. He wanted the Gods to see their mistake in separating him from his family.

As Phaethon stood on the very precipice where the stables let out onto the world, he imagined what it would be like to achieve his heart's desire.

HYMN IV

CHAOS RETURNED

8

THE EYES OF OLYMPUS

"What are you still doing up here?" Phoebe asked as she entered the stables.

Phaethon was sitting beside the last paddock gazing out at the day and the River Ocean as it flowed ever on. He looked up at his sister and she spotted the change in his eyes.

"What has happened?" she asked.

"I know what I need to do. I know what my destiny is."

"What?"

"I must drive father's chariot for one day."

"Why?"

"What do you mean, *why*? You saw the beauty of it, the power..." Phaethon gazed into the blue void. "If I can give the world a glorious day, then Zeus will have no choice but to allow us to remain here with father, and to bring mother here too."

"No, Phaethon. It's not possible. You are strong, yes. But father is a god. He *is* the light of the world. Not you."

"But I could be."

Phoebe shook her head. "But why? Zeus hasn't even forced us to leave, and we have been here for weeks."

"It's my destiny, Phoebe. I've never been more sure of something." Phaethon paced the space between the paddocks. "All these years I've sat gazing at the sun, wanting to be close to it, to touch it! And all that time, I didn't even know he was my father!" He stopped pacing and faced his sister. "I want to make him proud, Phoebe. As he is of you three, as mother is of Prometheus."

"Prometheus is a Titan, Phaethon."

"And our half-brother."

Phoebe felt a prickle of dread.

"I suppose you can ask father and see what he says."

"I will, Sister. I must."

Phaethon turned, his arms pulsing with a strength and energy he had never felt before, and a smile crossed his face for the first time in many days.

THAT NIGHT, the Chariot of the Sun arrived home and Helios began to unhitch his foaming team. He wondered whether he had rushed the day in his excitement to come home to his children.

He was eager for the company of his offspring; they lightened his heart and reminded him of Clymene, for whom he still yearned daily. They were all so like her.

"You've grown nostalgic, Cousin."

The voice startled Helios, but he recognized the lilt of the Gods' messenger immediately and felt the apprehension creeping in upon him.

"Hermes," Helios said, turning and walking toward the tall, lean figure framed by the blackness of the night outside. "What brings you to the Palace of the Sun?"

Hermes smiled and crossed his arms before coming forward.

"I believe you must know. Zeus has sent me with a command."

Helios chafed at this but held his peace. He moved to the stallion, Plegon, and stroked his muzzle.

"What command?"

"Come now. You know and see all. And so does Zeus." Hermes came around to face Helios from the other side of the stallion. The moonlight glinted off the wings upon his lean back, setting the white wall of the paddock alight with blue fire.

"Zeus is much displeased with the presence of your children in the Palaces of the Sun and Moon. You know how precious the order of all things is to him."

"I know."

"Then you must know what Zeus' command is?"

"Yes. But, my children have done nothing wrong." Helios came around to face Hermes.

"It's not what they have done, but rather what they are capable of doing that worries Zeus. I speak especially of your son, Phaethon."

The stallion looked up then and Helios rested a muscled arm upon him.

"I can trust my son."

"Are you so sure? You have, after all, only just met him."

"You're wrong, Messenger!" Helios' voice rumbled in Hermes' face.

The latter stood tall and defiant, backed by his god-given authority.

Helios continued. "I have watched him all of his days, and he has ever acted with honour."

"Among humans," rejoined Hermes. "Not among gods."

"By Zeus' command-"

"Yes!" Hermes' eyes blazed. "By Zeus' command! As are all things. None were supposed to approach the Caucasus to see Prometheus chained, and yet your son did, and offered him Hydra's blood!"

Helios' face fell, but he tried to stay strong.

But Hermes pressed on. "You're fortunate that Zeus did not strike your children down before they ever reached you."

Helios realized the truth of the words, their sting. He also knew, deep down, the resentment he felt for Zeus.

So many years apart from them...

Hermes rested his hand upon Helios' shoulder and smiled. "I know you are pained. We have all felt Zeus' justice harsh at times, but we also know that without it, without the command of Zeus, we would once more descend into Chaos. For the sake of your children at least, send them away."

Helios looked out at the night and felt the despair rising again in his chest.

He had thought it gone.

"How much time do I have?" he asked Hermes.

"Zeus commands that you send your children away before the close of three days. You should not think beyond that."

"I understand." Helios turned back to Hermes. "Go back and tell Zeus I shall do as he commands."

"Good." The messenger smiled and moved to the edge of the

void. "You have chosen wisely, Helios," he spoke over his shoulder. Then the relief of blue wings upon Hermes' back sprang to life and unfolded to their full length. He then dove headlong into the night sky like a star skimming the surface of the ocean.

"Father?"

Helios whirled around to see his son at the entrance to the stables.

Phaethon spotted the fiery tear that ran down his father's golden cheek.

"Who...who was that?"

Helios took a deep breath. "Come." He walked over to Phaethon and held him close to look at him. "I must speak with you and your sisters. Now."

In the great room of the Palace of the Sun, where they had all spoken, and laughed, and done their utmost to recapture a measure of lost time, Helios now stood facing his son and daughters.

They all looked at him, mingled portraits of admiration, adoration, dread, and joy.

The great charioteer paced before them, his massive frame struggling to defy an occasional shudder before finally speaking.

"Hermes has just come to see me."

Phoebe gripped Phaethon's hand, and Aetheria gasped.

Merope was stern and silent, her black head hanging slightly.

Only Phaethon did not know what the news meant.

"What did he want, Father?" Phaethon had asked before, but Helios had wanted to tell them all at once.

"Zeus sent him."

"No..." Aetheria whispered.

Helios came closer. "I am commanded by Zeus to send

you all away three days hence. If I do not comply, Zeus' wrath will fall upon you."

"But we only just arrived," Merope said.

"It has been some weeks, my daughter," Helios replied, the look on their faces an agony to him.

"Compared to a lifetime of separation." Phoebe's words were as the cracking of the Earth.

The father knelt before his children, making sure to look at each of them. He wanted to remember every detail of their faces up close, their personalities, before they were gone.

"Listen to me, all of you." He took Phaethon's hand on one end, and Aetheria's on the other. "You have given me the greatest days of my existence. After your mother was taken from me, I never thought to reach such heights of joy...but I have." Helios titled his head and his fiery locks hung about his face. The feeling of anticipated loneliness was more than he could bear, and it threatened to swallow him up.

"You must know that I love you all, and that I will ever be with you, whatever the Fates have in store."

"Perhaps if I could explain to Zeus?" Phaethon tried, but Helios began shaking his head. "There must be something, Father? Let me prove myself to Zeus -"

"There is nothing you can do!" Helios' voice burst out. "None can prevail upon Zeus when his mind is set. You should know, Phaethon. You have seen poor Prometheus."

"Yes, I have!" The young man sprang to his feet. "And he stood up to Zeus."

"And look what it got him!" Helios could not dislodge the haunting images of his tortured children from his mind. "I could not bear it to lose all of you. For if Zeus were to strike you down, all my world would crumble. You have all brought light and love to the Palace of the Sun, and I would not have that snuffed out. I would remember it that way."

With a cruel intonation, the great conch horn then sounded the coming of dawn and Helios stood.

"We yet have time, my children. Three days are ours."

But Phaethon stormed away, leaving Merope and Aetheria teary-eyed and clinging to their father.

Phoebe sat still, her heart full of the pain brought by the news, especially the thought that they would never return to the place that had eternally changed their lives.

WHEN HELIOS RUSHED into the stables, he found his team harnessed and waiting. Phaethon stood beside the chariot, tears running down his face.

Helios went to him, silent as he touched his son's muscled shoulder and observed his fine work in harnessing the team.

"It is well done, Phaethon." Helios stepped into the cab and took up the reins.

"Let me come with you!" Phaethon yelled above the rush of fire as the light shot through Helios' powerful frame.

His father shook his head. "We will speak tonight!"

And with that, Helios snapped the burning reins and the team shot off into the sky, a red sun cutting through stormy clouds as far as the eye could see.

Phaethon stood on the precipice, the winds tossing the hair about his face as he fought back the tears. He had had his fill of tears, and was determined to shed no more.

The young man looked down at himself, his solid arms, legs, and torso. He turned over his hands and observed the veins and calluses wrought by a strong hold on sword, spear, and shield. In Ethiopia, he had always been the strongest in the hunt. He had slain lions with naught but a dagger and his bare hands!

Phaethon felt his potential, the strength that flowed within his body. He knew he could set all to right had he but one chance to prove himself.

9

ARCING FIRE

Phoebe was standing at the colonnade, gazing silently at the River Ocean when Phaethon found her.

Aetheria and Merope slept side by side upon the couches, having drifted off to sad sleep at dawn.

"Where did you go?" Phoebe asked her brother as he approached.

"To harness father's team."

"You know how?"

"Of course. I watched him do it. He didn't even need to make any adjustments."

"I'm sorry you won't get to go with him at all," she said. "I know how much it meant to you."

Phaethon turned his back and leaned on the railing. Outside, the wind howled above Ocean's waves.

Phoebe looked at him. "Though we must leave, this journey was meant to be. I'll miss father terribly, but if it were not for these days given us, Phaethon, we would not have met you, nor had any time with father. How can we fault such a gift?" She reached out and touched her brother's cheek. In her heart, Phoebe found joy in what had happened.

"You need not return to Ethiopia." She smiled, a radiant, caring smile. "The four of us can guide father's golden boat, and it may be that we will see him again. At least we shall have you with us."

Phoebe looked from Phaethon to her sleeping sisters and thought that the prospect of the four of them living day to day together could be a blessing.

"It may be that we don't have to leave the Palace of the Sun." Phaethon's eyes gleamed as he spoke, and Phoebe's smile wavered.

"How do you mean?"

"If I can drive the Chariot of the Sun, for just one day, it will show Zeus that I am capable of greatness, and that I am not someone to be feared or dismissed. I can show Olympus that I am our father's son!"

Phaethon had clamped onto Phoebe's shoulders as he spoke. His intensity frightened her a little, and yet the possibility of what he said kindled hope.

"How can you be sure?" She pulled away slightly. "You have never driven the chariot. No one except father ever has."

"I *know* I can do it!" Phaethon smiled, hands on his hips. He could already imagine the joy he would feel as he raced across the heavens, a giver of light and life.

"I'll do it for all of us. But I'll need your help."

WHEN NIGHT FELL, and Selene had rushed off after spending the day with her nieces and nephew, Helios came into the great hall to find a feast laid, and his children awaiting him.

Aetheria, Merope, Phoebe, and Phaethon all rushed to him, their previous arguments, their sadness, forgotten.

Helios thought he would burst for all the joy they gave him, and he knew he would miss their company more than anything. He vowed he would speak to them in their dreams every night and tell them he was proud, and that he loved them.

"What is all this?" he asked.

"We would sit and be with you every chance that we can, Father," Merope said.

"Sit and eat with us." Aetheria led Helios to the couch in the centre.

Phaethon poured wine for all of them and reclined. He looked outside to see the indigo firmament blanketing the world.

That night, they were a family. Even Clymene was there for all the talk of her.

Helios spoke of how he had first seen their mother, of how he had always admired her from his golden chariot. As he spoke of his oceanid love, sounds of the sea and of sparkling laughter filled the hall about them.

Helios wished that it would never end, and Phaethon believed it never would.

The Heliades sang for them, and lightened their hearts with their godly voices that told of serenity and overwhelming joy, of golden days when the world was young.

But, as is always its way, joy's time was fleeting, and before they all knew it, the night was nearing its end.

Phaethon could feel it without looking beyond the pillars into the world. He knew that dawn was upon them, quick, and bright, and cloudless. He squeezed Phoebe's hand before rising.

"I shall return. Keep singing."

Phoebe watched him leave and with a pleasant smile to their father, she suggested they sing another song. "The one given us in our dreams. You remember? The day we came to the Palace of the Sun."

"Oh yes!" Aetheria said.

"Perfect," said Merope. "Listen, Father. It's the most beautiful song you have ever heard."

The Heliades stood up to face Helios, side by side, and closed their eyes...

The paean emerged from their young lips once more, the melody rising soft, and bright, and clear as the first green shoots of Spring.

Helios closed his eyes as the song washed over him, and he felt that he wanted to stop time forever in that moment.

But even he did not have that power.

Time pressed ever on, for gods and men. He was the Sun of the world, the great Charioteer. But for all that, he was bound to heed the coming of dawn. The great conch horn resounded and shook the palaces, and Selene's blacks thundered home.

Helios unwillingly raised his hand to stop his daughters' song.

"I must away, my souls. You have given warmth to the sun itself with your voices which will sing forever in my heart."

Helios stood and looked about the hall.

"Where is Phaethon?"

Aetheria and Merope shrugged, but Phoebe's eyes glanced up.

"Phoebe?" Helios began to panic. "Where is he?"

She shook her head and he saw the dread in her terrified, blue eyes.

"Oh no!" Helios leaped over the couches and powered up the corridor to the stables, fighting back such a fear within his chest as never a god or Titan felt before. "Ready the boat!" he yelled to the Heliades as he went.

In the Stables of the Sun, Phaethon had stood behind the great golden chariot, his heart pounding so violently he thought it would burst his chest.

The team had been harnessed and he had spoken to each of the immortal horses, asked them for their help. The stallion, Plegon, stomped an eager hoof as they waited for the great horn.

Phaethon stood still, ready then to bring in the day.

He fingered the medallion of the Sun about his neck and thought of how proud his father would be. He dwelled for a moment on how happy their family would also be once reunited, and his determination at last reached its zenith.

When the horn sounded, he stepped into the chariot's cab and took hold of the reins.

A power of fire, of unimaginable heat shot through Phaethon's body and he felt untold strength well up within. He smiled and cracked the reins and the team shot forward, launching the Chariot of the Sun as a shooting star, careening across the heavens...

"NO!!!" Helios cried out as he burst into the white light of the stables to see his son explode from the palace and into the sky.

Helios stood on the edge of that void, wind-whipped and crying for what was happening. He glanced sidelong at the Palace of the Moon to see Selene gazing at him, shaking her head in astonished fear.

He turned and ran down, and down to the quay where the Heliades were waiting.

THE FEELINGS that possessed every fibre of Phaethon's being as he achieved his heart's desire were overwhelming in that they all collided at once.

The sheer joy, passion, wonder, and excitement he felt as he blazed across the heavens were things not to be described by the injustice of mere words. He realized, as he watched his light come over the world, warm and life-giving to the earth, that nothing would ever compare.

The only thing that kept Phaethon from drifting away into bliss was the strain and strength of his team upon the reins as they plunged headlong into the orbit of their day. The heat had intensified, and the four immortal horses were all aflame, full of life as they blazed their familiar trail.

It took every minute ounce of Phaethon's strength to keep his footing in the inferno of the chariot. The strength in his arms wavered then as his team darted too high and too steep.

Phaethon's arms relaxed, their burning incessant as he gazed in wonder at the glimmering of the constellations beyond the black veil of heaven.

When he saw that the earth was growing dark far below, Phaethon yanked on the reins to put them back on course. With the sudden movement, the team veered sharply and sped back down toward the Earth.

"FATHER? WHAT'S HAPPENING?" Aetheria worried as the golden barge cut across the River Ocean. The shadows shifted and lurched unnaturally, though it was day.

At the prow of the vessel, Helios clung to the jutting beam, terrified of what he was seeing.

"Father?" Phoebe urged.

Helios turned to them all. "He cannot control them!" Helios pounded the prow. "Faster! Faster!"

HIGH ON OLYMPUS, Zeus, King of the Gods and Lord of All, leaned on a column and looked out at the world.

He had seen Phaethon mount his father's chariot, and now knew the cause of the racing light in the sky, reminiscent of past ages of Chaos.

He had *warned* them.

Zeus felt his anger rise then as he saw the sun come crashing back to earth.

He knew what would have to be done.

PHAETHON'S SCREAMS as the chariot sped toward the land were drowned out entirely by the rush of heat and wild fire.

His team was reeling as it came closer to land and sea.

Yellow light flickered to red fire, and black fear turned to sheer horror at the knowledge that he could not do the thing he had set out to do. Instead of the day of light and beauty he had wanted to give to the world, Phaethon was giving death and despair.

He cried out like a storm from the pain in his failing body. He pulled up just before crashing into the mountains of the Caucasus, but lost control upon the green plains of Mesopotamia, cutting a swathe of fire across the land and leaving a path of desolation in his wake.

The voices of thousands upon thousands of souls cried out in pain as he passed.

The team bounded up into the sky once more, their driver's fear overpowering.

When Phaethon reined in once more to avoid flying too high, the team wavered. The adamant harness began to burn under the intensity of the heat and flame.

All was a blur now to Phaethon as they crashed to earth again, setting fire to Ethiopia and all the lands to the West before bounding into the sky one last time.

"Forgive me, Father!!!" Phaethon cried.

THE BARGE RODE the crest of a great tidal wave all the way to the middle sea with Helios ever at the prow, and the Heliades wringing their hands behind him.

"Great Zeus," Helios pleaded. "Forgive him. Help him. I beg you, Lord."

In his heart, Helios could hear Clymene, her weeping in Ethiopia as it burned, almost as painful as the sight of the dying sun in the distance.

"Look!" Merope cried out, pointing to the sky behind them.

Bringing darkness in her wake, Selene and her blacks were racing as never before across the sky. The seas raged, and beasts cried out in the darkness as she went.

But she paid them no heed as she lashed her team after the chariot of her brother's son.

.   .   .

UPON THE PEAK of Mount Etna, Zeus stood towering over the world he so loved, pained at the destruction being wrought by a foolish youth.

The cries of dying mortals echoed in his ears and he knew it had to be done, for the sake of all.

With that, Zeus held out his powerful arms, followed the sun's burning brand across the sky and hurled his bolt with all of his terrible might.

"No!!!" Helios and his daughters cried out as they sped along, urged by sea creatures and oceanids.

All eyes were upon that fire in the sky, and it was at that moment that Selene arrived to eclipse the sun, and hide the horror of what was happening from all those who wept in the knowing.

Selene too wept as she watched, but she kept her team steady.

PHAETHON HAD NOT much time when he saw the blinding light come up from the earth. His awareness was only of screaming, of fire, and of pain as the flesh of his team burned away. He cried as his skin peeled back, black and bleeding.

When the bolt hit, the chariot erupted and Phaethon collapsed upon the floor of the cab.

The young man's soul clung to the image he had dreamed of - his family united and happy, their lives full of love, and song, and sunlight.

He did not see the death that raced in upon him with gaping jaws and an eternity of pain.

10

ELEGY

The golden boat of the sun came ashore a short distance from where the deep crater still smouldered beside the river Eridanus.

Helios ran, his body shaking with grief.

Aetheria, Merope, and Phoebe came after, their voices silent now, their eyes flashing with fear.

Helios fell among the charred remains of his immortal horses and the wreck of his chariot. But these were of no concern to the God of the Sun.

Upon his knees, Helios dug, and scraped, and searched for Phaethon, the son that had meant everything to him.

"Phaethon!" Phoebe wailed as she ran to the edge of the river. "My brother! No!"

Still burning, Phaethon's lifeless body lay sprawled so that half of him lay in the water.

Helios' cry shook the earth, and at once, the Heliades broke into a keen that could be heard from the heights of Olympus to the depths of Tartarus.

Helios held his son's burning bones and watched with

horror as they broke apart in his hands. At the same time, his beautiful daughters began to transform through their weeping.

At once, in their great grief, Phoebe, Merope, and Aetheria became bent, their beauty gnarled. Their tears continued to flow without end, falling upon the body of their brother until they were still.

All that stood in their place were three willows whose mournful branches would reach ever more toward the spot where they had found ill-fated Phaethon.

Helios wept, and shook, and raged upon his knees, clutching the four golden medallions that were all that remained of his children.

A flash of light in that lightless day brought Zeus to his side.

The God of the Sun struggled to his feet before Zeus. He felt hate take hold of him.

"I warned you of this," Zeus said. There was sadness there, pity. But there was also command, and challenge.

Helios moved toward Zeus, but the King of the Gods simply pointed at a new chariot harnessed to a team of winged whites.

"I have my duty...as do you. You must go, and begin anew. The sun must rise, now and always."

Helios closed his eyes, his muscled body tense and exhausted by grief beyond imagining.

"I will go and fulfill my destiny," he said through clenched teeth. "But I will not do it for you. *Never for you!*" Helios stepped into the chariot. "I will do it always for my daughters...and for my son."

Helios lashed the team and they shot into the sky.

When Selene saw her brother approaching, tears of flame

pouring from his weeping face, she pulled away and the sun came out once more.

THE HALLS of the palaces of the Sun and Moon echo with loneliness now. They are places of despair.

It is beside the waters of Eridanus where Helios now passes the night.

The trees still stand, their branches caressing the red-black earth and the clear water.

Oceanids, nymphs, and many others lay flowers and sing their mournful songs on the shore of the river, and they always will.

However, it is the sun that will ever be drawn to that sad place. It will shine for the memory of what might have been for that ill-fated family and the young man who loved them.

THE END

AUTHOR'S NOTE

Ancient Greek and Roman mythology have always fascinated and inspired me. First, as a child who was deeply affected by the film *Clash of the Titans*, but then throughout my life as a youth, a man, and as an author and historian. Mythology is always there, a comfort and inspiration and, at times, a much-needed escape.

In truth, the myths of ancient Greece and Rome pervade western history and literature. The archetypes are a part of the DNA of our culture. The stories are more often tragic than happy, but there is always something to learn about the world, about the human experience, and about ourselves.

Myths are, in a way, timeless, and the retelling of myths in successive ages has helped to ensure their survival.

The goal of the *Mythologia* series is not only to contribute in some small way to the survival of myth by introducing some of these stories to a new audience, but also to suspend disbelief and more fully explore the world and motives of gods and heroes. The gods of ancient Greece and Rome were, in a way, more human than deities from other religions, and so, more relatable. By humanizing the characters of ancient myth, we can better understand them as well as our ancient ancestors who worshipped and honoured them.

Why begin with the Phaethon myth?

That's a good question. Some years ago, I read about the son of Helios in Ovid's *Metamorphoses* (the main, surviving source for this myth) and was moved by the story of this young god whose motives were, to my mind, very human. As I thought about his burning chariot and the scorching of the world that created the Sahara desert, it occurred to me that this story had some very human themes such as wanting to belong, the need for love and approval, and the urge to prove oneself.

It is also a myth that is not often explored, and so I set out to tell it as I saw it. I hope I have done this tragic tale justice.

We are, after all, reminded of Helios and Phaethon when we look up at the sun in the daytime sky, and the Auriga, the constellation of the charioteer, at night.

Perhaps what I love most about the myths is that they enable us to feel and see our world and history with wonder, and that is a precious thing.

I do hope that as you read the tales in the *Mythologia* series, you will also be filled with wonder.

Thank you for reading.

Adam Alexander Haviaras
Stratford, Ontario
January, 2021

WHEELS OF FATE

THE STORY OF PELOPS AND HIPPODAMEIA

By Alfeios' ford he lies now, closely joined to the great feast of glorious sacrifice, his tomb oft visited, beside the altar where many a stranger treads. And the great fame of the Olympic Games shines far afield, in the course known of Pelops, where are matched rivals in speed of foot and in brave feats of bodily strength.

— PINDAR, *OLYMPIAN ODE* I

HYMN I

SINS OF THE FATHER

1

THE CHILD

The Chariot of the Sun scorched the earth of rocky Lydia that day as it soared into the West, its progress slow and laboured, as if the charioteer were loathe to lash his wild horses.

The calls of shepherds could be heard over the mountainsides as they emerged from the shady retreats from which they watched their flocks, to make their lazy way back to cave and hovel for the night. Many cast a backward glance as they went, for there was something in the air, a feeling to crush the stomach with planted dread.

Twilight was not a time to be out.

King Tantalus of Lydia stood on the obsidian terrace of his palace which was hewn into the rock of Mount Sipylus. He stood alone, staring out at the sea where it turned to fire in the light of the setting sun.

He stretched his thick arms wide, as smoke from two bronze, griffin-headed tripods wafted around him like spectral serpents at his behest. Then, he glanced at the small table where a golden bowl and goblet sat, glowing in the increasingly strong darkness.

Tantalus ran his hands over his bare chest, feeling the power that had coursed through his veins dwindling.

The bowl again...the goblet.

He watched them, thoughtful as he tugged at his long, black beard, and then strode over to take up the bowl in two hands. His breathing was rapid, but he smiled as he lifted the contents to his lips and opened his mouth to eat the last of the radiant ambrosia. He closed his eyes as he chewed and it slid down his gullet, filling him with heat and strength.

He put down the empty bowl and looked to the goblet - a few final drops of sweet nectar remained, the last portion of what he had stolen from Olympus.

He took the cup, not a drop spared for the Gods, and tipped the contents past his lips.

Tantalus' person shone off the blackness of the obsidian at his feet and he gazed defiantly up at the sky.

"You are no better than I!" he said, feeling the strength of fifty men charge through his body.

"What have you done?" a voice said from the entrance to his rooms.

Tantalus wheeled round, his eyes blazing.

"How dare you come upon me like that!" he raged at his chief battle commander and friend.

"How dare I?" the man said, staring back, the glow of Tantalus reflecting off of his bronze armour. "You'll destroy us all with your arrogance!"

"You go too far! You're weak!" Tantalus stepped closer, the muscles of his chest heaving and pulsing.

"The Gods, your father Zeus, invited you to Olympus - an

honour few mortals receive - and you decided to steal some of the sacred ambrosia and nectar. You're mad, Tantalus!"

"And you, friend...are dead." Tantalus leapt, swiping aside the blade that lashed out like a viper, and taking hold of his general's neck.

The man was lifted several feet off the ground, his eyes bulging, his face crimson.

"You think the Gods will find out? You think they know and see all?" Tantalus said, an idea forming even as the man suffocated within his grasp. "They only want us to think they see all, so that they can control us. But we are better! Zeus overthrew Kronos, his father, and so shall I overthrow mine."

"You...will...never..."

Tantalus' eyebrows raised. "Oh won't I? The Olympians come to dine here at my palace two nights hence. I shall give them a feast they'll not suspect, and the first shadow of doubt as to their omniscience shall be cast. It will be the beginning of their end."

"You're...mad," the general said, his fists slamming weakly into Tantalus' chest and arms. Tantalus looked up at the man he held in one hand, and reached for a nearby spear with the other.

"I am anything but, friend."

With that, Tantalus drove the spear up through the man's groin, along his spine, and then out of his gaping mouth before he turned and hurled the body over the railing into the flickering torches of the town below.

Screams rose up into the dusk, and even then, Tantalus laughed, his hands dripping with blood.

"Sinor!" he yelled for the servant whom he knew was standing outside.

Shuffling feet saw the man approach, his gap-toothed

grin and greasy hair belying the string of daggers he kept beneath his tunic.

"Yes, my lord!" the man bowed.

"We shall test the Gods, Sinor! It is time."

"You have something in mind, my lord?" the man asked, bowing, immune to the fear that would have overwhelmed even the bravest of warriors.

"Yes," Tantalus said, turning to look out at the sea where the emerging moon reflected on its surface. "Bring me my son Pelops."

BY THE SHORES of the black lake, safe on the lands of his father, King Tantalus, the boy, Pelops, watched the stars begin to wink from the glassy surface.

Birdsong and a flap of wings echoed from the dark depths of the wood about the lake, and Pelops scanned the fringes of that forest to see if his brother, Broteas, was there, or if his sister, Niobe, approached. But neither of them came, the one likely perched on the mountainside, continuously carving away at stone to honour Lydian Cybele, the other tending her many children in the depths of their father's palace.

Neither sibling had ever had time for Pelops, though he lived in hopes of their filial attention. Only the naiad of the black lake ever paid him any heed, and that night, she was not there.

Pelops stood, the dark water lapping at his bare feet as he gazed beyond the lake to the heights of Mount Sipylus, far above the palace, where he sometimes wandered to try and see how far the world stretched into the distance.

As he began to turn away, a hand touched his foot and he looked down to see the naiad gazing up at him.

Her eyes matched the darkness of the lake she guarded, the stars reflected equally in both.

"You leave?" she asked as she emerged from the depths to stand close to him.

She made Pelops nervous sometimes, but she had never been cruel, and for that he was grateful.

She seemed to guard him as much as her watery realm.

"I must. My father will be preparing for the Olympians' visit," Pelops said.

"Your father!" she said harshly.

Pelops looked at her, how her pretty face distorted for a moment that made his heart skip like a rabbit frightened on the path.

The Naiad looked down at him now, her wet hands touching the black curls of his hair ever-so-gently, coming to rest on his cheeks so that she could stare into his young eyes.

"It will be well," she said. "The water told me."

"What do you mean?" Pelops asked, unable to pull away.

But she said no more, only bent over to kiss his lips before backing away into the dark water until it rose above her breasts, chin, and eyes. Her hair wavered on the surface like sea grass in a stream, and then she was gone.

Pelops watched the water for a time before turning and taking the path that led back to his father's palace where it overlooked the sea.

He did not see the naiad emerge once more from the water to watch him go, her tears lost on her wet visage.

The path was growing dark, the branches of wild thyme that lined it turning to angry claws in the waning light. In the field to the right, the shapes of centaurs and satyrs darted about, ghostly shadows that emerged when the light of day dwindled.

A snake slithered across the path, making Pelops stop suddenly, just as he was about to step upon it. The beast rose to its full height, a terrible hiss upon its thin, reptilian lips lined with dripping fangs.

Pelops stood still, his face calm, though his heart raced beneath his ribs.

The serpent stared him in the eyes, its mouth closing, even as the tongue darted out to touch the boy's face. It then dropped to the ground and shot off through the tall grass.

When it was gone, Pelops ran and did not look back.

IT WAS COMPLETELY dark by the time Pelops arrived at the looming grandeur of the palace gates, the blackness of the arch made orange by the torches that flamed like a chimera's breath on either side of the road.

One of the guards stepped forward. "Someone's looking for you, young prince," the man said.

"Who?" Pelops asked, keeping his distance from the man.

"Sinor."

Pelops swallowed, and the man smirked.

Everyone detested Tantalus' man for one reason or another. The soldiers took him for a coward, the women for a lech, others for a cheat and a liar.

But Pelops always felt horror at the man, or the mention of his name. He terrified him more than his father, who had never been kind.

"Go on then!" the guard urged. "I'm not going to have my back lashed on your account. Go!"

Pelops passed beneath the gate and began the long climb up the wide, curving stairs to the uppermost reception chamber. If Sinor wanted him, he would find him along the way.

However, Pelops arrived without seeing anyone on his way there, and when he arrived before the chamber, the tall cedar doors were ajar.

Inside, beyond the polished marble table that stretched almost the length of the hall, Pelops could see Tantalus sitting upon his throne, his eyes grabbing at him even from a distance, and beside the king, Sinor.

For some reason, the words of the naiad popped into Pelops' head.

It will be well.

"Come here, boy!" Tantalus' deep voice travelled harshly over the marble and obsidian of the hall. "I need something of you."

Pelops forced himself forward, though something in his guts told him to run, to go quickly from that place. But he could not.

"Ye...yes, Father?" he said as he reached the end of the table and noticed Sinor sitting casually now upon the lowest step to the throne, sharpening a long xystis which rested across his knees. "What can I do for you?" Pelops asked, looking up into his father's cold gaze as the heavy hand took hold of his shoulder.

"You haven't grown for some time, boy. You're the same size as you were many months ago."

"I do eat father, and exercise as instructed by my teachers." Pelops looked at the ground and then back up when Tantalus squeezed his shoulder painfully, as if testing his strength, or his tolerance for pain.

"Do you remember the tales of your grandfather?" Tantalus asked.

Pelops nodded, though he did not like recalling them.

"Yes, Father. Kronos was devouring his children and Zeus,

the last of the children, was taken away and hidden from his father."

"And what did Zeus do?"

"Grandfather returned one day to defeat his father, and so the Gods crushed the Titans who now dwell imprisoned in Tartarus."

Tantalus let go and walked a few yards, his hand rubbing his black chin.

"Do you think Zeus did well?" Tantalus asked.

"Of course!"

"You are wrong. He should have destroyed the Titans once and for all, for while they live, there is ever a risk of their escape, of chaos."

"Surely they were well-imprisoned," Pelops said.

"Always be ready for the unexpected, and you will never be taken by surprise."

Sinor now stood and paced around the father and son as they talked.

Pelops watched the man out of the corner of his eye, but his father pulled at his chin. "Look at me!"

"Kronos was weak too. He was fooled by Rhea and did not expect his son to survive."

"Because he ate the stone she gave him instead."

"Correct. But..."

There was a long pause as Tantalus turned away from Pelops and raised his hands out to either side is if to hug the darkness.

"But what, Father?"

With his back to Pelops, Tantalus spoke.

"You are no rock."

Pelops spun, just as Sinor's blade came down onto his head and blood poured over the black floor of the chamber...

2

A FEAST FOR THE GODS

For two days, Tantalus' slaves scrubbed and polished every inch of floor, wall, and pillar, until the entire palace shone like the halls of Olympus.

Zeus and the other gods would be arriving very shortly, and the entire palace staff and slaves were busy preparing a feast for the Gods. The eagle had been seen flying high over Mount Sipylus - Zeus and the Olympians would be arriving soon.

Tantalus sat upon his throne, overlooking the banquet table, groaning with food that put even the cornucopia of Olympus to shame - swan and peacock, breads shaped as temples, the fruits of vine and olive tree, sweet drinks made from the resins of rare trees found only in his kingdom of Lydia. The kitchens at the back of the palace steamed with savoury delights and honeyed sweets from the hives of Mount Ida to the North.

Tantalus cared for none of it, however, only the stew he had ordered specially prepared - the true test of the Gods, as it were.

He spun his sceptre idly as he sat there, waiting for his father. Tantalus had never cared much for Zeus, or his aunts or uncles, his cousins Apollo and Artemis.

True, they had favoured him, invited him to timeless Olympus to dine and be privy to secrets that few mortals ever discover.

It will be their downfall, Tantalus thought, as he smiled and walked down the stairs to the black floor.

"What if they discover what you've done?" Sinor's slithery voice emerged from the right where he stood in shadows with a sword of adamant at his hip.

"They won't," Tantalus answered confidently. "One bite is all it takes. If they truly see everything...if they are truly all-powerful, then they will already know."

"You are bold, my lord," Sinor said, actually laughing.

"It's our time, Sinor. From here, we can rule the world..."

Sinor backed away into the shadows to take his place.

As he did so, a tremor rippled the atmosphere above Mount Sipylus. Tantalus spun to face the great double-doors of the reception hall where they looked out onto a balcony overlooking the city and sea.

There stood Hermes, the Gods' messenger, tall, lean and brilliant. His storm-tossed eyes raked over Tantalus, but he smiled.

"Greetings, Brother," Hermes said with a polite nod.

"Hermes," Tantalus answered.

"Father Zeus is here..."

Hermes bowed and backed away to reveal his fellow Olympians behind him, as they began to move into the hall, Zeus and Hera at their head.

Tantalus bowed curtly, then clapped his hands loudly so

that music burst from the mouths of five women in an alcove, and servants began scampering around the hall to offer wine to the Gods as they approached.

Zeus and Hera smiled as they walked arm-in-arm toward Tantalus. They shone with the otherworldly brilliance of immortals, their persons strong, vital and possessed of beauty that no mortal or half-mortal could ever dream of.

Behind the king and queen of the gods came Poseidon, the smell of the salt-sea in his wake. Athena and Ares followed, their eyes quick and aware, and dangerous. Artemis and Apollo followed, their silver bows ever at their backs, their matching blue cloaks billowing like a cloud-filled sky.

Aphrodite came next, to take even Tantalus' breath away, but close to her husband Hephaestus. Dionysus, clad in a leopard skin and holding a golden kylix to his lips waited by the doors for the last two Olympians, Hestia and Demeter.

The latter was clad all in black, her eyes red and worn as she was supported by Hestia whose fiery robes rustled about her.

Tantalus looked at each of them, and thought he spied weakness there, complacency and ignorance.

They've no idea what I've done.

Zeus and Hera stopped before Tantalus, who looked his father in the eyes before bowing slightly.

"Welcome to Lydia, Lord Zeus," Tantalus said. "Queen Hera."

"Your palace suits you well, Tantalus," Zeus said, nodding to his son and leaning forward to kiss him on the cheek as ever he did. But Zeus paused momentarily and sniffed the air about his son. "I smell...a divine feast," he said.

Tantalus smiled broadly.

"You do indeed, Father Zeus. I hope the Gods find it pleasing!" he said, motioning to the richly adorned stools about the long table.

The chatter began immediately as the Gods seated themselves around the table.

"Where is my granddaughter, Niobe?" Zeus asked. "Will she join us?"

"I am here, Grandfather," a high, confident voice bubbled from an adjacent hall, followed by the laughter of many children.

Niobe, Tantalus' daughter, entered the room, resplendent in white and gold, with glittering rubies about her long neck, hanging over her breasts.

"Sit, Daughter," Tantalus said, "and send your children away."

Niobe turned to the crowd of children behind her and nodded to the eldest who led them all away.

"And where are the rest of your children?" Poseidon asked, a faint sound of crashing waves filling the room as he spoke.

"My eldest son is upon the mountain, labouring at an image of Cybele."

"A worthy endeavour!" Hephaestus said from the far end of the table as he ripped apart a loaf of steaming bread.

"And your youngest, Pelops?" Poseidon asked.

Zeus reached for a great golden goblet where he sat at the head of the table, Hera to his left and Tantalus to his right.

Tantalus stared across at his uncle, the Earth-Shaker and tamer of horses.

"Pelops is a disappointment to me. He spends all his days beside the black lake, fawning over the nymph there. He will be here shortly."

The lies dripped like honeyed wine from Tantalus' lips, but the Gods seemed to take no notice, further encouraging his hubris.

"Love, or lust, is healthy for a young man," Aphrodite said to Tantalus.

Tantalus nodded, unashamed to stare directly at the Goddess of Love. "Please eat!" Tantalus said suddenly. "For we have prepared many delights for the Gods of Olympus!"

As MUSIC PLAYED and slaves floated among the Gods with platters of delicacies, conversations hushed. All enjoyed the food and drink that was brought. Tantalus, they thought, was one of the few earth-bound men who knew how to reciprocate the hospitality of Olympus.

The King of Lydia, however, was annoyed by the constant weeping of Demeter, Goddess of the Harvest, as she stared absentmindedly into her golden cup, constantly comforted by Hestia, whose hands rested always upon some part of her as if she were a helpless child.

Dionysus ensured Demeter's cup remained full, and they chatted in hushed tones that Tantalus could not overhear.

"Why does Demeter weep?" Tantalus asked Hera as she picked at a piece of fruit upon her platter.

"Hades has swept her daughter, Persephone, away to the Underworld. The girl cannot leave there for many moons."

"She appears consumed with grief," Tantalus observed.

"Would *you* not be?" Zeus asked suddenly.

Tantalus smiled and shook his head. "I would not be so weak, for I could get me more children."

"Quite right, Father," Niobe said, putting her cup down with a clang on the marble surface. "Look how very many children I have! Twelve! Why, that's many more than the lady Leto gave birth to."

The table went silent and Tantalus considered slapping his daughter for her ignorance.

Apollo and Artemis were on their feet, staring across the table at Niobe.

"Sit yourselves down," Zeus growled, pulling at his beard with a muscular hand. He stared so hard at Niobe that she felt her hands begin to shake for fear of the anger in his eyes. "You should teach your daughter respect," he said to Tantalus.

"Agreed," Tantalus said, annoyed. Then he turned to a slave waiting nearby and whispered some instructions.

Young men and women emerged from the alcoves to remove dirty plates and replenish empty cups. Then, golden bowls were brought out.

"I have asked my people to prepare a dish none of you will have had before," Tantalus said, standing beside Zeus to address the table.

There were curious murmurs among the Gods, except for Demeter who stared at the hands crossed in her lap, the hands that had gripped her daughter's as she was pulled into the bowels of the earth by the clawing hands of Hades.

Great golden bowls were placed before each of them, the images upon them moving around the sides animatedly as hot broth, filled with chunks of dark, rich meat and bone splashed into them, ladled from a broad serving bowl The air was filled with a rich, meaty scent.

"What is this?" Zeus asked, staring at it.

"A meal like no other. One-of-a-kind, Father, and only for the Gods."

The Gods stared into their bowls of crimson broth, meat and bone, and made no move to eat.

Tantalus grew nervous, sweat forming on his forehead as he watched them. All the music and dancing of the slaves faded away, and he could only see the Gods' faces as they stared at their bowls.

Only Demeter, distracted as she was by bitter grief, reached into the bowl and pulled out a large bone which she brought to her mouth and bit loudly, the crack of it bringing Zeus to his feet.

"What have you done?" he said to Tantalus, a moment before the rest of the Gods were standing, an uproar of protest and accusations of sacrilege upon their lips.

"What is wrong?" Niobe screamed above the angry words.

"I have done nothing!" Tantalus protested, but before he could say more, Zeus's hand lashed out to grab him by the throat and lift him out of his seat.

"How dare you feed us your son!"

Zeus' voice was so loud, it cracked some of the pillars surrounding the hall.

There was a loud cry and Demeter pushed back her marble chair and vomited the bone and blood she had consumed, her hand shaking, her heart despairing even more.

The Gods looked to Zeus, horror upon their beautiful faces, anger replacing joy, hope replaced by vengeance.

Poseidon stood before Zeus where he held a wriggling Tantalus aloft.

"He must pay," the Lord of the Seas said.

"He must pay dearly!" Athena said, pointing a glowing spear at Tantalus.

The latter tried to hit Zeus with all his might, but he could not, for if it were not for the enormity of his sacrilege, he would be no more annoying than a fly.

"You are not all-seeing!" Tantalus managed to say as his face turned redder from Zeus' grip. "You shall all die, the same as the Titans!"

"And you, Tantalus," Zeus said, walking over to the balcony that overlooked the valley far below, "you have sinned more than any man, and you shall pay for it in the depths of Tartarus for all eternity..."

For the first time in his life, fear entered into Tantalus' eyes and heart, a fear for which there is no word or possible description.

As Zeus held him over the void, the sky swirled black and grey, and lighting cracked the heavens. Far below, a black and fiery abyss opened up like a great land-bound Charybdis.

"To Tartarus with you for your crimes, Tantalus. You will pay forever!" Zeus yelled, making the Gods cover their ears as the winds ripped through the hall and the land of Lydia as Tantalus fell headlong, screaming into the depths of the earth.

Zeus wheeled around to Apollo and Artemis, his finger pointed at Niobe who stood weeping.

"And kill her and all her children!" he said, and the divine twins, whose mother had been mocked, drew their silver bows and loosed, sending Niobe's body across the hall to be pinned against the crumbling marble wall before they ran off in search of her brood.

The rest of the Gods stood before Zeus, Demeter still holding the shoulder blade of Pelops which she had partially eaten.

"My nymphs told me the boy was always kind and gentle," Poseidon said, gazing at the still-steaming bowls.

"We should destroy the palace completely," Ares said, standing beside his father, Zeus.

The King of the Gods stood in their midst, his chest heaving in anger and rage, and even a little grief at what had just happened. He knew he could not have allowed Tantalus to go unpunished, for he had sinned greatly and obviously sought to overthrow the Olympians.

"Perhaps the boy can be saved," Zeus said, walking over to the table. "Brother," he turned to Poseidon. "I leave it to you to gather his remains and take the boy Pelops to the Halls of Rejuvenation on Olympus. There, you will heal and raise him until he is ready to go back into the world of men."

"It shall be done," Poseidon said, the words sending ripples across the consciousness of his mind, as if a large stone and been thrown into the morning sea. "Whatever may come of it." He set about pouring the remains of every bowl back into the large serving bowl, and when he finished, nodded to Zeus.

"Go now," Zeus said, and in a flash of brilliant light, accompanied by the crash of waves, Poseidon vanished.

"We will return to Olympus with him," Hestia said as she held Demeter's arm.

Zeus nodded and there was another flash.

Screams then echoed throughout the palace as Apollo and Artemis hunted down the children of Niobe.

Hera bowed her head at the thought, but knew it had to be done, though she had no love for Leto.

"Destroy everything!" Zeus roared, lightning bolts suddenly throbbing in his fists.

Hephaestus, Ares, Dionysus and the others set about tearing the walls of the palace down as the skies above opened up and wept upon the fires that would not be quenched for several days.

The people of Lydia lamented their lands and lives as all

they knew crumbled around them for the sacrilege of their king.

THE HALLS OF OLYMPUS

High on the peaks of Olympus, water flowed through troughs of pure white marble to feed fountains that ran through gardens where the Immortals roamed barefoot. In the surrounding sky, the sun and stars glimmered with a constant beauty and could be seen at once, ranging over the peaks of thick cypress and golden apple trees. Ever fruitful olive trees dotted the slopes leading up to temples that glowed even in daylight, their pediments adorned with animated statues of the war with the Titans, fashioned by Hephaestus himself. Doves flitted from tree to tree, and phoenixes nested in the tallest of them, their fiery tails to be seen shooting across the mountains like comets in the evening.

A flash of light saw Poseidon appear on the grass of a small courtyard surrounded by a golden colonnade. He carried a broad, silver bowl carefully, as if it were riding upon the waves of the wine-dark sea, and walked up the steps into the Hall of Rejuvenation.

The god of the roiling seas, Earth-Shaker and Tamer of

Horses, stood silent for a moment to look about the great, circular room. Many of them, himself included, had lain in there to heal of the grievous wounds they had suffered in the wars with the Titans, and they would lay there again.

The hall was the calmest place he knew, more so than the darkest depths of the sea where sound could not penetrate.

Poseidon looked into the bowl he carried to see the broad, ivory shoulder blade which Demeter had given him. It was the final step in the healing of the mortal boy he had come to love more than the reflection of the sun upon the sea.

"For the boy I so wronged," Demeter had told him when she gave the piece to her immortal brother. "It shall give strength and purpose to his arm and the line of the Pelopidae."

Now he stepped close to the pool to peer into the shimmering depths with his stormy eyes to see the young man, his body whole again but for the shoulder blade on his right. Poseidon had heard the destruction of Lydia at the hands of Zeus as he had placed the boy in the pool, and the sound of that suffering had pleased him.

"I will right the sacrilege done to you," he whispered, as he leaned over the edge of the pool and, with the power vested in him by sea and sky and immortality, attached the ivory shoulder blade to the boy, making him complete again. When he was finished, Poseidon stood back, his eyes closed. "You will rise again. And you will be great."

IT WAS in the depths of the Hall of Rejuvenation that the body of Pelops healed and strengthened. Time passed, not in the manner of the earth, but in the way that the sea roils over and over, always the same, but passing nonetheless. In this way, the boy grew and healed and became a young man.

At last, on the day that was not a day, but a moment of Olympian beauty, Poseidon, Demeter, and Zeus himself stood beside the pool for the moment of awakening. Their flowing robes of purest white swirled about them in an unseen breeze that rarely penetrated the halls of Olympus, and Zeus looked up to the soaring ceiling and sky beyond.

"Much will come of this," he said to his brother and sister.

Poseidon looked at Zeus. "I know. He is destined for great things."

Zeus shook his head. "Mortals destined for greatness are like storms and fires... They can bring beauty and destruction wherever they pass."

"Such contraries are not only the realm of mortals, Brother," Demeter said to Zeus, and as she spoke, she could see her beloved Persephone whose absence from the earth brought destruction, and whose presence brought birth and beauty.

"It is time," Zeus said. "And in time, he must leave Olympus."

Poseidon bowed to the King of the Gods, removed his flowing robes, and stepped into the deep water to kneel beside the prostrate young man, cradling him in his arms. As he did so, he breathed, his great chest stretching out, his powerful muscles straining, radiating, as he held Pelops.

"Rise now," Poseidon said. "You are free, of pain, of suffering. The sins of your father's past are not your own."

Breath returned to Pelops' lungs, his chest rising and falling slowly. His heartbeat rippled the waters about him and the God of the Sea, his hair flowing like grass in a swift stream about his head. Slowly, the creases of his eyes opened, filled with light at first, and then revealing a colour of purest blue.

His muscles awakened, long and lean and stretching after a long sleep.

"Stand, Pelops," Zeus commanded, and even with his newborn sight, the young man knew the King of the Gods.

Poseidon set him down and, swaying upon his feet, Pelops bowed to the three Olympians.

All at once, however, a rush of memory struck at him, of blades and blood and of screaming pain. He began to shake, and weep, his fists clenched, his body flexing, feeling and unfeeling at once, as his mind reeled between joy and terror, hurt and healing.

"Leave him!" Zeus said as Poseidon went to hold Pelops. "He must travel the pain to be born again from these waters!"

The Gods looked on as Pelops struggled through his mortal traumas, as he gazed into the eyes of his murderous father, Tantalus, and as he reached out in vain to his suffering sister, Niobe... Then, it all began to fade and pull away. His mind spun with his body and turned toward a brilliant light filled with music and promise. He reached out, pulling himself from the depths, of his own accord, emerging from the waters and over the edge of the pool to collapse at the Gods' feet.

Poseidon climbed out of the water to stand beside Zeus and Demeter and, together, they looked down upon the mortal upon whom they had bestowed such favour.

"You have little time with him," Zeus said to Poseidon before turning to leave the hall. "Mark it well. Prepare him for his toils."

Poseidon and Demeter knelt beside Pelops and laid

hands upon him, calming him, steadying his breathing, soothing him.

"You are safe now," Demeter whispered, her tears falling over his brow, for even as she touched him, she could hear the crack of his bone within her godly mouth. *I would never willingly harm a child,* the goddess told herself, and hoped that in that moment, as his son rose again, Tantalus suffered deeply in Hades from eternal thirst and hunger. She touched Pelops' shoulder with her lithe hand. "Be at peace. Grow strong, and rise like the oak out of the earth."

"I will teach you, Pelops," Poseidon said as he and Demeter helped him up.

Pelops gazed from one to the other. He nodded, and quickly found his feet as they led him out into the light, like a hopeful foal finding its strength.

As THE STARS flickered about the peaks of Olympus, and Helios and Selene took it in turns to race across the skies, the youth Pelops grew and learned strength and wisdom from the Gods themselves, not least from Earth-Shaking Poseidon who came to love the youth for his beauty, skill, and his quick wits. Poseidon taught him the ways of horse-taming and equine skill upon the ever-green fields surrounding the palaces of the Gods, such that the herds of immortal horses followed the youth wherever he roamed, and obeyed his every command.

He watched Pelops roam the song-filled gardens of Olympus and the palace of the sea, the God's Olympian abode, and he wondered at his attachment to the youth, his wish to see him achieve greatness.

He knew that the Gods expected Poseidon to possess the

mortal youth - such was often the way of things - but he would not sully him.

"Even I would not touch the sun," he said to Zeus, when the King of the Gods asked him. "I am content to admire him from afar."

"His father, my own son, was an abomination, whom I was willing to destroy. He enjoyed too much favour of the Gods, and so became hubris itself." Zeus' eternal eyes narrowed as he peered down the long slopes from his eyrie to see Pelops beside a pool in the wood. "Pelops has grown strong, eaten of ambrosia, and filled himself with nectar...but he is not meant for our world. He is of the earth."

Poseidon's bearded head assented, for he knew his kingly brother was right, knew that it was also Zeus' command, for Pelops' presence in their pillared halls made the other Gods to whisper, not least Ares and Hermes, who felt the youth's presence as a threat.

"Grant me another moon, Brother, so that I may prepare him."

"I grant you that. But if he remains here after that, I will cast him down myself." Zeus disappeared, and the light of heaven flickered as Poseidon continued to watch Pelops.

IT WAS the case that men upon the earth often looked up to the Gods, wondered at the world in which they dwelled and at the timeless halls of Olympus where the sun ever shone, and the moon was bright and clear in the night, where neither wind nor rain existed, and where music and beauty were a constant.

For Pelops, however, having already dwelled upon the slopes of Olympus, the older he became, the more he wondered at life upon the earth. He often leaned over the edge of Olympus' heights to gaze down the long corridors of the sky toward the earth, his true home. He now longed for that home, though he knew it not, longed for that distant realm that held some faint familiarity.

He wondered what that place was that such a chorus erupted from its depths, a symphony of joy and of pain, of elation and torment, a place where people laughed and cried, were born and died. The more he scented the offerings upon the Gods' altars far below, he wondered at the reasons for those offerings and what drove men to pray to Olympus amidst the constant chaos in which they lived.

Poseidon watched Pelops one day from the glade of golden apples, and he could feel the youth's longing for his world. Olympus was not a prison, but nor was it a haven. The command of the world lay heavy upon all immortal shoulders, and being near such a burden was enough to drive a mortal mad. He did not want that for Pelops, nor did he wish for him to suffer the wrath of Zeus, such as Phaethon had long ago.

"Did you send me a dream last night?" Pelops asked as Poseidon approached him. The young man stood, his muscular body almost gold in the dwindling light of the passing sun, his hair brilliant, as if it were on fire.

Poseidon looked into his charge's sea-blue eyes and shook his godly head. "No. I did not." *He has had a calling,* he thought sadly. *It is time.*

Pelops turned back to peer over the edge again at the broad spread of humanity's realm, and Poseidon came to stand beside him.

"What did you see?" the god asked.

"I saw the roiling seas, and soaring mountains. I saw the

turning of chariot wheels and the charging of horses. And I saw..."

"Saw what?" Poseidon pressed.

"I saw the most beautiful mortal woman."

Poseidon's heart sank like a stone into the dark depths of the world.

Pelops continued as if still in his dream, as if he were looking upon her. "She is tall, and draped in silks. She lives in a palace with all that a mortal could ask for, and yet she is sad beyond reckoning. She lives in constant fear."

"Most mortals do."

Pelops shook his head. "But she is strong. I can see it. She seeks to protect others, but she cannot." He sighed. "As I was seeing her...watching her sleep...she awoke to look directly at me. I cannot stop seeing the tears upon her cheeks, the pleading in her eyes for an ally."

Poseidon stood beside Pelops and looked to that far-distant point upon the earth to which he was drawn and there, he saw her, felt her terror and need, her strength and will, and he knew she was the equal of the young man he loved.

"It was no dream that I or any other god sent you, Pelops. The Moirai are calling you to your destiny. It is the will of Zeus that you leave Olympus."

"Leave?" Pelops said, though he did not tear his eyes from the earth below.

"Yes." As Poseidon looked upon Pelops, salt-sea tears formed in the corners of his eyes. He had bid farewell to many a son and daughter, not a few lovers, and every time, it had pained him, for he knew the world was cruel and full of peril. *But sometimes, a hero rises to inspire others. Perhaps that is what the Moirai have showed you?* he wondered. "Are you ready, Pelops?"

"For what?" he now turned to Poseidon, his brilliant blue eyes full of terror and excitement.

"To go back and begin your toils upon the Earth?"

"Yes. I am ready."

Poseidon nodded and then his great arms reached out and pushed Pelops over the edge of Olympus as an eagle casts its young out of a mountain nest.

Pelops screamed as he fell, tumbling out of the skies like a star from the heavens.

"To your fate then," Poseidon said as he watched, and Olympus grew quiet about him.

HYMN II

THE WOEFUL KINGDOM

4

A HOUSE OF SADNESS AND DEATH

It was on a distant plain in the kingdom of Elis that many cries of the world of men were born at that time, just as a great roar can rise up from the belly of a terrible beast to haunt men, women, and children, wherever they may be across the land.

The king of Elis, Oinomaos, had ruled for many years from his palace in the middle of the sea-neighbouring plain where horses roamed wild, churning the earth with their thunderous hooves. It was once a joyous place, for Oinomaos had been blessed by his father, Ares, the God of War, and his mother, the naiad, Harpina. No neighbour dared invade, and the people enjoyed peace beneath a canopy of stars at night, and the brilliance of Helios during the day. Crops blossomed as if the land were set in the middle of the Garden of the Hesperides where the withering face of death was rarely found, and a gentle music echoed among the groves of olive, pine, fig and cypress. Naiads, dryads, nymphs and satyrs wandered without worry among the forests and along the streams and shores of Elis, blessing that land even more.

It is the way of things, however, that even those blessed by the Gods will face their trials, and when they do, they will either emerge victorious, to have their names sung in later ages to mark a time of golden light in man's history, or, be used as a warning of the Gods' themselves, a thing of terror in the night.

As with most men, Oinomaos was born with hope and optimism in his heart, and he was indeed blessed in his marriage to Evarete, one of the daughters of Acrisius of Argos and his queen, Eurydice. Together, Oinomaos and Evarete were loved by their people, and they loved each other, and their love grew with their children, Leucippos, and Hippodameia. Wherever the family went, the people cast flowers at their feet and made offerings on their behalf upon the altars of the Gods.

But, just as offerings burn, wither and fade, so too do the lives of mortals, even those blessed by the Gods.

The burning of Oinomaos' life, and the arrival of darkness in Elis, began with the death of Queen Evarete who, despairing of the fate of her beloved sister, Danae, fell into a despair the likes of which would drown any mortal. It was all Oinomaos could do to watch his beloved wife roam the stone, fire-lit halls of the palace as an empty shell of the woman she had been. Even promises of waging war upon her father, Acrisius, would not bring her out of darkness, and so the seeds of helplessness were sown in Oinomaos' mind.

It was on a winter's night besieged by storms that Evarete left her husband for the last time, wandering out to the churning shores of the sea to throw herself into the depths of Poseidon's realm.

"We have found the queen, lord."

Oinomaos would never forget the weeping slave who had

come to tell him what had happened, that the Gods had taken his beloved from him.

A cloud settled over Oinomaos' mind as he drove his chariot back to the palace, the body of his pale, lifeless love in the cab beside him. His tears burned as they fell, and the son of War felt shame turn slowly to anger.

The Gods, however, were not finished with Oinomaos, for in his own despair, Leucippos, his only son, departed Elis to roam the broad plains and mountainous passes of the world. Darkness followed the youth as well, for one cannot escape the Fates.

For his love of the nymph, Daphne, the favourite of Apollo himself, Leucippos met his end far away from home, torn to pieces by the nymphs themselves for daring to spy upon her.

The news of his son's death was too much for Oinomaos, and so a Stygian night settled over the kingdom of Elis, the music became sullen and muted, and crops began to fail.

The plain about the palace no longer rang with cheers and the thunder of wild hooves, but became a place of sadness, a tomb for the living in which Oinomaos fell into the oblivion of wine, and his surviving daughter roamed the corridors dreaming of halcyon days when the sun could still be felt upon her face and soul.

YEARS PASSED, and as Oinomaos filled himself with the nectar of Dionysus' vines, Hippodameia grew into womanhood. It was she who kept the altars of the Gods burning and lit, she who emerged to lay hands upon the despairing people of Elis.

Hippodameia also caught the attention of suitors from

across the lands of Arcadia, Achaea, Sparta and beyond. She had grown tall, quick, and lithe, a true descendant of Ares. Her beauty and kindness were renown, as was her skill with spear and bow, or at the reins of a horse-drawn chariot.

It was the appearance of these suitors that brought Oinomaos out of his eternal despair. But he emerged from it as a different man, a violent man, a tyrannical ruler who had cast hope, and joy, and love aside. In the many suitors who came to ask for Hippodameia's hand, he saw only men who wished to break the last of his family, to take away all that he had left in the world.

Oinomaos prayed to his immortal father for ways in which to prevent the final breaking of his family.

In the night, as he watched the thigh bones and fat of a ram burn upon Ares' altar, Oinomaos stood still beneath the writhing night sky to see the stars for the first time in what felt like an age.

"Oh, warlike Ares...Father... I beg you to help me keep my daughter from the covetous grasp of others. I will do whatever it takes, but let her not be taken from me. She is all I have left in this world."

As the shadows swallowed the forms of his guards, and the sounds of the mortal plain were sucked out of the very air, the thrum of the drums of war could be heard in Oinomaos' mind, and when he turned, he saw his red-cloaked father standing above him.

The fire in the god's veins burned brightly as he looked upon his son, his black-bearded face, so alike to his own. Ares had lost as well, and he would have kept his son from the same pain if he could, despite the laws of the Gods and Zeus himself.

"Will you help me, oh Father, oh War?" Oinomaos asked, bowed before the god.

"I will," Ares said, his eyes closing as he brought forth the manner of his aid in that lonely stone courtyard lit by fire. "Open your eyes, my son, and see what I have given you."

Oinomaos opened his eyes and saw the warlike gifts. There, leaning against the altar were a cuirass, helmet, and greaves fashioned in black and gold, a long spear with the shaft wrapped in leather, the tip of which would have torn the head from a gorgon in one thrust.

"This armour will never be penetrated, and the spear will never miss its mark."

Then, out of the shadows, four stallions, as black as the night above, stepped forward. Their eyes burned with life and their manes writhed like black flame as they tossed their heads. Behind them was a chariot to match, with wheels that would never break and a cab that would never throw its driver.

Oinomaos looked up at Ares, daring to gaze upon the fire in those warlike eyes, and it was then that his determination was forged.

"When a suitor comes to take your daughter away," Ares said, smiling, "you will challenge him to a race across this land, from Elis, across the mountains to the altar of Poseidon in Isthmia."

"But what if they win?" Oinomaos asked.

"They will *never* win. And you will never lose your daughter. Make offerings at the outset of every race, during which time, you must allow the suitor to set out. Once you have completed your offerings, you will then chase after them, gazing down the shaft of this death-bringing spear, until you catch up with them."

"And when I do?"

"You will slay them so that they may no longer seek to tear your family."

"She is all I have left," Oinomaos said, bending down to take up the god-forged spear. He held it aloft and looked to his father. "I will do as you say."

"And victory will be yours," War answered.

ARES HELD sway over the land of Elis, and the rivers and fields ran with the blood of any man who dared approach the palace to seek the hand of the princess, Hippodameia, who was said to be one of the most beautiful women in the land. Stories of her piety also accompanied those of her beauty, but so too did the tales of suitors who had gone before, and the ends they had met as a result of the contest with her father, the king.

It had been known far and wide, over the mountain passes, and in every village, that the kingdom of Elis was all but leaderless, its ruler lost in a silent despair. But when suitors arrived, they found King Oinomaos not sullen and quiet, but strong and ready with spear and sword to protect his high palace and daughter.

Over the years, Hippodameia watched as suitor after suitor braved the borders of Elis and her father's throne room to seek her hand. And she was made to watch, from the seat beside her father's throne, as many confident young men, men of beauty, courage and renown, walked up the aisle of that stone throne room to take up the challenge set by Oinomaos.

Hippodameia always sought to dissuade her suitors, finding them in the court of the palace to plead with them not to race, not to throw away their lives, but these men - confident and blind to the fickle ways of the Gods and the danger into which they plunged themselves - they would not listen. They promised her that the Goddess Nike would grant them victory, and that they would return to free her, to give her a new life and honour.

Hippodameia smiled at each, one last look of doomed encouragement before they rode to their deaths.

She could still see them, those hopeful, young men destined for ignominious ends. Their names and faces haunted her nightly, and nightly she wished for an end to the deaths as she recited their names in the darkness.

"Marmay...Alcathos...Euryalos...Eurymachos...Crotalos... Acria...Capetos...Lycurgos...Lasios...Chalcodon... Tricolonus...Aristomachos...Prias...Pelagon...Aeolios... Cronios...and Erythras."

When she finished her recitation of deaths that night, she then thought of the name she would have to add on the morrow, for Eioneus, a skilled horse-tamer and lord from Thessaly, was set to race. When this latest suitor had entered the wine-stinking throne room earlier that day to challenge Oinomaos, there had been a moment when Hippodameia believed that perhaps he was the one to break the cycle of death. His horses were fleet-footed and strong, his chariot broad-wheeled and light, and his radiant green eyes keen and far-seeing with a look of kindness that warmed her.

However, Hippodameia tried to dissuade Eioneus too, for though she felt he had a chance at victory, she knew that the Gods would not allow it. They never did.

"Make offerings for me, my lady," Eioneus said to her, his warm hands upon hers as his charioteer prepared his team the next day upon the plain. "The Gods have blessed me in this. The Pythia at sacred Delphi confirmed it for me. I will win and we will be happy together. I've seen you free."

"I will make offerings for your victory," Hippodameia smiled, struggling to keep the sadness from her lips. "May Poseidon guide your team to victory." She then released his hands and looked to where her father stood beside his god-given team, their muscles writhing beneath their black skin. Her father smiled at her, wine dripping from his final sip before he stepped into the cab of his chariot with his great spear in hand.

"Eioneus!" Oinomaos called. "I give you the lead. Begin your journey to the altar of Poseidon in Isthmia now while I make offerings to Zeus in the altis of Olympia."

"But lord," Eioneus called back. "I will race honourably and wait and make offerings with you."

Oinomaos shook his dark, bearded head, his armour glinting in the morning sun. "That is not the challenge. Go now, and seek your victory...or your death." Oinomaos smiled and for the first time, Eioneus' confidence wavered, even as he gripped the reins of his team.

Hippodameia tried to catch her father's eye, to plead with him to stop the madness, but he would not look upon her. Beside him, his charioteer, Myrtilos, the son of Hermes, did look back at her and smiled sadly, shaking his head of golden locks, urging her not to have false hope yet again.

Oinomaos' charioteer and servant felt pity for Hippodameia, for he had known her all his life, had loved her from the shadows, never daring to approach her for fear of his master's wrath. He had been content to watch the princess from afar, to smile when he caught her eye, secretly happy when a suitor fell to his death, for it meant that no other man should have her. He wanted Oinomaos to win, though he hated him deeply for his cruelty toward his daughter.

Hippodameia bowed her head, turned away from Myrtilos, and went to the altar of Hera to make her promised offerings as the thunder of hooves echoed over the plain and the race began.

As she walked to the grove where the altar was set, Hippodameia let the quiet of the place envelop her, away from the palace and pitying glances of the people who had seen her smile and run as a child, in the company of her mother and brother, and the caring man her father had once been. She supposed that all longed for those happier days before darkness and blood.

The grove of Hera was the only place in which she could find some peace, where she would offer her prayers to the goddess for hope and victory, for her, for a suitor, for freedom. Many a time, as she had laid flowers and herbs, and poured oil and milk over the pocked stone of the goddess' altar, she had added her tears to it as well. Whenever she returned, the altar was clean again, the goddess having taken her gifts, and heard her prayers.

That day, Hippodameia heaped her offerings upon the altar and then sat against it in the long grass about its base. The sun lit her face and she felt its warmth as if for the first time in an age, and she let that heavenly light lull her to sleep.

As she slept, the Gods took her over the peaks and valleys of that sad land. She saw the marching of armies, the births and deaths of men, women, and children, and she saw the passage of time as only the Gods see it, quickly and slowly at once.

But then, time stopped, and Hippodameia stood upon a

lonely, tree covered path along the edge of a mountain. There, she saw a man walking, and her eyes were immediately drawn to him as to the spring sun after a long winter. His face was smooth, and his auburn hair rested upon his muscular shoulders. He shone with a brilliance no mortal man could possess, and yet, she felt he was a man. Still, there was something different about him as he walked the long road, his brilliant and storm-set blue eyes taking in every inch of the world about him. He looked at the road, the grooves of chariot wheels cut deep into them, the blood that ran there. He stopped and dipped his hand into the blood of those ruts and, without an inkling of fear, carried on walking. Then she noticed that he walked toward her, toward Elis, in the opposite direction of the tracks, and that the blood that had stained his fingers was gone in a matter of seconds.

Who are you? she asked as he passed, but he could not hear her in that land of waking dreams.

He could, however, see her and his eyes softened, and his lips smiled as he walked past her, on his westward way. *I'm coming...* he whispered without stopping, and it seemed that the trees arched protectively about him as he walked, and the birds in the trees trumpeted his passing.

Hippodameia stood alone again upon that mountain road, but the feeling of despair to which she had become accustomed seemed challenged, unstable. Instead, she felt hope spring, like the first green shoots after a long winter when Persephone returns to her mother upon the earth, no longer beneath it.

For so long she had longed for the return of the loving man who had been her father, who had roamed the halls of their home, the paths of that once-happy land, and who had held her up to the light, but she knew in that moment that he was gone.

She could hear the charging chariots and frothing stallions pulling across the ragged land. She could feel the blood rising about her feet in the wheel ruts about her as she saw Eioneus' team race past with careless speed.

He did not look to her as he passed, but his mind was set on the finish, on victory, and for a few moments, she believed it could happen.

But then came the grinding voice of Oinomaos, like a fury pursuing a sinner. His chariot gained ground and his team, with fire in their divine eyes, leapt chasms and rocks at great speed until they were directly behind their prey.

It was then that Oinomaos raised his great spear above the head of Myrtilos, who gripped and lashed the reins. The point of that death-bringing weapon sought the point between Eioneus' shoulders, steady, hungry, and patient.

Few of the Gods could have made such a throw, but Oinomaos, son of Ares, was well-practiced, and as soon as he had picked his spot, he let loose the weapon so that it soared at great speed, ahead of the charging horses to slam into the suitor's back.

Eioneus let out a great cry that rent the high mountain air and made the dreaming Hippodameia, and every nymph, dryad and satyr in the land cover their ears for the painful death-cry that was uttered by the brave charioteer as he slumped over the rail of his cab and his team plunged to their deaths over the mountainside.

Against the altar of Hera, in the darkness now, Hippodameia opened her eyes and knew that her father had been victorious, and that brave Eioneus was no more.

But the lingering thought she had, even in the midst of

renewed grief, was of the beautiful man with storm-blue eyes who walked alone across the land, and who had truly seen her.

She knelt before the goddess' altar and leaned upon it in supplication.

"Oh, Mother Hera, let this be an end of things...and a beginning," Hippodameia prayed, and about her the trees shuddered in the wind.

5

ARCADIAN IDYLL

The winds howled around the rock face of the mountains, in and among the boughs of the pine-scented trees, their dark heights blotting out the blueness of the sky above. Nearby, the sound of a mountain waterfall could be heard, rough in spring as it cascaded from an unseen height.

Persephone had only recently come back from the land of Hades, but already the joy of her godly mother could be seen in the emerald shoots that rose out of the forest floor, and in the soft-faced leaves that graced the boughs of plane trees and the olive groves in the valley far below.

Somewhere, in amongst the rocky caves where mortals rarely set foot, the god Pan set his black lips to his flute, and the music weaved its path about the mountainside like a serpent newly-come out of the earth.

In the middle of a grassy clearing shielded by soaring black pine, Pelops lay sleeping with his face turned to the heavenly blueness of the sky out of which he had fallen from the heights of Olympus. He did not see the dryads staring furtively at him from behind the broad trunks of trees. They could see he was mortal, but also that he was not of that land. They had heard and seen him fall and be lain upon the earth by the Gods themselves as a newborn is lain upon a rick, or in a cot by caring hands.

Pelops did not move at first, but began to breathe slowly, in and out, feeling the mountain air fill his lungs. He noticed the twitch of his muscles in the morning chill, a feeling he did not remember having from...

For a moment, he forgot where he had come from, but soon the scattered images and feelings in his whirling mind began to steady and slow, and he formed a story of memories that at once terrified him and inspired him.

"My life began with pain...far away..." he whispered. "But then..." He looked up to the soaring sky where an eagle circled and cried, and he remembered the faces of the Gods, the peace, the beauty of Olympus. "I wished for this."

He suddenly felt his body ache everywhere but in his right shoulder, and he slowly sat up, unaccustomed to the new sensations that began to fire in him like the flames in Hephaestus' forge.

Thirst was the first urge to attack him, and he turned to the nearby torrent of mountain water, crawling toward it. The smell of damp moss, dirt and rock was strong as he leaned over a boulder to dip his hands in the icy water to drink and splash his face. When the urge was quenched, he stood and noticed the soft, woollen tunic and leather jerkin he wore, and the sandals bound snuggly about his feet.

He looked at his long limbs, the muscles stretched and strong upon his arms and legs. He could feel them upon his chest, beneath his clothing, and the sensation of strength returned like a wave crashing upon a lonely shore. "Lord?" he whispered, thinking immediately of Earth-shaking Poseidon, memories of his kindness rushing back like the tide. "Thank you."

Your destiny is within your grasp, a voice said in Pelops' mind. *You must take it if you wish it, along with its glories and consequences.*

Though Pelops could not see Poseidon looking down at him from the cliffs of Olympus, he knew the god was there, that he would watch over him.

But the young man did wonder in that moment, why he chose to live upon the earth rather than in the heavens... Then it dawned on him as the chariot cracks the eastern sky and lights it with fire.

The woman.

He remembered her - tall, strong, beautiful, and beset by an overwhelming sadness. He recalled the spinning of wheels and the cries of horses and of men, and the memory set his heart to pounding within his mortal chest.

But the music of that mountain soothed him, and he saw something rustle in the ferns behind a nearby tree.

"Who is there?" Pelops asked, stepping slowly forward in the long, wavering grass. "Are you friend or foe?"

At first, a head of long brown hair the colour of bark turned toward him, and then the eyes as dark and green as Dodonian oak leaves flashed. Slowly, the dryad emerged to stand before Pelops. She stood naked in the sun's light, but for the twined strands of ivy that were wrapped about her body.

As she stepped closer to the mortal before her, the others hidden in and among the trees retreated in fear, and the music that had floated so softly upon the air suddenly stopped.

"Where am I?" Pelops asked her.

When she would not speak, he showed his hands with palms open.

"I won't hurt you," he said.

She smiled shyly. "And I will not harm you, mortal man," she said, holding out an armful of newly-picked forest mushrooms and soft greens. "You are hungry."

Pelops had not thought of eating, but as soon as the words were uttered, he knew that he was and so he reached out to accept the food she offered.

The dryad watched him eat, curious about the movement of his mouth and jaws, the way his hair was tickled by the winds.

When Pelops finished eating, he thanked her. "I am Pelops," he said.

Her eyes widened. "I have heard your name whispered as a thing to come. The Morai have sent you?"

"I have come of my own desire." He stood again and looked up at the passing sun, and then back at the dryad who stood even closer now. "What is your name?"

She stood back again. "I am Axioche." She reached out to take his hand and he gave it freely. "Where is your home, Pelops?"

He looked at the grassy ground and back up at her. "I have no home. For a time, Olympus was my home...after the great pain... But now, I would seek and create a home that none could take from me, or from my children."

"Do you have children?"

"No."

"Do you have a wife?"

"Not yet. But I have seen her."

The dryad was silent, but nodded after a time. "I can take

you to her." Though she did not say so, Axioche had seen the man before her, some moons past, at the height of a Dionysian night when the wine flowed and Selene's silver light graced the clearing where she now stood. "I will travel with you."

"If you wish," Pelops said. "I would be happy of the company."

"Where is she? This woman?" There was a hint of sadness, jealousy perhaps, in the dryad's voice.

Pelops, though unused to such emotions, had an urge to gently squeeze her hand. "I know not. I know that she is surrounded by the cries of men and horses, and the spinning of wheels. She is sad beyond measure."

The dryad's features darkened and her eyes closed, giving her the brief likeness of a new-formed sapling in the middle of the clearing.

"It is the lady of distant Elis you have seen," the dryad said. "It is death to seek her out."

"Death?"

"Many have died." She shook her head. "You must not look for her. She is-"

The dryad suddenly winced as if someone had lashed her, and the words she had sought to speak died in her throat.

It is not your place! The words rumbled in her mind, the voice chiding and full of danger like the swing of an axe before a sinewy pine.

"What were you going to say?" Pelops asked.

His eyes are full of kindness, she thought, *but they hold a stormy danger too. He is beautiful, but he is not mine.* A single tear ran down her cheek as the morning dew runs off of an outstretched leaf.

"What is wrong?"

"We must leave now," she said quickly, gazing back at her friends, her family, hidden among the forest shadows. She turned back to the mortal man and smiled. "Come."

Axioche waved her hand, and a moment later, the forest growth spread wide to reveal a path that led downward among the rocks.

"The road," she said, and led the way.

IN THE RECESSES of his mind, Pelops held images of what a kingdom looked like - rocky, dry, inaccessible - but the Arcadian lands through which the dryad led him were beautiful and bounteous beyond his thinking.

Axioche led him by hidden paths, away from the gaze of men, from the sky-soaring peaks of the tree-crowned mountains, down through forests to plateaus filled with fields that were bursting with colour and life. Spring flowers of purple and yellow blanketed plains where wheat and barley grew in abundance. Sheep grazed, watched by shepherds who played lonely tunes upon reed pipes to pass the time. Eagles soared from their eyries in the attics of the mountains, and herds of centaurs shook the earth as they travelled through, appearing and disappearing as if hidden by constant, morning mist.

The more they travelled over the land, the more Pelops came to love it - the way the air smelled of pine and olive, how nature's music accompanied them always, how the broad skies shivered at all times of day. They walked in sunlight at the base of the mountains, and then upon the high, cliff-hugging roads, among the cool clouds that hovered about that mountain world.

That land, however, was not devoid of mortals, and occasionally, they came upon a small village, and heard the cries of babes in their mother's cradling arms. The sight of these gave Pelops pause, for it was foreign to him. As Axioche disappeared into the wood about a village to avoid the grasping hands of mortals, Pelops walked into their midst to look upon them, to speak with them, to understand their purpose and existence.

It was as if he was finally coming out of a dream, his senses prickling, his mind afire with questions and new-found knowledge with every word he exchanged, with every bite of apple, taste of olive or of cheese or bread molded by a peasant's hands.

The mortals he saw, the varying looks in their eyes, told him a tale of past laughter and joys overshadowed by fear and the heavy hand of Fate. Though there was suffering in their eyes, they were ever-hopeful, it seemed.

The men, women, and children whom Pelops did meet upon the high, westward road looked upon him too. When they saw him come down out of the mountain wood, they took him for a god, shining and strong with eyes like angry weather.

They backed away from him at first, but then he spoke kindly to them and asked the way. When they would not answer easily, he approached a solitary shepherd on the outskirts of the village, for it had become clear to Pelops that the shepherds of that land were not afraid, but respectful of the Gods and their ways. They knew the mysteries of that land, left offerings upon the remote altars, knew the paths run by centaurs, nymphs and satyrs. They knew where the dangers lurked, and where a man could sleep peacefully for the night.

Pelops approached the man who was dressed in hind-skin boots and a wolf pelt skirt. His dark beard was long and oiled, his bearing proud.

"They think you're a god," the shepherd said to Pelops when he stopped beside him at the far end of the village. "They've not seen a man like you before."

"I've not seen their like before either," Pelops replied, the chilling wind rustling his long hair. "They seem to have a good life here, but why do I see sadness in their eyes?"

"They were happy, once, as was this land."

"What happened?"

"Death. Many deaths."

"Whose?"

The shepherd looked upon the man before him. "It began with the king's wife and son. She died of grief, drowned in Poseidon's sea, and he was destroyed by the nymphs for love of one favoured by Apollo." He stared for a moment into Pelops' eyes and could hear the crash of waves then, finally given the pause that others had upon seeing the newcomer.

"Which king do you speak of?"

"King Oinomaos of Elis, the son of Ares. He ruled wisely once, kindly, but now..."

"Now?"

"He only leaves his wine-soaked palace to drench this land in blood."

"Why?"

"Who knows the ways of kings?" The shepherd shrugged but stood to look out over the cliff at the land below, leaning upon his wooden staff. "He has a daughter, the lady Hippodameia."

Hippodameia, Pelops repeated in his mind, immediately feeling the pull of his fate.

"Men turn mad for her, and risk all."

"How so?" Pelops asked.

"They seek her hand in marriage, but in order to get her hand, they must race her father, Oinomaos, in a chariot race across this land."

"A skilled charioteer could do so."

The shepherd shook his head. "No. There have been seventeen thus far, and all have perished."

"All?" Pelops tried to imagine so many deaths at the hands of one man.

"All. These suitors of the princess' must race from the hill of dreaded Kronos in Elis, all the way across the mountains to the altar of Poseidon at distant Isthmia. And Oinomaos gives them a head-start."

"And he still wins?"

"His horses, his chariot, his armour and spear are all given him by his immortal father, War. Of course he wins. The suitors ride like the wind, and just when it seems that they might indeed win the hand of Hippodameia, Oinomaos catches up with them, his spear levelled at their backs." The shepherd paused, as if haunted by the cries he had heard for so long, the litter of wreckage across that once-happy land. "He snuffs out their lives as easily as he downs another cup of wine. I know. I've watched it happen. I've seen young, hopeful men cut down like wheat in the valleys, and felled like trees in the mountains. Oinomaos does not want to give his daughter's hand to anyone, and he is merciless in his purpose."

"And what of his daughter, Hippodameia?" Pelops asked.

"What of her? She is Death's bait. To seek her out is to doom oneself."

That gave Pelops only the briefest of pauses, for he knew she was the one he had dreamed of on Olympus, the one he sought.

"How do I reach the king's palace in Elis?"

The shepherd looked up from his flock upon the mountainside below them, his eyes wide, unbelieving that yet another doomed suitor had stepped forward.

"You wish to win her hand still? After all I have told you?"

"Yes," Pelops said, tall and defiant before him. "Not all men are destined as food for the crows."

"All who race Oinomaos are." But the shepherd could see the youth before him would not be dissuaded. "Still, if you are determined... Continue on this road for three days and you will reach Elis. In two days, you will reach a fork in the road. Take the path to the left that leads down out of the mountains onto the plains of Elis, toward the place where the Gods themselves raced and fought around the hill of Kronos. Once there, carry on for a short time to the southwest, toward the sea, and there you will find the palace."

"Thank you, friend," Pelops said, but the shepherd shook his head.

"I am no friend to direct you there. If you do not wish to have your bones and blood litter this land like so many others, then you will not go. Stay here among these people... they have many beautiful women to give you strong sons."

"There is only one woman I seek," Pelops said, patting the shepherd on the shoulder before turning to look back at the watchful villagers. He smiled and carried on down the road that led along the cliffs where a great chute of water fell from on high.

The shepherd watched the man go, and when the villagers went back to their sad, simple work, he smiled to himself.

"Go then, favourite of Poseidon, and see what the Morai have in store for you." His countenance shimmered and shone, like golden morning light upon the still surface of a clear pond, and a moment later, fair-skinned Hermes, the messenger of the Gods, stood in his place. "You go to your doom, or to victory," he said to Pelops' back. "Either way, you will suffer."

He then plunged over the cliff's edge to soar through the air, back to high Olympus and the realm of the Gods.

THE STARS SHONE brightly that night, their gentle music thrumming in the silver light that penetrated every glade and clearing in that mountain world.

Beside a still pool, Pelops knelt upon the mossy ground to gaze into the water at his reflection. He felt apart from himself, as if a stranger looked back at him, a stranger with no place in the world of men or of gods. He could see the blue of his eyes, shining in the darkness, the fall of his hair about his muscled shoulders, his strong arms and broad chest. He turned his hands over to look upon them, and for a moment, they were young again, toying with rocks upon the dry, Lydian plain in summer. Even as the memory surfaced, it was lost, mercifully blown away by the will of Poseidon.

The surface of the water rippled in the mountain breeze, and there behind his reflection appeared Axioche, her arms softly twining about his body like the long branches of a willow about a stream-side boulder.

They looked at each other in the still surface of that starlit pool, and he could see a tear glisten and run down her cheek to fall over his shoulder.

"Do not go," she pleaded. "Stay here with me, and you will know neither death or pain. Run the mountain paths with me, Pelops. Watch the stars whirl and see the soaring arcs of sun and moon for all time with me. I have seen our son, and he is beautiful and strong...as are you."

Pelops stood from the edge of the pool and turned, still within the lithe embrace of her gentle arms.

Axioche's leaf-green eyes locked onto his and, before he could speak, her apple blossom lips pressed to his, softly at first, and then with urgency, as if the sands of time neared their end.

There, upon the grass of that hidden glade, away from the prying eyes of god, man, and beast, Pelops held the dryad and laid her down. Their lovemaking, in that moment, became a salve for their loneliness, their kisses bonds, their arching backs and groans a primal release that helped them, for a time, to forget their parting paths.

For the rest of that night, they lay together in the open air, Axioche's naked arms and legs twined about Pelops' limbs like ivy about a broad oak. They slept fitfully, contented and at peace with the world.

But such moments are not to last upon the earth.

In that land of god-sent dreams, Pelops found himself walking alone again, through stoney, firelit corridors with bronze, lion-clawed tripods. The sound of weeping, like to the gentle trickle of rain in a thick forest, caught his ear and he followed it to the end of the corridor.

Someone called his name from behind, but he did not look back, could not look back, for his urge to go forward toward that oak and bronze door at the end of the corridor was too great.

When he reached the end, the weeping louder in his ears, he set both hands upon the door and pushed it open. Inside, he found a large bedchamber into which poured moonlight, and by the arches of the windows was a table upon which a single lamp burned. At the table sat a woman with long hair falling down the back of her pure, white peplos fastened with golden knots.

She wept where she sat, alone and grief-stricken. Upon the table before her were also a bronze mirror beside a statue of the goddess Hera, incense burning at her feet to be carried away on the wind out the window.

It was cold in the room, and the woman shivered.

Pelops approached her slowly from behind, not daring to reach out and touch her shoulder, nor to speak. He was drawn to her, and could not pull away.

She held up the mirror to her face.

Oh, mother Hera, please make all of it stop...the deaths...my father's madness... That, or take my life, for I have no wish to continue in this living grief.

Pelops could tell that the woman did not want to die. He could not imagine someone so lovely, so perfectly fashioned by the Gods, to have their light snuffed out.

Suddenly, her eyes caught sight of him in the mirror that she held up and she turned.

Winded both, their hearts beating rapidly in that silent space and time, there was inexplicable recognition.

I've seen you before! the woman said.

Pelops looked back at her, remembered seeing her from the heights of Olympus.

Hippodameia? he mouthed her name in amazement, as if he had found a rare bloom in the vast gardens of the Gods.

She began to shake her head. *Do not come. Only death awaits you here!*

Pelops reached out to her, but as soon as his fingers were about to touch her soft, wet cheek, he was pulled backward through the door. He was hurtled down the corridor and out of the palace toward the mountains as the sun and moon swept the skies overhead.

The neighing of charging horses and the cries of a man suddenly rent the air in every corner of that vast land. Trees splintered and the mountain rocks cracked and fell, and then all was silence but for the fearful running of the nymphs and satyrs of forest, field and stream, and the panicked flight of birds as they shot into the skies.

Pelops' eyes shot open and he sat quickly, his heart pounding, to find himself sitting beside the pool, the naked dryad beside him.

Axioche listened to the forest's voice, and knew what had happened.

"What was that?" Pelops asked her.

She reached out to press her hand to his muscled chest, to lay him down again beside her, but his body and mind would not obey.

He is not mine any longer, she thought, her sadness returning. "Another death," she said, as Pelops stood up to put on his tunic and leather jerkin, his head tilted to the sky and his eyes searching the steep, forested mountain slope. "Another race. The king of Elis has killed another suitor."

Pelops turned to her. "Another?"

She nodded. "The world of men is full of death. Do not worry over things that are."

"I saw her in my dream...the lady of Elis. She was sad... alone."

"As am I," Axioche answered.

But he did not hear her. She was already fading from his memory.

"I must go to her," Pelops strode to the edge of the clearing and stopped where the path led away, back to the distant road. There he stopped and turned back to see the dryad standing alone beside the pool. He walked back to her and held out his hand. "Please come with me. I would end the deaths so that blood no longer runs in this land."

"You cannot promise such a thing in the world," Axioche replied, but as she looked upon the beautiful man with whom she had lain that night, she could feel the heat burning within her, the urge to make him hers, until she remembered the voice of the god warning her. She finally nodded. "I will go with you."

He smiled and squeezed her hand, and she felt joy for a little longer.

6

THE CHALLENGE

The darkness within the walls of Oinomaos' palace had grown deeper in the days following the race with the latest suitor, and when the king returned with the smashed body of his opponent tied to the cab of his chariot, it was to the bowed heads of a people living in deepest fear. None but his charioteer, Myrtilos, spoke to him, and that was as the king wished it.

Oinomaos ordered Eioneus' head set upon a spike beside the others that jutted out from the walls of his palace gate to gaze out over the Elian plain and warn off any more would-be heroes. Once it was mounted, the eyes staring out from a bloody, smashed mouth beneath the long, blood-matted hair, Oinomaos stared at it and thanked his heavenly father, Ares.

"Father, I thank you for my victory, and offer you the death of this man. Help me to continue to keep my kingdom, my throne, and my daughter from any more upstarts who would dare challenge me."

Oinomaos turned, expecting to see a crowd of his people gathered around to look upon the trophy of his victory, but instead, he found only the whistling wind in the tall plain grasses beneath the bronze, evening sky.

Thunder rumbled in the distance, an echo of the anger of Zeus directed at some distant place, but it did not worry Oinomaos, for the eighteen heads upon his gate were testament to his power and invincibility.

"Care for my horses!" he ordered Myrtilos, who stood waiting nearby with the horses and chariot.

"Yes, my king," Myrtilos said, bowing and flicking the reins to get away from Oinomaos and back to the peace of the sweet-smelling stables that were his only sanctuary.

Oinomaos looked a while longer upon the dreadful gazes of his former challengers whom, he knew, now walked broken, mute, and sightless through the lands of the dead. He had thought to bury the first two, Marmax and Alcathous, with proper rites, but he had decided against it, wishing more to set an example to all-comers, and to show the Gods themselves that the son of Ares was not to be toyed with any longer.

HIPPODAMEIA WEPT in the days since her father's return, but not for the death of Eioneus, as kind as he had seemed. She had tried to dissuade him, but it seemed men's desire for victory outweighed the value of life.

"Mother Hera," she prayed that night before the smoking altar in her chambers at the top of the palace. "I no longer wish to be the cause of death among men. If, by my own death, I can end this ceaseless suffering, I am willing to pay the price. Guide me, beloved Hera. I honour you."

Hippodameia's words travelled upon the winds to the palaces of the Gods and Hera, Queen of Olympus, heard them. She stood at the edge of her high balcony looking down over the women and children of the world, and felt herself moved by Hippodameia's offer of sacrifice.

"But what a lesser world it would be for the snuffing out of such a light," the goddess said to herself.

However, she had grown disgusted by Oinomaos' behaviour, his hubris, and knew that something had to be done. The deaths needed to end.

"And if the death of one girl will end it all, perhaps it is right?" She saw it then, Hippodameia's chamber that night to come, the bronze blade she would hold in her hand, and the deep cut that would let her lifeblood drain away. "Such a sacrifice will bear you to Elysium, near the stream of Ocean where you will never know despair, pain or death again."

Hippodameia, alone in her chambers before the goddess' altar then, stoppered her tears and felt hope. Still, she was not fully decided, and she hesitated. "I will wait for a sign from you, oh Goddess." And with that, Hippodameia lay herself upon the broad frame of her bed to watch the curtains flutter in the evening breeze and the stars alight in the heavens beyond that palace of death.

"You will be welcomed among the Gods," Hera whispered.

There was a rumble upon Olympus then, and almighty Zeus, appeared at his queen's side. "You cannot tempt her with death."

Hera looked upon her husband and shook her head. "She is death to many. She no longer wishes it to be thus."

Together they looked down the long pathways of the skies over that unhappy, blood-soaked land of man, and saw the possibilities of divergent future paths. Their grandson had failed as a ruler, and the land suffered under his boot, his arrogance and anger growing with every victory.

"I would free this girl from her mortal shackles," Hera said, her immortal eyes glistening like rain upon purest marble.

Zeus was silent as he stared across the firmament in search of the answers he sought. With each circuit of the sun's chariot about the earth, the King of the Gods sought a million answers to a million different questions. To rule upon the earth was an honour for men, but to rule upon creation, for Zeus, was an infinite burden, though he could not have chosen otherwise.

"She cannot decline her fate," Zeus said as he looked with his immortal wife upon the beauty of Hippodameia. "It is not hers to die so young a death, but to inspire victory."

"And more death?" Hera countered, placing her hand upon his.

"Let there be one more race," Zeus replied, and the heavens shook. "And the outcome of that race will put an end to all of it, one way, or another."

"As you wish," Hera replied, and Zeus disappeared in a flash of heavenly light. She looked again to Hippodameia as she slept, the dagger placed upon the bed beside her. "Do not touch that blade. Sleep...sleep and dream..."

Just then, Hera of the Heights, and Protector of Men, with her keen and caring eyes recognized the blue-eyed favourite of Poseidon striding over the mountain passes of the land below, urged on by his desire to see the lady of Elis. The goddess smiled, and wondered if such a union were possible, whether it would be joy to Hippodameia, and peace to that bloody land.

"Stay your hand from death awhile longer, child," Hera

whispered, her voice travelling on the long-winded ways to Hippodameia's mind. "Zeus commands one last race, and one last race it shall be. Sleep...and live..."

HIPPODAMEIA of the Long Tresses lay upon her bed, tossing and turning upon its surface in the night as if she were washed ashore after having been lost at sea. The death-bringing blade she had coddled beside her had fallen to the stoney floor as she moved, no longer a thing in her mind.

Instead, as she slept, she dreamed not of travelling to the land of the dead, but of the man she had seen previously in her visions, a man traversing mountain woods, accompanied by the sound of the sea, and as he filled her dreamscape eyes, a soft smile graced her lips for the first time in what seemed an age.

Zeus commands one last race...

The voice of the goddess roused her from her sleep and she sat bolt upright upon her bed to gaze out at a sky cleared at last of its rock-grey clouds. The light of the sun's chariot blazed in at the window and the song of a lark filled the room with new life, new hope.

But despite the brilliance of that golden-dawning day, the thought of death returned to her, and it was all she could do not to think of those blank-faced banners of Fate nailed upon the palace walls.

Her head spun, and her heart tightened within the cavity of her chest.

"I am alone," she said to herself, but even as she spoke the words, she saw new possibilities out of the realm of dreams. And so Hippodameia stood, and dressed, and went out of her chambers to meet the day.

. . .

THE SKY HEAVED with darkness and light, both pulling at each other, both at odds above mountain, river, field and grove. It had been thus ever since Pelops crossed from Arcadia into Elis with the dryad at his side, blown along with him like leaves upon the wind.

Axioche had given up her efforts to dissuade Pelops from continuing on his chosen course, for he was now set upon it like a wolf upon a scent. She had felt fear too, as she accompanied her mortal love, for in the whispers of the oaks, and the gurgling of the streams, the Gods chided her along the way, threatened her with terrible death if he did not reach his destination.

She wondered why the Gods should so desire Pelops' death, for in her eyes, he was kind and gentle and had already been wronged overmuch by the world. *Why can you not grant him peace?* she asked, but was silenced as thunder and lightning clapped over the broad fields of Elis as they emerged from the confines of the forest at the edge of the hills.

"What did you say?" Pelops turned to her.

Axioche looked on him from the safety of the wood, no longer willing to walk with him.

"I cannot go any further with you," she said, and there was sadness in her melodic voice.

Pelops walked back to her, took her hands. "Why?"

"You must go on alone now."

"But we are almost there!" Pelops answered, surprised that he did not want to let her go.

Axioche smiled sadly and shook her head. "The Gods command it, and I must listen." She closed her eyes and turned to the wood behind her, breathed in its spring scent and felt lighter.

Pelops stepped around the front of her and held her. "Will I see you again?"

Her eyes glazed over as she looked upon him, the leaves of the trees reflecting on their surface and she nodded. "I know you will," she whispered, her hands upon her flat, vine-clad stomach for a moment before she reached up to kiss his lips once more, and as she did so, sad spring poppies sprouted about their feet, their crimson heads bowed. "Go now, Pelops. If ever you need me, I will be in the hidden place in the mountain wood, that place where you first filled my eyes."

For a moment, he thought about going with her, was drawn to a painless life of peace and simple beauty in the wild, but then he pictured Hippodameia again, the sadness in her eyes, the desperation, and he knew he could help her.

"Thank you, Axioche," he said, and the dryad closed her eyes at the utterance of her name.

Without another word, he turned and began to jog across the new-green field toward the palace of Oinomaos.

"I love you," the dryad whispered through her tears, her thoughts lost on the hot breeze rustling the trees behind her.

As he ran, Pelops could feel his strength and determination growing, though there was an inkling of dread in the pit of stomach. The image of that lonely woman pushed him onward, however, across the rivers of the Gods, through groves of olive and orange, their new-born fruit bobbing in the wind as if raising their heads at his passing.

He did not understand how he knew which way to run,

but felt that the Gods were aiding him along his route. Soon, he came to a hill in the middle of the plain that was covered in dark pine and cypress, and that hill seemed to breathe and speak. Crows darted from its peak as he came to the base of it and peels of thunder could be heard though the sky was clear.

It gave Pelops pause, and so he moved away, wary of what lay beneath those steep slopes.

Do not tread upon the hill of Kronos! he heard Poseidon say in his head, and so he turned away from that dread monument of battle between the Gods and Titans and looked upon the broad plain where Alfeios ran in a cool, silver line across the land.

Pelops could not help but stop and stare at the beauty of that place, and as he did so, he saw and heard the Gods themselves running and fighting, competing in some strange pageant of strength and skill that shook the earth and made the green trees shudder. They faded from his sight, however, and instead the place was filled with smoking altars and temples. The statues of heroes rose up like a forest about him and, finally, the thunder of a thousand hooves and the turning of a thousand wheels erupted.

He fell to his knees, his hands pressed over his ears, unable to dampen the roar of victory and the crashing despair of defeat.

"Stop!!!" he finally yelled, and his senses grew still again. He knew the Fates were teasing him, baiting him, but he did not understand why. *Focus on her!* he told himself, thinking of the tears upon the woman's face.

As he pushed himself to his feet, not looking toward that dread, Titanic hill behind him, he noticed the rutted earth where chariot wheels had churned it, the imprints of hooves, and the faded colour of dried blood.

The shades of eighteen men hovered before him, dazed, confused, their strength and will sapped when once they had been filled with utmost confidence and hope.

Pelops would have spoken to them, asked what had befallen them, but he dared not.

Keep going, Pelops! Poseidon's voice crashed in his skull. *Do not linger!*

Pelops left that place behind, but inside, he knew he would return there soon, that he was fated to. His strong legs carried him over the low, lush hills of Elis to the southwest, taking the trodden goat paths that led among groves of spring olive and scented lemon. As the sun began to dip and paint the sky in shades of orange and crimson, he came to a road that ran parallel to the distant coast, and there he found an old woman walking with a basket of ruby cherries.

At his approach, she recoiled in fear, but when she looked more closely, she was put at ease.

"Greetings, lady," Pelops said, stopping short, breathing heavily.

"Young man, greetings," she replied, her voice crackling and dry, as if she had been walking a desert for days.

"I am looking for the palace of the king of Elis. Oinomaos is his name, I have been told."

"And why would you seek the walls of the dreaded son of Ares?"

"To challenge him!"

The woman dropped her basket and she bent to pick up the cherries with trembling hands. "Please do not do so," she said as Pelops bent to help her refill the basket.

"Why?"

"It is death. All who challenge him are taken from the light of day."

"Does he indeed have a daughter, the lady of Elis named Hippodameia? Or have I been led astray by my dreams?"

"Dreams?" The old woman looked at him, as if she now saw something different in him, something other than the other suitors who had come forth to take up the reins of death. But she grunted. "Our princess is cursed and abandoned." The old woman gazed across the plain to the palace hill in the distance. "This was once a happy land," she said wistfully, "but when Death came for the princess' mother and brother, it all changed. There is no longer joy here, nor light, nor music." She shook her head. "Go back to where you came from, young man. Live, be free and happy. Such things are not to be found here, nor in the arms of that woman."

Pelops looked at her keenly, and for a moment, he thought she smiled through her leather-skinned lips. "Please tell me where the palace is. I can waste no more time."

Slowly, the woman raised her withered arm to point directly across the plain to a mound where torches were beginning to alight in the growing darkness. "There, you will find that despairing and cursed house. There, if you choose it, Death is waiting for you."

Pelops felt his heart pound as the depths of his sea-blue eyes fell upon the distant walls. He nodded silently and took a couple of steps forward.

"It is not too late to turn back," the woman said, searching the young man's eyes for doubt, for fear. "The Gods will not think ill of you for it."

After a moment, Pelops turned to the old woman. "Thank you for your aid. Farewell, lady," he said before plunging down the gently-sloping rocks and setting out across the plain toward the palace.

The old woman watched him and smiled. "He has been tempted and tested," she said, and in that moment her skin stretched and filled, her hair lengthened and grew in brilliance, and her form grew tall and beautiful.

The Goddess Hera stood there watching Pelops run toward Hippodameia. "He has chosen," she whispered as she looked to the heavens and the emergent fires set therein. "Fates...be kind to them if you will..."

As Pelops made his way across the plain toward the flickering torches atop the thick walls of Oinomaos' palace, he felt as if he were making little progress. It was as though he ran as swiftly as he could, and yet, the palace came no closer. His lungs began to heave, and he sweat with the effort, and yet his proximity to those dark walls was little diminished.

"Gods! Let me go!" he called out to the night, pushing through the effort and pain until, at last, his feet drove him forward at great speed, and soon he was coming to a stop before the gates of the palace.

"Hold!" one of the guards called out, his spear levelled.

Pelops looked at the two guards standing there in great belts of bronze armour and with boars' tusk helmets atop their heads. His eyes however, could not help but look up and around the gates at the blank faces of the dead staring back at him. "What is this?" he asked.

The guards turned to look up and then back at the lone man before them.

"The heads of the suitors who have challenged the king

for the hand of his daughter." The guard lowered his spear. "Now tell me, stranger, what is your business?"

Pelops was mute, for the dead men who looked back at him were those same shades who had surrounded him, reached out to him, beneath the hill of Kronos that very morning. He swallowed and wiped his sweating brow. He could feel his heart beating quickly as the first traces of real fear began to invade his body like a slow poison.

I have already died and, by the Gods, I am here upon the earth again. I cannot turn back now.

"I asked you a question, stranger!" the guard repeated.

Pelops' sea blue eyes turned on the man and he cleared his throat as he stepped forward. "I'm here to challenge the king for the hand of his daughter."

The two men were silent, their features immediately full of pity and fear for the stranger before them.

"Are you sure you want to throw your life away?" the one whispered. "You see what happened to the eighteen men who came before you?"

"They all arrived at these gates, some hopeful, others arrogant...handsome and strong men all of them," the first added. "They were heroes in their faraway homes, but here, in this land, they all ended up food for the crows, their bones gnashed by wolves in the night." He shook his head. "Leave while you can, stranger. Live. Go back home."

"I have no home," Pelops answered calmly. "And my challenge stands."

The guards were silent for a moment, for they had grown tired of seeing good men sent to their deaths. Nevertheless, the one nodded and turned. "Follow me, then."

Leaving the one guard at the gates, he led Pelops beneath the great stone ramparts through the first courtyard where, from above, other guards of the palace watched them go silently as if in a funeral cortege. They rounded a corner where the road led up, through a second gate, and then onto the main courtyard before the palace itself.

Offerings burned upon an altar in the middle of the courtyard, and tripods cradling gently-burning fires cast their light inward from the perimeter.

The guard leading Pelops suddenly dropped to his knee. "My lady," he said. "Here is another."

Pelops stopped suddenly as if his feet were rooted to the very stone beneath him.

Walking quickly toward him from across the courtyard, like a new-formed butterfly in flight, Hippodameia approached, her silent robes fluttering all around her.

She stopped suddenly before Pelops, and their eyes locked for a moment as recognition dawned on them like the brightest of new days.

"My lady...it's...it's you." Only once before had Pelops truly felt the hand of the Gods at work, when he had come back from death, and now he felt it again.

"You?" Hippodameia said, her lips trembling, her eyes boring deep into his. "I thought the Gods were toying with me. I've seen you. I've wondered if you would come or not."

"And I saw you...in a...dream."

"No dream," she answered, daring to smile a little.

"I am Pelops. I've come to help you."

"Pelops," she repeated. "I am Hippodameia."

"I know," he said, his voice but a hoarse whisper. He caught his breath again and stared beyond her at the dark palace walls. "I've come to challenge your father."

In that moment, her countenance changed and the hope and light faded from her face as a great storm cloud covers the land and sucks all colour out of the world. "You must not," she said. "Too many have died." She knew she was countering the Gods wish, for Zeus' command had been for one last race, but as she looked upon the beautiful man standing there before her, she knew she could not bear to see yet another life taken. "Please leave, Pelops. Leave while you can. I will survive."

"You have been, lady. I can see that." He shook his head, his hair settling about his shoulders, his blue eyes bright in the firelight as he looked upon her. "But my place is here, with you, if the Gods will it."

She felt that familiar wave of sadness and despair rushing toward her. *I should have ended this last night,* she thought, and as the thought occurred to her, the flames of the nearest tripod flickered and danced, and within those flames, Eros appeared, sent by Aphrodite at Hera's command, to eliminate any doubt in the two mortals and stoke the fires of love that had already begun in the man and woman before him.

Eros pulled two arrows from his flaming quiver, nocked them upon his godly weapon, pulled back and sighted along the shafts at Pelops and Hippodameia. *Love is all,* the fiery god whispered. *You will not, nor ever shall you, waver in it.*

And he fired.

In that moment, any fear or doubt which Pelops or Hippodameia had been yielding to disappeared, for love is stronger than anything, even in the face of certain death.

"The Gods will it," Pelops whispered, "And so do I." He grasped her hands and the guard who stood not far off took a step closer.

Hippodameia stayed him with her raised hand and held Pelops' hands in return. "I couldn't bear to see them bring your body or head back here to the palace, and so I will not leave your side."

"I would stay with you always, lady," Pelops replied. But then he looked to the palace behind her and paused. "But first, your father must accept my challenge." He made to walk, but Hippodameia held him back.

"Wait! Please. Do not lay down your challenge in the dead of night when he is full of wine. Wait until the full brightness of dawn surrounds this place and fills the throne room. That is when you should lay down your challenge!"

"As you wish, lady." And he brought her trembling hands to his lips, the fate of the land sealed as much as the fate of those two mortals.

Reluctantly, Hippodameia left Pelops behind in the court-yard to go back to her chambers and offer prayers to Hera for success, and to her grandfather, Ares, to finally ease the stubborn will of her father that he might be the man he once was and return to her.

Pelops was led to one of the stables off of the main court-yard where he would spend the night to await the moment of his dawn challenge to the king.

"Here," the guard returned to him a short while later with a jug of wine and a clay plate of cheese, fresh bread, and roasted meat. "Offer to the Gods, and eat your fill, stranger."

Pelops stood from the freshly strewn hay and looked at the man. "You don't think I can win."

The guard was silent, and shook his head slowly. "No one can." He looked around and leaned in closer to Pelops so that only he could hear. "The king has lost all of his family, but for his daughter. He does not want to give her up to any man. His armour and weapons were forged by Hephaestus, and his horses were a gift from his divine father. They are the swiftest in the world. They cannot lose." He did not speak for a moment, trying to see if he had had any success in dissuading the man before him, but he could see that he did not. "Eat well and rest."

Pelops watched him go back across the courtyard to his post at the palace gates, and himself disappeared into the shadows at the back of the stall to lean against the olivewood wall. He filled the rough clay cup with wine and held it up in the darkness.

"Earth-Shaking Poseidon…Tamer of Horses…guide and protect me in the days to come. Protect me as my own father never did." And he poured the dark wine into the hay at his feet, leaving only a single sip for himself to bind his prayers.

ON THE HIGH slopes of Olympus, red-eyed Ares stared down from those divine ramparts toward his son's palace. He knew Oinomaos had had many victories with the horses and weapons he had gifted him, and his offerings had pleased the God of War more than any others, but even for the son of Ares, hubris was inadvisable.

"Your son is deep in Dionysus' again," the rumbling voice of Poseidon said beside Ares.

War turned to the Sea, his uncle, and felt his anger rise. "And your favourite mortal fool has but a day to live. Is it not hubris to think that he can come into the world and claim victory when he has never truly lived? To think that he can defeat my own son?"

"Not hubris," Poseidon said, turning toward the younger god. "Hope."

"Hope is the realm of fools," Ares spat, his hand crushing the railing beneath.

"How many deaths must it take to salve his pain?" Poseidon asked.

"Some pains can never go away."

"Pelops has asked for my help, and I shall give it to him. Try to dissuade your son. Get him to choose peace and the happiness of his daughter over victory and death."

"Peace?" Ares laughed. "Never! He will ride down this upstart and grind his bones beneath his spinning wheels. He will cut him to pieces and hang his head upon his lofty walls, and the land will bleed until every upstart who challenges the son of Ares wanders deaf and dumb in the fields of Hades."

"You will not help him any more!" Poseidon demanded.

"You do not command me!" Ares' glinting blade of adamant swept up and down, only to be caught in the teeth of Poseidon's trident, and the walls of Olympus shook.

"Stop this!" a great voice commanded, and the hand of Zeus fastened around the locked weapons, ceasing the shaking of the Gods' halls. "I warned both of you of the rift this would cause. I will not allow it!"

The Thunderer's voice shook them where they stood, and lightning filled the heavens for the briefest of moments, like a great net cast out to sea.

"It is within the law that Ares should help his son as he has been." Zeus, King of the Gods, turned to War. "But you have given him all that I will permit. No more!"

"He needs nothing more!" Ares answered, crossing his great arms so that the fire in his veins glowed beneath the surface of his divine skin. He smiled mockingly at Poseidon.

Zeus turned to Poseidon. "They will race, and one of them will die. Such are the choices they have made."

"Brother, I must protest-"

"Silence!" Zeus roared. "You gave Pelops renewed life in these very halls.... I will allow you to give him one last gift. One only!"

Poseidon stared across the broad chest of Zeus at War, and nodded gravely. "Agreed."

Ares smiled. "In the end, Pelops will pray that the Gods had indeed ground his bones in their mouths rather than feel the pain of my son's death-bringing spear in his back."

With those parting words, War faded from that Olympian balcony in a flash of red.

Zeus turned to Poseidon. "I understand your love for this mortal, but you must obey me in this."

Poseidon bowed his long-bearded head to all-powerful Zeus. "I will."

"When the day for the race dawns, we shall be there to ensure all is as it should be," Zeus said, before departing down the long corridors of Olympus.

Poseidon took a last look over the railing, through the clouds, to see Pelops sleeping alone in the warmth of horse hay. When he turned away, he was met by golden Hermes.

"I must speak with you," he whispered.

DAWN BRUSHED the sky above Elis in radiant hues of pink and orange, and there was a calm quiet over the land as if it had had its first fitful sleep in a long while. A warm wind tickled the groves, snuck in at windows, and rustled the senses of the populace, including the guards who stood watch over the blood-stained walls of Oinomaos' palace.

From the warmth of the scattered straw about him, Pelops opened his eyes to see the brightly-lit courtyard before him where some of the guards stood. But there was someone nearer and he sat up quickly when he caught a glimpse of golden eyes and a head of curly black hair watching him.

"Who are you?" Pelops asked, but the man departed quickly without a word.

"Good morning!" the guard from the previous night said as he approached with a pitcher of water, and some bread and honey upon a small wooden pallet.

Pelops stood and looked around. "That man just now...he was watching me while I slept."

The guard looked around the courtyard and spotted the familiar face of the king's charioteer retreating back into the shadows toward the far end of the stables. He set the tray down before Pelops. "That is Myrtilos, the king's driver. He's a nuisance, but we dare not beat him. He's the only one with the king's favour and some say he's the son of Hermes."

"Hermes?" Pelops repeated. "And he serves the king?"

"Yes," the guard answered, his face darkening. "Myrtilos takes a particular interest in every suitor who appears to challenge the king."

"I see."

"Speaking of which... Are you still intent on doing this? You seem a good man. You've seen what became of the others outside the gates. If you've changed your mind, I'll let you slip out and away, and no one will be the wiser."

"I'm decided... What is your name?"

"Leandros. Captain of the palace guard." He stepped closer. "And yours, stranger? I will need to announce you."

"Pelops."

"Of which land?"

That gave him pause, for he had some vague, painful recollection of his origins in distant Lydia, across the sea. *That was no home,* he thought. Yet, he knew that without a title, he would be considered little more than a peasant. "I am Pelops of Lydia, son of Tantalus."

"Tantalus?" There was real fear in Leandros' face then, and he backed away a little. "By the Gods..." he whispered. "But how is it possible? That sinner was damned to Tartarus for...for..."

"I'd rather not relive the memory, if you don't mind."

"But how did you-"

Pelops' stare silenced the captain of the guard who, in that moment, saw that perhaps the time had come, that the Gods had indeed decided to change the world in which he lived.

Leandros swallowed hard and wiped his sweaty brow. "The lady Hippodameia will be pleased you are still willing to take the risk. She asked me to ensure you were still here this morning."

"Tell her, I will risk everything for her."

"I will," Leandros said as he turned to go away. "I will return to bring you to the king's throne room shortly. You may wish to brush the straw from your hair and tunic after you eat."

Leandros walked away to the palace to speak with Hippodameia while Pelops readied himself.

Pelops began to feel fear gripping him again, strangling him, as the misty memories of his cursed youth intruded on his current hopes. He leaned against the wooden wall, his eyes shut against the pain locked in his mind. Then, he felt a warmth emanating from his right shoulder, and it spread over his entire body to calm him, to give him resolve and strength of body and mind.

"Thank you," he whispered, focussing on his faint memories of water and trees on the slopes of Olympus, the music-laced voices of the Gods who had cared for him. "Guide me in this quest."

You are not alone, Pelops, the crashing waves said deep in his mind, and in that moment, a stillness came over him. *After you make your challenge, tell them that you will go down to the sea for the night. Sleep there, and you will receive a mighty gift.*

Pelops nodded, his eyes still closed as the calm washed over him, prepared him. "Thank you."

A SHORT TIME LATER, Pelops stood in the middle of the courtyard looking up the stairs of the palace and waiting for Leandros to return.

A small crowd of people had gathered at the outer edges of the court, come to see the newest challenger. But it was different this time. In the past, those gathered might have whispered of the suitor's beauty and strength and how it was a shame for him to die so terrible a death. This time, however, they spoke of the impossibility of this man's appearance in Elis, of the stories told far and wide of his father's evil and of how the Gods had damned him. The fact that Pelops should appear before them now to challenge Oinomaos could only be the work of the Fates, could only mean that there was a possibility that this time would be different.

But the people knew Oinomaos, the son of War, very well, knew his pain, his anger, and his madness. There was, as ever, little hope, but as the sun shone upon their faces, as they watched Pelops standing and waiting in their midst, they could not help but hope.

Leandros appeared at the top of the palace stairs flanked by two more guards. "Follow me, Pelops of Lydia."

Pelops made his way up the stairs and followed the guards into the palace.

Inside, the daylight was sucked out of the world as they walked through the fire-lit darkness, along lonely stone corridors, until they reached guarded doors of hammered bronze.

"Open the doors!" Leandros commanded the men standing guard.

Pelops observed their long spears, bronze armour, and high helmets crested with horse hair as he passed, but he quickly forgot the warriors about him when he looked down the long hall toward the raised throne of King Oinomaos.

Fire crackled in tripods to either side of the hall which was dominated by a soaring statue of Ares which stood upon a plinth behind the throne.

The God of War appeared to look down protectively upon his son in his chair, and his granddaughter, Hippodameia, who was sat beside her father watching Pelops walk up the aisle.

The silent nobles and warriors of Elis stood in the shadows to either side of the throne room, watching, waiting for this next challenger to approach their king.

Leandros stopped before the king and bowed. "My king! Another challenger has come to Elis!"

King Oinomaos looked down on the captain of his guard and the man who stood behind him. He sipped from his golden winecup and then handed it to the slave kneeling beside him. Oinomaos stroked his black beard and his angry eyes probed the newcomer. Behind him, the divine armour and weapons his father had given him rested upon a stand, glinting in the fires at War's feet.

"Who is this challenger?" Oinomaos demanded.

"He is Pelops of Lydia, the son of King Tantalus!" Leandros shuddered as he spoke the name of Tantalus, as did the people there gathered, for it was like to uttering a curse.

"Tantalus?" Oinomaos laughed. "He did not fare so well, did he?" His eyes locked onto Pelops. "What makes you think the son of a cursed man can challenge me? What makes you think you are worthy of my daughter's hand in marriage?"

"King Oinomaos..." Pelops said, stepping forward. "I am not my mortal father, Tantalus. The Gods have punished him, and rightly so."

"He fed you to the Gods!" Oinomaos laughed, shaking his head.

Pelops focussed, tried not to let the pain dissolve his purpose. "And yet, I am here, by the Gods' grace..." Pelops stepped forward and looked from Hippodameia to Oinomaos. "It is said that you accept the challenge of all comers, noble or not."

"I do."

"Then I challenge you, King Oinomaos, for the hand of princess Hippodameia."

Oinomaos stood quickly, his anger suddenly up. "You speak so certainly to me, boy? Do you not know Death when you look him in the eye? Go back to your home if you know what's good for you, if you even have a home!"

"I will not," Pelops said, finding strength in the golden gaze of Hippodameia to the king's left. "Do you accept my challenge?"

Oinomaos turned and took up the long-shafted spear which his father had given him, and pointed it at Pelops. "Oh, I accept!" He looked at the people who had stepped out of the shadows the better to see and hear the son of Tantalus. "In three days, we shall race from the hill of Kronos to the altar of Poseidon at Isthmia." He looked back to Pelops. "In three days..." he stared down the shaft at Pelops, "...you shall die."

There was a murmur around the throne room as the people gathered, looking from Pelops to their king and the princess.

"Silence!" Oinomaos roared. "Captain?" he called to Leandros.

"Yes, sire?"

"Find this challenger secure rooms for the night."

Pelops stepped forward. "King Oinomaos... If you please, I will sleep beside the sea in preparation for the coming trial."

Oinomaos looked suspicious, but shrugged his shoulders. "If you wish to spend your final days in discomfort, so be it. The end will be the same, and your head will adorn my walls alongside the other men who thought they could defeat me!"

Oinomaos swept from the throne room then, through a back door behind the statue of Ares, leaving the people staring at Pelops.

Hippodameia slowly stepped down from the dais to stand before Pelops.

They longed to reach out to each other, to touch hands, to speak, but it was not the time. Her guards stood about her, and the people looked on, saw the bond that had already bloomed between them.

Myrtilos too saw it from where he crouched at the base of Ares' warlike form. He hated his master, it was true, but he also felt a growing dislike for this newest suitor.

Hippodameia stood tall, beautiful, and filled with hope in the midst of her admiring people, and it seemed that the throne room grew a little lighter in that moment.

"I don't want you to die," she said to Pelops.

Pelops smiled. "I have already died, lady. Now, I want to live." He knelt before her, and she laid her hand upon the back of his head.

The guards stepped forward, but she quickly stepped back.

"Go then, Pelops of Lydia. I will pray to the Gods that in three days, the victory shall be yours."

Pelops stood, took one last look at her beautiful face and brilliant eyes, and turned to leave the throne room.

Hippodameia watched him leave and prayed that that would not be the last time she would fill her eyes with his beauty.

Hera protect us.

7

GIFTS OF PERIL AND GRACE

The Gods' altars burned brightly around the kingdom of Elis as word of the latest challenger spread from the palace to the fields, hills and groves like the first soft exhalations of spring after a long, dark winter.

The people, however, still tempered their hopes, for in the past, when the first suitors had come, they had let the promise of those hopes tempt them overmuch. The older ones remembered a time long ago when the family of Oinomaos had ridden out among them, a time when the laughter of their children had been like the dancing of the Graces in the groves on dewy mornings.

They had prayed for their king to return to himself once again, that he would allow the love of his remaining daughter to lift his spirits as he bobbed on waves of grief and anger, but those who had once felt something other than fear for the king, had finally abandoned him in their hearts.

After Pelops laid his challenge, he disappeared in search

of the comfort of shimmering shore, there to wait as Poseidon had bidden him.

Meanwhile, as her father fuelled his anger with Dionysian strength, Hippodameia roamed the palace halls with prayers to Hera soft upon her worried lips.

When she had seen Pelops standing before the entire court to lay down his challenge to her father, beneath the warlike gaze of Ares, the prospect of the death of that beautiful man, of his head placed upon a spike beside all the others, threatened to overwhelm her. She fought back the rising fear as best she could, but as the sun began to descend in the crimson west, she prayed to Hera for a way to ensure that Pelops should win that doomed race.

As Hippodameia leaned upon the topmost part of the palace battlements, watching the sun and distant sea, she wondered what Pelops was thinking and doing, and prayed for some form of aid.

MYRTILOS, the son of Hermes, finished feeding and brushing down the king's black, iron-hoofed stallions. He had just sustained another bite from one of them, and sat across from their stalls staring into the bloody bucket with which he had fed them. With the other horses in the royal stables, he enjoyed the fresh scent of straw and the tumble of wholesome oats as he fed them. The divine horses which Ares had given to the king, however, refused such fare, preferring instead the raw flesh of goats and pigs which Myrtilos had to butcher himself.

The team trusted only himself and the king. None other could approach them or control them. He had been bitten only because, that day, he was distracted.

Seeing the son of Tantalus walk up the aisle of the throne room to challenge the king seemed different. With all of the other suitors, he had seen his divine father leading their souls to the Underworld, been able to see Hippodameia weeping for them even before their deaths.

But with Pelops, he had had no such visions, and this both worried him and filled him with dark hope. However, as he looked upon War's horses, he knew that none could win against Oinomaos, especially with himself at the reins.

Pelops will die like the rest of them, he thought, but even as the thought occurred to him, the stable slaves froze in their work, and all other horses nearby paused in their movements.

Myrtilos looked up to see divine Hermes, the giver of good fortune, standing before him. His image shimmered where he stood, the gold and silver of his chiton and helmet flickering above the swiftness of his winged sandals. "Father?" Myrtilos stood and backed into the stall behind him. "What are you doing here?"

Golden-eyed Hermes looked upon his skulking, dark-haired son, unable to smile, to reach out to him, for he knew the sort of man he had become, the thoughts he harboured. If Myrtilos had hoped for a warm greeting from his divine father, he would be ever-disappointed.

"I come to ask you to help Pelops to win this race against Oinomaos."

Myrtilos laughed, shaking his curly black hair nervously. "You cannot ask such a thing of me. Why would I want that? He would take away the princess."

"I command it then," Hermes said. "Pelops is favoured by horse-taming Poseidon."

"And the king is the son of War," Myrtilos said. "I would not anger either of them."

"Would you anger me?" Hermes loomed over his son, his light close to searing his skin.

"No...no I would not!" Myrtilos yelped.

Hermes stood back. "Good. You are the king's driver. In all of these victories, a portion of them has gone to you, as has a portion of the blood-guilt for the death of those suitors."

"They entered the pact willingly. They knew the risks." Myrtilos stood a little taller. "Why would I want Pelops to win? If he does, then Hippodameia will be his."

"My son, I know your thoughts... She is not, nor ever will be, yours. You are not destined to have this woman."

Myrtilos sat back down upon the polished olive-wood bench. A part of him wanted to refuse, to see Pelops' head upon the gates of the palace. But he knew that if Oinomaos continued, he would forever live beneath his boot, that Hippodameia would forever be out of his reach.

"You think you love the princess," Hermes said, knowing his son's thinking. "If you do love her, then you will help free her. If you do, both she and Pelops will show their gratitude and your life here on earth will be filled with light and happiness, rather than the dark despair in which you constantly sulk."

"I have everything I need," Myrtilos said stubbornly.

"And so does a dog." Hermes looked away from his son, unable to stand being in his presence any longer. "Help Pelops and Hippodameia in whatever way you can, or suffer the wrath of Olympus."

Hermes disappeared in a diminishing light and the sounds of the stables returned. Myrtilos sat alone, leaning on his knees across from the bone-gnashing stallions. He knew he was all but a slave to Oinomaos, that the only person who ever showed him any kindness was Hippodameia. *How can I help her?* he wondered. *How can I help myself?*

He could not poison the king, for that would be discovered. He knew that the Gods wanted the race to occur. It was a long road, and the race could last for days, even with those divine, black beasts.

Myrtilos looked around and then, at the end of the stables, where the firelight glinted upon its dark surface, he spotted the king's chariot. He stood and walked slowly toward it, a dangerous idea forming in his mind that, although it was unlikely, held the prospect of a new life.

I will not risk it... Not yet.

After looking over the chariot, Myrtilos then went out into the dusky night to find Hippodameia.

THE SUN'S light was gone, and the torches were fired along the battlements of the palace heights.

Hippodameia found that she could not leave, for from there only could she see the coastline and sea where she knew Pelops waited, alone upon the sand. She would have gone to him, but she knew the king had given orders to Leandros and his men to keep her within the confines of the palace as always.

As she stood there, she explored the pathways of her mind in search of a way to guarantee Pelops' victory over her father. Of course, she sought not her father's death, but rather hoped for an end to the blood. She hoped that the sight of her own happiness would mean an end to the madness which enslaved her father. She longed for the gentle-eyed man she had looked up to as a child, for song and smile to grace his bearded face once more, as it had when she was happy to roam those halls.

The thought made her weep, her tears glinting in the torch fires.

"My lady?" A voice interrupted her thinking.

Hippodameia wiped her eyes with the fold of her peplos and turned to see Myrtilos walking slowly toward her along the battlement wall.

"My lady, why do you weep so?" Myrtilos asked, his hands clasped before him in worry.

"Myrtilos," Hippodameia said, and he smiled at the utterance of his name from her rose-petalled lips.

"Do you need something, my lady?" he asked. "I may be able to help you...to ease your mind."

"There is nothing that can ease my mind or my heart but an end to the blood shed on my account."

"The Gods toy with all of us, lady."

Hippodameia shook her head. "No, Myrtilos. My father does."

Myrtilos sighed. "He will not be swayed. I have tried many times."

Hippodameia turned to him abruptly, shock upon her face. "You have?"

Myrtilos nodded and smiled. "I have...for you, lady. I can see how unhappy these deaths make you, though you did not feel love for any of the men who had come forward."

She was silent for a moment, and Myrtilos worried that he had said too much. But then, she nodded. "It is true, I did not love any of them, but I did not wish for their deaths. This time, however, it is different."

"You speak of Pelops?" Myrtilos asked, his smile quickly fading.

"Yes. Oh, Myrtilos, I do love him, and I would do anything to ensure that he wins, that he would live the rest of his days with me."

Myrtilos swallowed, a bitter taste at the back of his throat at the thought of Pelops and Hippodameia being together, with himself still relegated to the shadows. *Still, I could be rewarded...* he thought, and decided then and there, as her beauty filled his eyes, that he would put the idea to her.

"My lady," he looked around, "may I speak privately with you?"

Hippodameia looked to Leandros to her left, and the other guard to her right. "Please leave us," she said, and Leandros and the guard both moved farther away down the walls to give the princess and the king's charioteer space.

When they were far, Myrtilos approached her, nearly reaching out to touch her hand, but not daring. "My lady, I would help Pelops to win this race."

Her glassy eyes grew wide and expectant.

He nodded. "I would. I grow tired of death, of being the cause of it to so many."

Hippodameia then reached out to touch his arm, and he felt a surge of joy pulse through his thin limbs. "Oh, Myrtilos, would you?" Her voice was excited and desperate.

"I would...for you, my lady."

"But how would this be possible?"

"I will think of a way. I am the charioteer. The team listens to me."

"If my father were to suspect you, he might kill you! You cannot be less of a driver, ever, for he would know."

"It is true. The king knows my skills well." Myrtilos grasped her hand and looked down at the ground shyly.

When she did not pull it back, he felt even more hopeful that it would work. "I will think of a way, I promise you, lady."

Hippodameia squeezed his hand back. She felt for him, felt that he understood the enslavement of that palace, how cold it was in the shadow of her father. If Myrtilos could think of a way to help Pelops win, then it was worth the risks. "I trust you, Myrtilos."

He smiled, but looked away into the darkness of the night. "I trust you too, my lady. But, the risk if I am exposed is very great. I am afraid of your father. What will become of me afterward?"

"I will make sure you are rewarded, Myrtilos. If Pelops wins, then I will make sure you have everything you desire. You will no longer be a servant. You shall have lands of your own, horses, crops and more!" Without thinking, she leaned in and kissed him quickly upon the cheek, in the manner that friend greets friend.

But that kiss lingered on Myrtilos' cheek, burned it, and he formed an idea.

"Your gentle touch would be enough of a reward," he said as he dared to look into her eyes as he had never done before.

She smiled back and nodded as she released his hands and took him, arm's-length, by the shoulders. "I will be ever-grateful for your help."

He smiled and bowed to her. "My lady."

"I would ask only that my father is not hurt. Only that he lose the race."

Myrtilos looked up from his bowed head. "I understand. He will not win, lady. That I promise." *May the Gods do what they will with our wine-loving king!*

"Go then," Hippodameia said, her soft voice a whisper as light as a butterfly's wings near his ear, her thoughts filled with fear for Pelops and nothing else. "Make your preparations, Myrtilos, and when all is well, you will be free of the shadows."

Myrtilos left her there, his own heart filled with the prospect of his reward, a reward that only served to solidify his decision to turn against the son of dreaded Ares. *After so long,* he smiled to himself as he went back to the stables. *It is time!*

THE WAVES HAD BEEN gentle through the night, soothing in their sound, beautiful in their colour-filled swells as the night gave way to the dawn.

A warmth had enveloped Pelops where he slept in the soft sand among the tall beach grasses back from the water's edge. No one had bothered him in the night, spoken to him, or accosted him, but when he awoke, it was to find baskets of food - fruit, cheese, and fresh bread - and jugs of water and of wine laid carefully for him to find when he awoke.

He knew then that Oinomaos' people prayed for his victory, for they were finished with despair and the longing for days that would not return.

Pelops looked down on the offerings upon that rose-coloured beach and smiled. "Maybe I can give them new and brighter days?" he wondered.

A splash out at sea made him turn and there he saw an hippocampus soar out of the still surface of the sea to splash in the morning light. The sight of it reminded Pelops that the world of men was not all death and blood. *There is still beauty...and hope.*

He thought of Hippodameia then, for he had dreamt of her all night beneath the fiery canopy of the heavens. He had not wanted to think on what could be beyond the race, for he knew the risks were great, but it was impossible for him not to give way to the dreams he imagined in a life with Hippodameia. The love he already felt for her burned brightly in his heart, in his soul, and he would do anything to win her hand.

But how? he wondered. "I don't even have a chariot and horses!"

Poseidon had told him to wait upon the beach until the day of the race, and that is what Pelops decided he would do. "I still have two days," he said as he stood in the gentle surf, eating a fig.

The whinny and snort of horses startled him and he turned to see a group of riders crest the dunes at the back of the beach.

Hippodameia was at their head, her white robes fluttering in the sea's kissing breeze. She smiled to see him there, and Pelops went to meet her as her mare closed the distance between them.

Leandros remained behind with the guards, watchful but respectful. He too liked the newcomer and secretly harboured the impossible hope that many others did: that Pelops would win. He glanced at the pile of offerings the people had left in the night, and smiled to himself.

"What are you doing here, lady?" Pelops said to Hippodameia as he reached up to help her down from her mount. She looked beautiful to him, rosy-cheeked and excited, as if urgent news were about to burst from her lips.

Their eyes locked and, for a moment, they had an incredible urge to touch lips that gave them pause.

"We can't now. Not with my father's men watching," she said.

"You are right," he gripped her hands and kissed them. "I was worried for you."

"You needn't be. Especially now!"

"What do you mean?" Pelops asked.

"Myrtilos, my father's charioteer, came to me last night."

"Did he hurt you?" Pelops had seen the man, and knew he did not trust him, knew it in his guts.

"Of course not!" Hippodameia said quickly. "He is a kind and gentle man. In fact, he has always had my interests at heart. He even saved me from wolves when I was young and had strayed too far from the palace while riding. He happened to be out when it happened, and thank the Gods he was, for we would never have met."

Pelops doubted some of what she said, but could not bring himself to gainsay her, not while she was so hopeful. "What did Myrtilos say?"

She looked back at Leandros and the guards quickly, and then back to Pelops. Her heart was beating quickly, and she wondered if he could feel it standing so close to her, hoped he could.

"Myrtilos has offered to help make sure that you win the race."

"But how can he do that?"

"I don't know, but he is the king's charioteer. If there is a way, he will find it. I told him he would be well-rewarded for it."

"It could mean your father's death, Hippodameia. Are you ready for such a thing?"

She shook her head and smiled. "I asked Myrtilos to ensure that does not happen. I know my father will be good once again, once he sees how happy I am, once the blood stops flowing in this land."

Pelops released her hands and stepped aside to look out to sea. He shook his head and crossed his arms.

"What is wrong?" Hippodameia asked, standing beside him to look out to the colour-laced sea.

"I would win with honour, not by the guile of your father's charioteer."

"But there is no other way!" she said. "My grandfather, Ares, protects my father. The horses he has given him are divine, swift and furious. They have never tired, never lost."

"There must be another way, other than relying on Myrtilos," Pelops turned to her.

She shook her head and held his face in her soft, long-fingered hands. "There isn't. And we can trust Myrtilos. He is good and honourable."

Pelops wanted to protest further, but in looking upon her, in seeing the hope that had been kindled in her fair eyes, he could not bring himself to cast yet another shadow over her in addition to those that had been choking her for so long.

"Very well," he said, kissing her hands again.

Hippodameia then looked around. "You do not have a team of your own for the race?" There was new panic in her voice. "Shall I ask Myrtilos to harness a team for you?"

"No," Pelops said. *I want nothing more from him!* "I will find a team in time for the race," he said. "But you should go now, before your father misses you."

"I don't want to leave you," she said. "But you are right."

Pelops helped her up into the saddle and she looked down on him, her face lit by the rising sun.

"I will be there, in two days, beneath the hill of Kronos, to meet your father in this challenge."

"And I will be there to watch you race to victory," she said, and as she spoke she leaned down quickly and kissed him upon the lips. "By Aphrodite...I love you."

"And my love for you will bring me victory," he said. "Go now. Until we meet again."

With that, Hippodameia kneed her horse's sides and it charged up the dunes and back to the palace.

Pelops watched her ride away, his heart filled with love and the hope that love kindled. But he also felt dread, for the aid she had spoken of, the aid offered by Myrtilos, made him uneasy.

"Gods..." he said, turning to the sea. "Lord Poseidon... guide me in this...help me..."

For another day, the people came and went, leaving food and clothing and weapons for Pelops, and it was as if he were already their king. They did so at their own peril, but somehow there was a common feeling that none would speak of it, for Oinomaos was feared by all, resented by many in secret.

As the sun rose and fell and the moon brightened the night sky, however, Pelops began to panic and worry. Poseidon had been silent, and he still had no way to reach the hill of Kronos in time on foot, no way to carry out the challenge to the dreaded king of Elis.

It was before dawn on the third day that Pelops sat awake, feeling as though he stood upon a high eyrie with no wings to carry him safely through the skies. The hopes that he had, and that Hippodameia and the people nurtured, seemed to burn to ash before him, even as the sea darkened and a mist blanketed the once star-gleaming surface.

Pelops walked to the edge of the water and fell to his

knees, the waves lapping about his wrists and legs. He remembered the feeling of healing water on Olympus, and longed for that sensation again, a time when there was no sense of failure or regret, no pain, no anguish of heart.

"Gods...I ask for your help," he pleaded. "I would heal this land and help it prosper. I will build altars and temples to all of you across it. Please give me the strength and skill I need to achieve this victory, so that I can live with Hippodameia in peace and love. I have never known love...nor family... But I would if you will allow it. Please..."

The sea was quiet and still as Pelops knelt in the water, feeling the destiny that had drawn him out of Olympus fast slipping away. For a moment, he wondered if he should not go back to the remote cliffs and mountain forests of Arcadia.

Back to Axioche...

But as soon as the thought occurred to him, something began to happen. The stars sharpened in the heavens, their light beaming down on his lonely, sea-washed form. The gentle surface of the sea began to waver and shift, and then to bubble far out, slowly at first, but then with increasing turbulence, such that Pelops wondered if the Gods had tired of him and sent one of the great beasts of Poseidon's realm to finish him.

"Whatever you decide, lord," Pelops said, now standing with his arms spread wide to the sea and the waves coming slowly toward him. "I am ready."

As he waited and watched, the memories of his death at the hands of Tantalus rushed back, the pain, the ultimate betrayal and supreme loneliness acute. He wondered if the Gods would at least grant him a quick death this time.

The sea was bubbling with a fury now before Pelops, and he watched as one, then a second, and third, and a fourth head emerged from the deep. The beasts lit the night with an ethereal light and Pelops closed his eyes as they came toward him, covered in seaweed and foam.

Gods, make it quick.

Everything changed, however, with a great chorus of neighing, and the soft pounding of many hooves upon the beach.

Pelops opened his eyes to see four brilliant horses coming out of the sea toward him!

Their eyes were full of life, their muscled bodies strong and vigorous, their legs long and agile.

He stood back to allow them space to fully emerge from Poseidon's sea, their heads tossing, their manes long and shimmering in the moonlight.

He noticed that they were already harnessed, and when he looked behind them, he saw the cab of a god-made chariot rolling behind the team.

As the water ran off of it, its surface glimmered in shades of gold and nacre. The tall wheels cut through the sand easily, their adamant wheels glinting like blades in firelight.

The team came to a stop before Pelops and, for all his surprise and shock, he felt hope return as he looked upon their beauty through his burning eyes.

The stallions and mares nuzzled him in greeting and tossed their heads as he reached up to stroke their strong necks and manes, no words upon his lips to describe what he felt in that moment.

He walked around them to look more closely at the chariot and there, emblazoned upon the front he saw a blue trident.

Pelops looked immediately to the sea and there, standing

waist-deep in the dark depths, he saw Earth-Shaking Poseidon, still and watchful.

"Thank you, my lord."

"Go now, Pelops. Seize your destiny."

Pelops bowed, his hand upon his heart, and then stepped into the chariot's cab to take up the thick reins. He looked back over his shoulder, smiled, and then flicked the reins.

The horses sped away with unimaginable speed and grace, and Poseidon smiled as he watched Pelops charge toward his fate and the great trial set before him.

HYMN III

THE HERO RISING

8

THE SPINNING OF WHEELS

Day dawned across the kingdom of Elis, but it was not with the usual crimson-hued sky that slowly lit the forests and deep rutted fields of that sad land.

There was something different in the very air. The winds whispered to the people that the day would be momentous, that shepherds should leave their flocks to come to the edge of the field about the hill of Kronos, that villagers should emerge from their hovels to catch a glimpse of the Olympians whom, the winds teased, were watching all that happened.

When people arrived, it was to find the dark tents of King Oinomaos gathered in the field around the hill. The sound of his warlike chargers echoed over the land as they stomped in their paddocks, grinding their teeth on the flesh of animals.

None dared approach the royal gathering where, they knew, the princess also attended, having accompanied her father to witness the start of the race. All prayed for Hippodameia's sake that it would be the final contest, an end to death.

And so, the people watched, and waited, their eyes straining across the dew-covered fields of bright morning in anticipation of the gathering.

IN HER TENT which had been pitched in the shadow of the Kronian hill, Hippodameia knelt before the altar of Hera, her offerings smoking before her blurring eyes, her prayers to the goddess of utmost sincerity.

There had been no word of Pelops' arrival, and all through the night, as the hill of that dread Titan murmured and teased from deep within the earth, Hippodameia had prayed to the Gods for help for Pelops in the coming race.

But he is not yet come, she thought dejectedly. *He has left... and I do not blame him.* She chided herself, for this time she had allowed herself to bathe in hope for this one man, the only one of the suitors she truly loved and with whom she could actually envision a future life.

From her tent, she could hear her father's deep, raucous laughter as he drank with his men and talked of the coming race and what he would do to Pelops when he caught up with him on the road.

It was the longest night of Hippodameia's life.

When Dawn emerged to light the night-painted sky, Hippodameia stepped out of her tent to see the morning mist drawing back from the broad field where the Gods had run and wrestled, and where every race her father had undertaken had begun. And yet, nowhere was Pelops to be found.

Hippodameia stood beneath the supple branches of the olive tree before her tent, tilted her head to the sky and spoke. "Oh, Goddess Hera, let this day be an end to the misery of this life. Let Pelops arrive in time...let him be victorious...and let my father be gracious in defeat such that he is himself once more. I would be a good daughter, but I will not sacrifice my love for him. It is enough of death. If Pelops wins, I will build you a great temple on this spot, and hold games in your honour. Please, Divine Mother."

There was silence, but for the sound of her father's fierce horses, and the wind in the trees upon the hill of Kronos.

Hippodameia looked across the field to the paddocks and there she saw Myrtilos emerge from his care of the horses and the king's chariot in preparation for the race.

He had sworn to her that he would help Pelops win the race, but as she observed him, saw the smile upon his face, his relaxed manner, she began to wonder if he had changed his mind.

Myrtilos looked in her direction and he bowed to her, his hand upon his heart.

Perhaps he will still help? she wondered, smiling uneasily at him.

Myrtilos felt his heart pounding as he bowed to Hippodameia that morning, for he had been waiting all night for the king to close his eyes in wine-soaked sleep. And as he had waited, he had dreamed of his reward, played it over and over in his mind, felt himself stirred by the very thought of it. Sleep had not come for Myrtilos, no, but his resolve to achieve his end - even if it would help Pelops - had only deepened.

Since that moment upon the walls of the palace, when Hippodameia had smiled and kissed his cheek, he had set his mind solely upon the task of ensuring Oinomaos' loss and how it would happen. The roads upon which the race would stretch were long and, at times, treacherous upon the mountain passes. Many suitors' chariots had crumbled to pieces as they drove over the rocky earth, but Oinomaos' chariot was not like others. It was strong, and durable and never failed.

Then it struck Myrtilos that he could fashion pins for the wheels that were made of wax and wood rather than of the hard bronze that held them in place. *When the wheels begin to waver,* he thought, *I will jump from the cab. Let the Gods do what they will with the king after that.*

And so, that morning, upon the field before the hill of Kronos, Myrtilos had slipped away to polish the black chariot and oil the axle for the race. The guards had left him to it, for they knew the king trusted him, though they unanimously disliked him and always had. It was then that Myrtilos had replaced the pins of the right wheel, that side which would be nearest the perilous cliffs beside which they would be racing.

His heart had been pounding all the while, but when he emerged from the tent, his work complete, and spotted the princess, his heart began to beat from more than his treachery, and he relished the feeling. *Soon, my lady...soon.*

HELIOS BEGAN to rise higher in the East, and the murmur of a great crowd began to wash over the gathering of tents, to drown out the forceful neighing of Oinomaos' horses.

It was then that the sky grew brighter and thunder rumbled in the blue skies above where clouds began to gather with no sign of rain.

People covered their eyes and ears, and ducked behind boulders and behind the broad trunks of oak and olive trees.

But as soon as the day-storm had begun, it ended, and in that moment the immortals walked across the emerald plain, beside the fast flowing river Alfeios, toward the hill of Kronos where their divine light pushed back the shadow of that imprisoned Titan.

At their head walked Cloud-Gathering Zeus, and beside him, Hera Alexandros, the Protector of Men, her crown glinting in the growing sunlight like a beacon.

Red-cloaked War followed with Sterope, daughter of the Titan Atlas, and mother of Oinomaos. Their eyes were upon their son's broad tent where he had come out to greet them, dressed for battle, the long-shafted and sharp spear Ares had given him clutched easily in his right hand.

Poseidon and Demeter followed behind them, along with Golden-Eyed Hermes who sought his skulking son kneeling at the feet of King Oinomaos.

Other Gods arrived too, and the mortals gathered about the fields fell to their knees blinded, their ears filled with the music of Olympus, played even then by Apollo who was among the gathering. Swift-Footed Artemis appeared as well, like a deer out of the forest, and Golden Aphrodite whose order had bound Hippodameia and Pelops.

Zeus stopped upon the broad field, his all-seeing eyes taking in the Kronian hill, a reminder of brutal war and hard-won victory. He and the other immortals breathed deeply of the offerings upon the smoking altars as King Oinomaos and his charioteer drove out onto the field to stop before them.

Hera eyed her grandson with dismay, for he had been cruel and unworthy, ignored the pleas of his light-footed daughter who ever sought to preserve that part of his former self. *You do not deserve her,* she thought as she watched Hippodameia walk slowly across the field, alone, toward them.

"Where is your challenger, my son?" Ares asked Oinomaos as he stepped forward from among the Gods.

Oinomaos bowed low to them all, and answered with his eyes staring at the grassy ground. "He is not here. I fear that cowardice has overwhelmed him."

Poseidon then stepped forward. "He will be here," he said, and it was as if waves crashed upon the very field.

Zeus looked up at the sky then, his eyes like a storm, flashes of lighting in his irises. "If Pelops is not here by the time Victory arrives, his life is forfeit."

Oinomaos smiled at that and bowed.

Hippodameia struggled to keep the panic from her face, as she looked to Myrtilos, but he only smiled at her.

He will be here, she then thought, willing the words to Mother Hera.

The goddess looked upon the princess, but gave no indication of it either way.

It was Poseidon who looked to Hippodameia then and nodded. *He is coming, child. He will be here.*

IT HAD TAKEN Pelops some time to become accustomed to the strength and vitality his new team, but even so, he felt that some god had been working against him on his journey from the sea to the hill of Kronos.

Roads diverged, passes were blocked, and fields were flooded, all of it with the aim to waylay him and slow his progress. But the divine team of nimble and strong horses managed every obstacle with skill and renewed speed, racing through the remnants of dark night to finally emerge onto the road that led to the meeting place.

The sun was rising by then, and Pelops worried that his

team would be tired before even beginning, but when he looked, he saw no sign of sweat nor foaming muzzle.

You must come now! The sea-tinted voice of Poseidon crashed in Pelops' mind. *If you do not, your life is forfeit!*

"I'm coming!" Pelops yelled to the sky. "I'm almost there!"

THE PATIENCE of Zeus reached its limit, and the King of the Gods turned to the assemblage of immortals and the smiling son of Ares.

"It seems Pelops has given in to cowardice, like so many mortals..." There was disappointment in his voice, anger. He looked up again to see Winged Nike alighting from the sun-dappled sky to land softly in their midst.

"Lord Zeus," Victory said as she bowed, her robes billowing about her like clouds in a windy sky.

"There will be no trial this day," Zeus said to Victory, "for the challenger is not present."

Nike smiled and raised the long eagle feather she held in her hand, pointing it to the distant side of the river Alfeios that cut through the plain. "But he *is* here, Lord."

As the immortals turned their heads to look, Hippodameia felt her heart swell with rekindled hope.

Pelops raced across the field, urging his bright team onward, the earth rumbling beneath the cutting edge of his adamant wheels until he came to a stop before the gathered gods.

"Forgive me, Lord Zeus and Queen Hera," he said, breathless as he bent his knee before them. "The road was set against me."

The look in Zeus' eyes was dark, and he turned to look at Ares who met his gaze unflinchingly.

Hippodameia ran to Pelops' side and grasped his hand. She took in the beauty of his team, saw the trident upon the chariot cab, and looked to Horse-Taming Poseidon to whom she bowed.

"Give them water," Poseidon commanded her, kindness in his voice.

Hippodameia looked to the team of horses and took a water bucket from nearby. The horses each leaned down to briefly drink, and she stepped back, conscious of the Gods' gaze.

Zeus stepped forward to address them all, his mighty form taller and broader than all others there gathered. "The challenge has been laid, and glory is within your grasp." He paused to look upon the hill of his fallen foe, his own father, and then looked to where Hippodameia stood beside Pelops. "Battles are hard-won, and victory is not always filled with joy," he said. "But, to enter into this trial is to declare that you will accept its outcome, be it victory...or death."

Pelops felt the weight of Zeus' gaze, and bowed his head, heard the sound of the sea calming him inside.

Oinomaos smiled, and nodded to his father, War, before looking back to Zeus.

"Victories come at a cost. Are you willing to accept the cost?" Zeus asked Pelops and Oinomaos.

"I am," Oinomaos said.

"Yes, Lord Zeus," Pelops added.

Zeus looked to Pelops then and saw that he had no driver. "You have no second in this race? You drive alone?"

"Lord, Zeus, it is only myself and my team."

In that moment, Hippodameia stepped forward. "I shall ride with him!"

All eyes turned upon the princess, shock even clouding the immortals' faces.

"No!" Oinomaos cried. "I forbid it!"

In that moment, Hippodameia saw Hera looking to her with such pride as ever her own mother had in her eyes when looking upon her.

"Silence!" Zeus commanded, but Oinomaos was not so easily quieted.

"My Lord Zeus," Oinomaos pleaded, real fear now showing in his eyes. "My daughter is all that I have left in this world. She cannot take part in the race. As the object of victory in this trial, she must remain here, under guard."

"How dare you command!" The earth shook and thunder rolled in the distant mountains as Zeus' anger stirred. He looked to Hippodameia, and then back to her father, Oinomaos.

It was then that Hera leaned in to her husband, her eyes bright with pride at the courage displayed by the young woman.

Zeus nodded and laid his hand upon his wife's pale shoulder. "Oinomaos and Pelops...you both would put your lives in the balance to keep Hippodameia. So too, does she chose, and shall be allowed to do so." He looked to Hippodameia. "You understand the risk of death?"

"I do, Lord," Hippodameia said, forcing herself to look upon the King of the Gods. "I would risk all in this, if only to end the cycle of death in this land."

"Daughter, no!" Oinomaos pleaded, his facade of anger and rage momentarily broken. "Please!"

Hippodameia looked to her father, tears in her eyes. "How many times have I pleaded for an end to this, and been ignored? How many deaths have occurred on my account?"

She shook her head and walked to stand in Pelops' chariot. "I'll have no more of it! I race with my love!"

Even the Gods marvelled at the sight of that young, courageous mortal standing there behind the reins of that immortal team. Seeing their princess, so brave, so defiant, the people began to emerge from the fringes of the distant forest, their voices rising up, given courage by her own words.

The Gods saw this and, all but Ares and Sterope, smiled.

"The race shall proceed, and to the victor go this land and the Princess Hippodameia!" Zeus' voice sounded loud and definite. There was no gainsaying the King of the Gods.

Oinomaos stepped into the cab of his chariot, his great spear in hand as he stood beside Myrtilos who gripped the reins. The king then pointed his spear at his daughter and Pelops, the very last of his tears falling from his lids. "So be it!" He turned to Zeus. "Lord, I agree. As is my practice, I will allow Pelops to depart first, while I sacrifice a black ram in your honour."

"Your sacrifice is welcome," Zeus nodded, then turned to Pelops. "Are you ready, charioteer?"

Pelops and Hippodameia both looked up to the Gods, to the distant people watching, and then to Oinomaos whose armour glinted in the risen sun. "Are you sure about this?" Pelops asked her, his voice a whisper, his hands shaking as he took up the reins.

Hippodameia smiled and touched his hands to still them. "Never was I more certain."

Pelops nodded and felt calm. He looked to Olympian Zeus, the other gods, and divine Victory who hovered above them all. "I am ready, Lord!" he called.

There was a deep silence in that moment while Oinomaos began his offering in the grove behind them, the blood of the ram already spilling over the altar.

Zeus stared at Pelops for a tense moment. "Begin!"

THE EARTH SHOOK as Pelops and Hippodameia's chariot raced across the land, their team charging from the broad plain to where the road ascended the tree-clad mountain slopes of distant Arcadia.

It had all begun so quickly - the Gods' arrival, Hippodameia's decision, and Zeus' ruling - and now Pelops used every fibre of his muscles to strain at the reins, to keep those divine steeds on the track of the road lest they hurl him, and now Hippodameia, over the cliffs or into a rock face. He leaned with the whole of his body to steer, or backward over the edge of the chariot cab to slow down.

"Why did you come?" he yelled above the rush of the wind and grinding of the adamant wheels upon the earth. "It's too dangerous!"

Hippodameia stood beside him in the cab, holding on with white hands, her long arms straining, for her life depended on it. She shook her head, to get her long hair out of her face. "I won't leave you to your death!"

"Please, Hippodameia! Let me stop them and let you off. There is still time! We have a long lead!"

She shook her head. "I'm staying with you!" She crouched beside him, feeling the strength in her legs and arms rejuvenated, as if Love's soft breath reached and supported them both at their backs. *My father still loves me... He won't destroy us with me here.* She looked to the sky through the spaces in the soaring pines above their heads. *Goddess Hera, make it so, I beg you...*

The chariot swerved as the road curved sharply inward where a great crevice had been carved into the mountain. A white fall of water crashed beneath them as they crossed a short bridge, the mist shining on their faces.

"Heeaa!" Pelops yelled, flicking the reins upon the teams' backs.

They pulled away with unbelievable speed as the road opened up across the flat narrow of a mountain valley. Above they could see the sky already beginning to darken and the stars' lamps begin to flicker in the heavens.

OH, Olympian Zeus... I offer you this ram of purest black, its blood, the thigh bones wrapped in fat, that you may feast upon it and know that I honour you. Grant me victory in the race. Grandfather...let my god-made spear find its mark so that my daughter may know that her betrayal will not go unpunished. I have given all to her, and she choses Pelops over me. If she has given her heart and turned her back upon her father's love, then let her suffer the same fate. I am prepared to pay the cost for victory and my honour...

The wind was furious about the black chariot and chargers of Oinomaos' team as Myrtilos crouched beside his master, the reins expertly wrapped about his forearms. The king stood tall and defiant in the cab, grasping the rail with one hand and his death-dealing spear in the other.

Oinomaos could still hear his own prayer to Zeus in his mind, the words lingering on the air around the hill of Kronos like a morning mist to hide the sins of the night. He could still smell the ram's blood as it poured over the altar and down to feed the earth. He could still hear the crackle of the thick fat wrapped about the bones as they burned upon the altar for the Gods to feast.

Pelops made no offerings. He is doomed, Oinomaos thought, waiting patiently as his divine horses sped across the land and mountain passes to catch up to them. As he waited, he nursed his anger and sense of betrayal such that he would be ready to hurl his spear at them both when the time came, to avenge his shame and all the losses of his life. *Oh, Olympus... help your mortal son to victory!*

Oinomaos closed his eyes and felt the speeding winds upon his face and muscled chest, unbothered by the cold, the lashing branches, or screaming horses pulling him forward with such fury.

IN THE CAB beside his king, Myrtilos crouched and steered the team with his usual adeptness, watching the road rush toward them with incomparable speed. He had driven that death road many times already, knew every obstacle, fallen tree and rock, every precipice, sharp turn and crumbling bridge.

He also knew that they would catch Pelops and Hippodameia soon, despite the gift that horse-taming Poseidon had bestowed upon them. The glowing trident upon Pelops' chariot was burned into Myrtilos' mind as he drove, and it became a symbol of his freedom from Oinomaos' tyranny, and the reward Hippodameia had promised him. He was also determined that Oinomaos would not succeed, nor rob him of his reward, for he could see in his cruel master's eyes that he had decided to slay his own daughter.

That, I cannot allow! Myrtilos thought as he slammed the reins upon the flesh-eating team. *Never!*

. . .

THE CHARIOTS of sun and moon rose and fell as the days passed, echoing the race that raged upon the earth. Time swelled and contracted, departing from its usual path as gods, men and creatures watched and waited to see what would happen, for in the outcome of that dread race, it was felt that the effects would be far-reaching for them all.

The spinning wheels of that fateful competition scarred the land and stopped hearts in the night.

Only once had Pelops dared to stop to water the heaving horses. In that brief respite upon the rocky hills around Arcadian Orchomenos, the raging cries of Oinomaos' team could finally be heard coming upon behind them, like a curse upon the windswept funnels of the valleys to the West.

"He's coming!" Hippodameia cried, jumping into the cab before Pelops. "Hurry!" Her panicked voice made bird and beast shudder in the hills, and Pelops' cries, urging his team on, filled all who heard him with fear.

Impossible! Pelops roared inside, unable to comprehend how Oinomaos was already upon them as he lashed the team where he crouched beside the woman he risked all for.

The god-given beasts of Poseidon sensed the urgency in their driver's voice, felt the lash of his reins, and they pulled away faster than ever, with mingled near-madness and fear, as if all of them were trapped in a nightmare from which there was no escape. All there was to do was drive onward, faster and more perilously, in the hopes of outrunning death itself.

"I think your Myrtilos has lost his courage!" Pelops shouted as they sped past stinking Stymphalia. "He won't help us!"

Hippodameia shuddered to think it was true, that Myrtilos was too afraid of her father's wrath to help them. "We're on our own then!" she said, reaching out to grip Pelops' shoulder, feeling the warmth emanating from within.

As fast as they drove, as dangerously as Pelops steered, the sound of Oinomaos' team was ever behind them, drawing slowly closer and closer, despite the increasing speed with which the Horse-Tamer's team charged.

Another night fell, and the stars were alight in the sky once more, shuddering and shifting in and out, as if their light sought the racing team themselves.

"Look!" Hippodameia shouted as they sped past vine-covered Nemea where Herakles had slain the famed lion.

Pelops looked to the side of the road as they crossed the plain, bare-footed nymphs charged alongside swift-footed satyrs, urging them on with cries of worry and pain, even as their vine-leafed crowns fluttered and fell beneath the chariot's crushing wheels.

"Pelops! He is coming! You must go faster!"

Pelops recognized the voice of Axioche and as he looked, he could see her running alongside him for a time, her long legs matching his horses' stride for only a short time before she tired.

"Go! Hurry!" she cried, her tears glinting in the moonlit night.

But the night was to be a long one, for behind them, coming closer, glinting like a speeding star upon the earth, was the spear tip of Oinomaos.

.   .   .

MYRTILOS MARVELLED that the waxed pins he had put in the chariot wheels yet held, and a part of him wondered if the Fates had indeed sided with his master after all.

"Faster!" Oinomaos shouted as the night wore on and blood-soaked Nemea fell away behind them. By now, he had slain most of the suitors, but Pelops' team was swift and skilled, and horse-driving Poseidon had instilled in him the talents of the race. "If I have to slay him at the finish, I will!" Oinomaos yelled aloud to bird and beast and mortal along the side of the road, his voice haunting their dreams, and chasing their days. "I'll lay both their corpses upon Poseidon's altar myself!"

"SUCH SACRILEGE!" Poseidon raged as he watched from the heights of Olympus. He had been watching the entirety of the race, urging his team on to help Pelops and Hippodameia, but the horses of Ares were swift-footed and free of pain, driven by their wish to champ upon the flesh of the fallen as they had upon previous suitors.

Many of the Gods watched, and waited, for it was in the hands of the Fates then, and they were unable to affect any outcome, no matter how much they might have wished it.

It remained only for a victor to be crowned, and the other to be slain. It is at such times that the Gods too feel helpless, when they watch men drive toward uncertain ends by will and action alone.

BEFORE THE COMING of the last dawn, the road began to rise again, high, into the mountain passes before falling away to the sea and distant Isthmia where the altar of Poseidon ever glinted beneath the sun and stars.

Oinomaos' chariot closed, faster and faster, and the world about seemed to hold its breath, for even the winds did not blow as the shades of the dead watched from the rocky wayside. The earth shook as wheels spun as if they were on fire.

Exhaustion had beset Pelops and Hippodameia, and each would have let themselves gladly fall to their deaths for it long ago, but for the presence of the other beside. Together, their strength and will was strong, despite pain, and fear, and desperation at the closing of the gap by the black horses of Ares behind them and the glinting speartip of her father's rage.

Water streamed from Pelops' red and stinging eyes as the chariot charged up the mountain road, his heart beating wildly as the sun dawned over the distant sea, now visible as they peaked the mountain pass.

"Pelops!" Hippodameia shouted, pointing to a canyon where the thunder of their horses' hooves and the crush of their spinning wheels made the soaring bridge of the abyss crumble to nothing even as they approached. "Stop!"

Pelops looked back to see Oinomaos coming faster, closer, his smile one of bloodlust and rage. And so, he lashed his team harder and more furiously.

"What are you doing?" Hippodameia shouted, but even as she did, she saw the charge of hundreds of dryads to either side of them, running ahead of them, their limbs long and lithe, their hearts near to bursting as they leapt before Pelops' chariot, interlocking their limbs one over the other until they formed a bridge over the great chasm.

The chariot careened over the abyss, supported by the

spirits of that land itself, and as they crossed over, Pelops and Hippodameia turned to see Oinomaos' chariot following, nearly atop the dryads, his wheels spinning wildly as if out of control.

"He's not going to make it!" Pelops shouted hopefully, and the fear rose in Hippodameia's heart, even as her father raised his spear to hurl it at the two of them. *Father no!*

MYRTILOS LASHED the horses one more time, sending them onward, even as the strange bridge began to fall away before them. He had seen the wheel begin to fail at last as the wax melted and the thin wooden pins beneath began to splinter and crack, but they yet held.

As Oinomaos drew back his spear, Myrtilos let go of the reins and swung a leg over the side of the chariot to kick at the wheel hub.

"What are you doing?" Oinomaos shouted, but even as he reached for the reins himself, the chariot faltered and the wheel spun away into the rocky wall to the side. "Traitor!" he yelled, but Myrtilos had jumped away to fall upon the cutting surface of the rocky road. "I curse you Myrtilos!" Oinomaos shouted as the chariot spun and tangled into the horses' legs, over the dryads clinging to the cliff face, all to watch the king of Elis fall to his deserved death.

Father, why? Oinomaos thought as he saw the sky falling away from him, more quickly than a star out of the heavens, as he yet gripped his spear before his body was wrecked upon the jagged rocks at the bottom of the canyon.

Myrtilos stood on the cliff's edge looking down, holding his bleeding arms to himself, his eyes searching for any sign of life at the bottom of the chasm. As he strained his eyes, he saw only the broken, bloody body of Oinomaos, son of Ares, the cruel tyrant of his life.

"May the Gods damn you!" he shouted and spat into the void. When he looked up, he could see Pelops and Hippodameia's chariot speeding away toward Isthmia, and it was in that direction which he now sought a route.

MY FATHER IS GONE! Hippodameia's heart cried as the tears streamed down her dirty cheeks. *It wasn't supposed to be like that!*

But it was, and as they sped over the plains of fragrant orange, lemon and olive toward Isthmia and the sea, the reality of her father's death sank its bitter claws into her.

It was only Pelops' warm hand that kept her from total despair, the loving look in his eyes, the understanding of a father's betrayal that he too had felt.

"We've won," Pelops said to her as they came to the peace of Poseidon's sanctuary. "It's over."

The chariot rolled to a stop before the altar, in the shade of a broad and fragrant pine tree and there, Pelops and Hippodameia fell to the ground weeping together, in each other's arms, for the victory they had so dearly fought for.

"IT IS DONE," Poseidon said to Zeus and Ares with whom he stood on the precipice of high Olympus.

War fumed and vowed revenge upon the upstart Pelops, as well as the traitorous son of Hermes.

But Zeus shook his head. "It is finished. Oinomaos has lost, and his murderous reign is at an end." It was then that Zeus peered down from those godly heights at distant Elis, and that dark palace of pain and dismay. Raising his great fist, Olympian Zeus squeezed at the air and in Elis, the earth began to shake uncontrollably beneath Oinomaos' home.

Those high walls of death-stained stone were no match for the wrath of Zeus whose will shook the earth and crumbled the walls of that unhappy fortress. No more would men dwell there. The fallen rocks and dusty corridors of death would welcome only the wind, sun and rain.

And the Gods looked on, accepting the will of Mighty Zeus, as all must.

9

VICTORY

The victorious couple slept under the watchful eyes of the Gods and mountain-dwelling nymphs and satyrs for the rest of that day and the entirety of the next. So great was their exhaustion, their elation, and Hippodameia's grief, that it was as though they could not wake from a tortuous dream in which they relived every moment of that race. The cries of horses and crushing of rock, the splintering of trees and the spinning of wheels, all of it went round again, and again in their minds, even as they lay upon the soft ground with their arms clasped about each other.

On the second morning, Pelops awoke to the soft nuzzling of one of the stallions, the beast's hot breath blowing on his face to awaken him. He opened his eyes slowly to see the tree above him, whistling softly in the sea's breeze, the long altar stretched out before him, and the other horses gathered about it, drinking from buckets of water brought to them by the wary nymphs hiding among the sanctuary trees.

The stallion's large eyes looked over Pelops before turning to go back to cropping at the late spring grass about the altar.

Pelops sat up and turned to look at Hippodameia who yet slept beside him. He could see the tear stains upon her face, that she had wept in her deep sleep, and he knew why. She had won her freedom, but she had also lost her father, the only family she had had left in the world.

"I love you," he whispered, leaning down to kiss her cheek and stroke her hair.

Hippodameia's eyes flickered slowly open, and as she awoke from the terrible dreams in which she had been dwelling, she looked up at him, the morning sun full upon her face. Her eyes revealed the dawning of her new life, and the contrasting emotions that now harassed her, and would do so from that moment on.

Her tears now fell in the waking light, and she shut them against the image of her father raising a spear against her, of him plummeting over the edge of the cliff to his death. But then she felt Pelops' strong, gentle arms about her, lifting her off the ground to stand beside him.

"You are free," he said softly, uncertainly too, for the reality of his victory was but new-born.

Hippodameia wrapped her arms about him, pressed her lips to his, and buried her face in the crook of his neck. "I love you," she said. "Will you heal this land with me, Pelops? Do you promise me that?"

He looked back at her, and he felt his heart swell at her broken beauty. "We will heal it together, my love."

In that moment, Hippodameia knew that she had made the right choice, that the Fates had smiled upon them and handed them victory, though at great cost. "My father was cruel, I know," she said hoarsely as she looked to the blue skies above, "but he was driven mad by grief. It was not always like that." She looked back at Pelops. "I would build a monument to him back in Elis."

"Of course," Pelops said. "But first, let us honour Poseidon for our victory."

Together, Pelops and Hippodameia walked over to the broad, ancient stone altar that faced the distant sea. There they paused, filling their hearts with gratitude, as they had also filled the clay bowl with water from a nearby spring.

Pelops raised his arms to the skies. "Oh, Horse-Taming Poseidon...Lord...we thank you with all of our hearts for this victory. I thank you for my life, which you gave back to me so long ago." With the thoughts of his new life before him, Pelops then took the dagger from his belt, reached up, and cut a lock of his own hair. He then placed it upon the altar and took up the bowl. "Accept my humble offering...my gratitude... In Elis, I will build a hippodrome in honour of you and the team that you gave to me, who drove us to victory."

Hippodameia looked to see the four horses lined up behind them, their ears bent forward as if to listen to the words offered to their divine father. She then looked back to Pelops and, when he was finished, took the dagger from him, and cut a long strand of her own hair.

"Divine Mother, Hera...please also accept my own offering for this victory, and bless our future union..." She poured the water over her hair which lay upon the stone surface like golden filament in the sunshine. "Gods...we honour you..."

Pelops and Hippodameia, clasped hands and looked from that altar, beyond the trees to the sea. The Fates had been kind to them, and an entirely new world had now opened up before them.

.   .   .

IT WAS to be a long journey back to Elis, but before they departed, Pelops and Hippodameia led the horses to the sea's edge to wash and bathe upon the white-pebbled shore.

There, the horses splashed in the surf and charged happily back and forth at the border of Poseidon's realm while Pelops and Hippodameia swam and washed and held each other close in the light of another day.

The sun was dipping away to the red West when they put their clothes back on and sat watching the glittering night emerge on the still surface of the water. Both of them wished that moment in time to be frozen, that they could spend their lives laying together by the sunlit sea, free from fear and pain, from the grasping hands of others.

But such is not the way of the world of men.

Dark thoughts began to invade Pelops' mind, and he began to wonder how he would govern his new kingdom. He felt the weight of his new rule, even before it had really begun. *I will not rule as Tantalus did, nor as Oinomaos... I will be different.*

"What is it, my love?" Hippodameia asked as she stood beside him, looking out to the darkening expanse.

"I have never ruled before."

She smiled and laced her arm through his. "Nor have I," she said. "But we will find our way together. And we will love and cherish our sons and daughters."

That made him smile. "We will," he agreed, before taking up a one of the clay bowls they had brought from the sanctuary. "I'll be right back. I will get us some water to drink from the spring at the end of the beach."

"And I will be waiting," she replied, kissing him softly upon the lips she had already come to love.

Hippodameia watched Pelops' shadow move down the

dusky beach as the waves lapped gently about her feet. She sighed, finally feeling the joy begin to bloom within her.

There were steps upon the pebbles behind her, and she turned, expecting to see one of the horses coming to her, but as she looked, she saw the form of a man emerge from out of the shadows at the back of the beach.

Hippodameia stood, her heart beginning to pound, but then she relaxed. "Myrtilos?"

"Yes. It's me, lady." He did not smile. His limbs were badly scratched, and there was dried blood upon the side of his head, matting his hair.

"Are you hurt?" she asked, stepping closer to look at him.

"The king is dead," Myrtilos stated. "I stayed true to my word."

"I did not want my father dead," Hippodameia answered, her joy rushing out like the sea's waves before the earth shakes, her sadness returning. "You didn't have to kill him."

"But I didn't," Myrtilos said, shaking his head. "You did." He stared at her then in a way he had never done before. In fact, Myrtilos had been staring at her the whole of that day, watching her bathe and frolic naked in the sea, make love with the man she had chosen over him, the son of a god.

"Don't say that," Hippodameia replied, backing away.

But Myrtilos grabbed her wrist in his strong hands, and pulled her back to him. "I want my reward for all that I've done!"

"And you shall have it, Myrtilos, I promise! You shall have lands of your own, horses, riches...anything you desire."

"I don't want any of that!" he hissed. "I risked everything for you. I want what was promised! Your gentle touch, your kisses..." He moved closer to her, his grip getting tighter about her wrist, and his other hand moving to her waist.

"Myrtilos, stop!" Hippodameia cried, but even as she slapped him across his blood-encrusted face, he pressed his body to hers, his lips violently seeking hers as she turned her head to either side.

A moment later, Myrtilos pushed her backward onto the pebbles and fell upon her. His hands groped at her peplos, his breath heaved in her ears and face as she struggled and struck him, backing away.

At last, she found her voice and screamed. Her hand found the dagger that lay upon the ground with their cloaks and she gripped it, slashing him across the shoulder.

Myrtilos roared in anger and slammed his fist into her stomach, winding her, giving him a chance to rip at her clothing to see her body laid before him. "I want my reward, lady!" he hissed.

In his mind, he heard the rushing of the sea and the galloping of hooves to which he was so accustomed, and as he was about to take what he had always dreamed about, he felt himself knocked away from Hippodameia so that he flew through the air to land hard upon the beach. "Ahh!" he yelled.

Strong hands pounded into Myrtilos' gut and face, and his flailing hand found a large rock which he swung. There was a loud grunt, and he turned to see Pelops upon the ground beside him. Clumsily, and in his dazed state, Myrtilos drew the dagger that was tucked in his belt and lunged at Pelops.

"Look out!" Hippodameia shouted to Pelops, but Myrtilos' blade struck his right shoulder blade, its point stopping in the ivory of Demeter's gift.

Pelops swung his right arm and the blade fell to the

ground. A second later, he was running after Myrtilos who now turned to flee.

"I'll kill you!" Pelops roared, and even as Myrtilos stumbled away, he fell upon him, driving his fist into the charioteer's side and stomach, flipping him over in the silver surf to straddle him with his hands about his neck.

Pelops felt the rage and anger pulsing through his arms and hands, the strong will to take Myrtilos' life. "You will never touch her again!" he said, squeezing harder as the waves fell about the prostrate man's face, choking him.

"I...I curse..." Myrtilos gagged. "I curse you and your bastard children! For...for all time. I curse you and your line, Pelops!"

Myrtilos' wild eyes and gaping mouth stared at Pelops from beneath the waves, like an eel writhing in the deep.

Pelops felt he was close to ending that pitiful life, and would have done so but for the voice in his head.

Let him go! Poseidon commanded. *He is the son of Hermes!*

Pelops' grip loosened right away, and he picked Myrtilos up, and shoved him back into the water.

The charioteer gasped and choked. "I curse you!" he shrieked, seeing Hippodameia come to Pelops' side. "I curse you!"

But even as he raged and repeated his curse, he fell to his knees once more, the tentacles of some great beast wrapped about his legs.

"NO!" Myrtilos yelled, choking on sea water as he was pulled out to sea, and lifted into the air, only to be slammed bodily on the rocks over and over again until his lifeless body was dragged into the dark deep.

Pelops held Hippodameia close to his side, both of them

breathing wildly at the violent shattering of the peace they had been enjoying.

"It's finished," he told her, when he caught his breath. "He won't bother you anymore," he said, even as he saw the silver and black fins of sharks tearing Myrtilos' sad body to bits in the reddening water beneath the moonlight.

Hippodameia turned her head away from the horror of Poseidon's wrath then, and Pelops watched, shivering with cold and Myrtilos' echoing last words.

10

BLOOD GUILT

How can one bathe in the warm sunlight of hard-won victory when so many lives have been lost, and the means to achieve that victory haunt the memories like a lingering nightmare?

It is no easy task, less so for heroes, for they will slowly begin to doubt their deeds, constantly seek ways to improve upon them, or never be able to get beyond the memory of that one moment of glory that marks their evanescent life.

As they drove the chariot back across that blood-soaked land, Pelops felt the cold hands of the Moirai, those goddesses of fate, pushing him onward expectantly, and it gave him no end of restlessness. More so, however, he knew in his very bones and blood that the Erinyes, those unforgiving furies of the world of men and gods, had fixed their eyes upon him and the woman he loved so deeply.

If not for the presence of Hippodameia at his side, as if Aphrodite herself gripped his hand, Pelops would not have willingly returned to his newly-won kingdom. But the farther they got from the blood-soaked seashore, their offerings burning brightly upon Poseidon's altar once more, the more hope they felt.

Out of valley villages and hovels, from forests and dwellings beside mountain streams, people emerged as if into the light for the first time in an age, to greet the man and woman who had freed them from Oinomaos' rage. They threw flowers beneath their horses' hooves and the spinning wheels of their chariot, raised their children that they may look upon them, and smiled such that it was as if they breathed freely for the first time.

On the road, Pelops looked for Axioche, sought to glimpse her smiling face that he might thank her for her help in getting him to Elis, but hers was the only one absent along the mountain roads.

She, however, saw him, and watched, her heart but a little broken, thanks to the life that grew inside of her. From behind the thick trunk of a mountain pine, the dryad watched Pelops pass with his princess, and as she did so, she felt her heated heart sing sadly for the man she had loved. "Do not fret, Chrysippus, my son," she said as she caressed her already swelling belly. "You will meet him some day." And she watched the chariot disappear around a bend in the cliff-hugging road. "Someday..."

THERE WAS hope as Pelops and Hippodameia drove down the final mountain pass of Arcadia into the kingdom of Elis. People cheered and wept, and the clouds were swept away by all-seeing Zeus so that the sun's light might cleanse that land.

But fear accompanied them as well, still clinging to Pelops and Hippodameia when they arrived at the broad plain beside the river Alfeios, in the shadow of the Kronian hill.

As Leandros approached with the rest of the palace guard, Pelops stood beside Hippodameia, the crowd silent. For a moment, some expected the captain of the guard to arrest Pelops, but rather, every single one of those well-armoured men saluted the victor and bent their knees to him.

Cheers erupted in the surrounding groves near to the altars of Zeus and Hera.

"My lady," Leandros said, bowing to Hippodameia, and then turning to Pelops. "My king..." He smiled. "It is good to see you alive."

"We are alive, Leandros," Pelops answered. "But I am not yet your king." He looked to Hippodameia. "There is something I must do first."

The captain did not press Pelops further, but bowed and took his leave to ensure their quarters were set up.

"What is wrong, my love?" Hippodameia asked Pelops when they were alone.

Pelops stared across the heads of the assembled masses to the shadow of the Hill of Kronos and there he saw the shadowy figures he had been dreading, standing stalk still upon the tangled slopes.

Pelops smiled to Hippodameia, and kissed her. "I've won the kingdom, your hand, and your freedom...but there is much for which I must make amends."

She gripped him tightly and held him in her eyes. "Then we will do so together."

Together, they moved through the crowds to make their offerings of thanks to both Zeus and Hera for their victory, and for the people of Elis. The fragrant smoke of their offerings burned long into the night, the meat feeding the people over whom they would now rule.

THAT NIGHT, when Selene's silver light lit the plain about the tents and sleeping people, their minds distracted by the sweet weavings of Morpheus, the dark forms of Alecto, Megaera, and dread Tisiphone crawled from the shadows of the Kronian hill to stare out over the plain of sleeping mortals to the tent at their centre.

"There is a deep peace here now," Alecto hissed, her dark, gnarled hand reaching out to point at the people of Elis.

"Won, by murder and deceit," Tisiphone added, her voice a sound not of the world, but from the depths of the dark earth, full of anger. "He must make it right, or the burning of his soul will not be long coming."

"Hold, sisters," Megaera added, her voice softer but firm. "Poseidon's favourite comes."

As one, the three black-cowled heads turned to see the forms of a man and a woman walking slowly toward them.

"We see you, Pelops...son of Tantalus!" they hissed in unison.

The mortal man before them shook with fear as all men inevitably did in the face of those ancient furies. He held his love close to his side, and together they approached until their feet were but a pace from the edge of the dark hill of Kronos.

"We come to ask how we might make things right," Hippodameia said, a shaking courage in her voice. "We wish to atone for our actions."

"You, daughter of Oinomaos, have nothing to atone for," Megaera said, shaking her head slowly from side to side, her face hidden in the shadow of her cowl. "You did not seek your father's death. You sought to avert it."

Hippodameia looked upon them, and it was as if they made the smiling face of her father hover in the air between them. He was not angry, but rather full of love and care as he once was, and the sight of him made her weep for his loss.

The Erinyes let that linger for a moment before turning to Pelops.

Tisiphone raised a long, dark arm down which serpents slithered and twined, and pointed her finger at Pelops. "You, Pelops, have much to atone for."

"Murder and trickery!" Alecto screeched and Pelops covered his ears, shaking his head.

"There was no trickery!" he said. "But yes, I did murder, and I would make things right in your eyes that I might begin my rule in good faith."

"You believe you can rule more wisely and fairly than Oinomaos?" Megaera added. "You believe you are worthy to rule this land of gods and heroes?"

"I believe I can. I know in my heart that it is my fervent desire to do so."

The Erinyes stared at Pelops and Hippodameia for what felt like an eternity to the shaking mortals, and just when the latter thought a decision was to be reached, the three dread goddesses approached them such that the glow of their all-seeing eyes burned them.

But Pelops and Hippodameia stood their ground and awaited the decision.

"You will make amends before you marry, that you may begin your joint rule cleansed and in harmony," Megaera said, before taking a step back.

"Pelops, son of Tantalus...favoured by Earth-Shaking

Poseidon who keeps horses, you will bury all former suitors for the hand of your queen," Alecto decreed. "You will also bury the remains of King Oinomaos, son of Ares, whom you vanquished."

"I swear, I will." Pelops bowed his head, and Alecto stepped back.

Only Tisiphone stood before Pelops and Hippodameia then. They shook to stand before her, to smell the death that clung to her, to see the deep burning of her immortal eyes. They wanted to flee, to weep, even to die to make it stop, but they stood unmoving. Together, they endured the Fury's face, and the black fingered hand that reached out to within an inch of Pelops' forehead.

"You will also build a monument to the son of Hermes, whom you betrayed and murdered, whose body was torn by beasts in Poseidon's sea. You must do this, and that monument will be a bane on man and beast for all time." Tisiphone stepped slowly closer, as if to devour the mortal man before her, but she stopped short of smelling him, her possible prey in the shadows. "Do you agree, Pelops, future King of Elis?" Her voice was mocking, and deep, but she did not strike. She awaited her reply.

"I...I agree to that, and all other demands that I might make amends in your immortal eyes, oh dread Erinyes." Pelops bowed his head and Hippodameia did the same.

For a moment, Tisiphone looked upon their crowns, and caught a glimpse of what the Fates had in store.

She then smiled and stepped back.

"Go then...and rule," Tisiphone said.

Pelops and Hippodameia looked up, and saw that the Erinyes were gone, and that the shadowy slopes of the hill of Kronos were still and empty.

. . .

IN THE COMING MONTHS, Pelops set about the tasks that the Furies had given him, and the Gods looked on, helpless, unable to offer aid to such endeavours, for the tasks were his alone.

The remains of every suitor who had gone before were buried and their names inscribed on stelae among the trees as if they were heroes, and not the wealth-seeking men most of them had been. This act only served to ennoble Pelops in the eyes of the people, and it was said how honourable a deed it had been.

Tales were also told of King Oinomaos, of his early rule, of days when there had been joy and peace, before the blood. This, so that the people would remember their king before he had been eaten away by anger and grief and the fear of loss. People were reminded that all men, no matter the goodness in their hearts, were capable of falling into darkness, and so the great tomb that Pelops and Hippodameia built to Oinomaos served as a monument to that dark fate.

Wine was poured about the base of Oinomaos' tomb, and flowers laid, and it was said that the shades of him, his wife, and son could be seen walking about it, their faces at once joyous and disconsolate.

When it came to honouring Myrtilos, the slain son of Hermes, never was a task more distasteful to Pelops and Hippodameia. Where Pelops saw only the slinking, traitorous attacker of his love, Hippodameia tried to remember the charioteer as the young man who had once saved her from wolves, and who had been a friendly face in the corridors of her palace youth.

But try as she might, Hippodameia, upon thinking of

Myrtilos, remembering his face, could only see him in the guise of an attacker, violent and clawing.

It was with great solemnity and reluctance that the monument to Myrtilos was raised upon the field where the chariot races of Elis occurred and, in time, the turn where that monument was located, the Taraxippus, became a place of terror to man and beast, causing many a death by its very presence. And so the son of Hermes, lived on in dread memory.

Both Pelops and Hippodameia ensured that the altars of the Gods burned brightly in Elis, that they were never without offering and prayer, and the Gods answered them with gifts of blessing and greatness. Even Zeus granted Pelops a sceptre of gold, ivory and adamant, fit for a king.

The games were established in the Olympian Gods' honour, to be celebrated far and wide in those lands, to make the names of many a hero for generations to come.

Games were also established by Hippodameia in honour of her beloved Hera, the only mother who remained to her. In that first Heraia, the people saw their queen, Hippodameia, run to victory for the glory of the goddess.

The Gods were pleased with Pelops and Hippodameia... but for one.

In the quiet halls of lonesome Olympus, Hermes looked down on the world of men and remembered the son he had never loved, and who had never loved him in return. He had seen his death with his own, far-seeing eyes, and done nothing to prevent it. He felt no affection for Pelops who, despite the murder of Myrtilos, sought to appease the Messenger of the Gods.

Hermes watched Pelops standing before the tomb of his murdered son one night, days before he was to be wed to

Princess Hippodameia. The mortal man had tears in his eyes as he looked to distant Olympus, grasping at the faint memories of that immortal dwelling place.

"Oh Hermes..." Pelops said from beneath the cowl of his cloak. "I would not begin my reign without your favour. I did not seek your son's death, but I also know I am to blame. I have built this monument to him, and yet you, of all the Gods, are silent. I would make things right between us. If it pleases you, I will ensure that you are worshiped across the entirety of this land, that your altars are always bright and fragrant, and that your immortal ears are ever full of prayer and song. Send me a sign, oh Hermes. Let me know if this meets with your divine approval."

Hermes watched and listened to the mortal man's prayers. He knew he would have preferred a son such as that, rather than he who lay beneath the sea. In that moment, he shed a single tear for departed Myrtilos, and allowed the shame of both of them to be washed away.

Pelops stood before the moonlit monument, waiting and worrying, and when he was about to leave, the grassy mound began to glow with golden light and there, upon the slopes, sat the god to whom he had been praying.

Hermes looked upon Pelops then, and descended the slope, his golden light blinding, his caduceus extended as if to strike.

But he did not strike Pelops. Instead, he touched his staff to the mortal man's head and spoke winged words to him.

"I accept, Pelops, king of this land." Hermes smiled sadly at him. "I too am responsible for the demise of my son. Go. Marry she whom Aphrodite has chosen for you. Be blessed."

"Thank you," Pelops whispered, relief burning the rims of his eyes.

Hermes stood tall, towering over Pelops, and gazed about the surrounding plain. "This truly is a place of greatness, of great deeds and heroes..." He placed his hand upon Pelops' shoulder. "And you belong here. Rule well."

Light flashed, the wind rushing about the plain, and Pelops found himself alone again, a burden lifted at last.

11

CURSED

The long-dreamed of peace that the people of Elis had wished for finally arrived, and never was it more evident than on the day that their princess, Hippodameia, was wed to Pelops.

How could they not see that this was a blessed time? For at that midsummer, when the chariot of the sun rode high and bright in the heavens, when the evening air was fragrant with jasmine and orange, the Gods walked upon the earth, their all-seeing eyes like stars among them.

The Olympians had come to witness the wedding in the place where they had once battled Titans, and where they too had raced and battled among each other in friendly competition. It was a place of opposites, that plain beside the river Alfeios.

The people had gathered about the field to watch as Pelops and Hippodameia emerged from their tent, both dressed all in purest white, to make offerings at the altars of the Gods. The fires burned more brightly than ever before, and the burning scent of those offerings rose and weaved about the trees, the columns of the newly-made temples, and statues of the Olympian heroes, the first of many to come over the years.

When the Gods alighted from Olympus, drawn by prayer and burning sacrifice, Pelops and Hippodameia stepped forward and bowed before them.

Zeus and Hera looked down upon them, their smiles as brilliant as the morning sun.

"You have done well," Father Zeus said, the timbre of his voice unlike anything the people had heard before, an impression to mark the occasion in their minds and dreams. "There will be peace now in this land, thanks to you, Pelops." Zeus then bent and raised the mortal man to his feet. "Enjoy it. Nurture it."

"I will, Lord," Pelops answered, his voice low as he looked up at the King of the Gods.

Then Hera bent to raise up Hippodameia. Her smile and warmth melted hardened hearts who were used to hardship and grief, and it was as if spring were reborn again. She kissed Hippodameia upon the brow and spoke.

"Ever have you prayed to me with a full heart, and ever have I wished for your happiness." She reached out to take Pelops and Hippodameia's hands, joined them together, and bound them with words and a weaving of golden light. "Be as one. Act as one. Nurture this land and this kingdom like your own children, of which you will have many. Continue to honour Olympus with games and offerings, and Olympus will continue to honour you and your people."

The goddess then stepped back and the couple turned to each other, their hearts filled with love and a calm that is only experienced when two souls who have sought each other are willingly-bound.

Pelops and Hippodameia kissed before the Gods and people, and cries of joy rose up to the heavens.

As the feast began, and music from Apollo's lyre weaved a spell among the trees and the base of the Kronian hill, Pelops approached Poseidon and Demeter who stood beneath the overhanging branches of a soaring pine. He bowed to them.

"Thank you," he said, his voice full of emotion. "I never thought to...to live..." He shut his eyes against the unbidden memories of Tantalus' cruelty, and felt Demeter's hand upon his brow.

"Pelops," the goddess said, her voice soft and full of care. "He cannot harm you anymore, but the trials you endured are a part of you and your strength now. You have suffered, as both men and gods must, and now it is for you to rule and ease the suffering of others when you can." The goddess stood tall and her divine eyes looked across the valleys, rivers, plains and mountains of that land. "This land will bear your name for all time. People will remember you and your deeds in the utterance of its name."

"The island of Pelops," Poseidon then said, his bearded face smiling down at the mortal man.

Pelops looked up to the god who had brought him back from the edge of the black river Styx, who had nurtured and loved him as if he were his own, and who had helped him when no one else would so that he could achieve victory and begin life anew. "My lord...I..."

"I know..." the God of the Seas and of Horses said. "The wheel of time moves on in this place, and it is for you to live now, to seize every opportunity as you saw and seized your fate from the very heights of Olympus."

"Thank you, lord." Pelops bowed again and Poseidon reached down to pull him up again.

"You are a king of men, now. It will not always be easy, this life, but it will be yours. Whatever you do with it, Pelops, I know it will be one of greatness." In that moment, Poseidon listened to the sound of his distant sea, the crash of the waves, the cry of gulls, and the singing of beasts in the deep. "Your sons and daughters will be strong, and you and your bride shall begin a line of greatness."

Poseidon's face darkened a little then, for he saw much of the future, though it was against the laws of Zeus and of the world that he should reveal any of it. "All will be well, Pelops." And he kissed his favoured one's brow in blessing.

Across the field, Hermes and Ares stood side by side, sweet nectar quenching their thirst as they watched Pelops. They smiled when Poseidon's face darkened, for they too sensed what was to come, that the words of their dead sons still rang in the young hero's mind, in time itself.

"Peace will not last in this land," Ares said, smiling.

Golden Hermes looked at him and then back to Pelops and Hippodameia, they who were the cause of his son's death. They had heaped offerings upon his altars, instituted prayers in his honour across the land, and yet...he felt little love for them. He looked to War standing beside him. "We need not do a thing. Their sons and daughters will be restless of spirit. Peace... It will not be their way."

Ares smiled again, even as he watched King Stymphalus of Arcadia approach Pelops and Hippodameia with his entourage to offer his congratulations. "Blood will flow again," Ares said. "Starting there."

EVEN AS THE wheels of Fate turn, the fortunes of men and women rise and fall as easily as the tides in Poseidon's wine-dark sea. Men are haunted by memories and by past actions, and as deeds fade into time, and age creeps in upon them, they will often pin their hopes upon their children.

Pelops and Hippodameia had many children, and their grandchildren, the sons of Atreus foremost, were born for war and blood, despair and death.

As the glories of the earth itself bloom and whither and bloom again beneath a bright sun or cloudy skies, so too do the fortunes of families.

Whichever way the wheels of Fate turn, there will be a god that smiles, and a god that weeps at the fortunes of heroes.

The End

AUTHOR'S NOTE

Pelops is one of the most important heroes from Greek mythology, but it is interesting that his story is one that has not really been explored in popular culture. Few people today really know much about him, whereas most people with a passing interest in Greek myth know about Herakles and his Twelve Labours, Jason and the journey to get the Golden Fleece, or even Theseus and the Labyrinth.

Tourists will travel the length and breadth of the Peloponnese - the southern mainland of Greece - which is named after Pelops, and they will crowd the museum halls of ancient Olympia to look upon the statues representing the great chariot race from the pediment of the temple of Zeus there, and still know very little about him.

Years ago, on my first trip to Greece, I was surprised to discover that that ancient land, the 'Peloponnese', or 'the island of Pelops' as it is called, was indeed named after this hero about whom I too, at the time, knew very little.

It was the research for my novel *Heart of Fire: A Novel of the Ancient Olympics*, that really opened my eyes to the story of

Pelops and Hippodameia, a story I knew that I wanted to eventually write.

As with all myths, the sources are scant and there are varying versions. With Pelops, however, there are quite a few mentions in Greek and Roman sources, including plays about Oinomaos by Euripides and Sophocles. The earliest mention of the great race across what came to be known as the 'Peloponnese' is from Hesiod (seventh or eighth century B.C.) who, in the great Eoiae fragment, lists the suitors who were slain by Hippodameia's father in the races.

The first, more fulsome mention of the story of Pelops and Hippodameia, and the race, comes from the poet Pindar in the fifth century B.C.

When the flower of rising youth shaded his [Pelops'] cheek with down, then for a speedy marriage he counselled in his mind, from her father...to win the maid Hippodameia, of glorious fame. And coming near to the salt sea's edge, alone at night, he called aloud to the loud-roaring Wielder of the Trident [Poseidon], who came, and stood before him. Then spoke Pelops, and said 'Lo, great Poseidon, if in your count Kypris' [Aphrodite's] gifts find aught of favour, then shackle Oinomaos' brazen spear, and bring me on speeding chariot wheels to the land of Elis, and grant me victory. For thirteen souls now has he slain, her suitors, and holds back the marriage of his daughter. Great danger calls to no coward's heard; but for man, who must die, why should he nurse a nameless old age through, in vain, in darkness, and of all deeds that glorious are have not a share? But for me shall this contest lie for my challenge. Do thou but grant fair issue my heart's desire.'

So he spoke, and his prayer uttered no words that failed of their achievement. But for his glory's honour, the god gave him a gleaming chariot and steeds that flew unwearied upon wings.

And mighty Oinomaos he slew, and took the maiden for his bride; six sons she bore, chieftains leading the field in valorous deeds. By Alfeios' ford he lies now [at ancient Olympia], closely joined to the great feast of glorious sacrifice, his tomb oft visited, beside the altar where many a stranger treads. And the great fame of the Olympic Games shines far afield, in the course known of Pelops, where are matched rivals in speed of foot and in brave feats of bodily strength.

(Pindar, *Olympian Ode* 1.66; trans. Conway)

Though there is a great deal more to the tale of Pelops and Hippodameia, both triumph and tragedy, I chose to focus on the more glorious aspect of the race, and Pelops' rise to prominence from terrible beginnings, and in doing so, I had to make choices for the sake of story about some settings, events and relationships.

Pelops was supposedly a Lydian prince whose father, Tantalus, cut him up and served him to the Gods to test their omniscience. The Goddess Demeter was the only one to eat part of the slain child.

In the myth, Poseidon, who was actually in love with the beautiful boy, took him to Olympus to be healed, and Demeter gave him the ivory shoulder blade which became an important relic, especially during the Trojan War.

I was quite moved by the beginning of this story, the abuses of Pelops' terrible father whom Zeus sent to Tartarus to be tortured by eternal hunger and thirst. It is for that reason that I chose to make Poseidon more of a father figure than a lover, for I imagined Pelops' disappointment, the void left by his own father, and how it could be filled by the God of the Sea.

This story, is in fact, a story of Gods as much as mortals, for many of the main players, including Oinomaos and Myrtilos, were sons of gods such as Ares and Hermes. Tantalus too, was a son of Zeus, making Pelops the grandson of the King of the Gods.

For the location of Oinomaos' palace, nothing is known, and so rather than opting for the known capital of that ancient kingdom, which is Pisa, in Elis, I set the palace at a place called 'Kato Samikon' near the sea. This is a mound rising out of a plain in Elis that had some ancient occupation on site. Because Zeus is supposed to have destroyed Oinomaos' palace after the race, I imagined that Pelops and Hippodameia would have then moved the royal seat to Pisa, close to Olympia.

When it comes to Oinomaos, the father of Hippodameia, I did veer from the usual path. Roughly translated, his name means 'wine man', and in the myths, he is power-hungry and violent.

I wanted to get to know Oinomaos more, to give him more of a motive for his deeds, and so I created the story of the death of his wife and son. With Hippodameia his only remaining family member, he was now unwilling to let anyone take her away from him. She was all he had left of the family he had once loved so dearly.

Even good men can become evil, and we see this a lot in mythology and storytelling in general.

The beginnings of the story of Pelops and Hippodameia are romantic indeed. There are sculptural depictions of them both in the chariot for the race, and so I used that as a way to illustrate her strength and courage. Their story is one of the foundation myths of the Olympic Games, and indeed the chariot races were one of the marquee events of the ancient games. The *Pelopion* within the *altis* of ancient Olympia was said to be the tomb of Pelops himself, and it became a centre of worship for this hero.

You can read more about the foundation myths of the Olympic Games, and about Pelops, in *The World of Heart of Fire* blog series.

After the victory, it is also said that Hippodameia instituted the Heraian Games in honour of Hera, the sort of Olympic Games equivalent in which women could compete in footraces. At ancient Olympia, within the temple of Hera, there was a couch that was said to contain the remains of Hippodameia. To read more about the Heraian Games, visit the Eagles and Dragons Publishing website.

But their story, is also one of tragedy. After this part of the tale, Pelops and Hippodameia have many sons and daughters, including Atreus, Thyestes, Pittheus, Alcathous, Astydameia, Nicippe and Lysidice. Their daughters marry sons of Perseus, creating powerful political ties, while their sons spread over the Peloponnese to establish their own kingdoms.

In *Wheels of Fate*, I have planted the seeds of the coming tragedy for this family, and the curse of the Pelopidae which Myrtilos brought upon them.

In myth, one of the events that begins the rift in the family, and tears Pelops and Hippodameia apart, is the emergence of another son of Pelops by the nymph, Axioche (sometimes called 'Danais'). In this version of the story, I have Pelops meet the nymph before he meets Hippodameia, at a time when he is lonely and lost. She provides him with tenderness, and this tenderness is reflected in the love he later bears for their son, Chryssipus, who was apparently abducted by Laius, the King of Thebes. When Chryssipus comes to Pelops, his father brings him into the family and favours him, vows to protect him.

Sadly, Pelops cannot protect him from his own family.

In the myths, Atreus, and possibly Thyestes, murder Chryssipus, some say at the urging of Hippodameia herself. This act fragments the family with the sons banished from Elis, and Hippodameia fleeing to the Argolid peninsula where she later died. Pelops had her remains brought back to Olympia where they were supposedly placed in the temple of Hera.

Obviously, this story does not explore these later tragedies. But the curse of the Pelopidae, and the fragmentation of the family, only serve to illustrate the dual nature of Greek mythology. Triumph and tragedy go hand-in-hand as the wheel of Fate turns for everyone.

And it will continue to turn for the descendants of Pelops. The sons of Atreus, Agamemnon and Menelaus, will eventually find themselves at the heart of one of the most destructive events of the late, Greek Heroic Age: the Trojan War.

But that is another story.

Thank you for reading.

Adam Alexander Haviaras
Stratford, Ontario
May, 2021

A SONG FOR THE UNDERWORLD

THE STORY OF ORPHEUS AND EURYDICE

Oh, if I had Orpheus' voice and poetry
with which to move the Dark Maid and her Lord,
I'd call you back, dear love, from the world below.
I'd go down there for you. Charon or the grim
King's dog could not prevent me then
from carrying you up into the fields of light.

— EURIPIDES, *ALCESTIS*

HYMN I

THE JOYOUS HEARTS

1

THE GOD AND THE MUSE

Every event in this world, on the mortal and immortal planes of the cosmos, in those hidden places between time and space, has a song. It starts with a single note, and that note resonates, spreading wide like the ripples of a great pond in the heavens, until it touches man and god alike.

Some songs will last, while others will be short-lived, though the memory of them lingers for those few who have been touched by their sacred notes.

Then there are songs that resonate for eternity, songs that grant those who listen a glimpse of the mysteries of the world, that make the heart shudder as if for the first time in an age.

On a bright, midsummer night, when Selene cast her silver light over the length and breadth of the land of Boeotia, just such a song began, so strong and beauty-filled, that its notes reached the halls of Olympus itself.

It was then that the Gods took notice and knew that

something momentous was about to happen, and so they turned their timeless eyes to the eastern slopes of high Helicon, where the boar and bear roam, to peer into the lush, silver-green of a valley.

A song was about to begin...

"COME, SISTER!" said Clio as she and Euterpe supported Calliope between them. "We are almost at the spring. There, you can endure your labour."

Calliope cried out, the pain too great to bear, too much for her immortal legs to carry her. Sweat poured from her brow, matting her dark hair to her skin. She felt another tremor of pain beginning deep within and braced herself for its peak. When it came, her voice shattered the night, sending owls screeching from their nocturnal perches.

Erato, Melpomene, Polyhymnia, Terpsichore, Thalia and Urania walked in a circle about the three, their torches casting a protective light as they made their way along the rock and dirt path beneath the boughs of pine and cypress to the spring.

"There it is!" Erato called out, rushing ahead so that the others could follow her light. "The spring of Hippocrene!"

Clio and Euterpe went forward to a mossy bed about the base of a nearby oak tree and set their sister down upon it.

Calliope's breaths were quick and measured, but the pain was becoming unbearable, and she cried out again.

"Where is your husband?" Melpomene asked. "Where is King Oeagrus?"

Calliope shook her head. "He is not near. He is fighting."

"He is always fighting!" Clio said angrily as she pressed a

cup to Calliope's lips. "Here. Drink of the spring. It will soothe your labour."

Calliope drank and felt reserves of strength within opened up. Then another pain racked her body and her sky-blue eyes shot wide. "Ahhh!"

The cries travelled up the mountainside such that they would have cracked the sapling bodies of green trees.

With tears for her sister's pain running in rivulets from her star-searching eyes, Urania stepped into the moonlight where it painted the soft grass, and raised her hands.

"Oh, venerable Eileithyia, we call upon you, sister of the Fates. Come to us here that you may bring relief to our sister in labour's dreadful hour..." Urania closed her eyes, her thoughts and words reaching up into the heavens, and when she felt the rustling of the wind in her hair, she opened them to see the goddess before her. "Thank you."

Eileithyia smiled and nodded and her keen, dark eyes looked beyond Urania to where Calliope lay beneath the oak, braced against its sturdy trunk, her sweaty peplos hoisted about her knees.

"There, there now," Eileithyia soothed, her voice calm like the surface of the sea on a summer morning. "I am here now, and just as I helped bring Bright-Eyed Athena into this world, so too shall I help your child." The goddess closed her eyes and placed her hands upon Calliope's swollen belly, and by her very touch, it was as if both mother and child relaxed, the pain subsiding like the waves of a crashing tide pulling back out to the deep.

The other muses looked on as the goddess went to work, placing her hands upon Calliope, her own breathing guiding her, setting the rhythm needed for birthing. "Prepare now," she said, allowing Calliope to brace herself against her.

"Ahhh!" Calliope cried out, tears falling from her eyes. "My lord!" she called out desperately.

It was then that the wind picked up, cool against her sweaty skin, and from out of the dark, wooded slopes, Far-Shooting Apollo came running, his cloak billowing behind him as he dropped his bow and fell to his knees beside Calliope and Eileithyia.

The muses bowed at his coming, but he had eyes only for Calliope whose hand he grasped and kissed.

"I am here," he said to her, ignoring the goddess beside him who had not deigned to aid his own mother in her painful labour. "Look at me," he commanded, and Calliope gazed into his star-whirling eyes. "Your son is here. His song is about to begin. You have seen this moment."

Calliope nodded, her breathing steadying.

"It is time," Eileithyia said, her voice tender as she helped the muse to position herself. "You must push... Now!"

Calliope held Apollo's gaze as she pushed, once...twice...three times...until, at last, the cries of the child pierced the night air.

With water from the sacred spring, Eileithyia rinsed the child and swaddled him in Apollo's blue cloak. She turned to Calliope who lay exhausted against the body of the oak. "Your son, oh Mousa. He is beautiful and healthy."

Calliope reached out to accept her child into her arms, and in doing so she felt her pain dwindle as though it were a fleeting memory. Her heart beat as her child rested upon her breast, his crying subsided. "Welcome, my son." She looked up at Apollo.

The god knelt beside her and smiled. "He is beautiful," Apollo said as he looked upon the child and stroked Calliope's hair and cheek.

The other muses gathered around to gaze upon their sister's son, and as they did so, their voices were raised in song, and that song spread from the sacred spring, through the trees, and up the mountain slopes to break free of the valley into the sky where Dawn was only just beginning to paint it with shades of rose, blue and fiery orange.

Eileithyia saw to it that the child suckled at his divine mother's breast, and then stood to wash her hands in a broad wooden bowl of the sacred water.

"Thank you for coming to her, Goddess," Urania said to Eileithyia. "She was in great pain."

Eileithyia smiled, but in her eyes there was something of sadness. "I bring relief from pain." She put her hand to Urania's cheek. "It is the lot of my own sisters, the Morai, to bring pain." She glanced at Calliope and her son. "But they were not here," she added. "Not yet." The goddess bowed politely to the muse, and then turned to leave, to disappear into the darkness of the wood beyond where the morning light had not yet presented itself.

Apollo stepped to Urania's side to watch her leave, and with a final glance back at the Far-Shooter, Eileithyia was gone.

Apollo lingered with the Muses there, at Hippocrene, for some days. They were days of music and song and peace. They were days of hope, such that Apollo believed the child, by his very presence, cast a spell over the world, soothed all of their toils and worries. Even the child's wailing did not strike the plaintive notes that so often burst from newborn's mouths.

And the child's eyes... He had his mother's eyes, radiant

like the bluest skies on a clear summer day. But there was more, for in them there was a sense of deepest feeling.

As Calliope suckled her child in the shade of the broad oak, she could not help but gaze into those eyes and smile, and so it was for all of her sisters who danced and sang and played upon the reed flute from dawn until dusk. As she looked upon her son, Calliope could see that with every note, every beautiful word her sisters uttered, he paused and took notice. "You shall be a wonder, my son," she whispered to him, kissing the crown of his dark head.

Other creatures were drawn to that place too, but not to cool themselves at the spring created by Pegasus himself. No. Through the glade, birds and beasts passed in a constant procession - deer and wide-antlered stags, wolves and bears, glistening serpents and broad-winged eagles - they all passed through as though to glimpse the child, drawn by the song that had begun there.

The centaur, Cheiron, also came from the slopes of Pelion to gaze upon the child he had heard whispers of in the distant woods of Thessaly. "If ever you wish to send him to me for training, lady, I will welcome him and care for him," the centaur said to Calliope.

"I thank you," Calliope responded, though in her heart she knew that her son was destined for other things.

When the centaur departed the glade, and night began to descend upon them once more, a gentle glow crept in through the darkening trees. It became brighter and brighter, until the lithe form of the Huntress appeared, her golden bow slung over her shoulder.

Apollo stood and went to her. "Sister...you have come."

"Yes," Artemis smiled, her brilliant, grey eyes taking in the child in Calliope's arms. She laid her hand upon her brother's shoulder as she passed and went directly to Calliope. "How are you?" she asked the muse.

"I am well. Eileithyia came to ease my pains."

"I know." The goddess knelt upon her bare knees beneath the hem of her chiton, and reached out to touch the child's brow. "Such beauty...and kindness. He is gentle and full of feeling."

"He is," Calliope said, smiling.

"This world will be harsh with him," Artemis said, and her words silenced the other muses about the glade. The goddess looked up at her brother. "He must be armed in other ways."

Calliope clasped her son to her breast and kissed his soft head.

"He will be, Sister," Apollo answered, his eyes filled with the sight of the child and his mother. "I will make sure of it."

"I do not see your husband," Artemis said, looking around as the music and song began again as the fires were lit. "Why do you remain with Oeagrus? He is unworthy of you."

Calliope sighed. "I care not for him, it is true. And I am glad he is not here." She looked up at Apollo again, and Artemis noted this.

"And have you seen Oeagrus' other son, the satyr Marsyas?" Artemis turned to her brother.

"I have not," Apollo answered. "Why do you ask?"

"He has been roaming the Phrygian and Thracian plains, playing upon the aulos and lyre, telling all that he far surpasses you in skill and beauty of notes. He claims he will challenge you."

Apollo's eyes darkened as if the stars in them were eclipsed by far-reaching shadows, but when he looked upon the babe in Calliope's arms, his anger faded. "Marsyas' time will come, and his hubris will be stripped. For now...let us have music and beauty."

"Will you play for us, Lord?" Erato asked, and the muses gathered around to stand shoulder to shoulder with the Huntress.

Apollo looked to Calliope and she smiled up at him. "Bless him with your song, Lord," she said, smiling brightly.

The great cythara appeared then in Apollo's muscled arms and he sat upon a nearby rock to play for them all as they sat in a circle before him. With the god-made instrument resting upon his lap, Apollo's fingers plucked gently at the strings.

The night was then filled with such music that the stars grew brighter in the heavens, the winds grew still, and any mortal or beast who was nearby felt rested and calm.

Polymnia raised her voice in soft accompaniment, followed by Erato and the others until a chorus of life and love resonated in the middle of that sacred place.

And as Apollo played, his notes casting an intricate and invisible web over them, as the Muses sang, the child in Calliope's arms opened his eyes wide, taking in every note and feeling of joy and sadness, love and loss.

All the feeling of the world filled the child and fed his psyche, his limbs, and informed his destiny such as it was and would be.

When Apollo's song had finished, and the Muses' voices subsided beneath a starry firmament, the child slept fitfully in the warm embrace of that eternal music.

"Have you decided upon a name for him, Sister?" Clio asked, wiping the joyous tears from her cheek.

Calliope smiled as she looked upon her sleeping son. "I have," she said as she brushed his cheek with a lithe finger. "I will name him Orpheus."

2

THE GIFT

Music and song, and the ways of grace and creation became a part of the life of that child as he grew up among the Muses in and around the forests and fields, and crashing seaside near Pieria, in the shadow of Olympus.

He was Calliope's son, and she doted on him, taught him all that she knew of the secrets of art and creation, but he was, in truth, adopted by every Muse who had been present at Helicon on the night of his birth. All nine of those goddesses had a hand in raising the child, of teaching him the secrets of their arts. Their hearts were bound to him, and he to them, and the forests, hills, and plains echoed with the joys of that sacred pact.

Orpheus, however, stood apart from the world of men, lost in song and thought, and words to make one forget the pain of the world. As he grew and clung to independence, he had a thirst for roaming that led him along the darkening paths where wolves and centaurs roamed, and where satyrs and nymphs danced by midnight fires in forest glades. All that he saw informed his songs, and his voice could be heard echoing up the slopes of Olympus to delight the Gods.

The Muses spotted his dark head of hair often, along streams and mountain paths, and knew that he was creating with every step, that they needed to let him be, and grow. They knew that he would always return to Pieria, his brilliant, sky-blue eyes gracing the threshold of their dwelling, a smile broad upon his face as he sang for them all that he had seen.

He brought joy to the Muses, as did they to him, but for all that sun and bursting colour of creation, there was a long dark line that cut invisibly across the joy in their midst.

And Urania could see it.

The words which Eileithyia had uttered to her, after Orpheus had come into the world, had continued to haunt her with the passage of time. Every night, as the Chariot of the Sun fell into the West, she walked the forest pathways, up the slopes of Olympus, until she could clearly see the night sky and the eternal fires there lit. She hoped to see a change among the stars, to spot the erasure of that dark line she knew was there, but she was ever disappointed. It worried her.

"My Lord," she said one night when her worries reached a crescendo. "I must speak with you."

A moment later, Apollo's light erupted in the darkness behind her and he stepped to her side. "I am here," he said.

Urania turned to him. "I feel the encroachment of time, Lord. I remember the words Eileithyia spoke to me."

Apollo looked to the heavens where the stars' faces were reflected in his immortal eyes. He nodded sadly. "I can still remember her departing. There was much in her gaze."

"Then you know. Orpheus will face trials worse that many in the time to come."

Apollo closed his eyes and clenched his firsts. "Yes."

"The Morai are not kind, Lord."

"No. They are not." Apollo looked at Urania. "What are you trying to say to me?"

"You must arm Orpheus now, before the shadow envelopes him completely."

"He is not meant to swing a sword or cast a spear."

Urania shook her head and looked back at the sky as if seeing something in the time to come. "Not mortal weapons." She turned back to Apollo. "Give him a gift to help him overcome the greatest obstacles. I fear he will need it soon."

Together they looked at the firmament again.

"It will be done," Apollo said, and his voice echoed among the trunks of the forest pine below them.

FAR-SHOOTING APOLLO COULD FEEL that something was coming for Orpheus, but whether such a momentous event would bring joy or pain, was hidden even to his far-seeing eyes.

Even the Gods tread an unknown path... he told himself, and it was then that the thought came to him, made him smile. He travelled to the edge of the sea and there called for Poseidon.

The sea began to bubble, and the shore to shake, and after a time, the Lord of the Deep emerged from the foaming waves to stand before his nephew.

"Lord Poseidon," Apollo said, inclining his head.

"Nephew," Poseidon replied, the waves crashing more

furiously about their feet so as to mask their speech from mortal ears. "Why do you call to me?"

"I need something from the deep. Something no one has ever seen or heard…"

MIDSUMMER HAD COME AROUND ONCE AGAIN, and Pieria echoed with the sounds of celebration. Music and poetry were sung and spoken around every fire, and wine was poured for the Gods in even the most humble of dwellings. In the deep woods, frenzied Bacchae reveled and danced and spun out of control. The centaurs feasted beneath the stars, noting their fleeting pattern in the night sky.

Even on Olympus, the Gods celebrated Helios' long day of arcing sunfire, the corridors of Olympus lit by golden light where Apollo played the cythara for his fellow Olympians. Great craters of nectar and ambrosia had been set out and the smoke of many millions of offerings wove a welcoming spell about those halls rarely beheld by mortal eyes.

When he had finished, Apollo walked to the edge of a gilded balustrade to look over the edge of the Gods' world. He gazed down the long pathways of Olympus to Pieria where he could see the Muses gathered about a great fire, garlands of summer flowers in their hair, dancing and singing, and reciting their sacred words to the starry night.

When Orpheus stepped into their midst to recite in the sacred meter, his sky blue eyes seemed to look up beyond the rocky peaks of Olympus, and the words of his Orphic poem began with an utterance of Apollo's name.

As the god listened, he thought that never had he heard such words cast from a mortal's lips, such beauty and thought.

Now is the time, Apollo thought, and he turned to depart the palace of the Gods and join the daughters of Zeus where they sat rapt by their young apprentice.

ORPHEUS COULD FEEL the heat of the fires upon his face as he stood in the Muses' midst, their eyes fixed upon him, their smiles soft and full of care, and not a little pride. It was as if he stood in the midst of the most heavenly of constellations, as if he felt their music flow from them into him so that he could render into song and word what could not be translated.

He invoked Far-Shooting Apollo, the lord of them all, and then the first words came to him, from beyond that inner veil through which he was able to reach whenever he chose.

The words astonished the night. Orpheus sang of the beauty of the world in a time before even the Gods' tread the pathways of the Earth. Of a time before pain and suffering, when the very stars had their own songs which could be heard.

The Muses wept to hear of this time that was out of reach to them all. They travelled with Orpheus among the lush gardens of creation reaching out to touch what no longer existed, taste the indescribable, and see unimaginable colours that had long ago faded into the passage of time.

And through Orpheus' voice and words, this was all possible.

When he finished, there was silence. The Muses stared at him and the fire before them, their cheeks glistening with tears.

Calliope rose from her seat and went to her son. "You are a blessing to this Earth. I never thought to hear such...such feeling...such prying sight in time..." She hugged him and placed a crown of olive and myrtle upon his dark head.

There was a flash of light then, a brilliance to drown out the great night fire before them. The garlands about the grove trembled where they hung, and seemed to brighten, and as the Muses looked up, there they saw Apollo standing beyond the circle of firelight.

He stepped forward into their midst, and they bowed to him as he approached, his hand reaching out to each of them. "Please...rise, oh wondrous daughters of Zeus. Stand with me so that we might honour Orpheus for the beauty he has brought into this world."

Calliope smiled at Apollo and turned to her son.

"My lord," Orpheus said, bowing low, his crimson and gold chiton glimmering in the firelight.

"Your music delights even in the halls of Olympus, Orpheus. I think all of us..." here he looked about the circle of the Muses, "...know in our hearts that you have skills unlike any other. But this does not tip the scales of our emotions toward anger or jealousy. No." Apollo smiled. "We are, all of us, proud of you."

"We are," Erato added, brushing aside a strand of her hair.

"So proud," Thalia echoed.

"You constantly touch us all with your words, Orpheus," Terpsichore added.

Apollo stepped forward then so that he looked down into Orpheus' eyes of blazing blue. "But you have more to learn."

"My lord?" Orpheus said, holding fast to his joy rather than the emergent pang of worry.

But Apollo smiled. "To that end, I have a gift for you." Far-

Shooting Apollo then held out his arms and in a flash of light, a silk-covered form appeared.

"What is it?" Orpheus asked as the Muses gathered around.

"It is your method, your implement of creation. It is your sword and shield in this world...and the next. It is your legacy, though you do not yet know it." The silence was deep in the night then as the Muses looked upon the shrouded gift, while beasts, Nymphs and Satyrs gazed from the shadows to catch a glimpse of the Olympian. "Take it," Apollo commanded, the anticipation sounding in his divine voice.

Orpheus' vision narrowed so that all he saw was the gift in the god's arms before him, and he felt that in the unveiling of that gift, a new, even more wondrous world would present itself to him. He reached out with a trembling hand to pull back the silk, and there he beheld a lyre the likes of which he had never seen. "For me, Lord?" Orpheus looked up and in Apollo's eyes he could see great love and care, that it was the sincerest of gifts from god to man.

"Yes, my boy," Apollo said, smiling over Orpheus' garlanded crown at Lovely-Voiced Calliope. "Take it."

Orpheus reached out and accepted the lyre. It was far lighter than it appeared, but sturdy. He had never seen anything like it, and nor had any of the Muses. "It is pure beauty," Orpheus said, looking up briefly before running his hand gently over the entirety of the instrument.

The soundbox and tailpiece of the lyre appeared to be a tortoise shell, but it was unlike any previously seen by man or god. It was made of the shell of a great sea turtle, but the hexagonal pattern of it shimmered with myriad colours, as if it reflected all the colours of the worlds of both man and gods. The shell lent a life force to the lyre itself. From the bridge, seven golden strings were as the veins through which that life force flowed upward to the tuning bulge and crossbar of polished bronze and adamant pegs that would never fail to hold their intended notes. On the sides, the lyre's curving arms were fashioned of carved olive wood with delicate laurel leaves in relief upon their surface which Orpheus' fingertips traced in awe.

It was no mean reed pipe which Orpheus held then. It was his destiny, and he knew it.

"It is beautiful, Lord," Calliope said as she stood beside Apollo, looking at her son and the gratitude upon his young face. "I've never seen its like."

"No one has," Apollo said, kneeling beside Orpheus. "The shell is from the deepest, most remote parts of Poseidon's realm," he whispered. "It will resonate with the sounds of the deep so that your music will be heard everywhere. The strings and tuning pegs were fashioned by Hephaestus. They will never break or fail."

"And the wood?" Orpheus asked, his fingers caressing the lyre's arms gently, exploring the instrument he knew then he would never relinquish and which he was bound to.

Apollo smiled. "The wood is from my sacred olive groves in the valley at the foot of Parnassus."

"Thank you, Lord," Orpheus said, tears in his eyes as he held the gift. "I don't know what to say...I..."

"Say nothing," Apollo said. "Learn to play this, and you shall be well-armed for all that this life presents you. Let it be your light in the dark, and a light for all others."

In that moment, Calliope felt an unfamiliar chill in her body, but Apollo's eyes turned their starry stare upon her, willing her to be silent just then.

"Play for us, Orpheus," Erato said, holding her own small lyre in her hands.

Orpheus sat upon a stone, and positioned himself with the lyre upon the right side of his lap. He slid the hand-strap over his left hand, and the fingers of his right hand hovered in anticipation over the seven golden strings.

He then plucked the strings.

It was gentle at first, hesitant, but with each newly-struck note, Orpheus grew more confident. Though the melody he played lacked structure, it was filled with the emotion of one who sets his eyes upon an entirely foreign and beautiful world for the first time. His mind darted this way and that, up and down the scale. He struck notes that had never before been heard and as he did so, the Muses' eyes widened at what they heard.

The soundbox of that magical beast from Poseidon's realm resonated so deeply that it felt at times that one was beneath the waves, the echoes of those limitless pathways of mystery and darkness rising to the surface before fading out. The shell's colours changed with the music from the deepest crimson and indigo to the brightest of yellows and pinks.

Calliope said something to her son as he played, but he did not hear her, for he was lost in the world he now explored for the first time, unaware of the teary awe upon the Muses' lovely features.

Apollo too felt that this was something even beyond him, that he had been a mere player in the destiny that now took shape before him, though that destiny was in its infancy. The music enveloped him, and he felt the scars of his past toils melt away.

Not even in the deepest halls and most beautiful gardens of Olympus has such music ever been heard.

He would have wept then for the beauty of the grace that hovered about his ears, but then he saw what was happening in the world around their circle of creative fire.

They were surrounded by birds and beasts who had come out of the midsummer shadows to listen, drawn to the haunting echoes of what they heard. Here and there, great boulders hovered above the earth, and the trees themselves leaned in to be that much closer.

Apollo looked up, and in that moment, it seemed that the very stars in the heavens were closer and brighter than ever they had been. *What is happening?* he wondered. He looked to Orpheus, whose eyes were now closed, his fingers going faster, playing more urgently as if he were a storm-tossed ship carried away upon the sea.

The trees began to rustle wildly, and the earth to shake.

Calliope gripped Apollo's arm and the Far-Shooter then reached out to Orpheus.

"Stop!" Apollo commanded, his hand upon the young man's shoulder.

Orpheus' eyes shot wide open to see the trees and earth shaking, the birds and beasts taking flight, and his fingers stopped immediately. The strings continued to resonate until at last he laid his fingers gently upon them to mute their sound. He was breathing heavily, his heart pounding wildly out of tune until Calliope placed her hands upon him.

When calm returned to Orpheus, and the birds and beasts retreated back into the darkness of the wooded valley, he looked up at Apollo and the Muses, exhilaration and confusion dancing in his eyes. He looked at the shifted boulders and broken tree limbs upon the ground. "Forgive me," he muttered.

But Apollo stood before him. "Forgive you?" The god

smiled and shook his head. "There is nothing to forgive, Orpheus. We have never heard or seen anything the like, and you only just took up this instrument." He knelt before Orpheus and put his strong hand aside his head. "It is your destiny to be the keeper of this lyre, the same that its own destiny is to be both a sword and shield of creation. You are bound to each other, it seems. I did not plan this, but so it is. But you must learn to control the music you create. Explore slowly, and fully so that you are the only one who knows the pathways of that realm and then, only then, will you be able to fully depict in sound all that you see, all that you feel for the rest of the world."

Orpheus stood, the lyre cradled in his arms. He looked about at the Muses, those who had taught him to sing and feel and create and appreciate beauty, and he saw a change in how they looked upon him. They were at a distance now, awe-struck, almost reverent.

It saddened him not a little, and Calliope noticed this.

"Orpheus," his mother began, but he pulled away.

"I...I must be alone...for now," he said. He then turned to Apollo. "Thank you for this mighty gift, Lord. With all of my heart, thank you!"

With those parting words, Orpheus turned and ran into the wood.

"Let him go," Apollo said as Clio and Euterpe made to run after him. "He must be alone now. It is time."

ORPHEUS ROAMED the wilderness far and wide after that, absorbing the world about him, every sound, sight, and smell, every colour and texture. His music was imbued with all of it. In those first weeks, he played that gift of Apollo's until his fingers bled, until the instrument and he were one, both entangled in a magical symbiosis that not even the Gods themselves could have contrived.

He wandered across the plains of Thessaly to the mountains of Macedonia and Thrace. He played by the seaside at Chalkidiki where the land jutted out into the turquoise sea, and he whispered melodies to the shuddering oak at Dodona, where Zeus listened to the unearthly music made by his grandson. Wherever he went, Orpheus found that he could tame great flocks of birds, and quieten the most feral of beasts. Those parts of the earth - rocks, rivers and trees - that should not have moved of their own accord became animate when his music wound round them. He even tamed the roiling waves of the sea when he played upon a pebbled shore, and as such he became a friend of sailors who braved Poseidon's deep.

His greatest skill, however, was not in swaying the emotions of the Gods, which he did often without intending too. It was among mortals where Orpheus' music effected great change. Once the notes of his lyre, so skillfully plucked, were heard by human ears, they could not forget such music and grace. The notes that erupted from his lyre weaved a deep spell, something that spoke soothingly to the lost and longing child in everyone. Battle-hardened warriors, who lived by the sword and spear and who regularly bathed in the blood of their enemies, set aside their weapons.

When the armies of Thessaly and Thrace came together upon the dancing floor of Ares, Orpheus, from a rocky perch overlooking the place of battle, played for some time and it was as if the Gods had whispered in the ears of every man there. Warriors who had been ready to kill or die, were convinced of the folly of their actions. The kings there present exchanged gifts, and turned their chariots homeward, their men in tow, singing as they went.

Thieves and murderers found trades and turned to helping others. Mothers covered their children in kisses, and wives made it so that Estia's fire burned brightly in every home. Wherever Orpheus went, young men and women, upon hearing the music that flowed through the land, saw the potential of their lives, ways in which their future toils could be bearable, indeed ways in which their lives could be joyous.

Once immortals and mortals heard the music, they could not forget it. Nor did they wish to. They clung to Orpheus' melodies like their most fervent dreams, for he showed them a world which could be better than they ever imagined.

AFTER SOME YEARS, ORPHEUS' path led him back to the place where he had come into the world. Walking slowly through the land of Locris, and down into Boeotia, the long slopes of Mount Helicon came into view, and in seeing that place again, he felt as if he were finishing the first part of a wondrous song. As he approached the spring of Hippocrene and the moss and ivy-clad glade about it, a sadness came over him and his fingers were, for the briefest of moments, still above the golden strings of his lyre.

He set it down, and bent to drink from the spring. He splashed his face, neck, and hair and sat upon the ground, against the very oak that had seen his coming into the world.

The feelings of return he experienced in that place chased him, danced in his mind, and once more he took up his lyre to play them out, to follow their lead. As he did so, he could see the stars turning quickly in the heavens. Day passed into night. Cries of pain and joy echoed in that place. He saw the Muses standing about his mother, and caught fleeting glimpses of purest joy upon all of their faces. There was no sign of the Thracian king who had begot him, but Apollo was there in their midst, and the thought filled Orpheus' music then with deep gratitude.

"You create beauty unlike any other, Orpheus," a voice said from the trees upon the gently rising slope of Helicon.

Orpheus' playing slowed, and he looked up to see Apollo emerging from the forest, a bright light in the receding darkness. He bowed to the Far-Shooter, notes of that same gratitude rising up and around them.

Apollo smiled, his immortal, star-whirling eyes wide and glassy as a sacred pool. "Your skills have improved beyond imagining."

Orpheus smiled, purest joy upon his features then. "I will forever be grateful to you, Lord. For in giving me this gift, you have given me entire worlds to see and feel."

"In giving you this lyre, I have created beauty in the world."

Orpheus looked around the glade. "Is my mother not with you, Lord?"

"She is not. She has gone to Thrace and her husband, Oeagrus, to convince him to dissuade his son, the satyr Marsyas, from speaking ill of me and the daughters of Zeus."

"What does he say?"

"He spreads lies throughout the land that the music I create is nothing as to the notes that flow from his aulos."

Orpheus looked up at the sky and then back at Apollo. "Lord, I think that nothing upon the Earth could sound as sweetly as the music you give us all."

Apollo smiled sadly. "Marsyas' time will come...but you are wrong in what you say, Orpheus."

"How so, Lord?"

Apollo looked at Orpheus and was struck with wonder that there was no sign of hubris there, that he had never even given thought to the possibility that he was the best musician among gods, men and beasts.

Orpheus was immersed in his music, and that gave him a purity that was as rare as the glowing shell of the lyre he cradled in his lap.

Apollo felt joy then, and he took out his own cythara. "Let us play a game, you and I."

"What sort of game, Lord?" Orpheus asked, sitting up then as Apollo settled himself upon a nearby boulder which, as he touched it, became covered in soft, gleaming moss.

"We shall take it in turns to name a feeling or emotion, and then each of us shall play that emotion to the best of his ability. Do you understand?"

"Yes, Lord."

"I will play first," Apollo said, settling his cythara upon his knee, his fingers hovering over the strings. "Choose."

"Exhilaration," Orpheus said.

Apollo closed his eyes and, as a quickly as lighting strikes, his fingers began to dance across the strings, shivering the trees about them.

Orpheus felt the quick rise of the notes and the sustained, dramatic tones filled him. In a moment, he was running at full speed across summer fields with the sun on his face, riding toward a cool mountain stream where he splashed and played. He could feel the droplets of water upon his face, icy cold in the light of Helios' wake. His heartbeat danced and pounded and then, the music stopped.

Apollo smiled. "Now it is your turn. Exhilaration. Play it for me."

Orpheus closed his eyes, his fingers plucking mutely before they touched the golden strings and then the notes struck out.

Apollo felt himself swept away from that quiet glade at dusk, an inkling of excitement in the air, building slowly, and then its pace quickening until the Earth fell away and he found himself among the stars, clinging to a comet racing across the heavens at such a speed as he could not have imagined. The Earth turned round and the fleeting passage of all life joined in sight and song in the matter of a few moments before the notes dwindled, not suddenly, but with ease, allowing him to catch his breath and settle fitfully upon the mossy rock which he had in fact never left.

The god opened his eyes and looked upon Orpheus. "I have not the words to describe it."

"Words are not always suited, are they, Lord?"

"No. They are not." Apollo smiled again. "Now, I shall name a feeling... Peace."

Apollo set his fingers to his cythara and began.

At once, Orpheus felt a stillness within, born of those first few notes, and he found himself alone at the banks of a mountain stream with steep, tree-clad slopes to either side. It was neither too hot nor too cold. Birds sang in the trees all around, and bees flitted from flower to flower. The leaves in the trees rustled, their whispers soft in the ears, accompanied by the swaying of pampas grasses. It was a pastoral idyll in which all melded together in perfect harmony to create the peace that all men dream of but almost never achieve. Orpheus felt he could linger there forever, and then, the music stopped and he opened his eyes slowly.

"Peace," Apollo said softly.

Orpheus began to play...

Immediately, Apollo's eyes were filled with a brilliance of stars. The stars rose up before him, his eyes drawn downward to Earth and an endless, grassy plain. The simplicity of that place was perfection, the tone, the colour, the perfect speed of the wind as it ran over the skin and rustled the hair. It was a peace in which Apollo himself found that his immortal mind, despite all the horrors he had seen over the ages, the conflicts and wars with Titans and Giants, the pain, could all be set aside as he willed it. His immortal thoughts could be stilled as he wished, to sway as gently as the infinite grass about him, un-phased by the wind. And he found he could linger in that peace, that sweet nothingness, and come out of it feeling more calm and strong than ever he had thought possible.

"Oh, for such a world as that, Orpheus," Apollo said, wiping a tear from his cheek. "We know not the burden we carry until we set it down."

They continued long into the night, the slopes of Helicon witness to such music as had never existed before then. They played to turmoil and war too. Then their notes enlivened beginnings and endings, family pride, and the beauty of hearth and home. There was victory and defeat, and the greatest awe of the world too as the man and god played for each other. And every time Orpheus finished, Apollo grew more and more certain that he had, at last, been outdone.

And it pleased him greatly.

"Now, Orpheus," Apollo said. "One last emotion. Perhaps the greatest."

"Yes, Lord?" Orpheus replied, an excited smile upon his face.

"Play true love for me."

"Shall I play to the image of divine Aphrodite?" Orpheus asked.

"No. True...Love..." Apollo repeated, but as he spoke the words, he was saddened to see Orpheus' smile fade.

His fingers hovered uncertainly over the strings. "I...I know not, Lord." His heart began to pound wildly. There was panic in his uncertainty. "I cannot."

Apollo played calmly for Orpheus then, and the panic subsided like a summer storm that passes quickly overhead, leaving the world fresh and brilliant afterward.

"Will you play it for me, Lord?" Orpheus pleaded.

Apollo shook his head. "Not that. Such love, true love, you must feel on your own in time."

"You have shown me much, Lord," Orpheus said. "The victory is yours." And he smiled, that wonder-filled mortal.

Apollo stood to look at the rising sun where Helios' chariot arced in the pale blue sky above.

"Orpheus..." he said, turning to the young man. "When you play, the victory is everyone's."

3

THE BIRTH OF LOVE

Orpheus left the slopes of Helicon behind, but he carried with him Apollo's words, and so he continued to play across the land, to learn more. He observed the world about him, and though he did not know the truest of love, he was not so naive as to think he could go searching for it. If anything, all that the Muses had taught him, the songs they had sung, made him realize that such love was elusive, that it was folly to search for something few mortals were ever granted.

He travelled from the mountains of Epirus, across Thessaly and then over mountainous Macedonia and into Thrace, and all the while he played and sang and brought solace to all living things. He was welcomed for a time among the warrior tribes of the Thracians who allowed him to roam freely from the sea in the South, across the forests, river valleys, and plains, and into the mountainous North.

The peace of that land was something that Orpheus enjoyed beyond measure, the wild beauty exploding with colour and life the likes of which he had not seen elsewhere.

Herds of centaurs raced along the riverbanks to hear him play, and gryphons and myriad birds of prey left the pine-scented heights of the Dadia forest to circle above the spot where Orpheus played.

Wherever land had been ravaged by the fires of summer, there Orpheus played and healed it. Wherever crops failed or were blighted, he helped them to grow. And during the winter, when the snows blew wild and the people grew cold and hungry, there Orpheus' music warmed their hearts and hearths and helped them to get through the long winter months.

When Spring arrived at last, Orpheus wandered into the wilds once more to be alone, and to explore what he had learned among the Thracian families of that long winter, of family and loyalty, of courage and hope. He breathed deeply of the freshness of that Spring air as he walked. His path led him to the smokey valleys in the North where he followed a river in amongst the silent trunks of black, sentry pines. His song joined those of the ranging stags and wolves, and the playful rush and trickle of water over falls and rocks.

He finally stopped in the middle of that lush green world where the trees rose high and bright and the sun cast dappled shapes onto the mossy earth through the leaves of the surrounding oaks. In that angled sunlight, Orpheus laid himself down to rest for a while, his lyre beside him, the light emanating from it as muted and still as he.

THE WAYS of the Morai are impossible to understand, for what causes one to be in a certain place at a particular moment in time? Why should Orpheus, now famed throughout all the lands of the South, find himself in that lonely wood far to the North, alone beside that rocky riverbank?

Although, he was never alone. Not really. For as he slept, animals approached to surround him in his sleep, to doze fitfully near the source of the peace they unknowingly felt. They were drawn to him as to the warmth of the winter dens, or to the hidden places where they need not have feared the hunter's spear or bow.

Beyond that ring of wildlife, others came too. A joyous army of nymphs and satyrs had gathered in the shadowy wood to peer shyly from behind the dark and gnarled trunks of pine and oak at the sleeping man and his lyre.

Among these throngs of fleet-footed deities, was a young and fearless nymph who dared to step closer to the sleeping man, more than any other of her group. She had not heard him play before, as others had. She was drawn by something else, something inexplicable.

Her chiton hiked around her knees, she waded into the gurgling stream, watched by the others still hiding in the wood beyond. She bent to cup water and drink, then ran her wet hands through her long, tousled auburn hair. She looked up from the stream at the sleeping man with the lyre, and there she froze, rooted to the spot.

She felt something strange and sudden. She looked down, panicked, worried that a hunter had shot her, but her chest and stomach were free of blood. Instead, she felt a strange joy begin to weave in and around her mind and body. It pervaded the whole of her being then, and only became more acute when she looked upon the brilliant, dark-haired man sleeping beside that forest stream.

Ignoring the whistles and calls of the nymphs and satyrs

on the other side of the river, she approached Orpheus and knelt beside him.

The wolves, bears and other beasts about them looked upon her as she came close, but merely watched and waited, unafraid of the nymph in their midst.

She leaned close to look upon him, to admire him. She observed the strong line of his jaw and the gentle fall of his black, slightly curling hair about his ears and brow. She watched the rise and fall of his chest as he slept, and observed the long, gentle hands that would pluck the golden strings of the instrument lying beside him.

In her heart, the nymph felt a tightening, and she knew that the Gods were, in some way, speaking to her, telling her she was exactly where she was supposed to be. She felt like weeping and laughing all at once, and as the world about her faded away so that there was only her and the man before her, she spoke softly.

"I *know* you."

The man's eyes shifted beneath their lids and his hand reached to his side for his lyre, but instead, the nymph slid her hand into his, and his brilliant blue eyes opened.

ORPHEUS HAD BEEN DREAMING of playing in the halls of Olympus for the Gods. It was the most peaceful he had ever felt, and when he had finished playing the last, resonant note upon his lyre, the Gods had applauded him and wiped the tears from their eyes.

Aphrodite had come to him, out of the midst of those gathered Olympians, and her smile had been as the first rays of sun in Spring. The goddess had not spoken, but leaned over him and kissed him upon his brow, her sweet breath tickling his skin as she held his face in her soft, lithe hands.

Orpheus' eyes had closed at Love's touch, and when he opened them again, he was met by a brilliance he had never seen or imagined until that very moment.

"I *know* you," a voice said, and it was unlike any music he had heard before.

Beside him knelt the nymph, her auburn hair falling over her shoulder onto his lap, her warm hand clasping his, and her wide, wondrous green eyes looking upon him in a way no one had ever looked upon him.

Orpheus felt his heart pounding in a rhythm to which he was unaccustomed, but which was sweeter than any he had ever heard or played.

He squeezed her hand in return and took her other hand. Words failed for a moment, but as he looked upon her, he felt recognition dawn, strange and inexplicable, and he knew this was the moment all would change. It was the moment in which his songs would change.

"Who are you?" he asked the nymph.

She smiled, and it was a moment he wanted to linger in the rest of his days.

"I am Eurydice," she said, unafraid. "You are Orpheus?"

"Yes. But how do you know me?" he asked, confused.

"The others have been speaking of you." She looked down for a second, then shyly back at him. "The dryads heard you were here, in the wood, and wanted to show me."

Orpheus glanced to the surrounding trees where he saw darting eyes behind the trunks of rough-skinned pines, like little fires in the dim forest light. He would have called to them all, offered to play for them, but all he wanted to do was look at the nymph kneeling beside him on the mossy ground, to hear her voice, and only her voice.

"They are shy of you," she said, smiling a little.

"You are not," Orpheus said.

"No. I..." she reached up to brush the dark hair aside on his brow, "...I feel like I have been waiting to meet you for so very long."

Orpheus felt that new rhythm in his chest, deep and thrumming, like the beginnings of a new song that would forever be a part of him from that moment on, and his eyes were wide with wonder. He had no words to describe it, and it felt strange to attempt to do so to the beautiful creature beside him. They had only just met, and yet he felt with a great certainty that he had known her for ages. There was only one thing he could do to help her understand.

"May I play for you?" he asked.

She nodded, never taking her eyes from his, and leaned back against the tree opposite.

Orpheus turned and picked up his lyre. He positioned himself and admired her for another moment, the way a sculptor gazes upon his subject, his fingers poised over the strings.

Soft, slow notes crept about them, about that forest clearing beside the stream, as Orpheus began to weave a dream that, as he played, he realized was the love of which he had no notion until that very moment in time. He explored the feeling, felt the world of possibilities open up before him as if he had climbed a great mountain only to reach the top of it and see a paradise in the valley below.

As Orpheus played, he and Eurydice stood alone in the midst of that paradise, eyes only for each other. They were the epicentre of all joy in the world, and as the light cast by his otherworldly lyre cast countless shades of light upon their faces, she wept tears of absolute joy.

Music flowed through Eurydice's body, awakening it, enlivening her heart, her very soul, so much so that she wondered if even the Gods themselves felt as much.

Orpheus' music grew more joyous, more lively, as if it were filled with the greatest life-force. It the middle of that paradisiacal field, his fingers danced over the strings as Eurydice danced before him, around him, unable to contain the absolute exultation of her life in that moment.

When Orpheus' fingers slowed again and the explosion of light dimmed, they found themselves once more in the middle of that Thracian wood, surrounded by satyrs and nymphs, birds and beasts who had been drawn to that spot.

But they saw none of them.

Orpheus and Eurydice's eyes were locked, and as he stopped his playing and set the lyre gently upon the ground, they stepped toward each other, their arms entwining, their lips meeting in the gentlest of embraces.

Even though the music had stopped, a brilliance of light shone out from the two of them as they stood there in the middle of that distant forest, a sun upon the Earth itself, radiant, hopeful, and filled with life.

From the edge of a gilded balustrade in the sweet-scented halls of Olympus, Aphrodite gazed down the long corridors of time at Orpheus and Eurydice. She smiled, her golden hair flowing about her like soft grasses in a timeless ocean.

"Such love...," the goddess said to herself, smiling, feeling what the two young lovers felt. "Long may it last."

.   .   .

ORPHEUS' song changed from the day of that meeting. It changed forever, and was filled with a greater sense of hope and joy than ever it had been before, even under the tutelage of the Muses who, even from the slopes of Olympus and Helicon, could hear the changed song from across the sea and mountains.

From that day forward, Orpheus and Eurydice were bound to each other by a force greater than any other. They never left each other's side, but travelled over field and plain, over mountains and across rivers and seas, he playing and she laughing and dancing.

Their mutual joy enlivened the world wherever they ventured, gave a renewal of life to those whose ears chanced to hear that changed music.

It was the beginning of the greatest of songs.

4

OH HYMENAIE!

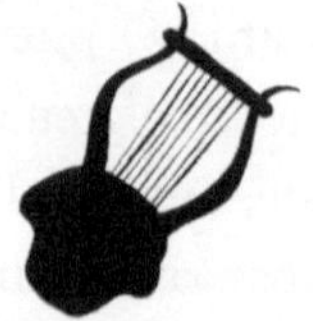

Never apart.

Such was the state for Orpheus and Eurydice who felt the constant warmth and life-force of Love within, burning as brightly as any star. Theirs was a song all its own, benevolent and all-inspiring; it drew others too, the birds and beasts of the world, gods and goddesses who watched with keen, timeless eyes the unfolding of a mystery elusive to them. As for mortals, they too watched, listened, and hoped for such a love.

But not all are fated to live such a life, and those who feel the Morai set against them are filled more with bitterness. Some were jealous of the music Orpheus played, of the love that bound him and Eurydice, the happiness that graced the land wherever they travelled.

It made no matter to the lovers, for they walked in a light that was all their own, a light that outshone wickedness. Wherever they roamed, wherever Orpheus played, crops thrived, people smiled and felt gratitude for their own worlds and lives, and there was a sense of peace not seen since after the great wars of the Gods and Giants.

On a clear night in Spring, on the banks of the river Strymon, in the lands of the Edonians, Orpheus and Eurydice lay in each other's arms beneath a thick blanket.

They gazed up at the broad firmament and saw the stars of Centaurus, Hydra and the Great Bear shifting and dancing in the light-pocked darkness.

Every day since they had met had been a wonder, and it was for moments like that, lived together, that they drew breath. Orpheus held his lyre and played softly to the night sky, and it was as if the stars themselves could hear, their constellations shivering and dancing to the music that rose up from that earthly plane to weave in and among their distant beacons.

Eurydice watched in wonder, her hand resting upon his chest, feeling it rise and fall as he played.

"I never thought to hear such beauty, my love," she said to him when he finished playing, resting her head upon his shoulder.

"And I never thought that such joy as that which I feel now was even possible, in this world or in any other." He turned to look upon her, and the light in his eyes was as the rising of the sun over the sea. He set his lyre down once the final note faded, and knelt in the sand before her. For a moment, his words caught in his throat as he looked upon her. *Gods... Can I be so fortunate that she would love me as much as I love her? I would live at her side and play for her for all eternity...*

"What is it, my love?" Eurydice asked, her hands reaching up to hold him. She observed every part of his face which she loved and which she could not live without.

"Eurydice...I...I love you beyond all things. You are my world, and my truest love and friend. I never thought to know the meaning of that, but when I look upon you, when I hear you, and when I hold you close, by the Gods I feel absolute certainty. You are everything to me, my love. Every breath I draw, every song I play...it is all for you."

Eurydice smiled, but there was one thought that harried her every sense... *Do the Gods permit such joy as this? How can it be that we are allowed such love?* She felt a little fearful then, but in looking upon Orpheus, the light in his eyes that shone directly onto her, she felt the welling of love's courage. "I would fly into the face of the sun if it meant that I could only have one day with you, Orpheus. I never dreamed I could love as I love you...but I do. I love you, Orpheus." She looked up at the night sky. "I love you more than any star or song," she said, tears of purest joy falling from her eyes as she looked back at him. "This world, and everything I see and hear and feel, are all better and brighter because of you and how much I love you."

He kissed her then, their hearts and souls completing the final, invisible and eternal binding, making them one great, life-giving force.

In that moment, on Olympus, Aphrodite smiled and wept to herself, for such was the perfection and the possibility of her domain, of Love's eternal realm. *No god can be jealous of such purity,* she thought.

WHEN SUMMER'S hot breath blew among the mountains and coasts, the time arrived for the joining of Orpheus and Eurydice. A great feast was to take place afterward in the land of Pieria, beneath the soaring slopes of Olympus.

It was a gathering of gods, heroes, and mortals, all of them drawn to that blessed event for the thread of a song that they could not hear, but felt in every fibre of their being, in the land itself. They came as if to gaze upon a wonder of their world and time.

Apollo and the Muses were present as people gathered and filled the valley with boisterous song and speech as they waited to see the lovers bound before Zeus and Hera.

The day passed in a blur of music and colour and smiling faces for Orpheus and Eurydice, but every look and touch that passed between them was as clear as a favourite memory. They would never forget holding each other's hands as they watched the Olympians arrive in procession from their lofty halls, Zeus and Hera at their head, followed by Aphrodite, Athena, Earth-Shaking Poseidon, Golden Hermes, and Swift-Footed Artemis. Ares arrived too, despite his discomfort with the widespread peace, and Hephaestus and Demeter. They all gathered closest to the altar and waited, their brilliance shining out from where they stood as they smiled at the couple.

Eurydice smiled when she saw the throngs of Thracian Dryads come out of the North to watch from the nearby trees, tears in their eyes at the sight of their friend. Cheiron arrived from Mount Pelion with some of the centaurs, and from the shore of the sea came Amphitrite and her Nereids in a procession out of Poseidon's deep, great conch horns heralding their arrival.

The mortal men, women and children who dwelled about the foot of Olympus were inexorably drawn to that place, some because they had the eyes to see what was happening, others because they felt something momentous was about to occur within the light of the brilliant aurora that shone out from that place with the Gods' arrival.

Even King Oeagrus, Sweet-Voiced Calliope's mortal husband, arrived to see Orpheus wed, his warriors in tow, unarmed and ready to feast among the Gods.

"Now, he comes?" Apollo growled beside Calliope.

But the muse held her lord's hand and spoke soft words to him, her lithe hands caressing his cheek. "Today is for Orpheus and Eurydice, Lord. Oeagrus is nothing now, and so he shall always be. But he did order Marsyas to stay away."

Apollo nodded and caught Orpheus' eye. The sight of Orpheus and Eurydice made Apollo smile and forget the willful bitterness that could fill even the heart of an Olympian.

"He is here!" Erato called out and the entire gathering of gods, heroes, beasts and mortals grew silent as a young, beautiful man walked into their midst.

"Hymenaios!" Zeus called out to the young god. "Welcome!"

Hymenaios walked shyly but with purpose among the parted crowd toward the altar where Orpheus and Eurydice stood surrounded by the Gods. He smiled when he saw them, but then he paused before a goddess with a lion, and a young shepherd who stood with her.

"Whom does Hymenaios stare at, Lord?" Orpheus asked Apollo.

Apollo leaned closer to answer. "That is my son, Aristaeus, and his mother, Cyrene. Aristaeus wished to come and meet you, to thank you for all that you have done, for his flocks and bees have thrived like never before as your music has passed over the land. He provided meat and honey for the feasts this night."

Orpheus smiled at that thought, but Apollo did not, for he could see the look that Hymenaios, he who blesses marriages, gave to Aristaeus. It was the only cloud to pass over that great gathering.

Even as Hymenaios turned away from Aristaeus and Cyrene, the cloud departed and light shone on Orpheus and Eurydice who watched him approach.

Hymenaios held aloft his bridal torch of gold which contained a blaze of sunfire, the light that touches all. All eyes were upon him then, for he was as beautiful as any man could be, and more so. His thick hair fell in dark brown waves, and his skin was as pale as any goddess'. He was not muscular like a warrior, but slim and quick as the deer who run the wood with Artemis. In the light of the torch he carried, however, it was Hymenaios' luminescent, grey eyes that drew the onlooker, for they could see much. Where Aphrodite and Eros could see and make a love match among mortals, Hymenaios' could look into the hearts of any man or woman and know the truth of their love and, sometimes, the outcome of that love.

The beautiful god bowed low to the Olympians as he came into their midst and stood before Hera and almighty Zeus.

"Hymenaios," Zeus said, thunder sounding in the great distance. "What do you see? Shall this union proceed?"

Hymenaios turned to Orpheus and Eurydice then, his eyes wide and glossy. He smiled to himself and tears formed about his far-seeing eyes. He nodded slowly. "I bless this marriage, Lord Zeus," Hymenaios said softly. "It will be most joyful!"

Immortals and mortals cheered at that down the length of the valley.

Hymenaios, however, grew severe in countenance, and turned so that only the Gods, Orpheus and Eurydice could hear him. "But every great union, no matter how true, will feel the sting of pain in its lifetime..." He looked directly at the couple where they stood, hands clasped. He could see their hearts were already joined. "Would you give up your love to avoid the pain to come?"

Orpheus and Eurydice held each other's hands tightly at that, but they did not let go. They shook their heads without delay, though they were afraid for the first time.

"I will never give up my love of Eurydice," Orpheus said.

"Nor would I turn my back upon my love for Orpheus," Eurydice said.

"Then give me your hands," Hymenaios said, extending his left palm so that they placed their joined hands upon it. With his right hand, he held the bridal torch beneath so that its flames caressed their joined hands. "May the fire that burns within your hearts burn brightly, and as one, for all time. May it guide you and warm you, and may your love be an example to all who walk this Earth. By the Gods...I bless your union."

Hymenaios withdrew the torch and watched as Orpheus and Eurydice kissed tenderly, the applause from down the slopes of Olympus and into the valley as thunderous and toilsome as though great waves were crashing among them.

"Oh Hymenaie!!!" shouted every God, man, woman, satyr, nymph and centaur who was there.

"I love you, Orpheus," Eurydice said, her heart bursting with a joy that had already overwhelmed the warning they had received.

"And I love you, Eurydice. I will love you forever."

· · ·

THE FESTIVITIES BEGAN in earnest with wine and offerings of food being set upon the Gods' altars far below, and ambrosia and nectar passed among the Olympians.

Music too, and words of such sweetness from the Muses' lips fell down the mountainside to rush among the gathered masses, like clear mountain waters in the springtime, bringing life to all.

The Gods came to present their wishes to Orpheus and Eurydice where they sat at a broad ivory table set with a bounty of food and wine. The couple received the Gods' wishes with gratitude and humility, and this pleased the Olympians, for though they too might have felt the sliver of jealousy, the power of the love between Orpheus and Eurydice was such that all who saw and felt its presence were enriched by it, be they mortal or immortal.

The cries of *Oh Hymenaie!* broke out long into the night and passed the lips of every being there at least once, every being that is, except for Aristaeus, Apollo's son.

Aristaeus, that most skilled hunter and herdsman, the keeper of bees raised by the Horae, and trained by Cheiron himself, sat silent in his cups of wine, watching Orpheus and, mostly, Eurydice. He had indeed come to thank Orpheus for all that his music had achieved, but when he had set eyes upon Eurydice, he quite forgot his purpose in being there.

Though he was respected among gods and men for his skills, he was as a rough presence among the colourfully-clad, brilliant throng, appearing more as one of the beasts he hunted, with his pale, dirty hair, rough beard, and grey piercing eyes so used to searching in the dark woods of the world.

"Why do you stare at her so?" his mother, the goddess Cyrene, said to Aristaeus at one point in the evening. She stood beside him, her hand stroking the head of the lion that never left her side. "She is beautiful," Aristaeus said, turning to his shining mother, the light glinting off of her golden necklace. "I am Apollo's son. Why should I not also have the gift of music, and be blessed with such a love as that?"

"The Morai have different plans," Cyrene said, her voice firm and unyielding. "Not even your father can counter them."

"I help so many, and yet I am ever alone. If only I could-"

"Could what?" the goddess said, cutting off his words. "I know not what is in your mind, but it seems that Hymenaios did, even before you. Whatever it is, leave it. You have your own paths to tread," she turned to look at Orpheus and Eurydice, "and they have theirs."

Aristaeus heard his mother's words, and knew the truth of them. But he could not ignore the thoughts that ran round in his mind like the cycle of the seasons, unstoppable and ongoing. Slowly, he made his way through the mass of celebrants like a hunter through the wood, his eyes ever on the shining place where the Olympians were gathered about Orpheus and Eurydice.

Then, with his great arms raised above all, Zeus stepped forward and turned to the newly-wed couple. "This union pleases us greatly, and we bless you this night."

Orpheus and Eurydice stood from their seats and bowed to Father Zeus.

"I would ask one thing of you on this joyous occasion," Zeus continued.

"Anything, my lord!" Orpheus said.

"Play for us, Orpheus," Zeus commanded with a smile that made even Hera link her arm through his. "Let us hear your joy in this moment that we may remember it always."

"With all my heart, Lord," Orpheus said, taking up his lyre. He kissed Eurydice then and left his seat to stand among the Gods.

Eurydice watched her husband as he stood, a shining light among the Immortals. As she watched and waited, she felt the comfort of the Thracian dryads, her family, as they crowded around her, joyful at her own good fortune at Love's hand.

A silence swept over the entire valley then, and all eyes sought the light from Orpheus' lyre as one searches the night sky for the first twinkling star at dusk.

Orpheus looked upon his wife then, his fingers poised, his face as happy as it had ever been.

He began to play, and immediately, it was as if the sun began to rise, bright and clear in the middle of the darkest night. The notes were soft and heartfelt, the melody telling of a loneliness healed by the truest of loves. It rose slowly and with constancy, filling the heart with warmth as a golden cup is filled with the sweetest wine.

As Orpheus played, all who heard his music saw and felt an inkling of the joys and laughters he had already shared with Eurydice, and it gave them hope for the world, for their lives. Worries and doubts were doused with the beauty of that song, though he did not sing. Words were not needed, nor poetry, for the music was a language all its own, pulling at threads of feeling that had been long-buried by some, until it was all they could think about.

It was not lost on any when Zeus held Hera's hand in his and kissed it as gently as ever he had.

Throughout the performance, Aristaeus watched, but he did not hear. Among so many, he was the only one whose thoughts were on another path, as one who goes against the flow of life itself. He wandered alone through the world.

When Orpheus finished, the Gods applauded him, and Eurydice rushed to her husband's side to kiss him and hold him tightly.

"Oh Hymenaie!" all shouted again.

Erato and Apollo then joined to play lively upon the cythara and lyre and all began to dance as wine and nectar flowed and the firelight blazed in the land of Pieria.

Orpheus watched Eurydice dance with the Dryads, a picture of utter joy, free of worry, and he knew that he had never been so happy in all his life.

"Oh, Hymenaie," a voice said beside him.

Orpheus turned to see Aristaeus beside him, watching the dancing along with him.

"I offer you my congratulations," Aristaeus said.

"Thank you," Orpheus replied turning to look upon the huntsman. "My gratitude for the meat and honey that you provided for the feast."

"My father asked for the best," Aristaeus said. "And so it is." He tore his eyes from Eurydice to stare at Orpheus. "I must thank you."

"For what?" Orpheus asked.

"For..." Aristaeus watched Eurydice, the way she moved, and danced, the way her lustrous hair clung to her sweaty brow. "For the music you play. Never have my crops, herds, or bees thrived as they have since you played over the land."

"I am glad it worked so, though I did not intend it. I play because I am drawn to."

"The Morai have a plan for you then?" Aristaeus asked.

"As they do for us all, I suppose," Orpheus replied,

smiling broadly at Aristaeus. "Though I am grateful that they have smiled upon me and my wife."

At that moment, Eurydice held her hands out to her husband. "Dance with me, my love!" she said.

Orpheus laughed and joined her, leaving Aristaeus behind.

The huntsman watched, and as he watched the Gods laugh and sing and dance about the couple, he saw one who did not.

Hymenaios stood still among the Gods then, staring directly at Aristaeus. The young god's eyes bore into him, accused him, threatened to show him the outcome of his thinking, but before Hymenaios could, Aristaeus tore himself away and melted into the night beyond the celebratory light.

HYMN II

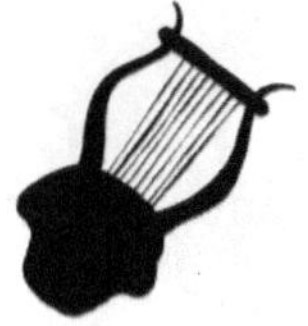

THE DARK HANDS OF FATE

5

THE COVETOUS HERDSMAN

She was the most beautiful creature he had ever seen, and he believed the Gods had finally smiled upon him when he came to the edge of the river only to find her swimming naked. She splashed in the sun-gilt water, laughing like a child, but as he settled in the rushes to watch her, he could tell that she was no girl.

But then she stopped her frolicking and, the water up to her throat, its sparkling surface now still about her, she pressed her hands to her face and wept.

He has hurt her, Aristaeus thought...hoped. *He doesn't deserve her!*

He shifted in the grass as a serpent slithered past him, and Eurydice looked up quickly.

Their eyes locked for a brief moment of pure intensity, and then she smiled.

Such a smile! So beautiful!

Aristaeus thought that he had never felt such elation as he did in that moment.

She motioned that he should come to her in the water.

He paused for a moment, looking about for anyone else who might happen upon them. No one was there but the two of them. Aristaeus stood, removed his chiton and his sandals, and waded through the swaying rushes into the sunlight and water to stand before her.

"I have been thinking of you ever since I laid eyes upon you," he told her.

That smile again.

She was about to step toward him, to touch him in that water that was now sacred to him, but then she stopped abruptly, her head cocked to listen to something.

He stepped toward her, but she stepped back, a hand out for him to wait.

"My love?" she said to the sky and stars beyond the blue expanse of heaven. "You haven't forgotten me?"

She swayed where she was, her eyes closed as if the music were played directly before her, for her and her alone.

"Who are you speaking to?" Aristaeus asked, trying to inch closer and within reach. He listened for what she heard, but all he could hear was the buzz and whirr of summer bees and cicadas in the fields beyond the river.

The river turned black then, and the sky darkened.

Aristaeus felt a rising panic in his chest as the water turned hot, and coiling black shapes churned in the water about them.

"Take my hand, Eurydice!" he yelled, but she would not turn to him, did not even know he was there anymore.

Then, *he* was there. Orpheus. He stood upon the other bank of the river holding his lyre in his left hand, and reaching out to Eurydice with his right so that she could climb out of the blackened river.

Aristaeus charged to grab her, unable to stop himself, but

just as he was about to catch her, his body was thrown skyward so that he soared through the air over the field opposite. He waited for the fall that would break him and then...

ARISTAEUS AWOKE with such a jolt that his head spun and he vomited in the long grass where he had been sleeping against the bole of an oak. Dizzy, he pushed himself onto his knees to try and remember where he was, what had happened.

"Morpheus, why do you torture me?" he growled. He stood and looked around. Before him, he saw the broad Boeotian plain dotted with vineyards, and down the line of trees where he had been sleeping, the orderly rows of bee hives. To the South, he could see the acropolis of Orchomenos, and remembered that the king had invited him to come and help with their vines and apiaries.

He had gone south after the wedding of Orpheus and Eurydice, to work, to try and forget. But Aristaeus had not been able to forget. Truly, the more he tried to push the nymph from his mind, the more he thought of her, dancing, singing, smiling. She was all he thought about, through the long summer days, and dark nights. He wanted her for himself, but knew that the Gods would punish him for even attempting to break such a pleasing union. And so he had gone back to his work, the things he was good at, those things which pleased the Gods and men.

Still, wherever he looked, whenever he closed his eyes to sleep in the summer shade of a tree, or gaze up at the stars from a ripening harvest field, there he saw her: Eurydice.

It angered Aristaeus too that his father, Apollo, had so doted on Orpheus, who was the son of the Thracian king.

Why? he asked himself. *Because he can pluck a few notes upon a dead tortoise?*

He had always sought his father's favour, but his arts of shepherding, bee keeping, hunting, and tending the vine were never so grand in the eyes of the Far-Shooter as the ability to make noise and paint the air. Everyone was fooled by Orpheus' music, even the Gods!

In truth, all Aristaeus saw when he looked upon Orpheus was an effeminate youth who preferred music to hunting. *Dainty Orpheus! He doesn't deserve Eurydice!* he thought, over and over again. Then, one day it occurred to him that the Gods had manipulated her, tricked her into into loving Orpheus.

"That is why she was weeping in my dream!" Aristaeus said to the air and the bees hovering about him in that summer field. "She needs someone to protect her in the wild world, not someone to pluck broken notes upon a lyre. She needs - wants! - someone to throw the spear, and wrestle away giants. Someone who can run as fast as any centaur in the land!"

He thought of the centaurs, with whom he had a definite affinity, for he spent much time among them. They did not shy from taking what they wanted, no. In fact, he had heard recently of a battle that took place at the wedding of the Lapith king, Pirithous, when the centaurs had tried to carry off the women, including the bride.

They were too brazen, and they were drunk, Aristaeus remembered hearing. *That is not the way of the hunt! One must be patient, and stealthy, and then strike with speed and accuracy.*

He knew he could not break the hold that Aphrodite had placed upon Orpheus and Eurydice, but he could cut it. It was then that the solution presented itself to him, even as his muscled legs carried him away from Orchomenos, north toward Pieria.

If Orpheus dies, then Eurydice will be mine!

The hunt was on.

6

SLITHERING DEATH

The land had not known such a summer as that. It was a time free of war and of ravaging fire. Crops across the land of Pieria and Thessaly thrived like never before, and the hearts of mortals overflowed with goodness and gratitude that pleased the Gods, whose altars constantly burned with offerings.

The world was bursting with life, colour, light and, of course, song. The earth about lofty Olympus was truly the Gods' garden, the Hesperides almost paling by comparison.

On a lonely cliff overlooking the world, along the hidden pathways and hunting grounds of the Gods, Apollo sat upon a rocky outcrop. His sky blue cloak billowed about him in the hot summer air, his silver bow across his lap as he sat listening to the music that wove its way up to him from the remote paths of Pieria far below, where Orpheus and Eurydice roamed.

So beautiful... he thought as he listened to the music as gentle as summer rain that refreshes life and limb. Of all mortals to whom he offered aid and skill, all whom he had fathered, it was Orpheus who made him most proud. He smiled at the thought, and wildflower blooms sprung up out of the rocks about him.

But his smile faded, for ever since that day of music and beauty when Orpheus and Eurydice had wed, there was one thing he wished to forget, but could not. The way in which Hymenaios had looked upon his son, Aristaeus. It was the one time in which he had seen the beauty of that young god fade and darken and, fleeting though it was, Apollo knew it would bring misery.

"Why is this future veiled from my eyes?" Apollo said to himself as he stood and took up his bow. "Aristaeus, my son... Where are you?"

Normally, as was his gift, Apollo could spot whomever he chose to see, to bestow favour and protection, or to punish and destroy as the need may be. But even as the sun's chariot blazed overhead, and Helios cast his eyes down upon every part of that land, saluting Olympus on his fiery trajectory, Aristaeus remained hidden from Apollo's eyes.

The huntsman had ever been skilled in moving without notice in the world, stealthy and strong, able to blend in with the rocks and trees, to immerse himself in waters clear and dark, then to emerge wherever he wished. And all the while, he could remain hidden from the eyes of Olympus itself.

"I must find him," Apollo said to the crow who had just perched upon the bough of a sweet-scented pine nearby. There was a brilliant flash of light, and the god was gone.

The crow took flight and soared down from the mountainside of Olympus to the valleys far below.

.   .   .

Since the day of their wedding, Orpheus and Eurydice had moved through the world, through each hour, every day, as though in a dream perfectly cast for them by Morpheus and the Morai. Their joy, oneness, was boundless and ever growing. They were content to simply exist, wherever that might have been, so long as they were together. Their hearts were their hearth fires, and their bodies their homes. Orpheus' music, and Eurydice's dancing grace, were the air they breathed.

They helped all whom they encountered, never discriminating or condemning, for such feelings were not to be found in the fibre of their beings.

They lingered in the land of Pieria that summer, still basking in the elation of that magical day of music, song, reverence and love that had shone out so that the stars themselves felt warm joy in their distant, icy placements.

Orpheus and Eurydice walked, and he played, his music exploratory and ever-changing, delving into unknown depths of feeling, of affection and deepest love, that few ever believed existed among the Gods let alone mortals. Animals followed them, eager for the peace and safety that proximity to the lovers brought. Birds saluted them from the bough of every tree, and Zeus' eagles danced in the skies high above them, rising on Orpheus' music as if it were the most powerful thermal.

If one had roamed into that land, be he warrior, centaur, farmer or beast, one would have thought that Peace and Order had finally overwhelmed and imprisoned Chaos and Discord.

Almost.

But the laws of Gods are such that there must be balance, and so there is never Gratitude without Jealousy, or Good without Evil. No, nor Love without Hate. The dark leanings of the world are cunning and patient, and can enter into the most unlikely of places or creatures and times, even upon a perfect summer's day, when the light is bright, the sky of purest blue, and love ever-present.

For the last three days, Orpheus and Eurydice had been spending their time along the shore of a shallow river. On one side of the clear river was an ancient olive grove of gnarled trees, their aged limbs bent under the weight of their still-green fruit. On the other side, a vast field of summer wheat stretched away to high and hazy Olympus rising in the distance.

It was the first time in some while that they had not been disturbed, and they revelled in each other's company, speech, scent, laughter and touch. During the hot days, they splashed in the crystal waters of that river, and dozed in the shade of an ancient tree, listening to the wind whispering in its silver-green leaves. At dusk, as the stars' fires began to blaze, and Selene drove her silver chariot across the firmament, husband and wife made love and held each other close, grateful for every moment together, constantly trying to put into words the feelings, hopes and dreams that they shared and which burst inside of them.

And Orpheus played upon his lyre, and sang such sweetness of being, that there was a renewal of life at every level of the Gods' making.

Olympus echoed with his songs, by the will of Zeus.

WHEN THE SUN rose on yet another day, streaking the eastern skies with soft hues of pink, orange and blue, Orpheus and Eurydice's eyes slowly opened where they lay, holding each other tightly. They stared silently into each other's eyes and smiled, never tiring of that second sunrise, wishing it to go on forever.

"I love you, Orpheus," Eurydice said, her fingers gently brushing away the dark strands about his eyes. "You are everything to me."

Orpheus smiled. "And you are my entire world, my love, my Eurydice. I will sing to you always. Every song I compose, every note that passes my lips, shall be for you evermore."

"Oh, my truest love..." She felt such joy, such impossible happiness in the expanses of his wide, blue eyes. "You cannot sing for me alone."

"I do. I will," he answered.

"Then our child would not grow and dream and be loved as I am." She took his hand and placed it upon her abdomen.

"Our child?" he repeated. "You are with child?"

She nodded. "I am certain of it. Orpheus, my love, we have made this child together. I am so happy. I love you so much, it hurts sometimes."

"I never thought..." Orpheus would have spoken, but he was lost for words as his face beamed with pride and purest joy. He took up his lyre and stood, and together they both walked into the singing river, she to splash and he to play to her and the rising sun.

As Orpheus played, Eurydice could feel the jubilation that he felt and she knew that he was as happy as he had ever been. It was the most beautiful melody he had every played.

"You will make the most wonderful father, my love," she said, looking at him and bending over to splash cool water upon her face and hair. As Eurydice stood again, her smile quickly faded, for coming up slowly behind her husband was a huntsman with a long dagger. "Orpheus, behind you!" she screamed.

The music stopped abruptly as Orpheus spun, narrowly dodging the blade as it sliced downward, only just catching his forearm. "Aristaeus?" Orpheus said, and then he saw the look of purest hate in the huntsman's eyes, the unwillingness to talk, the urge to kill. "Eurydice...RUN!" Orpheus yelled.

The abrupt and disordered notes that exploded from Orpheus' lyre seized Aristaeus' arm and flung the glinting blade back into the trees.

Aristaeus ran at him, his thick fingers reaching for his neck, but Orpheus' music laid hold of his limbs and pushed him back, then flung him onto the far bank of the river, spinning him. Each staccato note was as a bloodless sword thrust that drove his attacker back.

When Orpheus saw Aristaeus knocked to the ground against an aged olive tree, he turned with his lyre and ran after his wife, across that swaying summer field in the direction of Olympus. As he ran, he could see the sky darkening overhead, hear the thunder of Zeus' displeasure in the heavens, and the rushing pursuit of Aristaeus in the dried wheat behind him.

"Eurydice!" Orpheus called out, the rushing panic in his heart driving him forward. "Eurydice!"

EURYDICE RAN AND RAN, like a deer, fleet-footed and filled with panic as a hunter pursues her through a winter wood. She had seen the look in Aristaeus' eyes and never had she felt such utter fear.

Her long legs had carried her swiftly, but she kept looking back for Orpheus, tears beginning to dim her eyes until she heard his voice. She stopped to wait for him and saw the swaying wheat and a head moving swiftly toward her.

Aristaeus burst into view and she turned and ran again. "Orpheus!" she cried out.

The huntsman was upon her, his breathing fast, his scent ranker than any beast. He lunged like a lion leaping for its prey, and she tripped and tumbled forward through the wheat, her world spinning as if the sun overhead fell out of orbit.

She made to rise and run on, but she could not, for there was another feeling that invaded her senses, a painful, piercing bite that sapped all of her strength, and stunned her muscles. Her heart began to beat wildly as if some invisible force had grabbed it in a fist of adamant, squeezing it unrelentingly. "Or...Orpheus!" she gasped.

Aristaeus' face appeared in the darkened sky above her, his eyes wide, the hate and lust replaced with deep panic and fear. He looked down at Eurydice to see the glistening serpent fastened upon her left arm, its fangs set deep in her flesh, its body heaving as it wrapped itself about her leg and thigh.

He froze, realizing what he had done, but before he could speak, he felt his body seized by sudden pain and felt himself thrown a great distance through the air, away from the prostrate nymph.

"Eurydice!" Orpheus cried as he rushed to her side. "My love, my love!" The sight of that serpent stopped his heart. A few notes upon his lyre removed the creature, that slithering death, from his wife's body and sent it away into the depths of the sullied summer field.

"Orpheus..." Eurydice stuttered, her body shuddering. Her eyes were wide and glossy, filled with panic and tears.

"No, no, no! Stay with me, my love. I will play out the

poison." He set his fingers to the lyre where they stumbled clumsily, unable to play.

She shook her head, her once lovely lips in a rigor, pale and foaming. She stiffened suddenly, convulsing a few times, her hands reaching up to Orpheus' face but falling still just before she could touch him.

"Eurydice!" Orpheus flung his lyre aside and grasped at his wife's still body, cradling it. The only music he could make were his cries, and the deep-born tremors of grief that welled up. "My love...no, no, no! I can't live without you. I won't!" He forced himself to grow still, to breathe.

Great Father...Zeus... Do not let her leave this world. Save her, please! I beg you! My lord, Apollo, shine your light upon her. Bring her back to me!

Orpheus' prayers had never been in such earnest, and as he knelt in the swaying wheat, cradling his wife's body beneath a darkened sky, he felt that his heart would explode. His eyes closed, he bent over to kiss her face, to press her body to his, to will his life into her.

But all he felt was cold. The movement of her limbs had been arrested, the rhythm and beat of her loving heart permanently stilled.

Then, he felt heat and light approaching, and he felt that the Gods had heard his prayers, but when he opened his eyes, it was not to see Zeus or Apollo standing before him.

It was Hermes, tall and golden, his face stern and filled with regret.

"NO!" Orpheus shook his head wildly, tears falling from his eyes over the body of his beloved. "Please, no!" he begged.

Hermes stepped closer and pointed his caduceus at Eurydice's body, and even as Orpheus looked on, her shade rose up from Death's sleep, confused, a pale reflection of who she had been in vibrant life. She stepped behind Hermes, ready for her long walk.

"Please no," Orpheus begged.

"I am sorry for you, Orpheus," Hermes said, a foreign sadness written upon his godly features. "It is the way of things." He turned then, and the shade of Orpheus' love followed mutely and obediently until they disappeared.

Orpheus' body began to shake and shudder, and at last the great waves of grief that had been building far out in the sea of his soul crashed, and his cries echoed and exploded into the world such that birds and beasts fled and died, and even the walls of Olympus shook and cracked.

In that moment, Aristaeus rose up from the ground and ran north, like he had never run before, aware that Furies would pursue him the length of his days. He did not see the drawn, silver bow of his father, pointed at his back for a fleeting moment.

But Apollo, slacked his pull, and turned away from his fleeing son, turning toward Orpheus where he screamed wildly to the weeping skies.

There were no words or songs in Heaven or upon the Earth to describe the well of sadness felt by all in that moment as Orpheus cradled his wife's body in his arms, more alone in the world then as he had ever been.

7

THE SILENT STRINGS

Summer came to an early end. Men rushed to bring in their crops early before they rotted beneath darkened skies. War erupted in every corner of the land, and sickness began to spread among flocks of sheep and goats, and herds of cattle.

The Gods' altars were heaped with offerings, smoking and fragrant before the bowed heads of mortals everywhere, and yet, the halls of Olympus were dark and quiet, unable to gleam beneath the pall that had been cast over all things. Even the Gods were confounded by this, not having fully comprehended the impact of the silencing of music in the world.

And it was indeed silent. For all the efforts of Apollo and the Muses to fill the void, to inspire even the smallest of tasks and breathe life into the land, it was never the same as when Orpheus had played, when he and his love had travelled over the land with a purity that was now lost. All longed for days now erased.

Such longing kills action and hope.

From the side of a silver pool in the gardens of Olympus, Apollo sat with his cythara upon his lap, his starry eyes dim as he watched the world in the surface's reflection. He played, and played, but his own grief had sapped his skills. He watched and searched for any sign of Orpheus in that all-seeing surface, and there spotted him roaming the rocky landscape of Boeotia, absent his lyre, without a will to live.

"You have to help him," Aphrodite's wispy voice arrived at his shoulder, and she sat upon the grass beside Apollo to look upon Orpheus. "I have not been able to reconcile the loss of such a love." She closed her eyes, the fire flowing through her immortal veins burning lethargically. "Surely, something can be done. Not just to help all of us to breathe new life into the world again, but to help him."

"Life is a dirge to him now." Apollo looked at Love. "And the laws of the Cosmos are solidly written. We cannot undo death." He looked back at the sloping realm of the Gods, erected in hues of emerald, green and blue, white monuments of timeless beauty now faded and sad. "Not even Father Zeus can do this."

"Only one who has loved so furiously as Orpheus can. All of us...immortal though we be...how can we mend what we never fully understood?"

The wind swept over Apollo's face then, and the strings of his cythara vibrated in that breeze.

Aphrodite stood, her long-flowing himation hovering about her beautiful being, and he stood with her. She smiled. "Few of you understood just how much Orpheus and Eurydice loved each other...how much they still do. This is no mere mortal attachment or wish not to be alone. Their souls, their psyches, became one. Nothing can every break such a bond. Not even Death."

Apollo looked at her suddenly, only now understanding.

Aphrodite nodded, her golden hair falling about her shoulders, her sky-blue eyes growing brighter like the still summer sea reflecting the sky at midday. "His soul has been suddenly and violently hollowed out, for she is gone from his side." Love turned to leave, to go back up the godly paths of Olympus, but she turned back to Apollo. "Your son needs you, now more than ever before. Go to him now that you understand the depth of his loss. Help him mend what cannot be mended."

It was then that the sun's rays penetrated the high-soaring clouds that had besieged Olympus itself, burning slowly through to light the pool into which Apollo gazed down upon Orpheus. "The world needs you, Orpheus... We all do." And the Far-Shooter wept to see his son bent over and alone at the side of a trickling stream, weeping and clawing at the hard ground in grief.

ORPHEUS HAD NOT KNOWN it as he wandered, but his chaotic, grief-stricken path had led him back to the slopes of Helicon. The creatures of the wood had roamed near to him, at a distance, shielding him from harm on his way, though he had sought conflict with other mortals, ways to quench his savage grief with violence. But that was not him, and though the land suffered at his silence, all wished for his revival.

Orpheus' lyre had been silent ever since Eurydice had been taken from him. He had hidden it in a cave, buried it so as to permanently muffle its voice and erase the memory of it.

He bent over the water of that mountain stream and looked upon his contorted face. For a fleeting moment, however, she appeared at his shoulder...Eurydice.

She wept and would have placed her hand upon his shoulder, but when he turned to look upon her, he saw only the darkness of the wood behind him, and the raked clouds in the sky above.

In that darkness, a dove or purest white alighted upon a tree branch, but Orpheus turned away from it to search the water for his love's face once more.

She was not there.

"I can't go on..." he muttered, his face near the water's surface, his hands and arms churning the mud of the river-bank. "I want to die...I want to die..."

Orpheus wept then, wishing for Death to take him as he remembered the swift passage of the short time he had with his truest love, that first glimpse of love's true face in that far northern wood. He remembered her smile, more brilliant than the sun of Helios' chariot, the hope her very presence instilled in him and how a single glance from her did more than ever the Gods could.

He sat up and looked one last time at his feeble reflection in the water. "I am finished," he said, and his hand reached for the dagger tucked in his belt. Orpheus then held out his wrist and began to cut into his own flesh so that the blood wept from his body into the flowing waters of that stream. He closed his eyes then, and would have waited to fall into eternal sleep if not for the music that floated toward him through the dark wood at his back.

The notes came closer, and wove about him. Then, they were matched by a familiar voice. Their was beauty there, oh yes, and a love full of care and nurture.

Orpheus looked down at his wrist where the wound began to seal of its own accord. "No!" he protested, but the music soothed him, the voice calmed him, and a brilliant light began to engulf him until he turned and saw them, Apollo and Calliope, reaching out to him, their arms there to receive him as he fell. "Let me die, I beg you!"

They said nothing, but pulled him away from the water to a bed of moss nearby. Calliope's voice hovered around him, casting a spell over her distraught son, even as she wept to see him so, her heart breaking for what had happened to him, for his shattered joy and torn life. "We are here, my beautiful son. You are not alone." She continued to sing, the beauty of her immortal voice such that even grief took notice.

As Apollo looked down upon the mother cradling her stricken son, he played softly, music to hold, to heal, to plant the seeds of purpose and courage.

For he will need that courage in the time to come...

THE SILENCE WAS deep in the wood beside the river. Orpheus woke from a dreamless sleep put upon him by Apollo. The early morning air was scented with dew and jasmine, and the only music to be heard was the sound of the stream and forest, gentle and pensive.

But Orpheus did not want to think, for that only brought pain. He kept his eyes closed, there to hold onto the image of his lost love, but even then the tears seeped through the rims of his fastened lids and he sat up with a start to see Apollo and Calliope sitting before him, watching and waiting.

There were tears in his mother's eyes as she looked upon him, feeling the grief that flowed through him, that had replaced joy and inspiration and the will to create.

"Why do you interfere?" Orpheus asked. "I want an end of it...all of it."

"Do not say such things, my son," Calliope said, reaching out to him only to have him turn his head away.

Orpheus did not want the tenderness offered by his mother, nor by Apollo whose starry eyes held him fast and willed him to look upon him.

"Orpheus," Apollo said, plucking a single, appeasing note upon his cythara. "In the halls of Olympus and across this land, we all mourn the death of Eurydice."

"Do not mock me!" Orpheus snapped, looking at his wrist where there was no sign of the cut he had made. *Had I imagined doing it?*

"It is not mockery to speak of the dead," Apollo stood, and set his cythara down against a rock. The wind played with his blue cloak as he turned to face Orpheus. "What would Eurydice wish for you? Would she want you to silence your strings, to go through the world numb and mute, or to remember her, and to play so that your music shines out like a beacon for all, mortal and immortal?"

Orpheus laughed, and cursed the urge in his fingers to move, to play.

Apollo continued. "Would you deny your purpose in this life?"

"What purpose, Lord? There is nothing now but grief that poisons every moment with bitter hate. What life is that?"

"No," Apollo answered, the certainty in his eyes, his voice much more than Orpheus could have anticipated. "Do you remember what life was like before you met Eurydice?"

"No. I've no wish for that."

"I do. I remember your music. It was beautiful, but only so much as the green shoots of springtime are delicate and new in the time before they achieve their full bloom."

"I was naive and ignorant of love." Orpheus' voice softened, but he did not smile, wanted only to remember his life in the time he was with his truest love.

"Yes. But only by experiencing love at its fullest was your art bettered, and more than anyone thought possible."

"Please let me die, Mother," Orpheus tore his gaze away from Apollo to look at his mother, tears in his eyes.

Calliope was silent, pleading in her manner. "Listen, to your father."

Orpheus' eyes widened as he looked to Apollo. "My father?" He shook his head. "King Oeagrus is my father."

"No, my son," Calliope said. "He is not. We told you that to protect you. But it makes no matter now. Listen."

Apollo stepped forward. "Of all my children, Orpheus, I am proudest of you. I see in you what is best in mortals."

Orpheus was silent. He knew he should have felt shock, perhaps some dismay at being lied to, but he did not. He felt numb to the revelation, if not relieved to some extent. But whenever a feeling outside of grief emerged, he set it alight so that it turned to ash in his mind and heart.

"Your music, Orpheus, brought joy, healing and peace to the world in a way that my own, or that of the Muses never could. The love you felt enriched your music once you experienced the full force of it."

"And now my love is dead. She is gone." He would have wept again, but for Apollo's strong hands pulling him to his feet.

"Love was a crucial stage of your life's journey, Orpheus. And now, you have been forced to wade through loss and grief."

There were tears again in Orpheus' eyes as he looked closely at Apollo. And a great fear began to dawn in those blue eyes.

"Yes," Apollo continued. "Loss and grief are the next stage of your journey. Harness them," he commanded.

"No!"

"You must, Orpheus. Fight for what you hold dear. See your toils through to their end, even if doing so strikes terror into the deepest reaches of your being."

"To what end, Lord? Tell me, for if it is to achieve a life without Eurydice, I want no part of it. Let my song fade from memory, never to be heard or remembered again."

Apollo stood back. "The Morai have secret faith in the mortals they oversee, Orpheus. But they will not reward cowardice!"

"Cowardice? Is it cowardice to set aside my lyre for all time, to meet death willingly?

"It is cowardice to turn your back upon your fated toils, yes. And yours is to play for the world."

"To what end? It's not as if I can get Eurydice back, is it?"

Apollo was about to speak, but he stopped abruptly, his eyes closed. *Could it be possible?* he wondered. When he opened his eyes, he met Calliope's fearful gaze.

She shook her head.

"It is the only way," Apollo said to her, taking her hand.

"What do you speak of?" Orpheus asked.

"I cannot say now. For the moment, sit here," Apollo said, taking up his lyre and beginning to play. "Sleep, Orpheus," he said, his music matched by Calliope's voice, the two combined setting their son down to rest.

When Orpheus was asleep, Apollo turned to her. "Stay with him. I will return."

"You go to the dark halls?"

"Yes," Apollo replied, fear entering even his divine features. "I will plead for our son."

Light flashed and lit up the tears upon Calliope's face as she settled beside Orpheus to wait, to sing, and to hope.

UPON A SOARING cliff of blackest adamant, Apollo stood alone in the roaring wind. The sound of keening exploded in his hearing and made him feel more cold and alone than ever he had before in his ageless life. His far-seeing eyes searched for the sun, for starlight, or even the moon, but all he saw was an endless expanse of grey and black, a world constantly aflame with sadness and grief.

He would have wept for all that he saw and felt, for what he could not see or feel in that remote part of the Underworld. But he knew it was the only way...

"Uncle," he called. "May I speak with you?"

There was a pause in the wind, as if the sound had been taken out of it, and then the tall, shadowy figure of Hades was suddenly standing before him.

The Lord of the Underworld pulled back his black cowl to reveal his dark, bearded face, and his deep green eyes looked over Apollo. "Nephew..." Hades said, his voice deep and commanding, laced with menace and bitterness. "Why do you come to me unannounced?"

"My lord, Hades," Apollo began, not bowing, but spreading his arms wide. "I come to make a plea."

"For your son, Orpheus."

"Yes."

"He will join me soon enough. He longs for death." Hades smiled.

"But Death does not yet long for him."

Hades did not speak, for he sensed the truth of the words.

"My lord..." Apollo did bow then, his crown within reach

of Hades' grasp.

"Rise and speak, nephew. I have no quarrel with you."

"I come to ask for a soul."

"Eurydice," Hades said without hesitation.

Apollo nodded. "Yes. The world needs Orpheus, and he is lost without her. The world of men and gods was better, richer for the two of them being in it, together."

"You know what you ask is forbidden by the laws of the Cosmos."

"I do know, yes."

"Then you have wasted a visit to my realm." Hades turned to look out over the vast plains of his kingdom from that high cliff, to see the many millions of dead roaming without end, for all eternity, their wailing and weeping incessant and never-ending. He spoke with his back to Apollo. "You say the world needs Orpheus, that he and Eurydice made it a better place. But he never played for me. I was not present at their nuptials. I was not invited to Olympus when his music made the rest of the Gods weep with joy at its beauty." The Lord of the Underworld sighed bitterly. "Why would I even consider your request?"

"Because I humbly ask you, Lord." Apollo stepped toward Hades, smaller in his dark presence, though his light did reach out in that lightless place.

Hades turned back to him. "The only way to get a soul back from the Underworld is to give one in exchange. You also know this. Are you willing to sacrifice your son for his love?"

Apollo looked over the far realm of Death and knew that he could not, though Orpheus might have wished for it. He looked back to his uncle. "No. But he would sacrifice himself for her."

Hades' eyes widened, their green fires kindled anew.

"I ask that you allow Orpheus to come into your realm. Let him play for you alone, a song the Gods have not heard before. Let him play for you and, if you are pleased, you can then grant him the return of his truest love to life."

"And if I am not moved to do so?"

Apollo shivered then, for fear, for the thought of his son roaming those lonely plains of darkness for eternity. But he knew it was the only way. "If his song does not move you, he can remain here for eternity."

The wind roared about them, their cloaks snapping silently. Then, after a few moments, Hades nodded. "Very well. Orpheus may enter into my realm. But he may not travel here as a god. He must walk the Paths of the Dead, the same as his wife did. If he makes it to my halls unscathed, his soul unburned and intact, he may play for me. Then, we shall see."

"Agreed," Apollo said, and he departed that deep and dark world as quickly as he could.

APOLLO RETURNED to the forest stream with the first rays of sunlight to find Calliope and the muses sitting around the sleeping form of Orpheus.

They stood when he appeared, looking drained of light after his time in Hades.

Apollo strode to Orpheus and looked down upon him. "He is rested?" he asked Calliope.

"He is never fully rested," she answered. "But he is regaining strength."

"Good. He will need it."

"Our uncle has agreed then?"

"Yes," Apollo said, and at his answer the Muses wept for fear of darkness and death, of losing the sleeping man in their midst who had given them all the greatest gift of song. But Apollo turned on them, his voice firm but calm, as a song for marching to battle. "We must believe in him now, inspire him, so that he may believe in himself." He knelt before Orpheus and placed his radiant hand upon his brow. "Wake, Orpheus. Wake, my son."

Orpheus' eyes slowly opened, like clear blue water appearing in a crack of the Earth, spreading wider and wider. "I dreamed of Eurydice," he said, his voice shaking. "She was alone and sad...so sad..."

"I know, my son," Apollo said. "But I have gained you the chance you need to get her back."

"What?" Orpheus sat up, as alert as a stag in a wood surrounded by lions. "How? Please tell me!"

"You must journey to the Underworld to play for Hades."

"Play for him?" Fear entered into Orpheus immediately, a greater fear than he had ever experienced before. "I cannot play anymore!"

"You must," Apollo said. "For if you do not, you will never see Eurydice again, and your soul will be forfeit as well, never the two of you meeting in that dark, endless eternity."

"Surely, Lord, something else can be done?" Erato protested. "If we go to Father Zeus, perhaps he can prevail upon Hades?"

Apollo shook his head. "It is Hades' realm. His word is law."

Orpheus swallowed hard, holding onto the image of Eurydice in his mind's eye and in his heart. "How do I get there?"

"We cannot help you. You must travel there, alone upon

the road. Once you enter the gates of Hades' realm, you must descend into the Underworld by way of the Paths of the Dead."

"His soul will burn away!" Calliope protested.

Apollo shook his head. "It is the only way."

"I have no music left in me," Orpheus said, near to weeping for the desperation he felt. It was as if his gift had been taken from him. "I can no longer play!" he cried.

"You can," Apollo said. "Your grief has made you feel that you cannot. But you must harness this new experience, these feelings of turmoil and sadness and make all the world feel them as never before."

"You need a starting point, my son. Every song has an origin," Calliope said, taking his hand. "What were the last notes you composed and why?"

"I...it was when I was last with Eurydice. I had never felt such joy, such purity of being and of love. It was a song of deepest love... But that love was cut short!" He pulled away and buried his face in his hands.

"Finish the song," Apollo commanded. "I know that those few notes you wrote for Eurydice echoed across the land, all the way to Olympus. I saw the Gods weep for that song, for what you made them feel. We all did. That is your starting point. You had a love, and that love was lost. Help us all to feel the torment of that lost love, and the hope of regaining it."

"I do not have my lyre! I cast it aside, buried it in the Earth!"

Apollo stood then, and the Muses too, in a circle about him. He closed his starry eyes and held out his arms. A chorus of music rose up out of that wood, into the sky and across the land, reaching, probing, until at last, in a brilliant light that reflected all the colours of the world, Orpheus' lyre lay across Apollo's outstretched arms.

Orpheus gazed upon it, and even as he took in the sight of that timeless instrument, he wept with joy at the hope that was kindled in his heart.

"There is one more thing," Apollo said as he held the lyre out to his son. "You must not play this song before you arrive at the Gates of Hades' realm. It is to be new and unheard by mortal or immortal ears so that the first time it is played, it echoes through time."

"I am afraid," Orpheus admitted, his hands, his body, his heart shaking as he gazed down the long road ahead of him.

"Keep Eurydice in your heart, my son," Calliope said, standing beside Orpheus. "Her love for you will be your beacon in the darkness."

Orpheus thought of Eurydice, lost and alone in the Underworld. He forced himself to remember her bright eyes, her smile, the fall of her hair and the music of her laughter as she had danced in life. And the life that had been growing inside of her.

I am coming, my truest love, he said, wishing his words to her in the endless darkness, and he felt courage and strength return.

Orpheus stepped forward and took the lyre from Apollo's outstretched arms. He held the lyre, so familiar and comfortable, his fingers hovering over the strings, and his music rang out once again in the world, bringing light and colour and life.

Apollo and the Muses wept to see and hear and feel Orpheus' return.

HYMN III

INTO DARKNESS

PATHS OF THE DEAD

The sky was long and dark. It stretched painfully to the South, highlighting the great distance that Orpheus needed to travel, alone and without aid, in order to reach Tainaron and the gateway to the Underworld. He was living a nightmare, it was true, and the Gods wept for him at each step. But they also marvelled at the love that urged him to take those steps to the dreaded realm.

For months he walked during the day, beneath a sharp, steely sun that filtered through a canopy of sad grey, and at night he slept beneath trees, on the edges of fields, or anywhere else he might catch a glimpse of the stars and the hope they offered.

Never had he felt so lonely as he did in those months of travel from Helicon to Corinth, past thick-walled Mycenae, and across the plain to Argos. It was at the guard tower of Argos, a pyramid perched on a hill overlooking orange and olive groves toward the sea, that the soldiers urged Orpheus to take a ship south.

But he refused, telling them he had to walk, and then departed their stony post.

The soldiers made the sign against evil as he left, and were happy to see the back of him. Indeed, whereas before, man and beast had flocked to Orpheus' side to hear him play, to gaze upon him and his wife, now they avoided him, fearful of the curse they believed had wrapped itself about him like the serpent that had killed his beloved wife.

Orpheus pressed on, uncaring of what other mortals believed, preferring the time alone on his journey over the mountains and rocky plains of Pelops' isle into Laconia to play his lyre, to hone his skills like a sword before battle.

And he knew it was a battle ahead of him. He remembered Apollo's face as he described what he might meet during his ordeal, how the dead would be drawn to him, how they are pressed to devour the living in their midst. Apollo had nearly wept as he described the gateways and plains that stretched out for a dark eternity beyond the black river of Hades' realm.

"My son," Calliope had said to Orpheus as he prepared to set out, his lyre over his shoulder. "You must believe in yourself and the love you bear for Eurydice, in order to survive. Hold to that love in the darkest places of the Underworld. Remember and believe in it."

Orpheus had felt fear invading his being like a cold poison, but he nodded, hugged his mother and the Muses, and turned to Apollo one last time. "Thank you...Father."

"Have courage, Orpheus, and as you walk the Paths of the Dead, play like you have never played before."

Apollo's words haunted Orpheus as he travelled, and the tears in his mother's eyes tested his courage, but whenever he began to doubt, he thought of Eurydice, of getting her back, and of the joy they would have once more. He thought of the child inside her, their child, and the love that bound them to each other.

And as he thought of his truest love, the life they had, and the loss they had endured, he filled his mind with music to match it. His fingers strummed mutely over the strings, unable to play what he imagined until he reached the Underworld, and so he would walk, weeping silently to himself for the tale he told over mountains and across rocky plains and valleys.

In Laconia, as oceans of olive stretched out beneath soaring, jagged mountains, the people of that harsh land honoured Apollo's favourite and left him food and drink along the roads, though they came nowhere near to him. Orpheus passed as a shrouded shape, honoured and unharmed along the trackways that fell away south and away from high Taygetos.

Finally, after countless passages of sun and moon, of learning to control his fear, of arming himself with music as was never heard by gods or men, Orpheus stopped upon a dusty mountain cliff to find the edge of Poseidon's realm stretched out beyond a rocky peninsula.

I'm coming, my love...

THERE WAS music in that remote, wind-lashed place, but it was not music of Orpheus' making. There were howls on the incessant wind, keening cries and a deep dirge that seemed to rise up out of the rock and give Orpheus the impression that at any moment, pale hands might reach up out of the sharp ground to grab at him and pull him under. There was a constant feeling of drowning, be it in the rock at his feet, or in the angry sea ahead.

Orpheus suddenly became aware of people surrounding him, watching him from the cliffs, and doorways of squat, rough homes. All were shrouded in black, all silent, all observing him from shadowed cowls. They lived in Death's shadow, and Orpheus wondered at such a life, devoid of green beauty and light.

Such a plight became a part of his song, their silent shapes, like sentries at the cliff's edge.

The roar of the sea became louder, angrier, and Orpheus could taste salt upon the air as he descended the rock-hewn pathway, past two great, arching Tritons with crossed tridents, and into the sanctuary of Poseidon Asphaleios, the Bringer of Safety.

Orpheus, however, felt anything but safe.

There was a sense of creeping terror as he passed the altars of Poseidon and the Oceanids, draped with wind-tossed seaweed. The pathway led out into the churning foam of the sea, and Orpheus struggled to keep his footing, but then he turned and, for the first time, he saw that dreaded gate to Hades' realm.

Fear clawed at him instantly, for to stand before the doorway to the Underworld was to walk with Death itself.

The gateway stood as tall as twenty men, large enough to admit a Titan. It was carved out of the rocky cliffs, and adorned with all manner of symbols known to Death - peering eyes, skulls, sheep, goats and oxen. Orpheus looked to his right and there he saw the great altar of Death, dripping with blood and the bones of such offerings as those cut into the rock about the gate.

He stood there, staring at the gate to the Underworld. It

gaped like the maw of a Titan, jagged and deadly. The sea that flowed into that sharp bay seemed to be gulped down by the Underworld itself, greedy and ever-thirsty, the water disappearing without a trace.

His throat threatening to seize up, Orpheus took a step forward, and then another until he stood before the rock wall, expecting it to open.

It did not.

"Open," he said. "I ask to be admitted."

Nothing happened, and as the roaring wind and waves circled about him, Orpheus felt deep despair, even before he had set foot beyond that black threshold. He pounded upon the black rock with his fist, but felt only pain, and when he pulled back his hand, it was covered in blood.

The fear was very real then, a living, walking being beside him as he backed away and fell to his knees in the surf, the gate to the Underworld rising up above him.

For some time, he sat there, weeping and wondering how he could already have gone wrong. He wondered how far beyond that gateway Eurydice was, wondered at the fear she felt as she passed beneath that great maw of Death.

Soon, the sun began to drop away in the West, and Orpheus felt his desperation keen, his body shaking with rage, at himself, at the world.

Darkness fell, and Orpheus knelt in the deep gloom of that lonely cape of Tainaron, numb, feeling helpless.

Then, a faint light appeared to his left, coming down the pathway. He wondered if those haunting villagers were come to harass him, but when he looked, he saw the warm glow of Golden Hermes walking slowly, leading a procession of confused and tired-looking souls his way.

Orpheus scrambled out of the water and to the side, his heart pounding wildly as the dead approached, not wanting to touch them or look into their wondering eyes. He settled himself upon a barnacled rock to watch as they passed, and there he saw men, women, children, the wealthy and the poor, all walking together, mute and disoriented by their newfound death.

They followed Hermes, that solemn and silent god, his light leading them on to the darkness of the Underworld.

A sound could be heard out to sea then, and Orpheus turned to look where dolphins, messengers of the Gods, brought the souls of perished seamen ashore to join the procession, adding to the numbers of dead like grains of sand from a titanic fist, poured from a glass that never filled completely.

Hermes stood at the gateway, waved his caduceus, and the rock shimmered for a brief moment before the dead passed through in single file. The god watched them, pity upon his face, but determined in his duty to lead them.

It was then that Orpheus stepped out from his rocky hiding place, and approached the gateway behind the last of the departed seamen.

But Hermes' staff came down before him, blocking his way.

"Please let me enter, Oh Hermes. Let me follow."

Hermes looked down at Orpheus and shook his head sadly. "I cannot. It is forbidden." The look in Orpheus' eyes wrung even that god's heart, a heart accustomed to grief and death. "The living may not enter."

"But I was told I could!"

Hermes turned to go in, but then looked back. "Not with me, Orpheus."

"What do you mean?" Orpheus pleaded, his lyre held to his chest.

"The sun will rise soon," Hermes said quickly. "And when it does, then is the time to play." He then turned and followed the procession of souls in his charge, and the rocky gate blackened and shut once again.

Orpheus stood there alone, wind-lashed and dejected, tears streaming down his face as he looked upon the rock face and thought of his love beyond it, standing among the dead. He fell to his knees then and would have lain down to wait for the next cohort of souls to trample him, but for the ray of light and heat he felt upon his sodden face and shaking body.

The sun rose in the East as Helios' fiery chariot soared into the sky, the heat and light from the gracious Titan touching Orpheus' arm, shoulder and face, reviving him, giving hope and strength.

Eurydice's face emerged in Orpheus' mind then, the rising of his own sun, and he gathered himself to stand, looking out to the tossing sea. There, he thought he could spy the heads of Poseidon, his Oceanids and some creatures of the deep, bobbing up and down upon the waves of their watery realm, watching, waiting.

Orpheus followed their urging eyes and turned to face the gateway.

Play, Orpheus! Apollo's voice echoed in his mind. *Play now!*

Orpheus thought of Eurydice and all the joy they had shared. He thought of the depth of loss that invaded him when she was taken, and of the lonely road he had travelled to get to where he was, the faces of the dead he had seen.

He then brought up his lyre, his shaking fingers poised

above the strings, ready to play the notes he had created the length of the long road to Death's door.

The waves and the wind hushed, even then, as if the Gods themselves held their breath for the briefest of moments, and it was then that Orpheus began to play.

The first notes were faint, a prelude to the story he would tell. The music was so simple in its beauty, and the soft touch of his fingers upon the strings such that, were the living about him, they would have felt a catch immediately at the back of their throats. Those notes pried open the doorway that had been shut on all the thoughts and emotions that Orpheus had tucked away, and just as the light was thrown onto those painful memories, the rising rock face before him began to shimmer. The light of his lyre broke it down, little by little until it was gone and the long Paths of the Dead were revealed in the darkness beyond.

Go, Orpheus! Walk, and play, and don't stop! Apollo cried to him from the heights of Olympus.

Orpheus' first steps were reticent, but he pressed on, playing, his music lighting the way in the darkness, and before he knew it, the light vanished behind him as the gateway to the Underworld shut, shaking the ground beneath his feet.

Fear flowed through his veins as quickly and fluidly as his own blood. It threatened to arrest his senses, his thoughts, and feelings, at any moment, should he give way to despair and stop playing.

But he did not stop playing. He walked on over the rocky pathway as it descended and switched back, until he reached a lookout from which he could see the dreaded expanse of that dark realm.

The path led away into the distance, the dead appearing as faint, milky banks of mist hovering over the Underworld.

The road led on and then stopped at a thick line, a barrier blacker than black at which the dead paused, the light of Hermes a mere pinprick among them.

Beyond the black river, the distance was dark and endless, it seemed, going on forever. Orpheus felt his fear acutely, made worse by the scent of damp and putrefaction on the air. He stumbled then, his music faltering, and when he looked up, he was surrounded by angry, hungry shades of the dead.

They reached out to him with clawing, greedy hands, broken-toothed mouths agape as they made to feast upon his life.

Orpheus' fingers moved quickly to play upon his strings and the sweet, foreign sounds of his music stopped the dead in their tracks. He played memories of green fields and sweet-smelling summer flowers such that the dead forgot their rage and remembered, their souls struggling with the sensations lost to them long ago.

Orpheus pressed on, his notes cutting a swathe through the surrounding souls so that he could carry on his way down the long road to the river beyond.

Eurydice, my love... Where are you?

THE TIME PASSED STRANGELY as Orpheus walked and played in that world where neither Helios or Selene were known, where even they were but faded memories of a life lost. There was no way to truly measure time in that black world, for day and night were one.

Despair followed Orpheus like a rabid beast set on tearing him apart and stopping his transit across the plain of adamant. Wandering souls begged for a coin even as

Orpheus' music soothed them, for many wandered about, not having been buried with one for their passage.

Soon enough, Orpheus arrived at the still, black shore of the River Styx, and there the dead milled about a rocky jetty, waiting for a ship that would not take them, not ever.

Orpheus wept as he looked about him at the poor families huddled together, even in death, at the lone shepherds who had died in solitude upon distant mountainsides, their bodies unburied, left for the carrion birds and wolves. All of them sat with their hands outstretched to Orpheus, but he could no more give them coin than stop playing.

His song shifted again, and the dead took notice and began to weep at the rekindled memories his music brought them. Faint smiles flitted across the faces of the dead like shadows, as they remembered, as they felt again for the briefest of moments.

Orpheus pressed through them, no longer able to look upon their visages, his fingers plucking gently at the strings of his lyre as he arrived teary-eyed at the edge of the black jetty.

A great horn hung upon a the skull of a ram, but Orpheus feared stopping his music to blow upon it, for if he did, the dead would devour him.

And so, he stood there and played to the still, dark waters that stretched out before him. The souls of the dead crowded at his back, making him cold, prickling his skin, but he would not turn to look upon them. He played, and continued to play until, out in the distance, the dark outline of a barge approached, a single lantern dangling from the prow as the faint sound of oar-churned water joined Orpheus' music.

The barge touched the jetty head-on, the light dangling,

drawing the dead who crowded around, who pressed in to board, but who could not.

"Board," a hoarse, rocky voice said, as if they were the only words it had uttered in a millennium.

Orpheus stepped past the blinding light of that lantern, and found himself facing Charon, the ferryman.

Charon stood tall in the stern of his death barge, bobbing up and down where his hidden feet were fixed by time to the bottom. He stretched out his thick, aged hand, his skin mottled, grey, and thickly-calloused.

Orpheus had no coin, and as the realization dawned like a fire in the dark, Charon's bearded face turned upon him, furious and death-bringing.

Orpheus, however, continued to play, soft and sweet as he could muster, a memory of watching the sunrise from atop the highest mountain on his journey.

That very sun could be seen in Charon's rheumy eyes, now wide and wondering at the sight he had not seen for an eternity.

The outstretched hand slowly closed, and went back to grasping the gnarled oar that was his duty, turning the barge away from the shore of piteous souls to head out into the black water of the Styx.

Orpheus settled himself, exhausted, upon the bench, and continued to play as he gazed out into nothingness, his eyes searching for the far shore.

ORPHEUS HAD no way of knowing how long the crossing took. He played continuously, softly, the notes he played for Charon matching the lulling of the black waves lapping against the hull of the barge. He did not turn in his seat as he played either, not wishing to distract the ferryman from his duty. Nor did he gaze into the water about them, afraid of the untold horrors that might have lurked beneath the surface. He was aware only of a surrounding, deep darkness, as if one were caught in the heavens without the benefit of a single star's light.

Orpheus thought only of Eurydice, willed his mind not to wander from her, for he could feel the increasing pull of forgetfulness.

Just when he began to think, however, that they would be adrift for an eternity, the far shore appeared like a thinly veiled line stretching to infinity. Directly ahead was a great pier flanked by soaring columns atop which enormous flames erupted from great tripods.

The barge settled into the middle of a double jetty. As Orpheus was about to stand, he froze, for souls of the dead began to immediately disembark, brushing past him like a ghostly breeze that chilled him to his bones.

When the dead had finished passing, Orpheus turned, his fingers soft as they played upon the strings, to see Charon looking directly at him.

That aged ferryman's eyes were wide and teary, moved not by the denizens of dead and their accompanying regrets, but by the soft melodies which Orpheus had played for him the length of the crossing. Charon then raised his hand and pointed directly ahead down the long, wide road that led from the pier into the distance.

Orpheus disembarked and as he set foot upon the jetty, the barge was quickly pulled out into the darkness, leaving him alone and shaking.

When the water of Styx stopped rippling against the shore, deathly-still again, Orpheus turned to face the road ahead. His feet felt heavy, his limbs tired, but he pressed on, his fingers upon the strings, the probing music like a shield before him, soft, melodic, arresting, but he nearly lost his place in the music for what he saw next.

As he passed the great columns, the deep darkness dissipated to reveal an endless plain of asphodel before him. He felt an immediate urge to weep then, not for himself, but for the dead. He walked slowly, gazing from side to side of the broad, black road to see myriad men, women and children, all wraiths, shadows of their former selves, roaming among the gleaming, white blooms of those tall, swaying flowers of Death's kingdom.

The dead ranged themselves across that white, swaying plain, bending to smell the asphodel which abetted their revisiting of their life's memories, both fair and foul. How long the dead spent roaming those fields, Orpheus did not dare wonder, for he was too moved by the dread symphony of murmuring, crying and howling grief that invaded his mortal ears. Such raging songs of death, hate and regret as he had never imagined possible beset the dead's memories of life.

He played to soothe them then, his music weaving a spell amongst the stalks of asphodel, pausing their grim remembrances and providing succour as he passed along the road.

The dead stood still and watched and listened as Orpheus passed, tears in their eyes, their ululating keens stoppered in their raw throats. They reached out for him, urged him to stay, to ease their suffering forever, but he did not stop.

He could not stop. Orpheus carried on down the Underworld's broad road, unsure of how far he had to go, how long he was to wander before he could make his plea to Hades.

I will walk forever to find her, he told himself.

· · ·

AFTER WHAT MUST HAVE BEEN days of roaming, of playing, and of deep despair in which he clung to the thought of his love, Orpheus finally reached the end of the plains of asphodel. And with the dead still about him, he arrived at the shore of the river Lethe.

He froze upon seeing it, for there was no bridge, no crossing however thin or faint, only the milky-white depths of the river.

The dead waded into the waters without hesitating, stooping, driven to drink, made to forget, to make death less painful. They gulped the white waters of Lethe greedily, unknowing of the oblivion that accompanied each swallow before they crawled up the far embankment.

On the other side, Orpheus could see families that had wept together among the asphodel begin to separate and leave each other's sides as though they were strangers, though they had had the deepest love in life.

He stood, looking down at the Lethe, the surrounding, thirsty dead, and felt his heart pound with the rhythm of his playing. He sweat profusely, for fear, for the face of unknowing forgetfulness that reached out to him.

I don't want to forget... he pleaded, looking down the length of the river bank to search in vain for any sign of a safe crossing.

His fingers slowed upon the strings in his despair, and almost stopped. One final resonating note nearly became his last, for its silence would have allowed the burning of his soul, his shield to fully dissipate. A fraction of a moment before that happened, he played again, the notes longing, urging and strong, notes of remembrance, and of creation.

Orpheus played, and in playing he remembered the goodness of his life, the love he now fought for with every fibre of his being. It was then that he raised a foot and stepped forward over the water, his footfalls suddenly supported by a bridge, by the architecture of all that he held dear.

He walked slowly, the dead craning their dripping faces to look up at Orpheus as he crossed over them, as he gave them courage for the coming trial, just as the sun encourages us toward the dawning of a new day. They would forget all with the Lethe waters, but they would not feel the sting of unknown fear.

Orpheus reached the other side of the river, and there he found that he could still remember. In fact, he could recall every detail of his life as if it were painted by the Gods before his very eyes. His heart was filled with an appreciation of all that he saw, all he had lived, and his song was the richer and more beautiful for it.

Even as he set off down the mountainous and pocked landscape that spread wide before him now, dark and fiery, stretching toward a distant wall of mountains, Orpheus felt his courage renewed as he pressed on along the Paths of the Dead.

Despair was not long in coming for Orpheus, and when it did come, it arrived in torrents. The road narrowed, and became more precipitous, a great fall of black rock and ash dropping away on either side to a dark and fiery abyss that was deeper and more distant than Orpheus thought possible, but which was entirely visible.

Tartarus, Orpheus thought at the back of his mind, and it was then that he felt his fear cut deeply.

That lower landscape of horrors haunted the dreams of

mortals and gods alike, and in that moment, it became a living nightmare as Orpheus walked, and played and strained not to look or to let his song fall into the despair that so desperately clawed at him from those dark depths.

Eurydice...my love...I am coming, he called to her, told himself. *I am coming.*

His song filled the sulphuric darkness, its recalling of love, sunshine, and summer rain among the fields and mountains of Thrace and Thessaly dousing the fiery caverns and plains of that eternal prison for the briefest of moments.

As he passed, Orpheus could hear the cries of the greatest sinners known to man and god, far below him. He could hear them reaching up to him with desperate, bloody hands, calling with gaping mouths, searching for the light of his lyre through teary eyes as though for their sole glimpse of the sun for eternity.

From Tartarus, Ixion's snake-writhing wheel of time slowed almost to a standstill, just long enough for him to see the light that passed overhead, and hear the music that fell upon him and made him remember a time before his attack upon the Goddess Hera, a time when he had been a better man than the wretched creature he now was. That glimpse of himself as he once was only served to increase his torture, despite the pause in his eternal spin and the stilling of the serpents that constantly sunk their fangs into his flesh. He wept and screamed when the music passed and the wheel began to turn once again.

Orpheus ignored those cries and pressed on, the image of his wife in his mind, his beacon, his light and inspiration as he made his passage.

Far below, upon the great mountainside of Tartarus, however, the cries of another rose up from where the great trickster of the Gods, the tale-teller, Sisyphus, carried out his endless and frustrating labour. At the peak of his mountain prison, the boulder sat still as the music rained down on him, and Sisyphus turned to see the passing light from Hades' realm. Immediately his mind and heart were flooded with thoughts of his long-lost wife, Merope, and of his son Glaucus, his grandson, brave Bellerophon, and of beauteous Corinth, the city which he built. He wished that he had not cheated Death as he did, and prayed to almighty Zeus in that moment of respite as tears streamed down his dusty cheeks, his entire body aching and filled with pain.

"Don't leave!" he cried from the top of his mountain, even as the great boulder began to crush the earth again, to roll back toward him. "No! Stay!" his voice echoed in the dark as the light passed away and his despair became real once more.

Orpheus heard his pleas rising up to him, begging and pained, but he forced himself to walk on.

The realm of Tartarus went on however, far below, stinking and dark and without end, until the cries of another sinner rose up, angry, aggressive and straining.

There, in a deep valley, Tantalus, the son of Zeus, stood chained for all time in the midst of a crystal pool, unable to drink, unable to eat from the groaning fruit trees of pomegranates, apples, figs and olives that hung over him. In the music and light that Orpheus brought, he found his deep regret for his hubris in cheating the Gods, of mocking their omniscience. But most of all, he despaired at what he had done to his young son, Pelops. He shut his eyes at the sight of the blood, at the sound of the boy's cries as he was cut to pieces to be fed to the Gods.

"Father...Great Zeus!" he cried in that moment. "I am sorry! Forgive me!"

But Zeus did not answer then, and he never would.

As the music passed overhead, however, the water rose just a little higher for the tears that fell from Tantalus' shuttered eyes. He was able to drink for the briefest of moments before the water fell away from him once more, the light and the music arching past him in the darkness above.

Orpheus wept to hear the despair on the wind across the Tartarian plain below, his fingers slowing on the strings as he pressed on, blood dripping upon the path to be soaked up by the blackened rock of the roadway. Just as he began to hope that he might be near the end of that tortuous part of the journey, the cries of another pierced his ears, accented by the tearing of flesh and the infernal screeching of vultures.

Orpheus dared to look over the edge of the road as the path narrowed even more at a dizzying height, and shut his burning eyes immediately.

Far below, upon a broad, flat and rocky plain of darkness, just visible in the light cast by his lyre, he saw the giant, Tityus, a son of Zeus who had tried to ravage the lovely Leto.

Orpheus tried not to pity such a one as he, but his state was one of such horror that it was almost impossible not to.

Tityus lay staked out upon the plain, his body splayed and naked as two enormous vultures bored into his flesh without end, digging, pulling, probing, tearing as his flesh and tissue regenerated and death never came. Tityus' cries were a torment to all, but as the music filled the darkness, the vultures paused and turned their hoary, blood-stained heads to look at the passage of that lone mortal high above.

"Thank you!" Tityus cried up to the sky and fading light. "Please stay! I beg you!"

But Orpheus felt his heart harden in that moment, for the

giant had attacked Leto, just as Aristaeus had attacked Eurydice, and for that, his punishment was just.

"No!!!" Tityus begged. "Stay!!!"

Orpheus played on, his steps quicker, his will to leave Tartarus behind all the stronger now for, in his heart, he could feel that Eurydice was nearer.

My love...my life...

And he smiled in the dark as the plains of Hades' realm opened up before him once again.

THE WIND BLEW wild on the dark plain, the blackness deeper than ever to either side of the path where Orpheus walked and played without end, his light a pinprick in that world.

He thought not of hunger, or thirst, or of rest, only of his love, and the long song of their life which he played out to the soundless night in the hopes that she would hear him.

The shades of heroes passed him in the eternal night, their diaphanous outlines roaming the fields toward the mountains, bearing sword and shield and spear, lions and eagles at their sides, smiling as they bestrode great stallions that carried them ever on toward their earned eternities.

Orpheus searched among them for his love, for she had been more pure than any he had ever known, but she was not among them.

The heroes passed him quickly by, his leaden footfalls holding him back, his every step more laborious as he played. Just as he felt the weight of his world ready to finally crush him into the black earth, he saw it: Hades' palace.

Orpheus paused to look up at the rising mountain, the dark towers and balustrades hewn out of the mountainside. Fires burned in windows, and columns of adamant rose and curled to support the heighest peaks of the Underworld.

His eyes followed the fires downward, searching for a passage, until he saw, at the end of the road, a great, arching gateway, broad and high enough for a Titan.

Orpheus wept to see it, for beyond the gateway was a land of sunlight and of green. Warm gusts of gentle, sweet-smelling wind reached him from that gaping gate to tickle the tears that ran down his cheeks.

He gazed at that blessed realm of Elysium from afar, his steps taking him nearer and nearer as he approached the gate. His eyes filled with light and love and longing for Eurydice, for they had lived such a life upon the Earth, at least for a time.

I will bring you back, my love...or I will die trying. He walked more briskly now, his music hopeful, determined and bright. But even as he neared the gateway and palace, the earth began to shake and a deep rumble rose up through the bones of his legs. Fear clawed at him once again.

The tremors, however, came not out of the ground, but fell upon him from above, and as Orpheus looked up, he felt more afraid than he had the length of his journey across the Underworld.

Before him stood Cerberus, Devourer of Souls, who guarded the home of Hades and blocked the unworthy from Elysium. His three heads gazed down at Orpheus, each with fires in their eyes, each hateful and wanting to kill. The hound that roamed the Underworld, haranguing the dead, heaping death upon those who were already dead, now stood before Orpheus like a black colossus, more terrible than a hydra, more hateful than the chimaera.

Cerberus felt not fear or pity, the face of each head devoid of any feeling at all. His gnashing teeth glistened in the darkness, and his jaws opened and closed and slavered as they bent over Orpheus.

I am sorry, my love. I tried, Orpheus wept, and as he set his fingers to the strings, his song changed again, this time to a dirge of sadness and lost love, he prepared himself for the searing pain of Death's dealing.

But the pain did not come.

Orpheus opened his eyes as he played, the light from his lyre shining out like a sun upon the faces of Cerberus as the hound backed away, the fires in his great glossy eyes doused. Therein, where death and unfeeling instinct ruled, there was a foreign calm, as if the sea itself were stilled, a mirror to the sky.

It was a mirror in which Orpheus could see himself. He looked dirty, and tired, and desperate. But he shone out in the dark for the music he played, and the love he felt pulsing through his soul, the love that had led him through the Underworld to Hades' door.

Orpheus stepped forward, passed the still Cerberus, whose rumbling breath shook the ground beneath his feet, and found a grand staircase beside him, to his left, suddenly lit by firelight. He paused, wanting to walk into Elysium, drawn to that realm of peace and plenty, but even as the thought entered into his mind, Cerberus' growl struck a new note of warning.

Orpheus turned and made his way up the stairs, his fingers finally still upon his lyre as he ascended into the palace.

. . .

THE STAIRS SEEMED to go on for some time. How long, Orpheus could not tell, but they turned and switched back, roamed past scenes of wars between the Gods, Titans and Giants. These images moved and shifted as he went. Each step he took was slow and hesitating, and he was cold, his bones aching, his hands cramped.

Orpheus moved his fingers, keeping them limber as best he could, for he knew that he had not yet played his song in full. He had breached the gate of Death's door, held back the souls of the departed, given succour to the sufferers of that world. But he had not yet won over Hades' heart and brought Eurydice out of darkness.

Keep going, Orpheus, he told himself as he plodded on and upward, more tired and weary than he had ever been the whole of his life.

Eventually, Orpheus reached the top of the staircase where it opened up into a broad, black throne room lit by fires in golden tripods. He entered the room only to find that he was alone, the great throne at the far end empty.

Orpheus looked around, a ragged traveller with his lyre in hand. The air smelled strangely of burnt cedar and ripe pomegranates, nothing like the charred and bitter world through which he had passed to get there. The adamant surface of the walls gave the impression that fire was every-where, and a gentle wind and sunlight swept in at a window to the right. Drawn to it, Orpheus walked to the jutting balcony to look out in wonder at the blessed lands of Elysium where green hills stretched on forever, lit by sunlight, fed by cool clear rivers and divine waters. Trees eternally bearing fruit were everywhere, and the heroes of the past roamed freely where they would, never hungry or tired, never sad or feeling of pain.

Orpheus wept at the beauty of that world, and for a moment, he wondered if Eurydice was there, his heart reaching out to her, searching among those joyous souls whose courage had won them a place in that otherworldly paradise.

But he could not see or feel her. Fearful now, he turned to see another broad window on the other side of the palace, a dark frame that promised ghastly visions. Orpheus moved toward it and there he gazed along the ruined pathways of the dead over which he had just passed, over black mountains and pocked plains where fires burned and the souls of the forgetful dead ranged like starving beasts over the plains.

He could not believe the distance he had travelled, nor that he yet lived.

Orpheus fell to his knees, panicked at the thought that he might have passed Eurydice and not noticed her there, reaching for him, pleading, weeping...or worse, that she had forgotten all, and had been unmoved by his passage.

It was then he felt a deep thrumming in the palace floor and walls. At first, the tempo was slow, but it increased in speed, matching the wild beating of Orpheus' heart only to stop suddenly.

"Rise, Orpheus, son of Apollo," a deep, commanding voice said.

Orpheus looked up slowly, the sweat and tears dripping from his face, and there before him, he saw Hades and Persephone, the Lord and Lady of the Underworld.

9

LORD OF THE UNDERWORLD

"You've come a long way," Hades said to Orpheus who seemed adrift upon that wide, shining black floor.

Orpheus stood weakly and approached.

The Lord of the Underworld sat upon his great black throne, his cowl pushed back to reveal his long hair and thick beard of deepest black. He was timeless in appearance, neither old nor young, and he exuded an air of great strength and menace, the same as his brothers Poseidon and Zeus.

Beside Hades, on a smaller throne to match his own, Persephone, his sad queen, reached out to Orpheus and smiled. "Do not be afraid, Orpheus. Come."

As she spoke, it seemed as if Spring bloomed in that dark hall. Blooms of brilliant narcissus erupted from vases, and jugs of water and wine, and bowls of fruit appeared.

"I thank you for granting me an audience, Lord," Orpheus said, bowing his head.

Hades held up a strong hand. "Before you make your plea. You must drink and eat. Regain your strength."

Orpheus looked to the long table groaning with Elysian food and drink, his eyes drawn to the great golden bowl of crimson pomegranates nearest to him, calling to him. He was about to take one when he turned to look at Persephone and there saw the dread and tears in her eyes as he reached for that fateful fruit.

She did not speak, or move, but her eyes told of a world of hurt should he accept anything.

His hand retreated, and he turned back to Hades and his sad queen. "I have promised not to enjoy anything until I am reunited with my truest love, Lord. But I thank you." He bowed again.

Hades stood and descended the steps of his throne to tower over Orpheus. "And how do you know you shall be reunited? You have walked the Paths of the Dead. Did you not see the eternal suffering and damnation of those who wasted their lives, and of those whose hubris led them to try and put themselves above Olympus?"

"I have walked far and seen unimaginable things, Lord."

"Then why have you come here to make demands of me? To ask for the impossible?"

Orpheus shook his head and rose up from his bowed posture.

"Lord Hades...Lady Persephone... I did not walk the dread paths of your kingdom out of arrogance. I came not with trickery in my heart." He swallowed and stilled himself. "I came for my true love."

"She is no longer among the living," Hades said, his green eyes boring into Orpheus.

Persephone stepped down from her thrown to her dread husband's side and laid a hand upon his arm.

Orpheus looked up, his eyes glassy in the firelight, but devoid of any subterfuge.

"Your father came to me. He told me that you would be coming to request that I release your wife, Eurydice. Is that not arrogance? To ask for the reversal of Death's work?"

"Lord, it could be perceived as such, but with my love... Eurydice...the world is a much better place with her in it. It is simply for my wife, my love of her, that I am here to ask you, Mighty Hades, to release her from Death's grasp. Let her enter the world of men once more."

Hades shook his dark head and turned away from Orpheus to remount his throne.

Persephone, the daughter of Zeus and Demeter, reached out to touch Orpheus' hand, a glimmer of springtime hope in her lovely eyes. She then went to Hades, and took both of his hands in hers. "Will you not reconsider, my husband? He has come farther than any other, and all for love of his wife." She looked up at Hades then, bringing to the surface the slight love that had grown between them, that softness to keep the fires at bay.

Hades nodded very slightly, and looked to Orpheus. "What do you offer?" he asked. "Your life for Eurydice's?"

"I would willingly do so, Lord, but then I would not be able to live with her, to play for the world, to better the world with our song."

"You have not played for me," Hades said, his eyes growing angry, resentful of gilded Olympus where he rarely roamed.

"That is why I am here, Lord. To offer you a song for the life of my beloved."

Hades laughed, and the sound was one of crumbling rock and blacked-out sun.

Orpheus felt great despair then, as if he would weep forever. *I've failed!* he cried inside.

But then, Hades spoke once more.

"Play for me then, and let us hear and see the true nature of your gifts."

Orpheus looked up abruptly and nodded.

THE BREATH FLOWED SLOWLY in and out of Orpheus' body as he stood in the firelit darkness of Hades' hall. Time slowed to a standstill in that very moment, the moment in which it was within his power to save his love or lose her for all time.

As he stood before the thrones of Hades and Persephone, his mind recalled all that was beauty and love in his life, all that Eurydice meant to him. The notes in his mind crowded at the gates of that moment in time, as his fingers moved silently, stretching and reaching over the strings of his lyre. Then, he paused, his eyes closed, and began to play...

The first notes were soft, so gentle and sweet that Hades himself leaned forward to hear, like a mortal hearing the first tiny droplets of life-giving rain after a scorching summer. Light and colour oscillated from the shell of Orpheus' lyre as well, to match the music, casting the muted colours of dawn upon the walls of that blackened throne room.

Persephone too looked around, and felt her longing for the upper world acutely.

As the music progressed, they were carried on the winds of a time neither had known, but which they had wondered about in the deepest parts of their being.

Orpheus' song told of a beautiful world free of hatred and war, a world exploding with potential, colour, and new-born creation, such a world to make the Gods feel awe.

And then it came, as they roamed fields bursting with life and colour, to the untouched, untamed forests of the North, the destined meeting of a man and of a woman.

It was a meeting that made the world a better, purer place, and the love that was born of that meeting resonated with the sweetest notes across oceans and rivers, through forests, and over the peaks of the tallest mountains.

Hades felt a pause in his great chest, and cocked his head to make sure he was hearing correctly, the weeping of the Morai, the Fates themselves, as they too heard all the he was hearing.

Impossible, that dark god of the Underworld thought.

But it was not impossible, no more so than that the mortal man standing before him, playing, had walked across Death's realm to reach that very hall and stand before him.

And it was then that Hades saw Apollo's son in a different light.

Persephone reached for her dread husband's hand and clasped it as tears rolled in beautiful rivulets down her cheeks.

Orpheus helped them to see and feel and smell and touch every aspect of that world filled with love, so foreign to them. Together, they experienced the sheer, innocent joys of truest love. They stood among the crowded, light-bringing gods at the wedding of Orpheus and Eurydice, for that moment of supreme joy and celebration of two lovers who had never thought ill of anything or anyone.

I see now, Hades thought, bringing his wife's hand to his lips, not wanting to let go.

Then, it happened. An abrupt change in the music shook them from the blessed reverie in which Orpheus had enveloped them as the peace and love which they had been bathed in turned to ash in a darkened world.

Hades and Persephone found themselves standing in a dry field, watching the painful scene before them in which a moment of supreme love and joy was eviscerated by jealousy and violence. They saw with their own eyes the attack...Eurydice's tragic death. They felt the extreme pain of loss, and the desperation of snuffed-out love, a love cut tragically short.

It was then that they saw Orpheus with new eyes. They wept with him, for him, and could now, at last, comprehend Orpheus' determination and courage, and understand the love that drove him through the great sadness of the Underworld for the woman who was everything to him.

This new perspective and understanding, the deep sting of pure feeling, struck at Hades' heart, for he had not understood, truly, what love was.

Orpheus had pried him open to let in the light, and he was grateful for it.

As the Lord and Lady of the Underworld stood together, arm in arm, listening to the final measures of Orpheus' song, they could hear the shift in the music, the notes of which drew them on, out of darkness. They could hear the heartfelt plea for the love of Orpheus' life. They could glimpse the possibilities and hope that their reunion would bring.

As Orpheus struck the final soft and lingering notes upon his lyre, Hades and Persephone found themselves standing before him, their eternal eyes wet with tears, their fire-filled hearts beating softly, together.

They were all silent for a few moments, feeling the music's resonance even after it had slipped away into the darkness.

When Hades spoke, his voice was soft and gentle, worlds

away from the warlike god of darkness who ruled that terrible realm.

"Truly, Orpheus, no mortal or god has every played or heard such music as that. I understand now."

Orpheus looked up, tears upon his still face, for he had relived his love and loss, pried open his own heart for the Gods. He was about to speak, to repeat his plea, but Hades held up his hand to stop him.

Hades and Persephone turned and Orpheus followed their gaze to see Eurydice's opalescent form standing there before them.

Orpheus fell to his knees before her.

"Your fervent wish is granted, Orpheus," Hades said as he and Persephone came to his side.

Orpheus looked up through glassy eyes, his heart beating in his ears and limbs.

But Eurydice did not move toward him. Nor did she speak. She stood there, gazing blankly at Orpheus, swaying like a lone shaft of winter wheat in a desolate field.

Orpheus made to reach out to her, to touch her, but Persephone grabbed hold of his arm.

"You mustn't!" she warned.

"But why?" Orpheus pleaded. "I've come so far for her."

"And you are not yet at the end," Persephone said softly as they looked upon Eurydice's shimmering form.

"She is still a shade, Orpheus," Hades said, his voice growing harsher with each syllable, though the pity and feeling roused in him still lingered, and would do so evermore. "She drank of the river Lethe."

"You mean she does not remember me, nor our life and love?" Orpheus felt great despair crushing in upon him, but the Lord of the Underworld took him by the shoulders and held him in his eyes.

"Listen to me now. She has forgotten, but she will remember. As you retrace your steps and return to the mortal world, remembrance will come back to her like the dawn after a long winter. But you must play your song as you played it for us, not only to help Eurydice relive and remember your life together, but to protect you from the raging and jealous dead who will crowd you the length of the road."

"I understand," Orpheus said, reaching out to Eurydice again, once more stopped by Persephone.

"You don't understand, Orpheus," Hades said, more clearly now. "You must walk in front of her the length of your journey back to the world of the living. You cannot speak directly to her. You cannot touch her. And most of all, you MUST not look upon her the entire journey."

"But how will I know if she is still with me, Lord?" Orpheus asked, panic gripping hold of him. "The road is so long and dark," he despaired.

"You must believe, Orpheus. Believe in the bond between you and Eurydice. Believe in your song and yourself. You must never waiver in your faith that she is with you."

"Just play, and don't stop, don't look at her, until you reach the light of day." Persephone held Orpheus' face in her hands. "A love such as yours is precious. Believe, and you shall have happiness and joy and love the rest of your days."

"Remember to have faith. If you touch her, speak to her, or look at her, Eurydice will remain here for eternity," Hades warned again. "And not even I will be able to change that."

Orpheus looked upon the shade of the woman he loved with all of his heart, his soul, with every fibre of his being. She stood there, beautiful and blank-faced, and he knew that the long journey and his song were the only ways to bring her back. "I understand," he said.

"Now go, Orpheus," Hades said. "Go, and play, and she will follow you."

Orpheus took a last glimpse of Eurydice then, turned, and began to walk, his fingers striking the first notes of that longing song to carry them through the Underworld.

"Follow him," Hades commanded the shade.

Eurydice turned her ghostly face and followed slowly after Orpheus, led on by his music and Hades' command.

"Will they succeed?" Persephone said to her husband once they disappeared down the broad staircase.

"I wish them only happiness," Hades said, turning to feel his queen's lips gentle upon his.

10

TOWARD THE LIGHT

The music spread out from Orpheus like ripples in a hidden pool when a pebble is cast into its midst. Light shone out like an aura that bound Orpheus and the shade together.

Eurydice followed closely, but as they reached the gaping gates guarded by Cerberus, Orpheus could already feel his faith wavering, the worry beginning at the back of his mind that she might not stay with him.

I must believe, he thought. *Stay with me, my love,* he begged as he played his song for the Underworld, for his love.

As Orpheus stood there, looking down the long desolation of the road ahead toward the Tartarian bridge, he could feel the deep, breathing bass of Cerberus towering over him, sniffing at his mortal frame and the shade that followed him.

She is with me, he told himself one more time before taking those first steps and setting out across the plain. *Let's remember the beauty of better days...*

· · ·

IT THREATENED to choke him even more than before, that deep, cold, Stygian darkness. The wind roared over the plains, and souls gathered around to claw at Orpheus and the shade of his love, the beauty of that longing song their only shield against their harassment.

Orpheus played as he had played for Hades and Persephone, and as the dead approached - heroes, kings, queens, children and more - they all fell to their knees weeping, as if each note sopped up the waters of Lethe like a sponge from Poseidon's sea. They remembered the beauty of the world they had departed, and the pain was written upon their faces for a few brief moments before Orpheus' light passed and Lethe's forgetfulness filled them once again.

He walked on and on, playing his song of summer beauty, of sunlight upon the seas and mountainsides of a green world, of peace and beauty and the discovery of love.

From Tartarus' depths, Orpheus could hear Tityus, Tantalus, Sisyphus and Ixion's cries as he passed, deeply pained by the knowledge that they would never enjoy another such moment of respite for all eternity.

But Orpheus thought only of playing, of putting one foot before the other, slow and constant as he journeyed across that realm of death with his love at his back.

At long last, Tartarus was behind them, and he came to the banks of the Lethe. There, he paused, playing, his fingers soft upon the strings, the light shining out from his lyre, cast upon the stooping dead who looked up from their grisly lapping of the water to listen, to watch as Orpheus walked above them like an arching star across a pitch night, followed by the shade of Eurydice.

.   .   .

With the River Lethe behind them at long last, the attendant shade stopped, unaware, confused, and turned to look back at the white surface of the water where millions of other shades crowded to drink, to forget, while she began to remember.

That shade wept to see them. She began to feel once more, and to remember as the notes of the lyre player's song penetrated and revived her psyche.

Where am I? the shade wondered, but even as the question floated up, it was like the first breaths of fresh air in the aftermath of suffocating death, so slight, so minute, but giving of respite and promising a return to something bright and clear. *I must follow.*

The shade gazed ahead to the lone player travelling the road that cut through the endless plains of asphodel like a ship in winter seas.

Those tall swaying blooms rose up to meet her, to tempt her as they tempted the surrounding dead, but the music led her on, and on, slowly and persistently.

I hear music... The thought exploded in the shade's reforming mind and memories. *Such music...*

Oh, how Orpheus longed to look back, to comfort himself that Eurydice was still with him, that she had not been engulfed and drowned by waves of dead!

Keep walking, he told himself. Keep playing! *Remember the beauty of life, of our life!*

The endless night of Hades' realm stretched on without end across the undulating fields of asphodel, longer and darker than Orpheus remembered, even as his song touched upon the loving bond and purest joy he and his wife had shared in life.

At one point, as the dead wept all around him, he could see their eyes gaze to a point behind him, jealous and longing, sad beyond measure, and he knew that they then spied the object of his love. The momentary comfort offered him the strength he needed to press on, to play on across the final miles of that death-flowered plain toward the dark line of the River Styx.

After some time, the soaring beacons of Acheron's pier rose up in the darkness, and Orpheus plodded on down the road, through the disembarking dead.

So many souls... he thought, wanting to weep for them, for the emptiness, the forgetfulness that awaited them as their memories spun away from them like thread from a spindle whorl. *I will not forget... I will not forget... I remember,* he told himself, playing the song of his deep and infinite love for Eurydice, the light of his life.

Orpheus? The shade remembered as she boarded Charon's barge, trailing that beautiful music. She looked down to see the clutch of asphodel gripped in her opaque hands and wondered at their beauty. She looked up at the back of the musician as he played in the prow of the empty barge, and then turned to see the ferryman looking down upon her with teary eyes.

The shade listened to the waves of that black water against the hull and oar, and to the music that bound her, made her feel more and more as they went.

Oh, my love! she wanted to shout, but could not.

It was then the first tears fell from her longing eyes, which shifted from white, to grey to palest green as the memories of that song entered into her being.

You came for me! Eurydice now thought, realization rushing upon her like a new dawn.

Then she felt something more come back to her, the notes of another, ever-so-faint song. Her hands went gently to her stomach, and she smiled as she travelled across the River Styx.

WHEN THE BLACK barge reached the other side of that lamentable river, the ferryman, watched Orpheus disembark, followed by the flower-grasping shade of Eurydice.

Even as the next wave of dead boarded, crowded around his tall form, confused, straining their hideous necks to listen to some final notes of the passing song, Charon watched. He watched and wept to see Orpheus' Underworld passage, envied him his return to the light and to love. He closed his eyes then, and pushed off of the jetty once more, as he always had done, as he would do the length of his own eternity. But he would remember the passage of that lyre player, and the song would haunt him, and comfort him in the darkness forever more as he travelled back and forth over that black river.

"HE IS ALMOST THERE," Calliope said without turning as Apollo approached her beside the spring of Hippocrene on Helicon, worlds away. "I can hear the beauty of those notes... so faint...so beautiful...spilling out of Death's gate at Tainaron."

Apollo's star-whirling eyes looked up to the night sky. "Then our son lives," he said, relief bursting within him as he held her shaking hand in his. "He is still in the deep darkness. He must believe now, more than ever."

"Believe, my son," Calliope said, her winged words caught by the winds. "Keep going, keep playing..."

In that moment, it was as if Olympus, and the entire world, held its breath, waiting for a reply to their prayers, to the most sincere of offerings, that goodness and love and light would return to their world once more.

All this, despite their unknowingness of the harsh trial in which their Orpheus found himself, and the darkness and despair he then struggled to overcome as he clawed his way out of Hades' realm with his true love in tow.

ORPHEUS FELT HEAVY, the weight of deep hopelessness pressing upon him. He played, his heart bursting, his soul burning as his fingers bled, and as he fought with every ounce of life still within him not to look back, not to speak to Eurydice.

The rocky road out of the Underworld twisted, rose and fell and rose again, unfamiliar, unkind and, seemingly, unending.

The descendant dead filed past them, horror-struck by their new reality, clinging to that song of remembrance and hope like it was a final lifeline in a stormy sea. They clawed at Orpheus' face and shaking hands, licked at the desperate and exhausted tears that streamed down his cheeks.

Orpheus...my love...we are almost there! Play for me. Sing! Eurydice begged from the darkness behind him. *I am with you. I love you!*

She was no longer a shade, or shadow of forgetfulness.

Memory had returned with each note of that song of love and hope. She could remember long ago days of living when the sun had risen as if for the first time, to plumb the emerald depths of her forest home and reveal the face of her truest love.

I remember, Orpheus, my love! she wept aloud, though her voice was permitted no sound or resonance except in her own mind. *Oh, my eyes...my soul...we shall know such happiness!*

But as Orpheus walked, and stumbled, and crawled over the black and jagged ground, the urge to lie down, to sleep, was almost overwhelming. He stood still as the road began to climb for the last time, playing as he swayed upon his feet, dizzy, spent.

And for the briefest of moments, the music stopped as he wept, cloaked in despair and deepest doubt.

The shade of Eurydice watched him and wept, and when the music ceased, she dropped the stems of asphodel which she had carried across the plains of the Underworld as a dark remembrance. *Do not give up, my love. I am here!* she wanted to shout to his shuddering form, but her words had no wings, no strength, not yet.

Then, the music began again, stronger now, courage renewed in every note as hope filled the song.

Eurydice's shade looked up, her eyes wider and greener than they had been in an age.

Orpheus' fingers, dripping with the blood of his labour, plucked at the strings of his lyre as if he were making a desperate last stand at Death's door. He filled himself with strength, the memories of his life, and the thoughts of what lay ahead pushing him on, and in that moment, a crack of light appeared at the top of the steep slope.

Sunlight.

As Orpheus rushed, a final charge in the night, Eurydice's

shade wept for joy as she bent to pick up the asphodel she had dropped. *I will plant these about our home, as a remembrance of our love!* she told herself as she looked up and began to follow the light and sound of Orpheus' lyre.

THAT FINAL DISTANCE WENT ON, and on, but the beacon of daylight rose up, lighting the orbs of Orpheus' eyes, renewing him with every step.

With every step, however, a serpent of worry writhed within him. He recalled the infinite distance of the road he had travelled over the dark plains of Hades' realm. He worried that he had not been strong enough, his song not loud enough in the soundless dark to be heard by his true love, the shade at his back.

We're almost upon the light! he told himself. *Just a little farther!* He wanted to shout out to her, to look for her in the eyes of the passing dead, but he dared not.

He could smell the sea then, salty, tangy, devoid of ash and the sulphuric sting of the Underworld.

But the pull of the dark behind him was deep, and strong, and unrelenting, and the shadows of doubt therein clawed at his back like a thousand bleeding blades, lacerating the faith with which he had set out.

The sun was his thread in that eternal labyrinth, his song his strength.

As he played nearer the Underworld's gateway, that yawning maw of Death, the light drew him on, faster and faster, more hurried than any other step he had taken. His fingers were quick upon the strings, filled with joy and hope nearing the madness of Bacchic ecstasy, at odds with the shouting doubt in his mind and soul.

And then he burst forth from the gateway into the blinding light of day!

Orpheus wept, his eyes shut tight, even as he continued to play the final, resonating notes of hope and joy he felt with every ounce of his soul.

Orpheus, wait for me! Eurydice shouted, mute in the darkness behind. *Don't look back! Not yet!*

Eurydice stumbled and clawed at the black rocks of the Underworld, the gate so close, the blinding light outlining the form of her beloved.

Then, those eyes which she had longed to see, that form she had desired to hold, that man she wished to love the length of her days, began to turn.

She screamed, her voice too faint behind the crashing waves of the outer world. *Orpheus, wait!*

ORPHEUS COULD HEAR nothing behind the panicked pounding of his heart, the dark distances of worry too much to bear any longer.

He had waited to turn, to look, to speak, but he could wait no longer. Either she was there, with him, or she was not.

He turned slowly, his fingers plucking the last couple of notes as if he were in a dream, his arms open to receive his lost love in the light of that brilliant day.

"Orpheus, wait!"

He heard the voice, but even as the scream reached his ears, he saw her pale, desperate form reaching out from the darkness beyond the gate, too soon, too far behind.

"NOOO!" he yelled, rushing Death's door only to catch one last glimpse of his beloved before darkness swallowed her. "NOOO! NOOO!" he shouted, pounding with his bloody hands upon the rock, the eyes and skulls arching over him in silent mockery.

"EURYDICE!!!"

His cries drowned out the crash of the sea, the roar of the winds, and swept over the world in waves of deepest grief.

11

A LIFE WITHOUT LOVE

The sound of weeping could be heard across the whole of the land, and in the halls of Olympus itself, like the sound of a winter rain that never ceases for days or weeks on end. The stars whirled in the heavens, fainter than before, the sun and moon rose and fell, and all the while, Orpheus continued to live.

But how does one go on after tasting, living, breathing such a love as that between him and his Eurydice?

It is an impossibility to do so, to go on, to roam the same plane of human existence, for every sound is meaner, every colour more pale. Add to that the bitter draught of guilt and failure, which Orpheus swallowed at every moment, and the result was not life.

No.

Orpheus' existence was now a living death, and not even the Gods could succour him in the midst of so much pain.

Though Earth-Shaking Poseidon had found Orpheus weeping, prostrate before Death's gate, and ensured his swift transport over land and sea from Tainaron to the safety of

Helicon, a part of Orpheus had remained there, still screaming, still pounding with bloody and desperate fists upon the Underworld's door.

But those gates would not open for him again.

The Morai, those dark sisters of Fate, had had their say.

And so time passed cruel and lonely for Orpheus, and filled with sadness and pain for those who remembered the days of joy and hope and love.

With deep love and pity in their hearts, Lovely-Voiced Calliope and Far-Shooting Apollo cared for their sad son, willing their own godly music to heal him, to mend him, but a heart so scarred as his, wounded so very deeply, was impossible to heal.

When Orpheus awoke, he took up his lyre like a murderer might take up a dagger before leaving his home, and left Helicon for the last time.

Apollo, Calliope and all of the Muses wept to see him leave, to hear the song which he now played.

Orpheus' music had changed and now, after roaming the plains of the Underworld, he sang sadly his notes of burden the world over, on the mountain slopes, forests, and golden fields of Thessaly. Crops failed, beasts fled, and the birds that had sung so sweetly in salutation at his passing grew silent.

Reluctantly, numbly, he thought to find favour with Death among the other heroes who sailed east upon the Argo. They travelled through perilous realms and wonders until they reached the shores of Colchis and still, after much battle and blood, they returned alive in triumph.

Orpheus' every song and action courted Death, but Death would not take him, for the sad beauty of the music he yet played was as nothing previously heard.

· · ·

At long last, Orpheus' footsteps led him back to Thrace and the spot where he had first seen Eurydice, hidden among the trees, and rivers and rocks. There he sat and slept for days.

It was then that he dreamed of her, of Eurydice, his love, and their child. He opened his sodden eyes in that hidden glade, on a morning in Autumn, and felt his heart, his body, his mind reeling, shuddering with pain and torment.

"My love..." he said upon his knees on the mossy ground, his fist and eyes clenched. "I miss you so much. I cannot do this."

Play for me, Orpheus, my love.

Orpheus sat up at that, his eyes searching the faded forest where a bit more colour entered into his sight, a little more light cracking through the thinning treetops.

But he was alone, as ever, and yet when he turned to see his lyre leaning against a rock beside him, he had the urge to take it up, to play.

"I will play for you, my Eurydice. I only ever play for you."

His notes rose up from his lyre then, his fingers gentle once more, his song one of soft remembrance and not the harsh realities of a tortured soul.

As Orpheus played, he wept, and he hoped for something more, an experience beyond the realm of Death which he had already trod and survived.

As he played, Maenads gathered in the wood about him, peering out from behind trees and rocks to watch, to listen, to weep at the stirring of their own souls, newly awakened with longing for the music they now heard, which they had forgotten.

Orpheus played on, blind to his audience, his mind travelling, seeking in the midst of his music, a music that caused the sun to shine once more.

And then he knew what he must do to win Death's favour.

I must stop playing.

No, Orpheus! Apollo and Calliope cried out from the slopes of distant Helicon when his thoughts reached their godly ears.

But Orpheus did not hear them, or see their desperate faces. He only saw Death's pause as the final notes were struck and faded. He saw Death's face turn toward him, dark and hungry and welcoming.

Orpheus stood from the rock where he had sat and played his last, and raised his lyre above his head to glint in the reddening sun.

"Oh, Mother...Oh, Far-Shooting Father...I honour you, and I thank you. I go now."

Please no, Orpheus! The Gods pleaded. *Stay your hand!*

Orpheus shook his head, tears streaming down his face as he smiled and thought of his wife, his love, and their child.

It was then that the Maenads broke from their green hiding places, surrounding him, weeping, begging for him not to stopper his voice or cease his playing.

Orpheus looked upon them, wondered how Death could be so lovely, and then he lowered his arms quickly to shatter his lyre upon the rocks and roots of that hidden place. Over and over he struck, and as he did so, the Maenads wept and tore at their hair and faces. They churned about Orpheus in a maelstrom of madness, closing in on him, filled with fury.

But Orpheus smiled as he looked upon Death's messengers then, even as they tore his limbs from his body, more savage than beasts, their hideous song and dance echoing into the night.

Orpheus, laying upon the ground, looked his last up at the first glimmering of stars and there saw Eurydice as he had first seen her in that place of beauty and wonder.

Then...darkness...

NOT ALL DARKNESS IS PERMANENT, however.

And the light of the next day saw Orpheus' scattered remains floating upon the river Hebros, downstream to the sea.

His head, still smiling, sang softly of the love which he sought, and would seek, forever more, until it came to rest upon the pink-pebbled shores of Lesbos.

There, the Lesbian women found him, and remembered his songs from a happier age of their lives, and so buried him with honour and offerings.

It was not long before Apollo and Calliope alighted upon that remote shore, tears in their eyes, filled with gratitude to the islanders for the honour bestowed upon their now-silent son. Their far-seeing eyes gazed through the earth to see his face, smiling in death, his muted song ringing out in the Earth itself.

Calliope turned to Apollo, the Lesbians about them bowed low in the midday sunlight of Helios' fire.

"He is gone now, our beautiful son." And the Muse wept then, her tears dried by the Far-Shooter's blue cloak.

Apollo smiled and turned his star-whirling eyes to the heavens. "He is not gone. His song will resonate forever."

And in that moment, Orpheus' lyre took its place in the heavens, a memory of his song, his love, for all time...

.   .   .

THE WORLD HAD NEVER BEEN SO green and bright, so filled with joy and elation. Pain and regret did not exist in that land of plenty where a lightness of being was the state of existence for all heroes and heroines whose toils had earned them their places.

Orpheus walked without a sense of time, for time was irrelevant then. There was only beauty and joy, and the beacon of love which drew him onward over rolling Elysian fields. Never had the sun shone so brightly, nor the sky been so blue. Never had the air smelled so sweetly, such that gratitude for life was at its pinnacle, and all was possible.

Birds and beasts and smiling throngs accompanied Orpheus on his path until they came to a familiar, broad, sprawling tree.

I remember this tree, he thought, and as it occurred to him, he saw her.

Eurydice, who had been waiting, stood beneath the tree to meet him.

"My love," she said, her smile as the sun upon his face after a thousand years. "I've missed you."

Orpheus walked to her, his life, his love, his soul, and held her tightly.

He was renewed. She was renewed. In death, they had found each other again, unaware of the godly tears that fell in Hades' hall, and from the heights of Olympus.

They were each other's world once more, and would always be.

Eurydice then bent to pick something up from the long, soft grass behind her, and turned with a child in her arms.

Orpheus looked upon the child, and then once more upon his truest love.

Thank you, he said to the Morai. *With all my soul, thank you.*

"Orpheus," Eurydice said. "Will you play for us, my love?" She stepped aside to reveal the lyre leaning against the tree.

Orpheus smiled and nodded and, seated beside his wife and child, he began to play.

The End

AUTHOR'S NOTE

The myth of Orpheus and Eurydice is, perhaps, one of the most romantic and tragic in the constellations of mythology that have come down to us. It is the ultimate, tragic love story, and as such it has inspired countless works of art, music, plays, operas, and literature throughout the ages.

With the *Mythologia* series, it is sometimes difficult to decide which myths to adapt. There are so many!

I was reminded of the story of Orpheus and Eurydice when I first listened to the song, *Orpheus*, by Sara Bareilles. The absolutely beautiful melody and Ms. Bareilles' voice wove a spell, and upon hearing the phrase "Don't you turn like Orpheus, Just stay here...", I knew that I had to write this story.

In a way, my own version of this story began with a song.

Once I began to research this myth more fully, I became more and more engrossed in the story, curious about its impact over the ages.

There are a few primary sources from the ancient world that relate the story of Orpheus and Eurydice. For this retelling, I've used parts from each, having decided not to limit myself to one particular version. For this story, I've used elements from Euripides' play, *Alcestis*, which is one of the earliest recorded tellings of the story, and from the more fulsome versions by the Roman writers Virgil (*Georgics*) and Ovid (*Metamorphoses*). There are references to Orpheus in many other ancient sources such as Pindar (the *Pythian* odes), Plato (*Symposium*), Apollonius of Rhodes (*Argonautica*), Diodorus Siculus, and Pausanias.

Though the *Mythologia* series is fantasy, and requires a suspension of disbelief, I have still tried to include places or settings that are tied historically to Orpheus and Eurydice. The sacred spring of Hippocrene on Mount Helicon, where the Muses were said to gather, was supposedly made by Pegasus when he stomped his hoof into the rock there. The ancient author, Pausanias, tells us that there was a statue of Orpheus in that place. The ancient region of Pieria, around the base of Mount Olympus, which I have also included in the book, was said to be where the Muses lived, and perhaps where Orpheus was raised. Both Mount Helicon and Pieria were major cult centres of the Muses in ancient times.

When it comes to the entrance to the Underworld, the cape of Tainaron in the southern Peloponnese was believed by our ancient ancestors to be one of the gateways to Hades' realm, a truly forbidding, rocky place with a sanctuary of Poseidon and, supposedly, an altar of Death.

In the story, Orpheus and Eurydice do range all over the land of what we know as Greece, but Thrace in particular played a big part in the myth for it was there that Orpheus was supposed to have met Eurydice, but also where he met his end. There was a strong Orphic tradition for millennia in Thrace. In mythology and the history ancient Greece, the landscape is as much a part of the story, and by exploring it we can truly get closer to the myths.

Traditionally, the Muse, Calliope, is Orpheus' mother, but there are a couple of traditions around who his father was. Often it is King Oeagrus of Thrace, but then sometimes Orpheus' father is Apollo himself. I decided to include hints at both in this story, but opted for the latter tradition since it seemed more fitting that Calliope and Apollo would be parents to the greatest musician. However, in mythology, King Oeagrus was indeed the father of the satyr, Marsyas, who did challenge Apollo. For his hubris, Apollo flayed the skin from Marsyas' body, and there is a famous statue of the satyr in this sad state. For my version of this story, I liked the juxtaposition of having King Oeagrus as Marsyas' father, and Apollo as Orpheus'.

When it comes to the death of Orpheus, he was torn to pieces by the Thracian Maenads, but for varying reasons. Sometimes, it is because they each wanted him for themselves and fought over him. Other times, it is because of his loyalty to the memory of Eurydice, and his refusal of anyone else. One tradition has Dionysus turn against him because Orpheus preferred to honour Helios over him. I chose a slightly different route by making the cessation of his music the reason that the Maenads turned on him. Either way, what is agreed upon is that after they slew poor Orpheus, the pieces of his body were thrown into the river Hebros and floated down to the sea, his head still singing in death. The head landed on the shores of Lesbos where the people there treated Orpheus' remains with honour. As a result, the Muses granted the Lesbians the special gift of music and art. This is fitting, considering that Sappho, one of the greatest poets of the ancient world, was from Lesbos.

Of course, one of the central features of the myth is Orpheus' journey to the Underworld to get back his love, Eurydice. One of my favourite challenges as an author is to write about the Underworld. How does one portray such a realm as that? One cannot fit in every detail, and accounts in ancient texts vary. No one can truly know the mysteries of the Afterlife, so conjecture is acceptable. Another attempt of mine to portray the Underworld can be found in my book, *Saturnalia*. I hope this particular interpretation is a just offering.

The story of Orpheus was so profound and imbued with such meaning that from it sprang one of the great mystery religions of the ancient world: Orphism.

I won't go into the details of Orphism here. We cannot know much because it was a mystery religion, similar to the Eleusinian Mysteries.

What we do know is that the *Orphic Hymns* were central to its practices and beliefs, as was Orpheus' journey to the Underworld and back. It is thought by some to be a reform of ancient Dionysian religion, with a focus on the suffering and death of Dionysus who also went to the Underworld. Humanity's dual nature was central to the philosophy of Orphism. It also had ideas in common with Pythagoreanism, notably an ascetic life free of contamination, including rules such as a strict vegetarian diet. It is believed that Pythagoras himself was an Orphic initiate.

Orphics, as the followers of this ancient religion are known, believed in an afterlife in which they would spend eternity alongside Orpheus and other heroes. Those who were not initiated into the mysteries were reincarnated.

As always, as an author and historian, I find this oneness of myth and religion infinitely fascinating, and will explore more of this relationship in subsequent stories in the *Mythologia* series.

For me, however, at its heart this is a story about love, pure and simple. It is the ultimate expression of that which makes life worth living, worth risking all for.

It's almost impossible to fully convey such love with mere words. I don't have the skills that Orpheus himself had. But I do hope that in reading this story, some part of your heart and soul has been moved, or sat up and taken notice.

Thank you for reading.

Adam Alexander Haviaras
Stratford, Ontario
May, 2021

Thank you for reading!

Did you enjoy this collection of tales from Greek Mythology? Here is what you can do next.

If you enjoyed *Mythologia: First Omnibus Edition*, and if you have a minute to spare, please post a short review on the web page where you purchased the book, or on the Eagles and Dragons Publishing website.

Reviews are a wonderful way for new readers to find this series of books and your help in spreading the word is greatly appreciated.

More books in the *Mythologia* series, as well as exciting historical fantasy set in the ancient world, will be coming soon, so be sure to sign-up for e-mail updates at:

https://eaglesanddragonspublishing.com/newsletter-join-the-legions/

Newsletter subscribers get a FREE BOOK, and first access to new releases, special offers, and much more!

Become a Patron of Eagles and Dragons Publishing!

If you enjoy the books that Eagles and Dragons Publishing puts out, our blogs about history, mythology, and archaeology, our video tours of historic sites and more, then you should consider becoming an official patron.

We love our regular visitors to the website, and of course our wonderful newsletter subscribers, but we want to offer more to our 'super fans', those readers and history-lovers who enjoy everything we do and create.

You can become a patron for as little as $4 per month. For your support, you can also get fantastic rewards as tokens of our appreciation.

If you are interested, just CLICK HERE or visit the website below to go to the Eagles and Dragons Publishing Patreon page to watch the introductory video and check out the patronage levels and exciting rewards.

https://www.patreon.com/EaglesandDragonsPublishing

Join us for an exciting future as we bring the past to life!

ABOUT THE AUTHOR

Adam Alexander Haviaras is a writer and historian who has studied ancient and medieval history and archaeology in Canada and the United Kingdom. He currently resides in Stratford, Ontario with his wife and children where he is continuing his research and writing other works of historical fantasy.

Historical Fiction/Fantasy Titles

The Eagles and Dragons Series
The Dragon: Genesis (Prequel)
A Dragon among the Eagles (Prequel)
Children of Apollo (Book I)
Killing the Hydra (Book II)
Warriors of Epona (Book III)
Isle of the Blessed (Book IV)
The Stolen Throne (Book V)
The Blood Road (Book VI)
The Eagles and Dragons Legionary Box Set (Books 0-I-II)
The Eagles and Dragons Tribune Box Set (Books III-IV-V)

The Carpathian Interlude Series
The Carpathian Interlude - Complete Trilogy Box Set
Immortui (Part I)
Lykoi (Part II)
Thanatos (Part III)

The Mythologia Series
Chariot of the Son: The Story of Phaethon
Wheels of Fate: The Story of Pelops and Hippodameia
A Song for the Underworld: The Story of Orpheus and
Eurydice
The Reluctant Hero: The Story of Bellerophon and the
Chimera
Mythologia: First Omnibus Edition

Heart of Fire: A Novel of the Ancient Olympics

**Saturnalia: A Tale of Wickedness and Redemption in
Ancient Rome**

The Etrurian Players
Sincerity is a Goddess (Book I)
An Altar of Indignities (Book II)

Titles in the Historia Non-fiction Series
Historia I: Celtic Literary Archetypes in *The Mabinogion*: A
Study of the Ancient Tale of *Pwyll, Lord of Dyved*
Historia II: Arthurian Romance and the Knightly Ideal: A
study of Medieval Romantic Literature and its Effect upon
Warrior Culture in Europe
Historia III: *Y Gododdin*: The Last Stand of Three Hundred
Britons - Understanding People and Events during Britain's
Heroic Age
Historia IV: Camelot: The Historical, Archaeological and
Toponymic Considerations for South Cadbury Castle as King
Arthur's Capital

Eagles and Dragons Publishing Guides
Writing the Past: The Eagles and Dragons Publishing Guide to Researching, Writing, Publishing and Marketing Historical Fiction and Historical Fantasy

STAY CONNECTED

To connect with Adam and learn more about the ancient world visit www.eaglesanddragonspublishing.com

Sign up for the Eagles and Dragons Publishing Newsletter at www.eaglesanddragonspublishing.com/newsletter-join-the-legions/ to receive a FREE BOOK, first access to new releases and posts on ancient history, special offers, and much more!

Readers can also connect with Adam on Twitter @AdamHaviaras and Instagram @ adam_haviaras

On Facebook you can 'Like' the Eagles and Dragons page to get regular updates on new historical fiction and non-fiction from Eagles and Dragons Publishing.

To watch Eagles and Dragons Publishing's mini documentaries and other fun videos, be sure to follow us on TikTok and subscribe to our YouTube channel.